tumbling

A Novel

Caela Carter

VIKING

VIKING

An imprint of Penguin Random House LLC

375 Hudson Street

New York, New York 10014

First published in the United States of America by Viking,
an imprint of Penguin Random House LLC, 2016

LIBRARY OF CONGRESS CATALOGING-IN-PUBLICATION DATA IS AVAILABLE
ISBN: 978-0-451-47300-4

Printed in U.S.A.   Set in Egyptienne   Book design by Nancy Brennan

1   3   5   7   9   10   8   6   4   2

★

For Sarah,

For the leotards and somersaults in your
girlhood basement,
for now,
and for everything in between

Contents

DAY 2

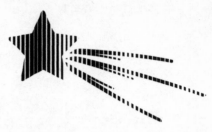

USA Gymnastics
Women's Olympic Trials

ROSTER

SQUAD A: Bars, Beam, Floor, Vault

SQUAD B: Vault, Bars, Beam, Floor

LEIGH BECKER, A:

Prediction: 1st Place in the All-Around

16 years old, 5'1"

Current National Champion, All-Around

Member of the Current World Bronze Medal Team

GRACE COOPER, B:

Prediction: 2nd Place in the All-Around

17 years old, 4'10"

Current World Champion, All-Around

Member of the Current World Bronze Medal Team

GEORGETTE PAULSON, B:

Prediction: 3rd Place in the All-Around

17 years old, 5'0"

Current National Champion, beam, bronze medal in All-Around

Member of the Current World Bronze Medal Team

KRISTIN JACKSON, A:

Prediction: 4th Place in the All-Around

15 years old, 4'11"

Current Junior National Champion

MARIA VASQUEZ, A:

Prediction: 5th Place in the All-Around

20 years old, 5'2"

Current Olympic Champion, All-Around

Olympic Silver Medalist, Vault

Member of the Olympic Bronze-Medal-Winning
Team, four years ago

WILHELMINA PARKER, B:

Prediction: 6th Place in the All-Around

19 years old, 5′0″

Junior Nationals and JO World Champion,
All-Around, three years ago

World Silver Medalist, two years ago

ANNIE SIMMS, B:

Prediction: 7th Place in the All-Around

16 years old, 4′11″

National Champion, Bars, 1 year ago

NATALIE RICE, A:

Prediction: 8th Place in the All-Around

15 years old, 5′1″

Current Junior National Runner-Up, All-Around

MONICA CHASE, A:

Prediction: 9th Place in the All-Around

15 years old, 4'10"

American Cup Runner-Up, Bars and Floor

CAMILLE ABRAMS, B:

Specialist, Vault and Floor

20 years old, 5'1"

Worlds Team Member, All-Around, three, four, and five years ago

SAMANTHA SOLOMAN, B:

Specialist, Bars and Beam

22 years old, 5'0"

Current Olympic Champion, Beam

Member of the previous Bronze-Medal-Winning Olympic Team

OLIVIA CORSICA, A:

Specialist, Floor and Beam

17 years old, 5'1"

Current National Runner-Up, Floor

Day 1

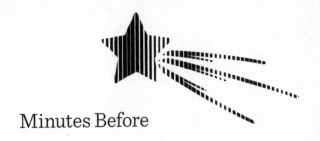

Minutes Before

The gymnasts gathered at the opening to the arena. From a distance, they looked like a mass of perfectly pressed red, blue, and bright white warm-ups; cheerful hair ribbons; precise makeup; and genuine smiles. But the mood was somber.

Somewhere on an edge of the gym floor in the Baltimore Metroplex, the announcers blathered on about the twelve gymnasts who were embracing each other under the stadium seats in the northernmost corner. They spoke of veterans versus brand-new baby seniors. They spoke of event specialists and all-arounders. They discussed the likely makeup of the final Olympic team—which names were destined to be called at the end of the meet the next night, and which positions were still up for grabs. They talked about comebacks and international debuts and likely breakout stars. Other names they didn't mention: the few who felt lucky to be present, who dared not hope to proceed.

"The top athlete in the all-around tomorrow night is guaranteed her place on the US Olympic team. She'll board the plane to Italy the day after tomorrow," announcers explained to television cameras and face-less fans at home. "Katja Minkovski and the Olympic selection committee will choose the other four members of the team. It's like filling in pieces of a puzzle: which five girls have the exact combination of talents most likely to bring home team gold? They may choose one or two specialists, or they may round out the team with four more all-arounders. We predict they'll choose at least one specialist, but nothing is guaranteed. Plus, they'll choose three alternates," the announcers said.

But all of these lines were drawn far away from the mass of young women inside the gray cave underneath the bleachers. There, among the USA's best female gymnasts, these rules did not matter. The divisions and distinctions, the rivalries and scores would fall on their shoulders as soon as they stepped onto the gym floor. But not yet. Instead, twelve girls faced one another knowing that, by the end of the weekend, five of them would be exalted, placed high above the other seven. Five would have dreams come true, seven would not, and right now twelve stared down the truth of that math.

So each girl reached out for the others, clutching the only people who could possibly understand the momentousness of her night, and the only people who could destroy it.

It was a moment shrouded in destiny and uncertainty, pressure and determination, and no one outside that little assemblage would understand the question running through each of their brains, the question that would be answered by tomorrow.

Was my childhood worth sacrificing for this dream?

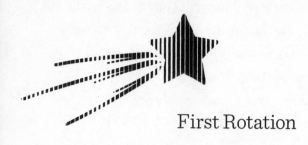

First Rotation

GRACE

Grace stared down the runway and squinted at her enemy. It stood strong, steady, and sure of itself at the end of the mat, like an elephant who would not move to let her cross. It was so confident that it could stop Grace, that it would rejoice in the victory of her landing on her butt or missing a crucial turn in her double twisting Yurchenko. But not today. Today, Grace would defeat the vault.

Vault was her least impressive event, but that was okay. She didn't want to see her name at the top of the scoreboard early in a meet; she liked the sneak-up approach. Of course, with Leigh starting on her own worst event, no one would know who was winning for a while. But by the end of the night, Grace would be on top. She was not allowing a repeat of Nationals earlier this summer and Classics this spring. Both times Leigh had beaten her by mere tenths of a point. And it wasn't that Leigh was better. It wasn't—as some reporters and coaches and commentators were speculating—that Grace had peaked at Worlds, a year ago. It was only because Grace had messed up on the second day of those meets earlier this season. She'd handed Leigh the gold at Nationals and Classics, and—no matter what the sports analysts for NBC predicted—she wasn't about to do it at the Olympic trials.

After each of those two meets, Leigh had morphed back into Grace's best friend and tried to giggle and congratulate Grace like it didn't matter which of them was first and which was second. But it mattered. To Grace, first place was all that mattered. Leigh might get wrapped up in school and television shows and secret crushes, but not Grace. Grace was a gymnast.

Being Leigh's best friend came second.

Grace shook out each leg and clapped her hands together twice, causing little puffs of white chalk to erupt beneath her face. She did not see Georgette exit the platform and hug her coach. She did not hear the crowd cheering for whoever was currently swinging around the uneven bars. She did not think about what her dad-coach was saying somewhere on the gym floor, and for one beautiful minute, she did not feel the organ-crushing pressure on her shoulders to win the Olympic trials.

She saw the vault.

Somewhere at the edge of her vision, the judges raised the green flag. She was dimly aware of the announcer's voice booming her name throughout the Metroplex.

Grace turned to the judges and raised her hands over her head to signal that she was ready. She didn't smile. She squinted at the vault one more time, bounced on her toes twice, and then she was off.

Foot, foot, foot, foot, foot. Her soles slapped the runway mat one after the other. Then it was *hand, hand*—the beginning of her roundoff. Her heels hit the springboard with her back to the horse and her toes exploded off it. Her palms slapped the smooth leather finish of the vault, her elbows and wrists sprung from bent to straight in unison and released her into the air.

Time froze.

She was high, floating, twisting, spinning over the first few bleachers, over the height of the uneven bars, over everyone in the gym. Now, as she rested in the air, she saw everything: her dad on the floor with his fists flung over his head in excitement, the gymnasts by the vault, fidgeting or watching her or warming up. She heard the screams of little girls throughout the bleachers. She swore she could pick out her little brother's voice from the mix.

Then her feet found the ground and, with the tiniest hop backward, she was standing again, her back to the vault. Pain rang through her ankle (remnants of a pesky old injury that wouldn't go away) but it didn't reach her brain. She put on a smile, turned, and saluted the judges. She caught that little nod. The only one that counted. The one from Katja Minkovski, the Olympic team coordinator.

Katja liked her, but Katja always liked whichever gymnast was best.

There, she thought. *One routine hit. Seven to go. Take that, Leigh.*

Grace's face twitched with guilt.

There's no room for friends on the gym floor, she reminded herself. Her dad's rule.

- - -

Last night, Leigh and Grace had been lying side by side on Grace's bed in their shared hotel room. They were roommates for the weekend. They had always been roommates, every meet, every place, for years. They had been sharing Leigh's earbuds, blasting Out of Touch songs into Grace's right ear and Leigh's left ear as the boys in the boy band danced on Leigh's laptop screen.

"You still think Dylan Patrick is hottest?" Leigh asked, mischief in her eyes.

Grace had flipped over onto her back. "Of course!" she squealed. "Look at his arms! His face! His moves!"

On the screen, Dylan Patrick put one foot across the other and spun around. He was dancing behind Greg Thompson, who was the lead singer and most popular heartthrob in the group. But something about Dylan's quiet ways, his humbleness, spoke to Grace. He was sort of Grace's opposite, she thought.

At long last, after seventeen years on the earth, Grace had a crush.

Dylan did a split and Grace squealed again.

Suddenly Leigh sat up, yanking the earbud out of Grace's ear.

"Hey!" Grace said.

"Sorry!" Leigh said. She pulled the computer onto her lap. "But I have an idea. Go in the bathroom! It'll be a surprise!"

Away from her Dad, Grace could never resist Leigh's cheerfulness. So she smiled back at her friend and disappeared into the bathroom.

"Okay!" Leigh called after a few minutes. "Come out!"

Leigh was standing outside the bathroom door. She shoved the computer at Grace before Grace had even fully stepped back into the room. "Check your fan page! Check your fan page!" Leigh squealed.

And there it was. A message from the real Dylan Patrick, confirmed and everything.

Good luck tomorrow, Gymnast Grace Cooper. I'll be cheering for you.

Grace had stared at it, stunned for a second, while Leigh squealed. "I just wrote on *his* page telling him how his number one fan is competing in the Olympic Trials tomorrow and seeing if he'd wish you good luck." Leigh was talking so quickly. "Look at that! I didn't think he'd respond so fast!" Then she paused and studied Grace's face. "What's wrong?"

"We've never done this before. We aren't those—"

Leigh interrupted her. "We've never been at the Olympic Trials before! We're about to get a whole lot more famous, Grace! And it starts with Dylan Patrick."

"If my dad sees it . . ." Grace's voice trailed off.

"Oh, come on!" Leigh said. "Your dad won't see it! It'll get lost in all the messages from all the boring people who always reach out before the Olympic trials. The politicians and old talk show hosts and stuff. And even if he does see it, who cares? This isn't a big deal, Grace, but we can act like it is, because that's the fun of being on television. Be a normal teenager for once. Dylan Patrick just messaged you. The. Real. Dylan. Patrick."

Leigh was right. He had. He said he'd be cheering for her. Dylan Patrick—Grace's one and only crush in her entire life, who she never thought would ever even know her name—was cheering for her. (Well, maybe not. Probably it was just a silly thing he did for a silly fangirl. But Grace would pretend he meant it.) Dylan Patrick of Out of Touch wanted her to win the Olympic trials!

So Grace gave herself over to squealing.

A minute later Leigh was pumping Out of Touch songs through her computer speakers without the earbuds and the two of them were dancing between the beds and it was friendship and joyful and perfect.

- - -

But that was last night. Last night didn't matter to real life.

Grace jogged to the edge of the platform and her father grabbed her under her armpits and swung her off it.

She could feel his fingers on her rib cage as if she were all bone.

"Your legs weren't as tight as they could have been," her father whispered as he hugged her.

I know, Dad, she spat back. But only in her head.

Grace had watched enough meets on DVR to know that on TV the announcers would be talking about how her dad-coach was congratulating her, about how happy they should be with whatever score she was about to receive. Whether they guessed he was congratulating or consoling, the TV announcers were wrong. He was always critiquing, always talking about how Grace could have been perfect but was always a millimeter short.

"Your right elbow bent a little more than your left on the vault. That's why you landed toward your left. That's why you hopped."

Grace nodded. She wandered over to her gym bag and pulled her warm-up pants on over her leo. It was red with three lines of crystals running from her left shoulder to her right hip and the USA insignia stitched on the side of her arm in gold. It wasn't her lucky leo. She'd need that one tomorrow.

Grace turned to hug Georgette and Annie and the others who each squeezed one arm around her and told her *good job*.

She said, "Thanks," "Thanks," "Thanks." Then she was alone again.

Who would Grace talk to today? Her dad hated hearing her voice in the gym. And Leigh was in the other rotation.

Grace squinted across the arena to find her friend. Leigh was sitting in the folding chairs next to the bars, a whole football field away from Grace. But Grace could still see her head leaning close to the girl next to her. Grace squinted deeper.

Monica. From GymCade, Grace's own gym. Leigh was palling around with Monica now, making Monica laugh and relax. Grace was sure they were having a great time. It still seemed impossible that Leigh had chosen her—stiff and sullen Grace—as a best friend.

Grace didn't understand how she could miss Leigh and also be so desperate to beat her.

Grace turned to her gym bag and closed her eyes. She didn't want to see her dad anymore, and she didn't want to see her score until the end of the first rotation. Grace and Leigh were determined to be numbers one and two. They talked about it all the time. And unless someone fell or messed up big-time, they all but surely would take the top two spots. Georgette would be close behind, but no one would know the exact order for hours at this point.

But what Grace didn't tell her best friend was that number two was not good enough. She'd only be happy if there was a one by her own name and a two by Leigh's. She didn't just want to go to the Olympics. She didn't just want to be one of the two Americans who qualified for the individual all-around there.

She needed to go to the Olympics as the favorite for gold.

Grace wouldn't watch Leigh on the bars or Camille on the vault or anyone else. She wouldn't talk to anyone. It was lonely, but she performed best when she could be a gymnast in a vacuum.

That's how it always used to be.

- - -

At Gym Camp USA—the sprawling campus adjacent to Katja Minkovski's New Mexico farm where the national team gymnasts, and those aspiring to qualify, were required to attend weeklong gymnastics training events throughout the year—Grace had been alone for years, secluded in her gymnastics. At home it was just her and her dad and her brother. Camp always felt overwhelmingly girly. Plus, Grace couldn't pull her mind off the beam or bars long enough to remember to smile at another girl in the dining hall or to sit with someone on the floor during team meetings.

A lot of the girls Grace had gone to Gym Camp with ever since she was eight years old were in this stadium right now. Maria and Samantha and Olivia and Annie. Grace remembered listening to them whisper and giggle into the darkness of their cabin while she lay on her side and repeated her mantra:

Don't worry. You'll beat them. Don't worry. You're better.

The mantra—and the loneliness—only stopped

when Leigh started attending camp. Only Leigh had been able to pull Grace out of her singular-gymnastics mind, and Grace wasn't so sure that was a good thing anymore, now that Leigh was starting to prove that you could go to school full-time and have non-gymnast friends and big, juicy secrets and still win.

- - -

"Camille will have the highest score." Her dad was behind her again, whispering strategy in her ear. "On vault."

Don't look at my fan page, Grace pleaded with her eyes. He usually looked at all her social media every day, but today he probably wouldn't. Today he'd be too obsessed with winning. If her dad did look, he'd be so angry. Even though it wasn't her fault. Her dad never understood a minute of her life outside the gym. Grace knew part of his harsh reactions to all-things-normal-teenager was guilt: guilt that there was no mom, guilt that he wasn't enough. He was enough for her gymnastics, so that's all there was. After her mom left when she was nine, gymnastics was the only thing they could talk about.

But he was only talking strategy, not social media: "Camille does the Amanar, and as long as she stands it up, it'll beat your DTY. Some of the other girls have an Amanar, too."

Grace nodded. "I know."

"But don't worry about that. Camille's a specialist.

She's not even competing beam and bars anymore. All we need to worry about is Leigh Becker."

At that same moment, Leigh's name boomed through the air around them, and their two heads—his a blond crew cut, Grace's a smooth, black ponytail—turned to watch her mounting the uneven bars across the gym. Grace looked away as soon as Leigh caught her first release move.

She swigged her water.

"You can get Leigh," her dad whispered. Grace hated it. As much as she wanted to win, she wished her basically guaranteed spot on the Olympic team would be enough for her father and coach.

He kept talking. "She's not better than you. You have to stop choking and get out of your own head. The only way she wins is if you have falls all over the place like you did on the second day at Nationals."

Grace shook her head, but she didn't say anything. *Gymnasts are made to be seen, not heard.* That's what her father said. But his analysis was never fair. Those meets hadn't been about choking.

He shoved his phone back into his pocket, and Grace managed to swallow the next sip of water. She was safe. For now.

"Even if she beats you today, she won't have a chance against you in the Olympic all-around. She's a crude gymnast. All about power and wow factor, but she doesn't have *it* the way you do. You have the long lines. You have the international look. You have it all, Gracie. You have grace."

Grace stared at her white father. It was the blood of her absent Chinese mother running through her veins that allowed Grace to embrace that "international look" in the first place. In today's day and age—when everyone was more concerned with nutrition than calorie counting, and weigh-ins had been banned by the USAG— if she were a white girl, a black girl, anything but an Asian girl, this "international look" she was sporting would have spawned suspicious theories from sports commentators and gym bloggers and possibly even USA Gymnastics. If the Chinese gymnasts from actual China weren't just as skinny, if she didn't look like them thanks to Nowhere Mom, she would never get away with it.

Grace couldn't believe her father used those words, like she didn't know exactly what they meant when you broke them down. *International look. Long lines.*

The rules would change for the Olympics because some judges outside the United States tended to be less concerned with the gymnasts' health. Because some of the other countries praised long, straight legs over complicated, daring tricks. Beating Leigh on an international stage would not have the same meaning.

She had to beat Leigh, and in order for it to count, she had to beat Leigh *today*.

Grace wanted to beat Leigh because she was the better gymnast. Grace did not want to beat Leigh because she was skinnier.

Although she was.

LEIGH

Leigh felt like her blood was pumping pure adrenaline, like her heart would leap out of her throat any minute. She took a deep breath where she sat on the folding chairs watching Kristin do giants around the high bar.

"Can you believe we're here?" Leigh whispered to the tiny girl sitting next to her.

The girl almost snorted. She kept her eyes on the floor.

Leigh turned to look at her. It was Monica, the mousy gymnast with huge brown eyes who also trained with Grace's dad.

"It's totally unbelievable, right?" Leigh kept talking. "Like, people are actually paying attention to this meet! I mean, the mayor of DC even wrote on my fan page this morning! OMG, and did you see that Dylan Patrick wrote on Grace's fan page? Dylan Patrick, from Out of Touch! I wish he'd written on mine. Don't you?"

That was dumb, Leigh thought. *Why'd I lie like that?*

Monica shook her head and looked down. She was short, even shorter when they were sitting because, unlike Leigh, she was built like a gymnast: tiny, but with legs so long they seemed taller than her total height. She was flat-chested and baby-faced. Leigh, on the other hand, was the tallest gymnast in the competition, with unruly blonde hair that shot off her head in a chaotic ponytail. Her body was all muscle except for her actual breasts, which were big enough to ache when she dismounted any apparatus with a thud. *Sports Illustrated* had recently called her the "linebacker of the US National Gymnastics Team." It was supposed to be a compliment, they'd told her publicist. Whatever.

"I guess it makes sense. People are paying attention. We're at the freaking *Olympic trials.*"

Stop talking! Leigh's brain screamed. Her mouth never listened.

The girl, Monica, was still studying her broken, mangled gymnast toenails.

"Are you okay?" Leigh asked. "Did I say something wrong?"

"No. It's just—" Monica looked up at her, the flash of joy dancing in her brown eyes matching the feeling in Leigh's heart. "Well, I can believe *you're* here," she said. "You're the national champion."

Leigh laughed.

She'd forgotten.

It was the best moment of her life, yet she forgot about it all the time. Yes, she was the national champion. Yes, she remembered a month ago when she'd finally worked the beam well, when she'd hit eight routines in a row, racked up high score after high score, and climbed onto the top place on that podium in the middle of the floor. But it was like a dream. It was foggy and full of magic. It was a happy memory, but it felt like it belonged to someone else.

The real Leigh was the one sitting on this folding chair, trembling at the hugeness of the moment. The real Leigh felt too small for her body, marveled at the muscles that were layered on her bones when she was watching her routines on DVR. The real Leigh was a little mad at her parents for parceling her life into a million pieces and then calling it normal. Inside, she was not the national champion. Inside, she was scared.

"I can understand why you're here, too," Leigh told Monica. "Your floor routine at Nationals was incredible. Seriously, the whole place was standing, like on their toes, trying to see every tiny move you made. You're a really good dancer, too. I could never dance like that."

Monica smiled. "Thanks."

She almost whispered it. Like they were in church and not the Baltimore Metroplex. It made Leigh feel tipsy, the way people had started talking to her. The way the little girls squealed when she'd stopped to sign a few gym bags in the stands today. The gymnastics goddess they saw in her—Leigh didn't know who that girl was.

"Did you know—" Monica said, then the gym erupted into applause. "Yeah, Kristin!" Monica cheered. Then, "Hey, Leigh." Monica said her name like she was nervous, like she didn't deserve to utter the single syllable.

Leigh smiled at Monica again, trying to help her feel comfortable.

"Aren't you up next?"

Shoot! Leigh hopped to her feet. Why was she always like this? She got pulled into conversations, distracted by signs in the stands, lost in watching other gymnasts' routines. She was always wishing she had another minute to stretch before mounting an apparatus. "A teaspoon of Grace's focus could go a long way for a gymnast like you," her coach, Phil, kept saying.

Now Phil stayed on the arena floor as she hopped up the steps to the podium and began chalking her grips.

Leigh heard Monica call "good luck" to her, and she smiled.

Leigh spat in her chalky hands and tried to imagine her routine, tried to see herself making her first release, tried to see the crystal-embroidered mesh sleeves of today's maroon leo stretch forward as she caught the high bar. She ran her right finger over her left palm, smoothing out the pasty combination of water and chalk. Leigh heard Grace's name ring through the gym.

She looked up to see her best friend shaking her legs at the end of the vault runway.

Come on, Grace-machine, Leigh said in her head. She wished she wasn't on the podium so she could yell it out loud. She continued chalking, but she watched out of the top of her eyes as Grace nailed her vault.

Yeah! Leigh thought. They were one step closer to being Olympic roommates.

- - -

That had been their plan ever since they first became buds at USA Gym Camp three years ago. Back then, Grace was fourteen and already the junior national champion, already being called a great hope for American artistic gymnastics. At the same age, Leigh had barely qualified as an elite. She wasn't even on the national junior Olympic team yet. But, for some reason, Grace had chosen her.

Leigh had been on the back beam at the camp gym, running though her routine, the same element catching her off guard every time. She'd go through a tumbling pass, nailing a roundoff back handspring with no problem, but then she'd lose it on the wolf jump. Over and over when she landed, her back foot would either miss the beam or she'd barely be able to grasp it with her toes. Her old coach had gotten so frustrated with her, she'd stormed away. Back then, Leigh didn't get much of any coach's attention. She wasn't anyone's best hope yet.

"You're not getting full extension," she had heard a soft voice say.

It was the amazing Grace Cooper. She was looking up at Leigh as if Leigh were the superstar and she were the nobody.

"It seems harder to go for the full extension," she was saying, "but it's not. You'll keep your body more aligned with the beam that way, so it's easier for your feet to find it when you land."

Leigh tried the wolf jump on its own and landed it easily. But she was often able to land it without all the elements ahead of it throwing her off.

"Yeah, you know," Grace was saying. "This time, when you do it, talk to yourself in your head. You've got the roundoff back handspring down, so the whole time you're doing it, say *full extension, full extension* in your brain. Then look for the beam."

Leigh followed Grace's directions, and she landed the element with only the slightest wobble. She hopped off the beam.

"Thanks!" she said. Even then Grace was almost a head shorter than Leigh and inches smaller in all directions. "Do you always talk in your head?"

"Not always!" Grace squealed. "Only when I do gymnastics."

They both gave a shy giggle and the giggling hadn't stopped in the almost three years since.

It was Grace who had taught Leigh the true meaning of focus and commitment. It was Grace who had convinced Leigh that her coach wasn't good enough and made her seek out Phil. It was Grace's career that allowed Leigh to win one argument with her family. Her parents always wanted her to be "well-rounded" instead of "exceptional," but they moved from Philadelphia to Washington, DC, so that Leigh could train with a coach who was the right fit for her. Grace was the only person in her life who understood Leigh's determination, her need to be special. And Grace—Grace, the gymnast who would do anything to win—had held on to Leigh's secret instead of throwing her vulnerabilities to the wolves, even the two times in their lives, both over this same summer, when Leigh had beaten her.

- - -

Leigh glanced into the crowd and found Katja staring at her. Katja believed in Leigh. Leigh had to find that belief in herself.

She had to focus.

She spat into the palm of each hand one last time, swung her arms in front of her chest, and walked behind the high bar.

As usual, a torrent of crippling fears ran through her bones like bolts of lightning as she watched the red flag, stone-faced, waiting for it to turn green.

I forget my whole routine.

I'm going to fall on my dismount.

I'm the Linebacker of Gymnastics: way too big to swing around these bars like a petite nothing, like Grace.

Focus! she reprimanded herself.

She felt like her whole life, every Leigh in every day of her past, was lined up behind her. Every missed sleepover. Every potential friend or girlfriend whom she didn't have time for. Every lie. Every time she chose to be exceptional instead of normal. It was a series of crushing choices that shoved her up to the space where she stood right now, on the blue mat, under the uneven bars, at the Olympic trials. And it would all be pointless if she fell.

Then the flag turned green, and the storm inside her *poof*ed away. A smile lit up her face, and she threw her hands over her head to salute the judges before popping immediately onto the high bar.

Her brain turned off. It was only her body on the

bars. Through every giant, every release, every transition, she was That Girl. The Other Leigh. The one who was national champion. The one who could fall every day in practice but would never let the bar slip out of her grasp in a meet. The one who smiled even as she held her breath through handstands and pirouettes atop the high bar, whose toes pointed without her telling them to, whose knees would never bend, the one who would never break.

Ninety seconds later, with a double twisting backward layout, her feet were on the mat, her hands over her head. She was That Girl again.

MONICA

There were cameras everywhere. Every red-carpeted pathway between every white-draped podium was swarming with reporters and camerapeople circling the gymnasts the way a vulture circles its next meal before sinking its beak into the rotting flesh.

There had been cameras at Classics and Nationals but they hadn't come anywhere near Monica. She was a nobody. But now there was a camera sticking its lens practically up her nostril as her coach, Ted, gave her a pep talk before her first event.

Did this mean she was on TV right now? Were the announcers talking about her?

She hadn't ever noticed cameras on her at other

meets, not even in that moment after floor at Nationals, the moment that had been the height of her career so far.

Monica had been standing in the middle of the floor, her right arm poised over her head, her left hand holding her leg up so it was practically touching her left ear. Her chest was sucking in air. Her muscles were jumping. Her eyes were wide open. For that split second—after the music stopped and before the clapping started—gymnastics belonged to her alone. There weren't any cameras, because she'd been a surprise. There were rarely good surprises in gymnastics. There were bad ones all the time—the steadiest gymnasts would fall, the most powerful gymnasts would miss a connection, the most consistent gymnasts would stumble on a landing—but the good stuff in the gym was pretty predictable. Monica on the floor one month ago had managed to be a surprise. And that was why she was here.

She was *lucky* to be here. That's what they were saying. But that moment after that floor routine at Nationals didn't feel like luck.

"Monica!" Ted whisper-yelled. He was standing over her, his large elbows on her shoulders, his coffee breath inches away from her cheek, as he assured her that there was no pressure on her.

"Look, it's not about the Olympics for you today, kiddo," he said, his bushy blond eyebrows jumping around his forehead.

She made herself focus on him. She hadn't expected

him to pay her any attention at all today, with Grace, his star athlete and daughter, competing alongside Monica for the chance of her life.

"But it is about something, okay? I know you're years away from college, but you'll go this Olympiad, right? Well, let me tell you, there are recruiters here everywhere. I've talked to Arkansas, Florida, UCLA, LSU, Stanford, all the biggest programs."

Monica stared at him, wide-eyed. Why would he choose this moment to lay out this information? Why would he wait until minutes before she was about to mount the podium for the first event in the biggest meet in her life to tell what her stakes were?

"And, kiddo, they're watching you. Almost every other gymnast in this room has given up her eligibility to compete in college gymnastics by taking endorsements and going pro. Not you. You are still technically an amateur. And that means the colleges, the NCAA programs, will be after you. They'll be paying extra attention to you today. And you're taking this gymnastics thing to college, right? That's always been our goal, right?"

Monica nodded. Most of the other GymCade elite gymnasts dreamed of Olympics and Worlds teams and nailing gold medals into the wall, but Monica wasn't that kind of gymnast.

Monica was a second-best kind of gymnast. An almost-good-enough-but-not kind of gymnast. It had been that way since she was a little kid: always the second best in her gym, the red ribbon at the meet, the silver medal. And that was okay.

"It almost doesn't even matter how you do today, Mon. You're at the Olympic trials! We get you through the weekend with no disasters, we keep you healthy for two more years, and you should have a college scholarship in the bag. That's the goal, right?"

Monica whispered to herself the goal she always set: "Don't fall."

Ted laughed. She hadn't realized she'd said it out loud.

"Sure," he said, like he was brushing her off. "Don't fall. Also, let's get you an NCAA scholarship one day."

"And now on uneven bars," the announcer's voice called through the Metroplex, "Monica Chase!"

Her heart pounded, her kneecaps vibrated with nerves. Here she was, about to begin the most important event of her career—what was he doing writing all her goals in this minute? Here she was competing alongside stars like Wilhelmina Parker (who was Monica's secret gymnastics hero) and Leigh Becker (who was as nice as everyone said she was) and Georgette Paulson (who had wished her luck before the meet today). Now was the time to be steady and focused and to *not fall*.

"Have a good day, Mon," Ted said. "That's all I'm saying. Just have a good day."

Monica nodded.

She approached the platform with that mantra running through her head. *Just have a good day. Just have a good day.*

She chalked her hands and turned to salute the judges. *Just have a good day.*

Before she threw her hands over her head, she noticed the cameras were gone. She glanced around. There were some at the vaulting table where Wilhelmina Parker was warming up. There were several gathered around Leigh where she sat on the floor munching on a Power-Bar. There was one still zooming in too closely on her coach. Even at a meet this small—twelve competitors as opposed to twenty-four at Nationals and fifty at Classics—Monica would be ignored.

Her heart slowed just in time. That camera had been interested in Ted, the Coach of the Stars, not Monica. No one was paying attention to her. It was as if she were invisible. It wasn't a happy thought, but it was a calming one as she stood beneath the bars. This was like any day at the gym, any day at practice, any silly Level 9 dual meet like the ones at which she'd won silver after silver a few years ago.

Just have a good day. Don't fall.

Monica saluted the judges and piked onto the low bar. She transitioned off it in a straddle, launching her hips over the height of it and extending her arms so that her entire body hung in the air for a moment before she grasped the high bar.

She raised her body into her handstand, knees straight, toes pointed. Then she spun on her hands, a double pirouette, and swung her entire body around the high bar in a giant.

This was Monica's favorite event. It was like ballet, but upside down. She felt precise whenever she worked bars: her legs extended and split, knees straight and toes pointed, making her look like a human arrow.

Most of the time, in her tiny body, with her sheepish smile, Monica felt awkward and silly. But it was different in the gym. On bars, she felt beautiful.

When she released the bar, she flew feet above it and heard a few gasps from the audience. By the time she grasped it again, she was smiling.

She did two more giants, then her twisting backflip dismount.

She landed on the blue mat as if she were a butterfly on a windowsill. She stuck it. She saluted the judges.

No falls, she thought. *A good day.*

"Good job, kiddo," Ted said when she hopped off the podium. He put one arm around her and patted her head. She stood still next to him, her blue-and-silver chest heaving for air, her muscles hot and taut, her abs flexing behind the silver fabric to keep the air in her lungs.

Then, in a blink, Ted was gone, the cameras trailing him across the floor as he searched for the real reason he was here.

"You were so good!" Kristin came up squealing behind her. She hugged her friend tight, then hugged the other gymnasts who lined up to congratulate her.

Leigh was last. "Good job, kiddo?" she whispered, mimicking Ted into Monica's ear.

Monica let go of her, took a step back, and lowered her eyebrows at Leigh.

"What's with that: 'Good job, kiddo'?" Leigh asked.

Monica swallowed. Did Leigh think she didn't do a good job?

"He's your coach. He owes you more than 'good job, kiddo,'" she said. "First of all, that was amazing. And, secondly, if you were Grace, he'd be telling you about every out-of-place pinkie toe."

Now Monica's eyes got wide. She didn't know what to say.

"Well . . . you know . . . it's the Olympic trials . . . and Grace . . ."

Leigh shook her head and bit her lip. "I'm sorry. Not my business."

Monica stared.

"I just think you did a really great job," Leigh said again.

Inside, Monica squealed.

Then the numbers came booming across the gym speakers. Immediately both of their faces fell—Monica's to shock and Leigh's to horror.

Monica had just outscored the national champion on bars.

WILHELMINA

Wilhelmina hated her birthday.

For the past four years, it felt like it had shown up just to remind her how screwed over she was.

No, it wasn't today. If it were today, August 2 instead of January 4, everything about her life would be just fine.

She stood next to Camille and Samantha, halfheartedly shaking out her shoulders as she watched tiny Annie Simms launch her feather-like body over the vault.

"Remember when we looked like that?" Camille laughed.

Wilhelmina stretched her lips like rubber bands, hoping they looked like a smile. Camille was the only other one left from their old group of gymnast friends. They'd been friends because they were around the same age and started elite gymnastics at about the same time. They weren't best friends or anything. There was a whole group of girls, and they were each members of it, but they rarely spoke just the two of them. Wilhelmina and Camille hadn't been a pair of friends until the rest of the group disappeared.

And now Camille really wanted to be Wilhelmina's friend, and Wilhelmina was trying not to be a jerk about it. She'd managed not to hate Camille all year, which was impressive, considering their history.

But Wilhelmina was mad that Camille was here a second time when she hadn't even gotten a first chance yet. And then Camille woke her up last night, disturbing her sleep right before the biggest meet of her life, for a truly silly reason. Mina couldn't help but be annoyed about that.

"Welcome to the fogies club, ladies," Samantha said. Once an all-around gymnastics sweetheart, Samantha wore her full warm-up suit because she wasn't even competing on vault today. At this point, Samantha competed only on bars and beam. But Wilhelmina knew that underneath the fabric she was still slender with rope-like muscles lining her pale arms and legs. Even her white-blonde hair, pulled into a bun, was thin.

Camille was built more like Wilhelmina—thick muscles clustering onto every bone, breasts and hips and a butt that made her look like an actual woman, enough body fat to have rolls on her stomach if she sat slouched over. They were like gymnastics twins: same shape, different color. But they weren't the same. Camille had been a skinny, feathery gymnast once, but Wilhelmina was always built like this. And, back when they were in their prime, Camille had been given a chance. Most of their friends had been given a chance. Wilhelmina hadn't.

"I wouldn't want to be that skinny," Wilhelmina said.

She liked being larger. She was built like a tree. Instead of flying above the equipment in the gym, she took it sailing with her, becoming a part of the vault, a part of the beam the way an oak is rooted to the earth no matter how fast the planet rotates. Wilhelmina was so solid that when you watched her perform—when you saw her flying above the vault or bars or beam all smooth, dark skin and bright leotard and muscles, muscles everywhere— you couldn't imagine her falling.

And she never had. Wilhelmina had pulled off the almost impossible: a long career in gymnastics with zero major injuries. Yet now Wilhelmina was almost unknown.

"It's awful to be a skinny mini," Camille said. "Trust me. I know."

Wilhelmina sighed and dropped into a split beside her. It would be impossible to avoid Camille all day. Wilhelmina was going to have to try to get along with her. After all, they were roommates for the weekend.

But it was hard to stand the sight of her because there was a good chance Camille was about to steal Wilhelmina's Olympic dream. There were Magic Markered, multicolored poster boards lining the stands with the phrase *Comeback Cammie* for a reason. Camille was a fan favorite as well as one of Katja's pets. And she was a hell of a vaulter. If she landed her four vaults in this meet, she was jumping on a plane to Europe.

Wilhelmina was like a ghost. The only people in the stands who remembered her name were probably her parents. And Davion. (Because he was here. He said he would be. But Wilhelmina wasn't going to let herself get distracted by any boy—especially not today.)

Phil came over to the group and pulled Camille away. Wilhelmina's mouth relaxed out of its forced smile.

It was too hard to think about being nice. Wilhelmina was here to prove something. To prove everything.

- - -

Four years ago, when Camille and Samantha were named to the Olympic team, Wilhelmina could have beaten both of them with her arms tied behind her back. But four years ago, Wilhelmina's sixteenth birthday was four days shy of allowing her to compete as a senior.

In the year leading up to that Olympics, the FIG—the International Gymnastics Federation—was rethinking the rules about what age constituted a senior gymnast. Decades ago, there was no age limit. Then it was fourteen, then fifteen, then sixteen. The year Wilhelmina was fifteen, an Olympic year, her coach Kerry kept telling her to keep her fingers crossed. "They're talking about moving the age back down to fifteen, huh?" Wilhelmina would nod. "If they do, you'll be ready, huh?" Wilhelmina would nod. She'd kept her fingers crossed so tight they hurt.

The weird thing about the FIG is that it doesn't care when your birthday is. It's all about your birth year. So if you were fifteen in August but would turn sixteen before the end of the year, you were considered a senior already. Wilhelmina was born at the beginning of the year. She didn't want that to screw her over.

But the FIG had maintained the age limit. A girl would not be considered a senior gymnast until the year she turned sixteen. And a junior gymnast could not compete at the Olympic level.

It was such an unfair, arbitrary rule that had robbed Wilhelmina of this experience when her body was most ready for it. She'd won the Junior National Championships and watched the Olympics on television. The next year, when Wilhelmina was finally a senior, she went to the World Championships as the USA star. She'd been one measly point away from beating the Chinese girl and winning the gold medal.

When she'd gone back to the gym after Worlds, Kerry had pulled Wilhelmina out of her warm-up drills. It was surprising. Kerry was more focused on warm-ups than any coach Wilhelmina had ever heard of.

"We have some strategizing to do, huh?" Kerry had said when they got to her office. Her Romanian accent was similar but not identical to Katja Minkovski's Russian one. And, though Kerry was sure of everything she said, she ended many sentences with "huh?" It was a tic Wilhelmina found endearing.

Wilhelmina had smiled. "Do you think I can do it?" she'd asked.

But Kerry wasn't smiling as she had been in Germany a few days ago when Wilhelmina had won that silver medal. "That's what we have to talk about. What exactly the *it* is," Kerry said.

Now, it was Wilhelmina who said "Huh?"

Kerry swallowed. She cleared some papers from the big desk between them. "I pulled you from the camp roster for next month."

"What?" Wilhelmina almost-shouted. "I have to go to camp. If I don't go, Katja will be mad. At me. I can't just skip camp right after proving I'm the best US gymnast!"

Kerry nodded. "I know. She'll be mad."

"So why—"

"I see you walking around that hotel in Germany with bags of ice taped to your hips and knees. I see you popping Advil like little candies. You think you can sneak these things from me, but you can't, huh?"

"I wasn't sneaking," Wilhelmina protested quietly.

"You know what happens at the camps. You're overworked on old equipment. You're working out too hard for too many hours. Then you come back feeling like everyone is ahead of you. Not you personally. All the gymnasts do. Those camps create competition between our girls. A little bit of competition is a good thing, yes. But what happens is you go and you work too hard and then you come home and you keep working too hard."

Wilhelmina had never thought about it like that. She liked the competition. She liked working hard. But Kerry was right. It always took weeks to recover from camp. Or from any event where Katja was in charge. And the camps happened almost monthly, so it was like she was always recovering. "I have to go," Wilhelmina whispered.

"If we go to that camp, you'll come back broken,"

Kerry said. There was no *huh*. Wilhelmina knew she was serious.

Wilhelmina didn't say anything.

"We have options, Mina. We have different ways to proceed now. But if you keep going as Katja wants, if you keep going to all the camps and all the meets, if you keep training forty hours a week for years, you won't make it to the next Olympics. You're getting older. It's something I hate saying to a sixteen-year-old girl, but the sport, the way we play it, it makes me."

Wilhelmina sat silent and shocked. Days ago she'd been on top of the world, on top of Worlds, literally. Now her heart was being broken.

"If the Olympics were next year, it'd be different, huh?" Kerry said. "So we have to talk about your goals. If you want gold at Worlds a year from now, if that's what you want most, we'll keep going like we have been."

Wilhelmina was shaking her head.

"That's what I thought," Kerry said. "You want the Olympics."

Wilhelmina sucked in breath; she summoned that moment when she almost won the World medal; she reminded herself that she was good enough. Then she said it. "I want an Olympic medal in the women's all-around."

Kerry didn't laugh. She nodded. "Okay, then. I need to keep you healthy for three more years. I need to keep you safe. I will not play by Katja's rules. I will not break your body. So here's what we do. We take a year to relax, to heal. We withdraw from all the camps, from the national team, from everything. You train and stay in shape, go to physical therapy and get the kinks worked out. Then you come back. But we only go to the three mandatory camps each year. We don't go to the other monthly ones. We keep you healthy. And . . . you only compete on vault."

"What?" Wilhelmina said. "No, I want to do the all-around."

Something about specializing didn't sit right with Wilhelmina. It seemed disingenuous for an athlete like her who loved all events, who excelled at them all.

"I know," Kerry said. "We'll train on them all. But in the years leading up to the Olympics—at Nationals, Classics, Worlds, Pan-American, whatever—we'll only enter you on vault, huh?"

Wilhelmina was shaking her head.

"It's scary, I know. But at the Olympic trials, you'll enter the all-around. You'll qualify by the vault, then enter that way, okay? And worst-case scenario, we'll keep you the best vaulter in the world, so you'll be a vaulting specialist. You know the best vaulter will always get to go to the Olympics."

"It just feels . . . I mean, Katja—"

Kerry interrupted her. "I know Katja likes you now, because now you are a star. But look back on the other gymnasts Katja has loved, huh? What has happened?"

Wilhelmina thought about it. And Kerry was right. A lot of her friends her age or a year or two older were starting to drop the sport, whether they'd made an

Olympic team or not. They were breaking backs and spraining the same wrists over and over again. They were in braces and casts. They were hospitalized due to eating disorders or emergency surgeries. A lot of them had once been Katja's favorites, too.

"I'm not saying this is fair, huh?" Kerry said. Wilhelmina realized she must look heartbroken. "It's not fair. The Olympics being only every four years is not fair to gymnasts, huh? And Katja—the way she does this, the amount of control she has—it is not fair, huh?"

Wilhelmina was surprised. People whispered about Katja. People invoked her name to tease each other. But people rarely stated this problem outright. Katja was too scary for that.

"You know you can try it Katja's way," Kerry was saying. "You know you can go to all of the camps and push and push and push yourself until you break, huh?"

Wilhelmina stared at her.

"But not with me. You'll need another coach for that. I'm only going to do this in a way that doesn't damage you. If you want to do it with me, you have to trust me. If you want to do it with me, you have to be okay with defying Katja. That's how we get you to the Olympics. That way, if you fail, you're still in one piece."

Wilhelmina knew Kerry was right. She trusted her with everything she had. So, she nodded.

- - -

"Mina," Kerry called her over to where she was pacing a few feet down the vaulting podium.

Wilhelmina turned, patting down her hair. It was cropped short, nestled close to her head and decorated with rows of sparkly bobby pins. Years ago, Wilhelmina's Level 9 team had insisted over and over again on matching hairstyles. As the only black girl on the team, she'd spent too much time wrestling her hair into silly positions like poofs or upside-down French braids to try to make it look like her teammates'. Eventually, she got frustrated. After all, she'd never asked all of those white girls to go for flat twists or dreads. But she couldn't say that, so instead she'd chopped it all off. This was gymnastics, not a fashion show.

Kerry put her arm over Wilhelmina's shoulders. "No one knows what you can do," Kerry said, her high Romanian cheekbones tilting close to Wilhelmina's creased forehead. Her parents still called Kerry's accent intimidating. But after so many years together, Wilhelmina found Kerry's voice the most relaxing sound in the gym. "Remember that. We know you can get one of the top four spots. But no one else does."

Kerry had been right about almost everything in that locker room three years ago. But she hadn't been able to keep Wilhelmina the best vaulter in the world. No, that spot had been stolen last year by Wilhelmina's one sort-of friend left in the sport, when Camille burst back on the scene in a new body with a totally new repertoire.

So they were blessed when the USAG announced that the Olympic team would be determined directly after the Olympic trials this year, publicly. The first-place gymnast would automatically make the team. The Olympic Committee (along with Katja) would choose the rest of the gymnasts. They were likely to choose Camille for her high-scoring vault, and then the next three finishers in the all-around. Wilhelmina knew that Grace, Leigh, and Georgette were great all-around gymnasts, but she was hoping to beat one of them. And even if she couldn't do that, the fourth spot was open.

One spot. And every gymnast in the room had her eye on it.

Mina wasn't sure she could do it, but Kerry believed in her.

She hated that she was vying for the last place on the team. She hated that she wasn't one of the gymnasts—Leigh, Grace, Georgette, Camille—whose position was almost certain. She should have been. She should have gotten her chance.

Wilhelmina stretched her forced smile wider until it felt like her lips would split. She made her head bounce up and down like she was catching Kerry's enthusiasm. She was supposed to be excited. She was not supposed to be bitter. She was supposed to forget all about how this would have felt four years ago. If the FIG was more fair. If the rules weren't so stupid.

It was what happened in gymnastics. Each girl who

was lucky enough took her turn at the top, and then slid down into anonymity as perkier, skinnier, higher-flipping teenyboppers climbed on her broken body.

"You can make this team, huh," Kerry was saying. "You get that position. Or, if you win on the vault, you get a different one, huh."

Wilhelmina squinted at Kerry. Vault was her best event, but did Kerry really think she could beat Camille on it? *Camille?*

"And worst-case scenario, if you come in fifth or sixth," Kerry said with a smile, "you're still going. You're an alternate, at the very least."

"I don't want to be an alternate," Wilhelmina whispered. It was another thing she wasn't supposed to say. She was supposed to be here as a gymnastics veteran, lapping up any of the Olympic Glory Juice that might drip off the girls at the top. But she would rather retire than be an alternate. At least she thought she would. Wilhelmina had no idea what retiring would look like (except the tiny part of it that would look like Davion). But she knew it would be impossible to stand the smell and sounds of the gym if she missed her dream that narrowly again.

And alternate was exactly where the analysts predicted her to land.

Kerry shrugged and, like Wilhelmina knew she would, said, "You only control you. You perform the best; you take what you get."

Wilhelmina nodded.

"You don't have to be an alternate, though, Mina-Mina. You can be *it*. Just hit, huh?"

Wilhelmina nodded.

It was infuriating how wise her coach was. She wanted to be able to control it all; she wanted the guarantee that if she hit all eight of her routines, she'd be on the team.

"Go chalk up," Kerry said.

"Go Team Fogies!" Samantha called out when Wilhelmina was climbing the steps to the podium.

Wilhelmina turned to give her a smile even though it wasn't fair. Samantha was twenty-two. She already got to be an Olympian. It made sense that she was close to retirement.

You can't control your birthday, Wilhelmina. You can only control your routines, she heard her coach's voice say in her head as she spread chalk on her palms and her feet.

She stood at the end of the runway, crossed her arms across her chest, making an X with her forearms, and visualized her Amanar, her upper body twitching back and forth.

Wilhelmina and the other athletes who were hoping to get the chance to compete in the individual vault event in Italy—Camille, Leigh—would each perform two different-styled vaults. But only the first one counted, really. Only the first one would be factored into the team score, and that's what Katja was most interested in: team gold for the USA.

Wilhelmina got the flag, bounced once on her toes, closed her eyes for a quick second of silence, and took off down the runway.

Roundoff, she told herself as she got to the end. *Jump off the springboard.*

So far so good.

Explode off the vaulting table. NOW!

She kept her legs together, her knees tight, her upper body held stiff with her arms across her chest. She was high enough, higher than anyone else except Camille would get, but not as high as she could be. She twisted two-and-a-half times before she sensed the floor coming up underneath her. She finished her final rotation and stretched her toes toward the mat, then—*boom*—landed on her feet with her back to the vault. She landed heavily, and before she could stop herself, her left foot darted out behind her to keep her steady.

Stand up! she told herself.

She pulled all the muscles in her legs to attention and straightened out her body. One big step. A three-tenths deduction. Not exactly the splash she was hoping to make, and vault was her best event.

So oh well on beating Camille.

Still, when she signaled the judges, the entire arena erupted in applause and whoops, and she heard a familiar Russian accent cheering her name. She turned from the judges to Katja Minkovski, and she saw a huge smile fill her grandmotherly face.

Well, she thought to herself, *if that's going to make you smile, today will be better than I thought.*

Wilhelmina jogged back to the end of the runway for her second vault, her heart pounding to the beat of the surrounding applause.

"You can do even better," Kerry called up to her.

I can, Wilhelmina thought.

And then, she did.

CAMILLE

With two feet on the ground and only the smallest hop forward, Camille landed her second vault and threw her hands over her head. The smile on her face was genuine for a fleeting moment. She forced it to stay there.

She jogged to the side of the podium but paused before hopping off.

"Comeback Cammie! Comeback Cammie!" the crowd chanted.

That was her name now.

"Comeback Cammie! Comeback Cammie!" the crowd roared.

Thanks to the great skills of her new publicist, these fans liked her story even more than her gymnastics. The story that was plastered on every gymnastics blog on the Internet, printed in the gymnastics magazines, high-lighted on espnW and CBS Sports and even the Jewish Week. Her story was everywhere, even though Camille, until the American Cup six months ago, had been no-where.

She was living the old fantasy, the dream she had during every gymnastics meet she watched as a little girl: that it would one day be her name squealed from the plastic seats of the stands; that it would be her face on the posters in little girls' bedrooms; that it would be her signature Sharpied across gym bags. That politi-cians and talk show hosts and even boy band singers like Greg Thompson would write "Good luck out there" on her fan page the day before the Olympic trials. Ca-mille had a second of joy when she saw that "Good luck" from the lead singer of Out of Touch on her fan page this morning. But it fell to pressure quickly.

At the edge of the podium, Camille threw her arms over her head the way she had seen so many gymnasts do before her. She waved both her hands at once and the audience got a little louder, as if they were saying hello back to her.

Camille always thought it would be more fun than this.

She imagined her mother's smile floating somewhere far above her head and made herself keep waving.

"That's my star!" her coach said, giving her a double high five before wrapping her into a hug. Camille hated that nickname. She hated that he was yet another person depending on her gymnastics. "You couldn't have done that any better. That's exactly what we need."

He put her down, and she was smiling. Because she liked making him happy. Because she liked making her mom happy. Because the blood pumping through her veins when she landed a vault like that one always felt like exclamation points.

Because they all expected her to smile.

When the cameras turned away and the gym focused on Olivia, the last performer on the bars, Camille seized a private moment to check her phone. No messages. No missed texts. Nothing.

The morning of Classics, Bobby had texted her to say good luck. The morning of Nationals he'd texted. And this morning, he'd texted nothing.

- - -

Camille remembered Bobby's voice coming through her cell phone last night. "Please, baby, don't do it," he'd begged.

Camille had pushed her frizzy dark brown bun against the tiled wall of the hotel bathroom in frustration. "Can you just come? If you leave Long Island tonight, there won't be any traffic. You can be here in four hours," she'd whispered, not knowing how to cover up her desperation and stay quiet enough that Wilhelmina wouldn't hear her through the bathroom door. "It won't be the same without you in the stands."

"You don't want to do this," Bobby had said, his voice heavy and masculine. Camille could picture him in his kitchen, his curly-haired head resting on the white tablecloth, his blue eyes blinking nonstop as he waited for her answer.

Bobby was so heartbreakingly cute. In the almost three years they'd been together, Camille forgot that sometimes, as if by getting used to his good looks, his dark hair and light eyes, his muscled shoulders and crooked smile, she could start to ignore them. But he always seemed hottest in the moments when it felt like they were ending.

"I need to . . . finish it."

"You're twenty now. You're still there. What does 'finish it' even mean?"

"It's my choice, baby," she'd said.

"No, it isn't." His voice sounded lethargic, like a barbell hung on each word. It was the conversation they kept having, over and over, for almost a year as Camille fought and strived for a comeback, as her body turned to rock and her brain turned to mush, as her vault got higher and her mood got lower.

After his initial objections when she said she was returning to the sport, Bobby had supported her. He helped her find Coach Andrew, listened to her play-by-play of every workout, massaged her sore legs and arms and back, and showed up to every meet in his lucky green polo.

But he told her to quit. Over and over again he asked

her to quit. And she thought about it, a little bit.

But her mom was depending on her. Her mom was depending on her gymnastics for everything.

Bobby's voice had a new kind of desperation to it the night before the trials began.

The tile floor was cold through Camille's pajama bottoms. She glanced at her watch. It was 10:55; Lights Out had been more than an hour ago.

"I have to go to bed," Camille had said at the same time Bobby said, "I can't do it."

"You can come," Camille said. "You have to." She hadn't gotten through a meet without him since before they met, since before . . .

"No. . . ." he said. "I mean I can't do this. I can't support you if—"

"I have to go to bed," she interrupted. "Please come. We can talk about this in person when the meet's over."

"Camille!" he'd gasped, like it was hard to say her name all of a sudden. "I'm breaking up with you."

She'd dropped the phone. It clanged off the tile floor in the darkness, and she didn't even care if it woke up Wilhelmina or the entire hotel.

His voice was coming at her ear so quickly when she'd picked it up again. "—I love you but gymnastics is killing you and you don't even want to do it anymore. I can't watch you flush more and more of our time down the toilet. I . . . will you stop? For me?"

"Bobby!" she'd said. "You can't ask me that."

She didn't want to stop, that's what he didn't get.

She didn't want to be here. She didn't want gymnastics to take over every little bit of her life. But she didn't want to *stop* cold turkey again, either.

He spoke quietly. "I feel like if I don't come, maybe I'll finally get you to stop. And then we can be together. Fully committed."

"That's not fair," Camille had whisper-screamed.

He'd sighed. "I don't know what fair is anymore," he'd said.

She was ready to tell him the stuff she hadn't before, ready to bare her soul if it would only mean he'd come to the meet. "My whole life I've followed the rules. When I met you, I was seventeen and I'd never kissed a boy. I'd never even stayed up until midnight."

"That's my point," he said.

"But—" she said. She didn't know what followed.

But I like being a girl who follows the rules.

But I don't understand your rules for me.

There was a long pause, and then he said, "I'm sorry. I can't." And hung up.

Rap rap rap. The sound was sharp on the door. "We should be sleeping." Wilhelmina's voice snuck under the wood, each word pointed like a pencil stabbing Camille's thigh. "Go to bed."

Camille's face had burned. Wilhelmina sounded like a teacher and, even though she was older, Camille felt like a misbehaving child. She couldn't face her friend, so instead she waited until she heard the squeak of Wilhelmina's mattress before promising herself she'd make it up to Wilhelmina tomorrow, somehow, and climbing into her own bed.

Camille had whimpered herself to sleep, half hoping that she'd be so tired she'd miss her vaults and not make the team so she could limit the gymnastics in her life without her mom blaming Bobby for it.

- - -

So, of course he didn't text. Of course he wasn't in the stands.

And of course Wilhelmina was still acting cold and distant.

All of that hadn't stopped her at all. Vault was the shortest event, so it was possible to get very few deductions on it. The best vaults earned more points than the best scores on any other event. The Olympic Committee would always choose the best vaulter for the team because the best vaulter added the most points to the team score, and the committee was always after team gold.

The best vaulter was Comeback Cammie.

Camille was two vaults closer to her second first Olympics.

STANDINGS
AFTER THE FIRST ROTATION

1.	Camille Abrams	15.350
2.	Wilhelmina Parker	15.050
3.	Georgette Paulson	15.000
4.	Grace Cooper	14.800
5.	Monica Chase	14.750
6.	Leigh Becker	14.550
7.	Maria Vasquez	14.500
8.	Annie Simms	13.850
9.	Kristin Jackson	13.700
10.	Natalie Rice	13.000
11.	(Samantha Soloman)	0.0
12.	(Olivia Corsica)	0.0

Second Rotation

LEIGH

Leigh stood next to the uneven bars podium, face-to-face with Monica. Monica's mousy eyes were wide, the pale pink lipstick unevenly applied on her little mouth shaped in a small O.

This stupid little girl just beat me. Leigh could barely believe it.

"I—I'm . . ." Monica stumbled.

"God, don't say you're sorry," Leigh interrupted her.

"I wasn't going to," Monica said quietly, but Leigh rolled her eyes. Of course Monica was about to say she was sorry. Seriously, what kind of competitor apologizes for doing well? Once again, Leigh found herself wishing for Grace's focus. Grace would never let something as bland as friendliness get her into this kind of a mess. Maybe if she were allowed to devote herself to the gym the way Grace and Monica and everyone else was, she'd learn how to focus like that.

But Leigh wasn't that lucky. Her parents insisted that she attend high school, that she go on family vacations, that she have a backup plan. All their rules and philosophies confused Leigh. Like: *Always be nice, even to your competition.* Like: *A balanced life is a better life.* Like: *Of course we'll keep your secrets until you're ready to let them go. That's your business.*

Leigh didn't understand why they decided some things (her sexuality) were her business and others (her gymnastics) were theirs.

They totally accepted Leigh as a lesbian. As a gymnast? Not so much.

- - -

It was only a little more than two years ago that Leigh had finally won that one argument with her parents. She'd lost all the other ones, before and after. But this one time, she won.

Leigh's mom and dad were both in the airport when she and her old coach, Julie, had arrived home from Gym Camp. She was trying to make the national JO team for at least one year before she became a senior. The decision would be made soon, Leigh knew. And Leigh couldn't get there with Julie.

Julie had never had a gymnast on the national team. Julie's goal—stated on all the material she sent for elite gymnasts and their families—was to send gymnasts to college, not the Olympics or Worlds or any of the National meets. But Leigh was the best gymnast Julie had ever coached, she thought. Leigh had a shot at a national team. She needed a coach who believed in her, and in Katja Minkovski.

At the baggage claim, Leigh's mom spread her arms open while Leigh was still ten feet away. Her dad smiled and called out, "Leigh-bee!" his embarrassing nickname for her. For a second, Leigh was happy to see them. But then her heart fell to her feet.

They were her parents and she loved them. But she was so sick of fighting.

The family greeted and then said good-bye to Julie in the parking lot. As soon as Leigh was strapped into the backseat of her parents' car, she breathed a huge sigh and said, "I need to move to Virginia with Aunt Carol."

"What?" Leigh's mom had said. "What are you talking about?"

Her dad laughed.

This is always how it started when she wanted to be taken seriously. When she wanted her gymnastics to be taken seriously.

"I need to train with Phil McMann. He pulled me aside at dinner last night at camp. He told me he could get me to the Olympics, and he can. He can, Mom. And he's nice. He's a good coach. He never yells and he had banned weigh-ins before the coaches even had to. He cares about his athletes as people, too. That's what he told me. He's a really good option. And he's right in Virginia, right outside DC. So I could just live with Aunt Carol. And Dad works there one week every month anyway, so I'll see him then. And I can come back on Sundays. It's only a few hours from Philly."

Leigh's dad was laughing like she was hysterical

now. Like she was a little kid who thought singing "I'm a Little Teapot" meant she could win *American Idol.*

Leigh was so angry, she was shaking.

"Dad!" she yelled.

"Sorry," he said, flicking the blinker and switching lanes. But he was still laughing.

"Leigh, come on," her mother said. "You're only fourteen. We aren't ready for you to move away from us."

"The Olympics, Mom," Leigh said.

"What about school?" her mother asked. "You already missed a week for camp, and you'll miss another in two months. What would happen if you moved to Virginia?"

"I didn't miss anything," Leigh said. "I did every bit of homework. I always keep my promises, and you guys never ever do."

"There's more to school than homework, Leigh," her dad said.

"There doesn't have to be!" Leigh wailed. She hated that she was too loud. She knew she had good and important things to say, but she always wound up sounding like that little kid singing about teapots. She could never make her arguments sound right to her parents. They were always so much better in her head. "If I move in with Aunt Carol, I can just be homeschooled. Lots of other elites do it. I'll go to school on my computer like a normal girl."

Her dad laughed again and Leigh almost growled, so he said, "Sorry."

She shook her head.

"But seriously, Leigh," he went on, "we want you to have the other parts of high school. What about school sports and going to football games? And making friends?"

"And going on dates?" her mom added.

Leigh's face burned. She hadn't told them yet that she wasn't sure who she would be dating once she started. But she knew she didn't want to start until after her first Olympics.

"Those things don't matter to me," Leigh said. "Gymnastics matters to me."

"You only get to go to high school once," her mother had said.

"I only get to be young once," Leigh said. "That's when I'm going to be the best at gymnastics. Sixteen is the average age for a gymnastics peak, and the Olympics will be when I'm sixteen. A coach like Phil McMann could take me there. But Julie is planning for me to peak when I go to college, years after the Olympics. I need a new coach."

Then Leigh swallowed. She was about to play her gold card. If this next statement didn't win the argument for her, nothing would.

"Why should I have to spend the next few years the way *you* would be happy and not the way *I* would be? I want to be homeschooled. I want a new coach. I want to commit fully to my dream. Why should I have to waste my time on football games when what I want is to be a gymnast?"

Her parents looked at each other. They said nothing. They were totally, frustratingly silent.

Leigh knew they were inching closer to her. But she couldn't take the silence. Finally she said, "Just call him, okay? Just call Phil."

And they nodded.

In the end, her parents had come up with a "compromise." That's what they'd called it. Her dad had requested a transfer to the DC office, and they'd all moved to Virginia. Leigh started training with Phil. She got that part. Her parents got everything else. She enrolled in public high school. She maintained friendships with normal girls because that's what her parents had insisted on. She went to the occasional movie and football game. She pretended to be a regular girl when she wasn't in the gym, because that was the deal.

She'd gotten Phil, and that's what she needed to get here.

But still, Leigh always thought, *imagine how great I would be if I were allowed to commit to gymnastics the way Grace did.*

- - -

Monica was still staring at Leigh. Leigh wanted to shove her.

Instead, she gathered her stuff so they could commence their ridiculously feminine march to the balance beam.

Leigh led the six gymnasts around the uneven bars

podium to the folding chairs next to the balance beam. She felt Monica's breath on her neck.

That pip-squeak just beat me on bars.

Sometimes Leigh hated her body. Not her whole body: just the mountains and globs of muscle.

Leigh watched as the other line of gymnasts approached on their march toward the bars. Really, Leigh was watching only one of them. She was about to walk right past! As much as Leigh hated her own muscles and curves, she loved Camille's. The girl's eyes were dark, dark midnight blue, as if they were masking her own secrets. She looked right at Leigh when they passed.

Leigh hoped Monica wouldn't see the goose bumps that suddenly dotted her shoulders.

She looked at me! She looked at me! Before she could help it, Leigh was smiling like a crazy person.

She shook her head. All crushes had to be turned off, shut down. They were only distractions. Especially when the object of her crush was a girl with a boyfriend.

Leigh ran through her warm-up, then paced the floor with her water bottle, keeping her legs warm and visualizing her routine. But mostly she was screaming at herself inside her brain: *Focus, focus, focus!*

She couldn't afford to think about Monica's score or Camille's cushy lips when she was up on the four-foot-high, four-inch-wide beam. Beam was the event that terrified Leigh the most. She had to be calm and steady up there—two traits that didn't come naturally.

And Leigh needed to hit on beam. Leigh knew she'd

make the team. She was the national champion, after all. But her beam work was lacking. Leigh wanted more than to make the team: she wanted to be selected as one of the two gymnasts who would compete in the individual all-around during the Olympics. In order to get that spot, she had to hit on beam today and tomorrow. At camp last month, Katja had noticed that her beam work had gotten worse instead of better since Nationals. Katja had made it clear that she'd better hit on beam today if she wanted a chance to compete in the individual all-around.

Leigh put down her water bottle and kicked into a handstand. It was easiest for Leigh to focus when she was upside down.

Stay on the beam. Stay on the beam.

"Hey!" Leigh heard. She saw Grace's pink toenails underneath her nose. "I'm last up on bars, so I thought I'd come cheer you on."

Leigh dropped out of her handstand and embraced her friend. "You were so good!" she squealed. "We're doing it! We're getting to the Olympics."

Grace smiled at her, but her brown eyes stayed steady. Later tonight, in their hotel room, they would bounce and yelp and gossip and plan out the rest of their summer together. But not yet.

"How'd you do?" Grace asked Leigh. "Sorry, I missed it."

Leigh knew what she meant: *I'm beating you, aren't I?*

Grace was competitive. She was even competitive with Leigh. And Leigh accepted that. Part of being

Grace's best friend was loving all of her, even the parts that were sort of ugly. But Leigh didn't answer. She said, "How's it going for you?"

Grace shrugged. "Safe for now," she said.

Leigh lowered her eyebrows, confused for a second. "Safe?" she said. Then, "Oh! You mean your dad didn't look at your fan page?"

Grace let out a hushed breath between lips that were almost pressed together. "Not yet. I should just delete it."

"No!" Leigh said. "Don't do that. Dylan would probably be so insulted. Besides, your dad is not going to care."

Grace bit her lip and Leigh sighed. Grace was always worrying about nothing.

"How'd you do?" Grace said again.

Leigh knew that Grace wouldn't want to talk about publicity or privacy or any of the layers behind what she was going to say, but she had to say it. Besides Phil, Grace was the only person in the arena who knew about Leigh.

"So . . . I mentioned to Monica that I wished Dylan had written on my fan page. . . . Well, it's not true, obviously, but I made it seem like . . . but only because I don't want anyone to think . . ."

Grace wrinkled her nose like Leigh was the one being crazy.

"What?" Leigh said.

"No one knows," Grace said, more annoyed than soothing. "No one suspects anything."

Leigh had seen that look every time she had worried

out loud that there might be some hidden meaning to the word *linebacker*. (As if the straightforward meaning wasn't hurtful enough.) Grace had always been the safest person to know about Leigh because Grace didn't care. If it wasn't about gymnastics, it was nothing to Grace. It was stupid that Leigh had to keep this secret locked up so tight anyway—it's not like most gymnasts had time for girlfriends or boyfriends, so what did it matter which one they'd eventually prefer? But there'd never been an out-and-proud gymnast before. Leigh didn't need to be the Michael Sam of the gym.

Her mother always said that the world could be a terrible place, but that wasn't even Leigh's first concern.

She was scared about more people writing enthusiastic articles about her in *Sports Illustrated* and *International Gymnast*. She was afraid her first mention on ESPN would be about her sexuality instead of her vault. She was worried that if she came out as a lesbian she'd become the Lesbian Gymnast.

"You really think no one knows? Or I mean, not knows. Suspects? Because that reporter said 'linebacker,' and, you know, linebackers are, like, husky or whatever, and—"

"Will you calm down about it?" Grace said.

Grace was right: she was being crazy.

Leigh changed topics. "What do you know about this Monica Chase?" she asked.

An emotion flashed across Grace's face for a second,

her eyebrows raising and her thin lips curling in toward her cheeks. Pure condescension. "Monica from my gym? Why?"

Leigh shrugged. "She beat me on bars."

Grace laughed lightly. "I don't think we need to worry about *Monica Chase,*" she said, as if the name itself smelled like a rotten banana. Grace was almost laughing in the middle of a meet. It was unheard of. "My dad's prepping her for the NCAA."

Leigh tried to minimize the superiority threatening to puff up her chest. She chewed her cheek to stop her smile. She was not here thinking about the NCAA. She was better than that.

"I don't think it matters how great a day she has," Grace said. "She could have her best day and you could have your worst and you'd still beat her twice over."

Leigh nodded. She took a deep breath to try to steady her twitching heart.

"I mean, look at her," Grace went on.

The two friends turned their heads to see the tiny gymnast crouching a few feet away with her back to the purple-mat-lined bleachers. Monica's arms were twisted behind her back.

Leigh couldn't help giggling. "What is she doing?" she whisper-squealed. "Is she . . ."

To Leigh's surprise and delight, Grace was giggling, too. And for a split second, they weren't talking in code about whose name was higher on the scoreboard. The sight of Grace's tiny, pesky teammate pretzeling her body in an attempt to pick her leotard out of her butt without drawing the attention of the crowd was too much for even the most stoic gymnast. "Cheap butt glue!" Grace whisper-squealed, a hand on her stomach so her laughter wouldn't be visible through her red leo.

"Oh, God," Leigh said. "Leo wedgie! And she's picking it! In front of everyone! Poor thing."

Grace brought a hand to her mouth. "Poor thing?" she breathed. "She could put her pants on."

"Or buy better butt glue! That's one way to not be the Wedgie Queen!" Leigh squealed.

Monica looked up.

Oh, God. Did she just hear?

No. No. She didn't. She couldn't.

Leigh would not let herself feel guilty. Today was not the day to be nice to every baby gymnast with delusional dreams.

With another quick squeeze from her best friend, Leigh took her place beside the beam.

I'm ready, she told herself. *I'm the best.*

When the green flag raised, she rushed at the springboard and flipped onto the beam. She moved on autopilot now, her muscles working through her dance positions while her brain spun in happy, thoughtless circles between her ears.

She heard Grace and Phil and Georgette cheer her name just before her first tumbling pass. She did a roundoff *(bang)* followed by two back handsprings *(bang-boom-bang)* and landed solidly with her heels *(boom)* barely edging off the end of the beam.

The crowd applauded and her name was shouted but all Leigh heard was the metallic crashing of the equipment below her.

Stop listening to the beam, she told herself.

The reporter meant it as a compliment.

She split leaped, another *boom*. She did a full turn and wobbled out of it. A wolf jump *(bang)*, she landed with her foot half off the beam. She squeezed her toes around the corner of it as her upper body swung dangerously backward. She squeezed all the muscles in her right leg, her right hip, her abdomen together and managed to send herself upright again. She missed another connection.

She did her backflip. *(Boom.)* Another wobble.

Is the beam always this loud?

She danced to the end of the five hundred centimeters for her dismount, and she stood still.

Back handspring, back handspring, double back tuck, stick the landing.

But her brain was echoing the metallic crashes. The noise that rang every time her feet hit the beam. Even with the whole stadium cheering her on, the crashing noise was the loudest in her ears. It was what that *Sports Illustrated* reporter had meant when he called her the Linebacker of Gymnastics.

Fluffy Monica and balletic Grace would never

make the balance beam echo the way she did.

She couldn't chase the thoughts out of her head before she was flipping down the beam, listening to the crashes below her limbs.

As soon as her feet launched her off the end of the beam, her head tucked into her chest so she could attempt her double-tuck dismount, she realized she didn't have enough height. She flexed all her muscles, trying to get around a second time, and landed crouched too close to the mat. Her knees were bent too deeply, her butt was hovering over the floor, her feet backpedaled, moving her away from the beam in a series of steps until she finally regained her balance. She didn't fall. But she might as well have.

Leigh saluted the judges and slunk off the podium.

She felt like crying.

Her coach intercepted her as soon as she hit the floor. He hugged her, patting her back. She tried to walk away, to get a moment to herself at her bag to wonder what happened between bars and beam. Ten minutes ago she thought she could rule the world. Now she was in damage-control mode.

But Phil put his hands on Leigh's massive shoulders. He forced her to stop moving, to look at him. "You nail floor and vault, and this won't matter, okay? You do your routines like you have a million times and it'll be fine."

This morning they hadn't needed a strategy. They were so sure she'd be placed on the team. Now, things were different.

"Do you think I should try it?" Leigh asked. "Should I try our new vault today?"

Phil thought for a second. "I hope you don't have to. Let's see where we are after floor. For now, don't think about anything else. Focus on floor."

Leigh stared at him. She didn't want to nod because that felt like it would be a lie. People were always telling her to focus on this or think about that, but it wasn't that easy. Leigh couldn't always control what she was thinking. Sometimes words and pictures and sounds snuck into her brain before she could stop them.

Words like *linebacker*.

"What happened out there?" Phil asked finally.

Leigh shrugged.

She and Phil hadn't talked about that article after Nationals a month ago, but she'd noticed that he didn't hang it on the wall in his office with the rest of the articles about his gymnasts. The reporter might have tried to claim "compliment" when Leigh's publicist called to complain, but the article was ugly. The sounds he said Leigh made on the beam. The way the bars flexed under her weight. The way the floor dipped under her "power."

Phil was still staring at her, so Leigh said the one word: "Linebacker."

To Leigh's surprise, Phil knew exactly what she was talking about. He swallowed hard and mumbled, "That asshole."

That's all he said. He didn't tell her to forget about it

like her dad; he didn't explain how it was intended as a compliment like her mom. He said, "That asshole," and walked away. Leigh almost smiled.

She kept her eyes away from the competition, her ears closed to her score, and fumbled in the bag for her ChapStick. Her pulse felt shaky in her chest, her gut wobbly, as if, in some alternate universe, she was still at risk of falling off the beam.

As soon as Leigh could handle it, Grace was by her side.

"That wedgie-picking queen is not going to beat you," Grace said.

Leigh nodded. "Yeah," she said. "I'll crush her. And her cheap butt glue."

Her eye twitched. It was funny, what she was saying, but it stressed her out, too. She didn't want to be focused on crushing Monica. She wanted to crush Grace.

No. God, these meets could get her so confused. Leigh didn't want to crush Grace or Monica or anybody. She only wanted to do well enough today to compete in the all-around at the Olympics.

"Monica's plain delusional if she thinks she'll make the team," Grace hissed. "She's like my-DTY-will-beat-Camille's-Amanar delusional." They were both laughing. "She's like Dylan-Patrick-is-in-love-with-me delusional."

It was a low blow. Monica was delusional about gymnastics, maybe, but not about everything.

But Leigh laughed anyway. They laughed and laughed.

WILHELMINA

The chalk-coated fiberglass of the uneven bars spun in Wilhelmina's palms. That's what it felt like when she was having an "on" day. Like her body stayed in one place while she manipulated the bars around her straight knees and her pointed toes. Instead of a straddle release, where she flew over the bars with her legs kicked out to each side, today she shoved the high bar beneath her and sat in the air while she waited for it to rejoin her hands. Instead of a transition kipping beneath the low bar to a handstand on top of the high bar, she threw the entire apparatus over her head, then spun it around in her fingers until it rested beneath her body, perpendicular.

Bars were widely known as Wilhelmina's worst event, but it was sometimes her favorite. She would receive deductions for imperfect lines and separation between her feet because of the way she was built. It was impossible to have the "long, lean lines" the judges love when you have muscular, curvy legs that never look perfectly straight. It was nearly impossible to keep your knees glued together when your quad muscles touched with your knees still inches apart.

The best bar workers were always built like Grace Cooper or Annie Sims. They were all limb and no torso. They were more bone than fat, more bone than muscle, even. Gymnasts like Wilhelmina were expected to dazzle with the space they managed to put between their bodies and anything that anchored them to the floor.

Still, Wilhelmina loved the bars. Yes, all of those deductions were frustrating, but when it came down to it, working the bars was like swinging on a playground.

She bent her elbows and launched her body away from the bar, curled into a double-double—two tucked backflips, each with a full twist—and made sure her feet stuck to the floor when she landed.

She turned to the judges with her hands over her head and a smile already on her face. There was so much cheering and applause behind her, she felt like taking a bow.

Surprise! she told the crowd, the judges, the other athletes.

Wilhelmina and Kerry had been working for this moment for the past three years and here it was. She wasn't a vault specialist. She wasn't only competition for Camille. She'd just nailed her worst event.

All-around, here I come!

She hopped off the podium and, after the obligatory hugs, stuck her earbuds in, hoping Beyoncé would block out her score when the announcer screamed it. She didn't want to hear her scores until the meet was over. She didn't want to think about her place when she should be focusing on her gymnastics.

If she had six more performances like this, maybe she wasn't here for nothing. Maybe she would make the Olympic team. Maybe the past four years hadn't been a waste and maybe her birthday hadn't cursed her completely.

She didn't have to beat Grace or Leigh or Georgette.

She only had to beat everyone else.

The dream had been so close and then so far, it seemed impossible that it was back within her grasp.

When she glanced at Katja, the woman was frowning right at her. But that was okay. As long as Mina made the team, Katja's feelings didn't matter. She'd come here to prove you could make the Olympics a different way, a non-Katja way. She was here to prove you didn't have to beat up your body with constant gym camps, you didn't have to push yourself to train forty hours a week, you didn't have to suffer through eating disorders and broken backs. You could do this gymnast thing and keep your body intact. Wilhelmina had come here to prove Katja wrong, because her body and her birthday had required that was how she do it.

"Where did *that* come from?"

The words cut through the music pumping into Wilhelmina's brain. She turned to find Camille behind her. She pulled a wire until her right ear was free and forced herself to smile.

"What do you mean?" she asked.

"That was amazing," Camille said. But she didn't sound enthusiastic. She sounded confused. "Where have you been?"

Wilhelmina stared.

Just because you became a dirty gymnast who

rests on one perfect Amanar doesn't mean I'm going to,
Cammie.

"Why weren't you at camp last month?" Camille
pressed. "Why have you only been there for the required
team practices? Why didn't you do bars at Nationals?"

Wilhelmina shrugged. She felt her personality
shrinking inside her at this barrage of questions. She
didn't want to let Camille in on her strategy. Camille had
her own strategy and it was clearly working for her a
second time around. Why couldn't she let Wilhelmina do
her thing in peace?

Strategy and safety: they were what brought Wilhelmina to this place. Unknown. But uninjured.

Of course it would upset some people. Of course
some of her competitors would think it unfair that they
didn't know exactly who they were up against before
this meet. Some of them might think this was dishonest,
like Wilhelmina thought it was dishonest of Camille to
suddenly adopt the vault, which had been her worst
event four years ago. But Wilhelmina knew her plan was
different. She wasn't being lazy. And she wasn't being
dishonest with *herself.*

"What's it matter to you?" she hissed. "It's not like
you're even doing the uneven bars."

Wilhelmina meant it as a dig, but Camille's face
didn't change.

She tried again. "Anyway, it's not like they'd take me
over Comeback Cammie. Even if I am as good on vault
and an all-arounder."

Camille stared. She wouldn't budge. She wouldn't get angry back.

"You don't even act like you care," Wilhelmina said. "Staying up all night cooing to your boyfriend, keeping me awake—"

Camille's eyes finally went wide.

Wilhelmina wanted to sit down. Being mean was as exhausting as being friendly.

Camille leaned her mouth close to Wilhelmina's one free ear. "You really want to go, don't you?" she whispered.

That knocked Wilhelmina's guard down so fast, she almost fell with it. "To the Olympics?" she asked.

"Yeah." Camille scrunched her lips to the side of her face.

Wilhelmina nodded. Of course she really wanted to go. Didn't they all? Wasn't that the only reason to be here today?

"Don't you remember Melissa?" Camille whispered, her voice barely audible above the gym-chaos behind them. "And Caitlin? And Danielle?"

"Yes. . . ." Wilhelmina said.

Those girls had been on her brain constantly the past few years. Those girls who also shirked the system. Who had coaches who refused to play by all of Katja's rules. Who skipped camps or added events last minute.

None of them had gotten to the Olympics.

"But I'm better than all of them," Wilhelmina said.

"Everyone is going to see that today. I can do the all-around. I can help us win team gold. The committee will choose me." Inside she said, *Be quiet. Don't spill your secrets.*

Camille shook her head. "Katja doesn't like surprises."

Wilhelmina wanted to scream, "Who cares?" across the gym. She wanted to pound Camille's head into Katja's knee.

Camille went on: "Katja is . . . She won't . . . If she's mad at you, you're done."

Wilhelmina rolled her eyes. Camille was trying to get under her skin. She didn't remember this dirty side of Camille from four years ago, but she hadn't spent this much time with her back then. "If I prove I'm one of the best five gymnasts here, or one of the best four *all-around* gymnasts," Wilhelmina said, "Katja will take me. She's not going to hurt the USA's chance at gold just because I didn't do it her way."

Camille was shaking her head. "That's what Melissa said, remember?" Camille said. "She was ready for the last trials. You weren't at the selection camp four years ago, but believe me. She was better than everyone, almost. She totally should have made the team. Katja refused."

"But—" Wilhelmina protested.

"You're better than she was," Camille said. "Or you might be. I don't know. I don't think it'll matter. It's too risky for Katja."

Wilhelmina stared, dumbfounded. Camille couldn't

be right. There was no way she knew what she was talking about.

"If you go to the Olympics," Camille was saying, "you prove that all of those camps aren't necessary. You prove that you don't have to train constantly six days a week, eight hours a day in order to be an all-around gymnast. If you make the team, you prove you can do it *without* Katja."

"Exactly," Wilhelmina said.

"Yeah . . . that's why she's never going to choose you," Camille said. "If you make the team, you prove she's pointless. You threaten her power. You kill her job . . . her whole life."

Despite herself, Wilhelmina froze.

"If you want to go, you have to make it impossible for her not to pick you," Camille said.

Wilhelmina wanted to tell her to shut up. She wanted to unleash an angry barrage of gymnastics right on Camille's wide cheekbones.

She said, "You're saying I have to win the meet?"

"No," Camille said. "Probably not. You just have to beat someone she wants to bring. You have to beat Georgette or Leigh or Grace. Or else you have to . . ." Camille trailed off. But Wilhelmina knew how her sentence ended.

She said it: "Or else I have to beat you on vault."

Camille snapped her jaw shut.

Truth: it wouldn't be as simple as eight great routines after all.

The other truth was that Camille was evil: the only

reason to say all of that to Wilhelmina in the middle of the meet was to try to get her to choke.

At least now Wilhelmina could stop trying not to hate her.

CAMILLE

Why did I say that?

Camille's chest was jumping with electric bolts of alarm for her friend. Wilhelmina stood in front of her, her eyes lit up with a fire that had drained out of Camille's a long time ago.

Camille remembered that fire. Camille and Wilhelmina had been friendly until four years ago, when their birth years and the last Olympic trials came up between them. It felt like Wilhelmina would never forgive Camille for being born eleven months before her. And since the last Olympics, nothing about gymnastics politics had gotten more fair. Katja Minkovski was still the only voice of power in determining who would make the international teams, who would make the national team, who would compete at different meets. Wilhelmina hadn't been at the last trials to see how unfairly Katja treated some of the girls behind closed doors. And Wilhelmina had missed so many of the camps in which Katja was at her worst also.

But it wouldn't help Wilhelmina to hear any of that today. It would only freak her out.

Camille had once again made everything worse instead of better.

Wilhelmina was staring at her, brown eyes narrowed and angry. Then she sucked in a hot breath, turned on her heel, and stalked away.

Camille knew she had just lost a friend again. Do gymnastics, lose her boyfriend. Quit gymnastics, lose her mom. Say something stupid, lose Wilhelmina. She always lost.

Except on vault.

Camille sunk into one of the folding chairs and dug in her bag for her water bottle.

- - -

At the last Olympic trials, Camille had been sixteen, the perfect age for a gymnastics peak during the perfect year, an Olympic one. The gym had been swarming with the stars of her youth, the girls she had looked up to four years before, when she'd screamed at her television throughout the entire Olympics. Now she was here, among the Gym Goddesses, and she was ready to beat them all.

Since she was a new senior, no one knew what to expect from her (except Katja, who kept pace on all the juniors). Camille had choked at US Nationals and barely made the cut for the Olympic trials. Back then Camille was a wisp, a weed, a skinny thing, all legs and elbows and frizzy hair. She had dreams too big for her tiny frame: multiple gold medals around her neck and tears in her eyes as she listened to the national anthem over and over. It was a long shot. Her old coach kept telling her to see what happened. She was projected to get the last of the five spots on the team or to be one of the alternates.

She wanted to be the star.

She debuted her Amanar and, though it was weak compared to her vault now, she stuck it. She did a double back off the beam. She had the entire stadium clapping and gasping throughout her powerful floor routine.

She hadn't won the trials: she placed third, behind only Maria Vasquez and Melissa Doyen, two well-established superstars. But it was close enough to get her name on the list of almost-definites.

Then she'd gone on to Olympic Selection Camp and nailed everything again, day after day after day. The articles about America's smallest athlete started popping up all over the Internet. She was getting encouraging e-mails and texts from everyone she'd ever spoken to: distant cousins, old neighbors and classmates, girls from her temple. Some girl in the suburbs of Seattle started a Camille Abrams fan site.

The summer was kismet. Her chances grew and grew, her future got brighter and brighter as the Olympics inched closer.

Then there was the day. She stood lined up with the fourteen other gymnasts who had been duking it out at camp throughout the week. She held her breath. She knew she deserved to be on the team. She stood, her tiny four-foot-ten frame filled with confidence, her dark blue eyes radiating that fire, and waited for her name to be called.

And it was.

She'd let out her breath in one hot rush, her heart feeling cool and slow all of a sudden. It wasn't joy she felt, or accomplishment, or even happiness. Not yet.

Instead, what overwhelmed her, what rushed through her blood like ice, was relief.

It had all been worth it. All the sacrifice. All the heart-wrenching choices. All the grueling practices even through injuries and the flu. The physical therapy. The diets. The pushing through off days. The names her coach had called her. She was one of the best. She was an Olympian.

For a few hours.

GRACE

Grace was a willow tree on bars. Something natural and beautiful to look at. Something certain and steady yet light and flexible. Something long and lean and wispy.

Grace spun on her hands on the high bar in pirouettes that looked like they were powered by the wind. She floated to the low bar like a leaf in autumn. She straddled, and her straight legs and pointed toes embraced the audience.

They watched her with reverence. They didn't scream

and whoop at the height of her release moves or squeal when she transitioned from bar to bar. Instead the stadium held a collective breath in devotion to the beauty before them: a beauty that exists only when a small and perfect body does impossible things.

Inside, Grace felt peace. She felt zen. She felt what she used to when her mother would put her to sleep as a little girl after telling her the tale of the spider and the silkworm. "*Wo ai ni*," she would say, and Grace would feel so loved. She'd kiss Grace on the forehead, and Grace would drop to sleep.

There was no adrenaline on her breath like there had been an hour or so ago when she was lined up on the vaulting runway. Vault was about being impressive. Bars was about being beautiful. Bars was hers.

Grace did a one-handed straddle giant, named a Cooper because she'd been the first to perfect it in international competition, and then re-grasped the bar with her left hand to begin her dismount series.

Her muscles were screaming, her breath was strained, her palms were burning despite her grips, but Grace didn't feel any of that. Her heart was pumping sunshine and fresh running water. She was alone, practicing bars in a cave next to a babbling brook. She felt like her mother was there, somewhere, watching her and helping her breathe. Once she landed her Mustafina, Grace would be back in the gym. She'd be back to the cameras and the numbers and Leigh and, worst, her dad.

But for now it was Grace and the bars.

Then, as she piked to start her dismount, she felt that flutter in her chest: her heart divided like a swarm of moths in her rib cage, and she was back in the gym sooner than she planned. Her entire body flinched and Grace hoped the judges didn't notice. It was so scary when her organs split like that.

Still, she released the bar and threw her legs over her head, twisting her body to the left, then finding the floor and thrusting her arms into the air. The gym swung dangerously, the judges a pendulum in her vision, but she managed to keep her body anchored and upright.

She was sucking down oxygen. It felt like she couldn't get any past her throat and into her lungs.

All gymnasts breathe hard after bars routines, she reminded herself. *No one will notice.*

To prove her right, her father lifted her off the podium and immediately broke into analysis of her routine, saying nothing about her labored breathing or the fact that Grace was sure he could see her pulse punching through the skin beneath her jaw.

"Good," he concluded with a nod.

Grace tried to smile, wishing her body would calm down enough for her to enjoy the rare compliment.

He handed her a water bottle and she sucked some down, her nerves finally slowing, her heart finally solidifying.

"Just watch the transition into the dismount."

Grace nodded.

He didn't understand. He didn't know. It wasn't her

gymnastics breaking down in that moment; it was her entire body.

It was good he didn't know.

Grace took shaky steps back to her gym bag. She tried not to collapse into her chair. She pulled out her phone so that she would look busy and avoid some of the hugs. She didn't want anyone to feel how she was shaking.

Even though it was normal. Everyone was shaky after bars.

There was a notification on her phone.

Bet you thought that message last night was a one-and-only, Grace Cooper, but I'm actually watching and cheering for you! That uneven bars routine was HOT! <3 Dylan

Hot. He'd called her *hot.* Her still-not-back-together heart did little dances all over her body.

She bit her lip to keep from smiling.

Dylan Patrick had written to her again. He was actually watching. And he'd called her *hot.*

"Put it away." Her dad was towering over her suddenly.

She threw the phone in her bag quickly. Too quickly? Did she do it too quickly? Was he going to guess there was something bad on there?

"You have to focus," he said.

Grace couldn't stop her cheeks from turning pink. It was the first time she'd ever been called hot. Why did her dad have to shove himself into the middle of it?

Grace leaned into her bag, pretending to go for her ChapStick, but really pushing the phone deeper into it, below her pants and jacket, to a place far from her dad's demands for focus.

It was just one little thing for her to have to herself today. Just one little thing that wasn't 100 percent about gymnastics. It was dangerous, but Grace wanted to hold on to it for as long as she could.

MONICA

Monica was awkward in her body as she paced back and forth beside the beam, waiting for her turn. Minutes ago she'd been a puffed-up member of the US National Gymnastics team. She'd been a legitimate competitor on the uneven bars, beating the national champion in her opening event.

Now she was the Wedgie Queen.

Her body was all angles. She tried to focus on her upcoming routine. She tried to push the clicking sound of Grace and Leigh gossiping about her out of her brain and, instead, imagine her long lines, her graceful transitions, her powerful tumbling. But there were too many nerves shooting back and forth between her ears.

Monica marched herself into the locker room for the millionth time since she'd heard Grace and Leigh's biting gossip and locked herself in a stall. She pressed the blue fabric into the glue on her right butt cheek, and it yanked at the raw, freshly bare skin of her crotch. She resisted the urge to yell out in pain, to rub her fist over the itchy-burny skin at the base of her leotard where the wax job from a few days ago had replaced her pubic hair with angry red welts.

"Fifteen is too young to be getting waxed *down there*," the woman at the salon had said. "Especially to be waxing away *all of it*."

Monica was lying half-naked on the table, a curtain hanging at her waistline so she couldn't see her own bottom half. She'd squeezed her mom's hand. She was scared. All the girls at the gym said this was going to hurt.

They laughed, though. Like it was funny they had to brand themselves to stay in the sport.

"It's okay," her mother said. "It's different for my daughter. Tell her, Monica."

Monica's mother was always pushing her to tell people she was a gymnast. She said the word so much at her mother's prompting, she almost forgot what it was like to claim it on her own. Monica was glad her mother was proud of her, she guessed, but she wanted a chance to be humble. She felt humble.

"I'm a gymnast," Monica had said.

"On the US national team," her mother added, too loudly. "She's competing with the best girls in the country. She's a gymnast."

The woman nodded and started stirring the wax. It was a magical word that made Monica older. She only kind of understood why.

She was an elite athlete. But her crotch burned like any other fifteen-year-old's.

Now, in the darkness of the bathroom stall, Monica lit up the screen of her iPhone and stared at the empty spaces of her fan page. Sure there were a few *good lucks* from cousins and a stranger or two, but that was it. Nothing from her classmates. Only one message from one teacher. The rest of the school probably didn't even know why she was absent. She was there so rarely—only attending half days and missing one week almost every month for Gym Camp—they probably didn't even notice when she was gone anymore. She'd looked at the other fan pages this morning—Grace's and Leigh's and Camille's and Georgette's—and they'd been full of messages. Grace and Camille even had some from the boys in Out of Touch.

Monica had sort of hoped that a few hours into the meet her own page would start filling up. That some people would recognize her name on television and . . .

But it was like she wasn't even here.

Grace and Leigh said she didn't deserve to be here. And it seemed like no one outside the gym, except for her family, even knew where Monica was.

Why was Monica always invisible?

Monica checked Wilhelmina's page quickly. It was just as empty as her own, and that gave her courage. Wilhelmina had always been Monica's favorite (though she'd missed so many camps and meets, she didn't even know who Monica was, probably). Maybe she could be a gymnast just like Wilhelmina.

Monica darkened her phone, pressed her palms into the flesh of her butt to solidify the fabric one last time, and made herself move back into the light and the crowd.

The minute she was within throwing distance of so many hundreds of eyes, Monica felt itchy again.

Yes, Monica was spazzy all the time and it was one reason she'd never be a Leigh or a Georgette or a Grace. But she wouldn't have felt quite this spazzy if she were currently wearing more than this skintight, revealing leo. It was so annoying how, in order to compete in this sport, you had to be basically naked. Monica knew it was necessary, but it still made her feel squeamish. Every line of her body was on display. Anyone who looked at her could see the dip where her quadriceps met her hamstring, the jutting out of her collarbone above the silver hem of her leo. The lines of her abdominal muscles and the edge of her sports bra were visible through the shimmery fabric.

She paced back to the other end of the podium just as Kristin did her leap mount. *Put the warm-ups back on*, Monica told herself. She usually spent the entire meet in her pants except when she was on the apparatus. Most of the girls did not. The average elite gymnast stayed almost naked for the duration of a two-hour meet, marching around the gym like she never thought twice to be self-conscious about her exact shape being on display for the whole arena.

Monica had pulled off her warm-ups too early this rotation, accidentally misreading Maria's name as her own. She thought she'd be up right after Leigh. But she wasn't until second to last, and now she was pacing like a leopard in a cage and completely failing at her mission to appear confident, because she didn't have her pants on and she didn't want anyone to notice that she put them on and took them off then put them on and took them off all between only her first two routines.

Not that anyone was paying that much attention to her.

Then again, that's what she'd thought before when she'd tried to readjust her own leo over her own butt, and clearly the Royal Duo had noticed that. Monica shook her head to try to chase their giggles from her memory.

She kept her pants off.

She paced back toward the front of the beam and *wham!* Leigh Becker walked right into her. They froze and stared at each other, and the memory of Monica's name in Leigh's disgusted voice echoed through her ears. *Monica Chase, Monica Chase, Monica Chase . . .*

"Excuse me," Leigh said, staring down at her like she was a rodent. And Monica moved around the star to prop her leg up on the podium. She bent to roll out her toes.

It had been surprising to Monica when her score trumped the national champion's, but it turned out she had a higher degree of difficulty, so that's what happens. When you added up the score potential for each of Monica's tricks on bars, it was higher than Leigh's. They both did most of their tricks well, so Monica's score stayed higher than Leigh's. So who cared? It's not like Monica would beat Leigh in the all-around.

But Leigh had been so bratty about it. "Don't apologize."

Like Monica *should* apologize or something.

It was trippy, though—she *had* almost apologized.

It was a wake-up call. Monica could be friends with the other gymnasts here, but she couldn't be a fan. She had to be a fan of herself alone.

If she wasn't her own fan, no one would be.

Monica switched legs and rolled out her left toes. Her body felt more like her own when she was stretching and doing gymnastics. When she was walking around for millions to see all her muscles and organs, she almost felt like her body wasn't hers anymore. Like it was a cage everyone else owned and she was trapped inside of it.

Monica kicked into a handstand to stretch her abs and finally started to visualize her routine.

"Just have a good day, right?"

Ted's voice came from high above her head. She nodded, her chin moving up toward her feet, and she dropped out of the handstand.

"That's the goal, right?"

No. Monica nodded even as she argued with her coach in her brain. *Don't fall. My goal is to do eight routines with no falls.*

"Good girl." Ted patted the top of her head like she was a dog playing fetch. "Go chalk up."

A few minutes later, Monica's hands grasped the four-inch beam, and her butt and abdomen pulled her legs up over her head into a handstand. She split into a full upside-down straddle. Then she walked on her hands so that she was on the edge of the beam and bent her back until her feet were on the beam behind her head.

Monica might be skinny and tiny. Her body might be all angles and her hair might not be shiny. She might sometimes have trouble getting distance on her vault and height between her tumbling body and the beam. But she was one of the most flexible gymnasts in the country. Her beam routine was designed to demonstrate that.

It worked.

For the next ninety seconds, Monica saw nothing but the beam. She did walkovers and handsprings and roundoffs. She did her double full turn, which got an *ooh,* so at least a few little girls in the audience were watching her. Her eyes stayed on the slightly fuzzy cream surface of the beam. She did an aerial cartwheel into a walkover that landed her seated on the beam, her legs hanging over it, her stinging crotch being flattened against the hard surface.

She laid her body across the beam, grasped it with her forearms, her chin pressed into the side of it, and kicked her legs over her into a beam-hugging handstand. Another *ooh.* She lifted herself onto her hands, did a back walkover, and landed at the end of the beam just in time to hear the warning beep. She had ten seconds.

Perfect.

She pointed her toe in front of her, took a deep breath, and dismounted: cartwheel *(upside down, right-side up)*, aerial cartwheel *(upside down, right-side up)*, double back tuck *(upside down, right-side up, upside down, right-side up)*.

She landed on her feet with a tiny hop.

Something somewhere in her gut made Monica's head lurch up, and her eyes landed on Katja Minkovski. She was leaning toward an ex-Olympic gymnast and laughing. She wasn't even paying attention.

Oh well. That much Monica expected.

She was on her way to her goal. She didn't fall.

STANDINGS
AFTER THE SECOND ROTATION

1.	Georgette Paulson	30.725
2.	Grace Cooper	30.650
3.	Wilhelmina Parker	29.650
4.	Maria Vasquez	29.540
5.	Monica Chase	29.350
6.	Samantha Soloman	28.980
7.	Leigh Becker	28.450
8.	Annie Simms	28.200
9.	Kristin Jackson	27.750
10.	Natalie Rice	27.000
11.	Camille Abrams	15.350
12.	Olivia Corsica	14.850

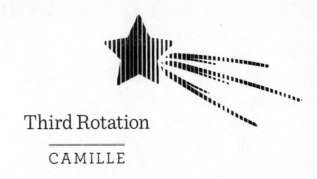

Third Rotation

CAMILLE

Worms of guilt crawled through Camille's heart as she watched Wilhelmina warm up for the second of the two rotations Camille would be skipping due to her specialist status. Her friend was shooting her confused and dirty looks that made her want to shrink. She should apologize, but how?

Her phone buzzed in her hand and Camille flipped it to study the screen. Finally! Her heart leaped to her throat. Bobby wasn't there, but he was watching from home, she figured. He was finally texting her that good-luck message.

But no. It wasn't a text or a phone call or anything. It was just another message on her fan page. This one from male gymnastics superstar Mario Alvarez.

Good luck, Comeback Cammie! Hoping we'll be heading to Italy together in a few days!

Camille sighed. She wanted to throw the phone into the stands and run away from this gym forever. But—

bing—a little, tiny thumbs-up appeared beneath Mario's message. Her mom had liked his post. Her mom had liked Greg Thompson's post and the mayor's post and her old high-school principal's post. Stuff like this was keeping her mom going.

Camille had no choice but to be the top scorer on vault today. *Sorry, Wilhelmina.*

Sixteen-year-old Camille would never have sat on the sidelines like this, worrying about boyfriends or parents or trying to determine another girl's chances because she recognized the fire in her eyes. Sixteen-year-old Camille's fire was too bright to see past it.

What had happened to that girl from four years ago? What had happened to the singularity of her mind, to the gumption of her dreams, to the joy in her competition?

- - -

Her mother had been there that day, of course. That single day when she was an Olympian. All the parents were asked to pay their way to New Mexico to sit on a set of bleachers and listen as their daughters' dreams were either confirmed or squashed.

The relief in Camille's chest had solidified into joy by the time she'd found her mother. Then, Helen was huge compared to Camille's tiny frame, a woman of more than two hundred pounds, all soft tissue and slow movement. At almost seventeen, Camille looked like she could be eleven—four foot ten and string-bean skinny with unruly brown hair and no hint of hips or breasts. Helen picked up tiny Camille and swung her around as Camille whispered in her ear, "Come on, Mommy. Let's go." Camille wanted to rush out of there, away from Gym Camp, where the busted dreams and tears of so many of her fellow gymnasts threatened to dilute her joy.

She would fly back to Long Island with her mother for a quick three days of family time (and training, of course) before she was required to return to the camp for a few weeks, and then ultimately board the plane to the Mexico City Olympics.

Camille and Helen were the first out the gym doors after a quick thank-you to her coaches and Katja. They burst into giggles as they made a break for the parking lot, and together they dove into her mother's rented Ford Taurus. While Helen backed out of the parking space and barreled down the winding camp driveway, Camille strapped herself into the front seat and hooked up her iPod to the car stereo. She blared "Wake Me Up Before You Go-Go" by Wham!—the song they both loved to sing whenever Camille had a successful meet.

And Camille was happy. Camille was so happy, it was almost surreal. She was going to the Olympics. She was one of the best gymnasts in the country, in the world, even. She was with her mother.

This was before Bobby and regular high school. This was before she even had the fan page for Greg Thompson or Mario Alvarez to find her on. This was when all the people Camille knew could be divided into three categories: gymnasts, coaches, and family. So her mother was her best friend. And the only thing that could possibly feel as good as hearing her name as part of the Olympic team was seeing her mother's smile.

They careened through the New Mexican country roads, screaming the song out the open windows, smiling and bouncing in their seats. This hoped-for, prayed-for moment was almost otherworldly, almost like she wasn't in the car but was instead floating above it, watching and saving the joy for later.

And it was good she wasn't in her body at that moment. Because that's probably why she didn't feel her head go through the windshield.

- - -

When Camille woke up, she wasn't on Long Island. She was still in New Mexico. She knew that right away from the air-conditioning—in New York's July, it would be blasting all the time, but it was barely purring on her skin. In New Mexico, you could turn down your air-conditioning at night. The state cooled off without the burn of the sun.

Camille's eyes shot open. Where was she? It was pitch-dark.

She pulled her elbows to her sides, trying to prop herself up, but pain rang through her scalp and her lower back like black flames. She crashed the two inches back to her pillow, and that's when she realized it. The tight way the sheet was folded. The beeping of a machine by her head. Her mother's heavy breathing somewhere to her right.

She was in a hospital.

"Mom?" Camille managed to push the one word through the fire.

Her mom was immediately awake, her eyes glowing in the darkness. "I'm so sorry, Cam-Cam. I'm so sorry."

Camille didn't ask where she was. She asked the only question that mattered.

"Am I still going to the Olympics?"

Her mother had stroked her cheek with a fleshy palm. "Of course. We'll get you back in the gym. We've come this far."

Camille leaned her cheek further into her mother's touch. She let herself calm down.

"We'll talk to the doctor tomorrow," Helen concluded.

- - -

"It's gymnastics that almost killed you."

That's what the doctor said the next day. He looked from Camille's face to Helen's, searching for a reaction, but they were both still. Gymnastics had almost killed her before. It almost killed everyone she knew at least once. Everyone had some sort of scare when she fell head-first off the bars or whacked her back into the balance beam from three feet in the air.

He repeated it. "It's gymnastics that almost killed you. I would advise you never to return."

"No," her mother corrected him. "It was a car accident."

"Mrs. Abrams." The doctor said her name like Camille's mother was the child. He turned to face Helen where she sat next to the bed, clutching Camille's hand. "What was this young girl doing in the front seat of the car?"

Camille's face pinched into a tight expression; her heart sped up in her rib cage.

Helen faltered. "She's . . . almost . . . seventeen. . . ." she said.

"She's only seventy-eight pounds," the doctor replied. "In New Mexico, it's illegal for any individual who is under eighty pounds to ride in the front seat of a car, and, quite frankly, it's inadvisable for anyone under ninety. In fact, they still make booster seats for children her size."

"But . . . she's sixteen. . . ." Helen tried again.

The doctor shook his head. "Her body doesn't know that," he said. He turned and faced Camille. "Do you menstruate?"

Camille blushed. She'd never heard a man talk about periods before. She shook her head.

"I didn't think so." He sighed. "Unfortunately, with that doll factory right up the road that y'all call Gym Camp, I've seen too many gymnasts to hope that these words will have any effect. But I'll say them anyway:

you need to rethink how much your sport is worth. If you were not an elite gymnast, you would have gotten in a fender bender, and you'd be on your way home, no more banged up than your mother, who is only suffering from a bruise on her arm. You would be taller and heavier, so you would not have to risk your life sitting in the front seat of your mother's car at sixteen years old, and you wouldn't have slipped out of your seat belt and crashed your skull into the windshield. Furthermore, if you weren't constantly beating your body with overtraining, you would not have the stress fractures in your back that caused it to break in three places during the crash. It's gymnastics that almost killed you," he concluded. "The crash just helped."

By now Camille's heart was beating in her throat. Sure, she'd seen nutritionists. She'd been told by regular doctors that she was too frail and small to be training as much as she did. She'd been warned that if she didn't start her period before her eighteenth birthday, that could mean something terrible about her health.

But she'd shrugged all that off. It sounded crazy. How could she be unhealthy when she was able to make her body move in ways most people couldn't even think about?

Plus, for every doctor and trainer who warned her, her coach seemed to be able to find another who wasn't too concerned.

But now she'd almost died. She knew it.

"But she was just named to the Olympic team!" her mother had yelled.

Camille's eyes ached, they went so wide. That felt like a year ago, a lifetime ago. Her mind was anchored in her broken back.

The doctor looked right at her. "You're not paralyzed. If we get you the right doctors back home, this situation won't be permanent. On your body, anyway. Your mind's another story."

"So she can try again?" her mother said. Then she seemed to decide it. "So next Olympics she'll try again."

The doctor still didn't take his eyes off Camille's bony frame.

"You shouldn't. But if you do . . ." He sighed. "And I know enough by now—you'll keep at it no matter what I say. So if you start training again, please put on at least twenty-two pounds, okay?"

GRACE

Grace clasped her hands over her breastbone. She was standing on the beam podium, waiting for the green flag.

Stay there, she said silently. *Stay still. I mean, keep beating, but don't fall apart.*

It would look like she was praying, but Grace didn't pray. She spoke directly to her inner organs. It was her own body she counted on, not some Great Unknown Creature in the Sky.

And today, it felt like her heart was listening.

You can't give out on me now, okay? she asked her heart. *I need you. I'm winning.*

Because Grace had done what she'd promised herself she wouldn't: she'd snuck a peek at the scoreboard. And even though her dad always warned her against comparing scores too early in the meet, Grace was shocked to see that Leigh's name was nowhere near her own. Her own name was almost on top. That was not surprising. Georgette was technically winning, but that's only because she got a lot more points on vault than Grace did. Grace's degrees of difficulty and maximum score were higher for every other apparatus, so Grace would catch her quickly. But both Grace and Georgette were beating Leigh. Wilhelmina was several slots in front of Leigh. And—this gave Grace the most confidence in her eventual domination—Monica was *still* beating Leigh. Monica was in Leigh's rotation, which meant their scores were comparable. And it was basically agreed upon that Monica didn't even deserve to be present that day. The gap between Grace and Leigh was not simply because they'd competed different events so far: it meant Leigh was having a terrible day. And Grace was having a good one.

Grace was supposed to be scared for Leigh. She was supposed to be her friend and feel her losses. But Grace wasn't. She couldn't be.

It was perfect.

The only thing that could stop Grace was encased

within her own skin. *Just do what you're supposed to.*

The green flag waved in the corner of her vision, and Grace dropped her hands and squinted at the beam. Her beam coach always told her "focus can make the beam grow."

And she was right. When Grace's insides were still and her mind was laser sharp, she could make the four-inch surface of the beam spread to six or eight. And on the rare day that Grace was off, the beam got skinnier. Sometimes, mid-routine, when she stood with her ten toes lined up for her single standing back tuck, her pinkie toes hung off the edges. Other times, the creamy cloth that covered it seemed to go on for inches on either side of her feet.

Today, she would turn this beam into a sidewalk.

She signaled the judges, stormed toward the springboard, and leaped onto the beam, the soles of her feet landing squarely with a *bang.* Her heart beat solidly in the pit of her chest. Everything was as it should be.

For the next ninety seconds, the gym disappeared and she saw only the glowing sidewalk-beam. Ninety seconds of only her limbs and her hands and her muscles. Then, with a roundoff double back layout, it was over.

Grace threw her hands over her head as she faced the judges, then brought them immediately to her heart. *Thank you, thank you,* she told it. *Only one rotation left. We can do it.*

Her father patted her sleek ponytail once she was off

the platform. "Not quite as good as bars," he whispered through his fake smile. "You can get more height on that dismount. You swung your arms before your switch leap, so you missed that connection. And you weren't solid on your full turn."

Grace nodded. His critique was unfair, as usual. She said nothing, as always.

He turned his back on her and scanned the gym, seeming to look at nothing.

Was he punishing her? Had he found her phone? Had he taken the time to go on her fan page on his phone?

Did Dylan post again?

If he kept it up, Grace would have to tell Dylan Patrick to stop. She'd be freaking out about him until the Olympics, even through the Olympics, if she didn't put a stop to it. They were stupid messages from some patriotic celebrity, and it would be 100 percent mortifying to acknowledge them with more than a simple "like" button. But she'd have to do it. All those silly fantasies that sometimes danced in her head when she was outside the gym—dates and candlelit dinners and midnight phone calls—she couldn't have them anyway. Even if that was what Dylan Patrick meant when he said *hot*.

So Grace would reply to him on her fan page and say, "Thanks for the good luck message! Please don't post on my page anymore. I can't afford to be distracted by boys." That would placate her dad. And then it would be over . . . Dylan . . . her crush . . . her distraction from the world of beams and bars and vaults . . .

It would be over. Soon. She'd take care of it before her dad found out, hopefully.

But Dylan had called her *hot*.

Maybe Leigh was right. Maybe her father wouldn't bother to check her fan page.

"I think you probably got what we need to take the lead, though," her dad said, turning back to her.

Grace nodded again, even though she knew better than that. She gave a stellar beam routine. It was more than they needed. Why couldn't he admit that?

A dinging rang between them, bursting out of Grace's gym bag. *Dylan again?*

Grace's father's eyes flicked to her bag and then back to her. He dared her to check her phone. She swallowed.

Then he was gone.

Where did he go?

Grace grabbed a water bottle, glancing around, trying not to be obvious as she looked for where she should be and who she should be talking to. She wished again that Leigh was in her rotation and she could go plop down next to her. Grace hated feeling lost and shy, especially in the middle of a meet.

She saw her dad then, his blond crew-cut head dashing between the podiums, rushing to the folding chairs beside the floor. *Oh yeah,* Grace thought. Monica stood in the corner of the floor, her head thrown up to the ceiling and her arms folded over her chest. *He has to watch Monica, too.*

Now would be the perfect time to check her phone.

Now, when her dad couldn't look at her. But there was a camera next to her. And that probably wasn't Dylan again anyway.

Grace wandered toward the floor podium. Fans liked when you cheered for your underdog teammate, she reasoned. It looked good. As focused as Grace was, it was impossible not to think of the people who might be watching her at home when all the cameras surrounded her like this. People like Dylan Patrick. And, maybe, people like her mom.

Not that Grace knew anything about where her mother was or what she was doing. It had been eight full years since Grace had laid eyes on her mother; the woman had been gone ever since a few months after Max was born. She hadn't heard a word from her since her twelfth birthday, when they had a brief phone call, but her mother refused to tell Grace where she was calling from. Then she had said she'd been reading about Grace online. She'd been following her career. Grace didn't know if her mother followed gymnastics anymore. But if she won Olympic trials, if she was the favorite for gold, if she was on all the magazines and in commercials and maybe even on *The Tonight Show,* her mother would have to see her face again.

Not that that's why Grace wanted to win.

"Hey!" Leigh said, walking up beside her.

Grace nodded at her friend.

"Did you see?" Leigh blabbed, the words falling out of her mouth too quickly and carelessly as if she didn't realize where they were. "I don't know if you saw, but he messaged you *again*. It's been after, like, every event. And you know what? I only asked him to wish you good luck the first time. He must be watching the meet!"

Grace turned to Leigh's bouncy smile. Didn't Leigh realize she was losing? Didn't she know a stupid new message didn't matter? And what did that message say?

"Are you gonna reply?"

Leigh was crazy. Leigh was a boy-crazy lesbian.

"No," Grace said, a little too loudly. What had Dylan written that made Leigh think Grace should respond?

Just then, the piano notes rained softly down on the gym, and Monica began her routine. She was a talented dancer. Grace knew that from the ballet classes her father insisted all his gymnasts take to support their floor and beam routines.

"He's right, too. Dylan is. You were great," Leigh whispered. "I think that's the best I've ever seen you do on beam."

Grace returned Leigh's fake smile. There was no way Leigh's smile and compliment were real. She was trying to get under Grace's skin, but she should know by now that it wouldn't work.

They turned back to watch Monica dancing.

Grace squinted at Monica's bottom, looking for signs of loose-leo. She tried to think of another butt-glue joke to bring her real friend back, but she found herself captivated. They both were. Monica controlled the floor. Her movements were graceful and precise and perfect. Her arms and legs commanded attention, pulled the spectator onto the floor with her. She was taller than her height should allow her to be. And her tumbling looked like dancing.

When she struck her final pose, Grace and Leigh clapped along with the rows of fans in the stands, their jaws dropped in awe.

Leigh's smile was gone. "Shit," she breathed.

Grace started adding up past scores in her head. Leigh could still beat Monica on floor. Monica's performance was close to perfect, but Leigh's difficulty was greater, so her maximum potential score was higher. Still, Leigh wouldn't be able to blow her away. At the end of the day, Monica was likely to still be ahead of Leigh.

And Monica was not going to the Olympics.

Leigh was the national champion (thanks to Grace's fluttery heart), so, to a lot of people, it seemed like Katja had to choose Leigh no matter how she performed today and tomorrow.

But Leigh was not only far from second—she was behind Wilhelmina and Georgette and Maria and Monica. Monica!

"If all these girls beat me . . ." Leigh trailed off, but she didn't have to finish the thought. Grace knew the end of the sentence.

Katja had some leverage as to whom she chose, but these trials were on television. If Leigh came in toward the end of the all-arounders, Katja and the Olympic Committee would not be able to explain picking her. So they wouldn't.

Grace paused her clapping and turned to study her best friend's profile. A thought went zinging through her brain, jolting her from her skull to her fingertips. A thought that she didn't like as much as she thought she would.

What if this meet isn't about beating Leigh? What if I'm going to the Olympics without her?

LEIGH

Leigh stood panicked as Monica saluted the judges and exited the podium to a storm of applause. Her heart hammered with anger, fear, shame.

"Monica is going to beat me," she whispered to herself. She said it out loud. Of course. Stupidly.

Good-bye, Olympics. Good-bye, lifelong dream.

"Use it," Grace said into her ear.

Leigh's head jerked toward her. She'd forgotten she was standing next to her friend. "What?" she asked.

"Use it," Grace said again, a twisted look spreading across her face. "Look at her. She can't beat you." They watched Monica's smile disappear like a switch had been flicked as Ted pulled her off the podium. "You're the national champion and *Monica Chase* is . . . her.

You haven't peaked. You're not done. Get angry. Let it motivate you."

"You're trying to help me?" Leigh blabbed before she could stop herself. Her blood was zipping quickly through her veins. If Grace was trying to help her, she was in trouble. Her voice was still motoring. As usual, Leigh was powerless to stop it. "How did everything get this bad so fast? How did this happen?" How was her Olympic dream in doubt?

"Get ready," Grace said before Leigh could speak again. "You're next."

Damn it, Leigh thought.

She rushed to her gym bag for a final sip of water and tried to re-clasp some of her hair clips. Phil came up behind her and put his palm on the spot where her left shoulder became her neck.

He said only one word. "Focus."

Leigh shrugged him off and stared into her gym bag until she felt the adrenaline build through her veins again. She had to be That Girl when her music began filling the stadium.

It's simple, she told herself as she climbed the steps to the floor podium. *I'm better than Monica. I'm better than Kristin and Georgette. I might be a little better than Grace.*

Leigh dipped her feet into the chalk and watched the white powder spread over her peach skin.

Leigh was a winner. Monica was not. Little wedgie-picking Monica should not be intimidating Leigh.

By the time Leigh stood in her opening pose in the corner of the blue mat awaiting the first notes of the guitar that would play her floor music, she was That Girl again. She transformed the blue mat into her playground. Her dancing was a bit clunky as usual, but her tumbling made her dancing invisible. Leigh had speed and height as she launched her body into double Arabians and twisting tuck punch-fronts. The audience would be sitting on the edges of their seats anticipating her next tumbling trick and gasping at the amount of air she managed to put between her upside-down head and the floor.

Then it was over. The music trickled away and Leigh stood in the middle of the mat, sucking in oxygen, listening to the roar of the crowd and attempting to savor the moment, to memorize it so she could replay it over and over in bed tonight when she was back to being Normal Leigh and she wasn't That Girl anymore.

Leigh jumped off the podium and threw her arms around her coach.

Leigh was going to claw her way back to the top, she decided. She wasn't going to let Monica or Katja or Grace or anyone else intimidate her. She was going to win the meet.

It was possible. Vault was next. It was all in her control.

"I want to do it," she told Phil. "I'm ready."

He took a step back and looked at her calmly. "You sure?" he asked.

She nodded. "I want to be winning at the end of the day," she said. "I can do it."

"Okay!" he said. "Keep your focus! This will either clinch the top shot or ruin your chances."

Leigh nodded. That was all fine. Nothing would stop her now.

Leigh hugged Grace and Kristin and Annie. Everyone lined up to hug her. She was passed from girl to girl to girl until she found herself embracing a body that was bigger than her own, her cheek only inches from the warmth of another cheek, her neck being tickled by curly hair, her chest pushed up against . . . It was Camille.

Leigh froze. Electricity zapped through her veins. Her heart pounded harder than it had on the floor. She was both burning up and covered in goose bumps.

Camille was hugging her, actually pressed against her body, like Leigh had imagined so many times in the privacy of her own head.

"Oh!" she said, before she could stop herself.

"Nice job," Camille whispered right into her ear.

It woke Leigh up and she let go of her crush as suddenly as she had clung to her. "Th-thanks," she stuttered. "I was really nervous. You know, I haven't been doing too well today, so I needed to do those double Arabians . . . to land . . . well, thanks." Leigh bit her lips to keep the words back. Was she smiling too big? Was she being totally obvious?

Camille shrugged. "You don't have anything to worry about," she said.

Yes, I do, Leigh thought.

Leigh didn't trust her voice anymore, though, so she kept her lips sealed and only smiled.

She watched Camille wander back toward the girls in her own rotation.

Stop it. Stop it. No crushes. Not right now.

Leigh had demolished the floor. She'd done so well, she'd pulled Camille over to the side of her podium like a magnet.

Turn crushes off.

Leigh shook her head and shut her eyes. She replayed that end-of-routine moment in her brain already, even though it was only a few minutes ago. It had to be the best floor routine she'd ever performed. She was on top of the world. She was so high, so empowered, so sure of her ability to control destiny.

She practically skipped over to her gym bag. And she almost tripped on two little legs sticking out from a body slumped against the back wall. Monica.

Monica was scowling at her.

That was not okay.

Then Monica looked away and pulled a PowerBar out of her bag.

What was wrong with this girl? No one was this petty just because someone else trumped a great performance.

Leigh had not acted *this* small after bars.

Leigh had to ignore the Wedgie Queen. She had more important things to worry about than being nice. She would have to beat Monica to get to the Olympics. She would have to pull herself several places above where she stood right now.

She had to have the vault of her life.

MONICA

Monica sat on the red carpet, her back against the purple-matted wall of the stands, her warmed-up legs in a straddle, her mouth munching on a PowerBar. She was grateful Leigh was gone, grateful to have a minute of peace and rest while the drama of the meet slithered around her.

She was always exhausted during the third rotation. By then, all her adrenaline had run its way out of her system and it seemed like the meet would stretch on forever. Plus, there were all the people. By the third rotation Monica had chatted with and hugged and smiled at so many girls so many times over and over, and it wasn't that she didn't like people, but they wore her out. She knew from previous meets that her fourth event would go much better if she took a little breather after her third routine. Meets were exhausting always, and today was worse. Monica could only stand crowds of *nice* people for so long.

She knew how to congratulate her competitors when they bested her.

She wasn't used to the opposite. She wasn't used to beating people. It was so tiring.

Right now, Monica needed to use a few moments to have a little snack and turn off her brain. She relished the solitude.

But within minutes, there was a cameraman crouched a few feet in front of Monica's toes, his lens pointed directly at her.

The same thing had happened a minute before Leigh came up to her.

Monica tried to look away and choke down her mouthful of PowerBar. She hoped there wasn't purply-gray goop gumming up her teeth or anything. She pointed and flexed the toes on her left foot repeatedly, staring at her navy-blue toenails as they vanished and then reappeared in her vision.

What was with all these cameras? Why were they in her face all of a sudden?

Monica caught a frantic movement out of the corner of her eye and turned to look at the man in black. He was balancing the camera on one shoulder now, leaning to the side so it looked like he was about to fall on his hip, and shaking his other hand back and forth in the air in hectic repetitions.

Monica squinted. *What is he doing?*

Grace appeared behind the squatting man. She smiled and waved. She was looking right at Monica like

Monica was a real girl and not a garbage can, and there was a camera there, so that didn't give Monica much choice. She smiled and waved back.

The cameraman gave her a thumbs-up and disappeared.

Grace didn't. She plopped down next to Monica. *What is she doing?*

"They always want you to wave," Grace said.

"Oh," Monica said.

"The people at home like when you smile and wave, like you care about them, you know?"

Monica wished she could tell Grace that the "people at home" were leaving messages all over Grace's fan page and none on her own, so she didn't care one bit about them or Grace or anyone else. But that was too risky.

Monica knew all about Grace from sharing a gym with her every day.

If Grace spread some ugly rumors about her, there'd be no way to get revenge. Grace didn't care what people said or thought about her. The only thing Grace cared about was gymnastics.

I should be the same way.

Monica needed to do her own thing right now. She could feel her blood running slower and slower. If she didn't get a few more quiet minutes to recharge, she might not make it over the vault at all.

Just as she was gathering the guts to ask Grace to leave her alone for a minute or two, there was another camera. The girls waved and it went away again.

"Why does that keep happening?" Monica whispered.

Grace smiled at her. It looked stretched and awkward on her red-lipsticked lips. "They're talking about you."

Monica tilted her head. They were? "What are they saying?" she asked. As soon as she asked it, she tried to swallow the words back from the air. There was no reason to trust Grace's answer.

"That you're having an amazing day. That you're beating people no one thought you ever could. That no one knew your name this morning, but now you might be placed on the Olympic team."

Monica's head whipped around; she studied Grace's profile. *What is she trying to do to me?*

"The Olympics?" Monica asked through her teeth. The word felt like an ice cube too big for her mouth. She didn't want to swallow it. She didn't want to hope.

Grace shrugged. "You've got a chance."

Monica chomped on her PowerBar. Grace cracked her skinny knuckles and stared out into space.

"You should at least be an alternate," Grace said, after too much time had gone by.

Monica turned. Grace's lips were twisted into that strange smile again.

"Wouldn't it be great? Being in Italy? At the Olympics? Together?" Grace said.

Monica forced her jaw not to drop, but her eyes kept growing.

Grace was up to no good.

But another camera focused on her face. It came so

close, she could tell it was looking at her alone, and not at the superstar next to her.

These cameras had to mean something.

Monica *was* having the best gymnastics day of her life.

It was possible that Ted never mentioned the idea of alternate because, to Ted, being an alternate wouldn't count for anything. Ted was an all-or-nothing kind of coach. He wouldn't care that much if Monica was the Olympic alternate. The country wouldn't care about the alternates. They wouldn't compete or be interviewed on TV or any of that. Monica's own family might not care if she was named alternate.

But Monica would.

She could see herself in an Olympic leo, boarding the plane to Italy. She could see herself smile and . . .

But the idea came from Grace. Who was still talking. Some part of Monica's brain detached and flew out to that fantasy world.

"We could get ready together. You know, go shopping for whatever we'll need. Get our nails done before our flight—"

"What are you talking about?" Monica said finally.

Grace snapped her jaw shut. "I was trying to be nice," she said. "God."

Then she was quiet. But she didn't move. She sat there, her shoulder almost touching Monica's, her breath ruining Monica's silent moment, her words destroying Monica's strategy.

Don't fall, she told herself. *Don't fall. Have a good day.*

But when she closed her eyes, the five Olympic rings were tattooed on the inside of her eyelids.

She had tried so hard not to want the impossible. Not to set herself up for disappointment. Her heart was breaking already and the meet wasn't half over.

Monica took a deep breath. She held the vault in her eyes and held her goal in her gut: *don't fall.*

WILHELMINA

Camille's words were running through Wilhelmina's brain as she warmed up for beam. *Katja doesn't like surprises.*

It was awful. Camille had seemed scatterbrained and distracted and lazy. Not like a cutthroat, manipulative, insecure gymnast who would start psychological wars. Turned out, somehow, she was both.

Wilhelmina hated those kinds of gymnasts. They made a mockery of her sport, her life.

Katja doesn't like surprises.

Katja loved winning more than she hated surprises. That's what Kerry said. That's what they were banking on.

Still, Wilhelmina hadn't thought about the full ramifications of trying to disprove Katja's system until Camille said it to her like that. And since a lot of the previous trials took place at private selection camps,

Wilhelmina could only be so sure that she was better than all the other girls who had tried to do it their own way before.

If Camille was right, here's what it meant: unless she managed to beat Grace or Leigh or Georgette, each time Wilhelmina performed well on any apparatus except for vault, she would be hurting her chances at making the Olympic team. Katja would view her dismount on bars and her tumbling series on beam as insubordination or trickery. It meant that Kerry was wrong, that Wilhelmina was dreaming this dream impossibly, and that—for the second time—she was destined to miss the Olympics by the skin of her teeth.

It meant that Wilhelmina was entirely dependent on Leigh messing up like she did on beam. Or else once again her talent and training would be dismissed for rules and politics.

Wilhelmina's entire life had been cursed.

She did her tumbling series, and her left heel landed off the tape on the floor that represented the beam.

The stupid, stupid comment. Four silly words had managed to rewrite Wilhelmina's entire day. *Katja doesn't like surprises. Katja. Doesn't. Like. Surprises.*

Wilhelmina walked away from the tape without practicing her dismount and went to her gym bag for some water. She would be last up, anyway.

Next to her, Annie and Georgette leaned across an empty chair to peer at Georgette's phone. "Do you see this?" she heard Annie whisper. "He's only writing on

Grace's page because Leigh, like, begged him to." Wilhelmina rolled her eyes.

Georgette shrugged. "I'm not really into Out of Touch," she said. "But it's cool for Grace, I guess."

Wilhelmina did not care. She and Georgette were probably the only girls at that meet today who couldn't name a single Out of Touch song. Black girls just don't do white boy bands. But it also wouldn't have mattered who messaged Wilhelmina or who called her in the middle of the freaking night (or who was waiting for her in the stands); all she would think about today was gymnastics. She was so sick of the fact that she was the one who knew where she was and how important it was for her to be right here, right now, and yet she was also the one who was almost certainly going to get screwed out of her rightful spot on the team.

Wilhelmina didn't like them poking fun at Grace. She didn't *like* Grace, but she respected her. At least Grace was in it for the gymnastics.

Wilhelmina shot Camille another dirty look where she sat next to Georgette. *Thanks, Comeback Cammie. So nice of you to point out the futility of my own comeback, right in the middle of the Olympic trials.*

Annie was still looking at her phone, holding it out to Maria, one seat over.

Then, since she couldn't take the unfairness anymore, Wilhelmina plopped her butt down right on the folding chair that had been serving as a stage for Annie's phone. She sat so quickly, Annie almost didn't have time to pull her arm away before it got snapped beneath Wilhelmina's muscly behind. The two girls shut up, and that was good.

There was an inch for her somewhere. Leigh had messed up on the beam. Grace had a few falls in Nationals and Classics earlier this summer. Georgette was not as good as either of them. But Wilhelmina had spent many hours with a calculator, adding up DODs and potential execution scores. A few mess-ups would not guarantee she could beat these girls. Every gymnast had a few mess-ups every meet, Wilhelmina included. There might be an inch for her to sneak into one of the top three spots. But it was narrow.

And of course this didn't account for anyone else. Every girl here was trying to wiggle her way into that inch.

She watched in silence as Georgette, then Grace, then Annie performed nearly flawless beam routines. Samantha mounted.

A tear started in the middle of Wilhelmina's heart, pulling the two sides of it farther and farther apart with each high score.

It was uncanny for three gymnasts to hit beam routines in a row, and Samantha was about to be the fourth. It was almost statistically impossible for five to do it. By the odds alone, she was probably going to screw up this rotation. And, if she did, that would help her, maybe. In a weird way.

Maybe she shouldn't be trying to beat the all-arounders. Maybe Wilhelmina should be thinking about beating Camille. If she was the best on vault, she'd be named to the team, for sure. And Katja wouldn't hate her for it.

But she couldn't beat Camille. Not unless Camille fell.

Wilhelmina could have been the best on vault if she was totally focused on it like Camille was. But Camille had outsmarted her.

And then gotten into her head.

Wilhelmina stood and did a quick back walkover, keeping her muscles warm as she waited for her name to be called, for her doom to be sealed.

Kerry came up beside Wilhelmina and put her warm hands on her almost-shaking shoulders. "Just yourself, right?" Kerry said.

Wilhelmina nodded.

They both watched Samantha nail a double-tuck dismount.

"It doesn't matter what these other girls do, huh? You only control Mina, huh?" Kerry said.

Wilhelmina nodded, even though now she knew she was better off doing just okay for the rest of the day. She was better off performing mediocre on beam and floor today, and on bars, beam, and floor tomorrow. And rocking the vault.

Would that be a dirty strategy, too? Would that make her just like Camille?

Camille was getting exactly what she wanted: Wilhelmina was thinking about her stupid hushed voice instead of visualizing her beam routine.

Wilhelmina's name rang out through the gym and she swung her arms in circles, loosening her shoulders before mounting the podium.

"Just your best, huh?" Kerry said, her voice so low it was almost a whisper. Like the advice was a secret. Like a coach who said to do your best was unheard of in that room.

Wilhelmina nodded again. But she wasn't sure anymore. What if her best hurt her?

A minute later, after the green flag and the signal to the judges, Wilhelmina ran toward the beam, her left foot pushed against the springboard, and she leaped with full extension of her legs. Her right foot landed on the beam with a solid *bang.* Her heart pounded in her chest, hard but not fast. It seemed to be saying, *You can do this.*

Wilhelmina launched immediately into her full turn and stopped without the smallest wobble.

She took a deep breath, preparing for her longest tumbling run, and she realized it. She didn't have the choice Kerry seemed to imply with that "huh?" It didn't matter if Katja would hate her.

When Wilhelmina was up on the beam like she was now, she didn't have a choice but to do her best. In the end, gymnastics was about this moment. Even more than the results. Even more than the scores. Gymnastics was about right now. The stadium captivated by the way she could control each muscle in her body. The beam staying exactly where she put it, beneath the soles of her feet or the palms of her hands. Ninety seconds of publicly flying, of joy pulsating through every muscle, of power marrying grace right in her soul. That was Wilhelmina's gymnastics.

Then she was back on the ground, the crowd cheering, the judges nodding, her coach jumping up and down.

Wilhelmina couldn't help but search out Katja Minkovski and stare at the ugly frown on her grandmotherly face.

Grace or Leigh or Georgette. I only have to beat one of them, she thought. *And everybody else.*

STANDINGS
AFTER THE THIRD ROTATION

1.	Grace Cooper	45.806
2.	Georgette Paulson	45.775
3.	Wilhelmina Parker	44.600
4.	Monica Chase	44.300
5.	Leigh Becker	44.000
6.	Maria Vasquez	43.850
7.	Annie Simms	42.225
8.	Kristin Jackson	42.220
9.	Natalie Rice	40.950
10.	Samantha Soloman	29.980
11.	Olivia Corsica	29.738
12.	Camille Abrams	15.350

Fourth Rotation

GRACE

Grace was winning.

She was mid-meet with a lot to lose, and so she knew she should have been focusing exclusively on her own gymnastics. But she couldn't.

Leigh was losing. In fact, there was now a small chance Leigh wouldn't even get chosen for the team.

Did it matter?

Grace's heart was calm now. Her body felt strong after half a bottle of water and a full stretch during the break between beam and floor, before she started talking to Monica.

Grace led a short line of gymnasts as they marched around the bars toward the floor.

The Olympics without Leigh. The thought made her tilt, like she might fall doing a simple march from one podium to the next. Grace swallowed air and blocked the thought. She couldn't start thinking about Leigh now. She couldn't let her own gymnastics suffer for the sake of her friend.

The solution was simple: if Leigh wouldn't be at the

Olympics, Grace had to make one new friend. It hadn't worked with Monica, but Monica probably wouldn't be there anyway. Grace would have to find a new-new friend.

Grace went to her new folding chair to reorganize her bag like she did at each apparatus. She pulled out a water bottle and took a long sip, feeling the coolness of it reach beyond her esophagus, down her arms and legs, and into her fingers and toes like her entire body was empty except for H_2O. She loved that feeling. She was ready for floor. She'd be up first.

She mounted the podium to run through a quick warm-up and practiced a few tumbling passes.

She did a roundoff-back-handspring-double-Arabian across from the north to the south corner of the floor. Then she stood frozen and watched Wilhelmina cross her X. If Leigh didn't make the team, it was possible the spot would go to Wilhelmina.

"Nice job," Grace called to her down the length of the floor.

Wilhelmina gave Grace a quizzical smile.

Camille came tumbling down the path Grace had just made and stood behind her.

"Do these trials feel the same? Like four years ago?" Grace asked.

Camille stared for a second, then shrugged.

So much for Operation New-New Friend.

No one liked Grace. No one except Leigh. She imagined the Olympic Village without Leigh: being the one member of the team without a roommate, always feeling awkward when they traveled to the gym, sitting alone on the bus every day.

No one liked her.

Except, maybe, Dylan Patrick. If Leigh was right, if he had somehow noticed Grace the way she had noticed him, if he somehow had a crush on her, too, would that change things? Was he able to see what Grace and her father and most people couldn't—the part of her that was deeper, the part of her that was sometimes not a gymnast?

She shouldn't be hoping for it, but she was.

Maybe she could win him, too. Probably, he didn't really like her specifically. Maybe Dylan Patrick liked the *idea* of a gymnast girlfriend the way Grace liked the idea of a pop-star boyfriend. Maybe something would happen if she flirted back.

Ha.

Grace landed a tumbling run and bounced off the podium. She ran over to her gym bag to reapply her ChapStick before she was called to chalk up.

Grace looked over her shoulder. Leigh's blonde head was clear across the room, on the other side of that vault. Grace expected to see her laughing or whispering with some other girl. Grace expected to see the smile her best friend wore almost like her skin was frozen that way. Instead, Leigh was squinting at the vault, staring it down the way Grace had three rotations earlier.

Almost like Leigh was afraid.

And Grace should be grinning. She shouldn't care whether she shared a room with anyone. She shouldn't care about a message from a crush or girl talk or pretty nails. All of that stuff mattered, but it only mattered when life didn't. Life only counted for the four hours this weekend that she'd be on the gym floor, the eight to sixteen hours during the Olympics that she would be competing. So, life, the part that mattered, would be easier if Leigh stayed here. Winning the Olympic all-around would be easier if Leigh stayed here.

Her heart pulsed and broke, unconvinced by her brain.

"What are you thinking about?"

Her father's voice was angry behind her. Grace buried her eyes in her gym bag and shrugged.

"You should know the answer, Gracie. It should always be the same thing."

Somehow, he always knew when she was thinking about friendship and roommates. When she was being a normal girl instead of the robot he loved.

The Same Thing was gymnastics. Everything was gymnastics. It was how they got through that first awful time eight years ago after Max was born and her mom left: gymnastics, gymnastics, gymnastics.

"My floor routine," Grace mumbled, turning to face him.

He stared at her for almost a full minute, like he thought he could open her skull and prove that her mind had been elsewhere a minute ago.

"Don't relax. You're not done yet, Gracie. Today doesn't count when you compare it with tomorrow, right?"

Grace nodded.

"And tomorrow doesn't count really, either. When you compare it with the Olympics."

Tomorrow doesn't count in his eyes?

Grace nodded.

"Okay," he said. He jerked his head up and down quickly like he was satisfied with his job of tearing down her almost-perfect day. He put his arm around her and smiled as he whispered in her ear, "Keep your legs together during your double Arabian. You had so much air between your feet during your warm-up, I'm surprised you didn't start a mini-tornado. Don't get sloppy."

Grace pursed her lips. "Okay, Dad," she said. The Olympics without Leigh would mean her dad would be the only person who talked to her for those two weeks. And Grace wasn't even allowed to answer him.

Without Leigh there, they'd drown in sorrow and unspoken words about how unfair it was that she was the star of the Olympic team without a parent in the stands.

He patted her lower back. "Go get 'em, Gracie," he said.

She closed her eyes and talked herself through her routine. *Throw head back. Arm arches. Foot-foot-foot, roundoff, back handspring, double Arabian.*

By the time she climbed the podium a few minutes later her brain beat with the rhythm of the music that was about to pour down on her, her body was solely focused on keeping her legs together during her Arabians and hitting each of her landings, finishing the day as well as she started it.

And, she did.

Then she made her way across the gym to the line of girls standing next to the vault. She knew how to fix everything. And who cared if she was a little mean?

Grace needed Leigh.

MONICA

Grace and Leigh were standing too close to her, snickering again. They were pretending to be whispering, but Monica could hear every word.

"You cannot let the Wedgie-Picker beat you," Grace said.

Leigh chuckled. "It won't be a problem."

Don't look at the scoreboard, Monica told herself, bending over in her straddle stretch. *Don't look. Walk away.*

They might not know the scores anyway. Most times, most gymnasts avoided looking at and hearing their scores. Most times they kept tabs on themselves and one another without doing much math. Or at least, they tried.

Monica hadn't heard or seen any of her scores since bars. And she hadn't meant to hear that one. Ted always told her that looking at scores would do nothing but mess with her mind. And he was right. Usually when she paid no attention to the scores throughout a meet, she was pleasantly surprised to see the final results.

- - -

Last month, at Nationals, Monica had ignored the scoreboard completely. Instead she'd focused on her individual routines, taken her quiet time after the third rotation, and ignored her overly enthused mother.

She'd looked at the board once the meet was over. She'd done well. She hadn't fallen. It didn't matter where her name was. Monica started reading at the bottom of the list of twenty-five names. She wasn't in the last five. Or the last ten. She wasn't in the last fifteen. At this point, Monica had held her breath until: there it was.

10   MONICA CHASE

She'd placed tenth. Everyone in the arena must have been shocked. Tenth was an automatic entry into the Olympic trials.

That night, Monica had been sitting back-to-back with Grace at the banquet that USAG hosted for the gymnasts and their families. She was at an entirely different table from any gymnasts because her family required their own table in order to fit her mother and father and grandparents and stepdad, brothers, and sisters. She was mortified at the size of her crowd. The only gymnast with a table close to her size was Leigh Becker, and honestly, Leigh deserved the fanfare: she was the new national champion. Monica sunk lower in her own seat as her family carried on way too loudly about how great she'd been and how they couldn't wait to see her in the Olympics.

"I have no chance to make the Olympics," she'd whispered to her mother who was talking too quickly and too loudly and waving her hands too much as usual. "Please be quiet."

Over Monica's shoulder, she heard Grace snickering. *Is she laughing at me?* Monica wondered.

"Man!" Monica's stepsister had yelled across the table, brandishing her iPhone. "There are, like, no hotels left in Rome. I can't find a single open room for the Olympics."

This time, Monica heard Grace speak. She was clearly listening to her family's conversation. "But Max got a room, right, little dude?" Grace said. "All of the rooms already went to the families of gymnasts who actually have a chance." Grace was singsonging like she was sharing some sort of wonderful news and not attacking Monica behind her back.

Monica heard a little boy answer, "Right!"

She turned. Grace and her dad and a little black-haired boy were at their table. Alone. Grace was leaning over the boy's plate, slicing up his meat.

"I get the first room we find!" Monica's mother had shouted gleefully. "I'm the one who pushed her out after all."

"Mom," Monica had whispered, her face burning. "Please be quiet. There's no point in yelling like that. It's not going to happen."

Behind her Grace was laughing. It was the kind of laugh you pretend is silent but that clearly is meant to humiliate someone. *Why doesn't Ted say something?* Monica thought. Why was her coach letting Grace rake her over the coals like this?

Her mother had turned to her, her tan eyes leveled seriously on Monica's. "This victory isn't yours alone, kiddo. We've all sacrificed to get you this far. We've all gotten up early to get you to practices and traveled across the country to see you at meets and put in thousands of dollars and hundreds of hours to getting you to this level, this level that is so much farther than anyone else predicted. You did not do it alone."

Monica stared at her, wide-eyed. Her mom could not hear Grace's laughter, even though it kept going and going. Or her mom didn't realize Grace was laughing *at them*.

"And we have proven so many people wrong already. We've gotten so far. So you need to let us have this moment of victory, you hear me, honey? You need to let us celebrate."

Monica blinked at her mother. She'd said that Monica needed to *let them* celebrate. Not to join in. Not to celebrate with them.

She'd said it like Monica was a tool to happiness, not a person whose success was her own.

Her father had leaned across the table toward her and said in a low voice, "Don't you want to go to the Olympics, Mon-Mon?"

He'd stared at her until Monica nodded sheepishly.

Of course she wanted to go. But that didn't mean she would. It didn't make her good enough. A lot of girls wanted to go to the Olympics. A lot of girls dedicated their whole lives to that goal and still fell short. Wanting it was not enough to make it happen.

There was so much she could do in the sport without going to the Olympics. It was something her non-gymnastics family would never understand. They thought the Olympics were a be-all and end-all. But Monica wasn't a gymnast because she dreamed of Olympic glory.

She was a gymnast because she couldn't be any other way.

Monica had leaned back in her chair to try to put some distance between herself and the picture in her family's head. The fantasy that shouldn't be theirs when it wasn't even hers.

She heard Grace whisper to her father, to their coach: "Are all gym moms as delusional as that one?"

Monica's cheeks had burned bright and her heart had sped up with the stress of anticipating what Ted would say back. Her mouth stayed shut.

"Let them have their moment," Ted had said.

Monica had risked turning her head at that point, looking at their table, and she'd felt a little sorry for Grace. She sat sandwiched between her father and brother. There was no one else. The other side of the table was filled with the spillover from Leigh's entourage. There was no mother. No extended family. No one to feel proud of Grace in the way her brother couldn't and her father wouldn't.

Monica had known Grace's mother wasn't around. She knew Grace's life wasn't stuffed with family the way her own was. But it was different to see it. Grace looked empty.

Monica's heart almost broke for her. Until she heard her say, "Well, you'd better not expect me to start treating her like some A-lister just because she beat Kelly Moss."

Ted had actually chuckled. He probably thought Monica couldn't hear over the racket her family was making. But she could. Ted said: "You know what I say. There are no friends on the gym floor."

It was a twisted moment for a family to laugh, but they did.

- - -

Now that Monica was at the Olympic trials, stretching and waving at camera after camera, she was glad she'd seen how Grace's family worked. She was glad she knew that Grace's life was contorted, so that she could force herself not to take it personally, when Grace was clearly trying to sabotage her for no good reason. She wasn't Grace's competition.

"I don't know what she's doing here," Grace said to Leigh, barely pretending to whisper. "I'd never show up to a meet that I was sure to lose."

Leigh laughed. "Yeah," she said, a little quieter, but still loud enough for Monica to hear without straining. "She's in the way."

Monica couldn't possibly be doing well enough to make Grace and Leigh alarmed, could she?

Don't look at the scoreboard.

Why were Leigh and Grace doing this?

Monica shifted into a split. *Don't look.* She swung her arms across her chest, back and forth, back and forth, trying to get her blood pumping. She hated that she'd missed her quiet time.

"Whatever," she heard Grace say. "I'm sure *Monica Chase* is about to screw up on vault. She's due for a fall."

Monica squished her eyes shut, trying to eradicate the image of her falling over the vault from her brain. *Don't fall. It's your only goal: don't fall.* Yet another camera caught her funny face.

She grabbed for her phone in the bag next to her knee. Her fan page was less dangerous than the scoreboard.

She opened it up, looked at her interactions, and . . . nothing. Not a word from *anyone*. She was a gymnast in complete anonymity.

Why were they trying to tear her down? What had she done?

And why was she letting them get to her like this? She wasn't even trying to beat them. *Don't fall. Don't fall. Don't fall.*

"She'll fall," Leigh said, so loudly. "But I hate that she's beating me now."

Monica stood, keeping her eyes on the vault. She threw her phone back in her bag.

She would not believe it. They were only trying to make her look, trying to mess with her head. After all, Ted, who said the scoreboard was their enemy, was Grace's coach, too.

She could not be three rotations in and still ahead of the national champion.

Monica's eyes narrowly missed the scoreboard. She sprinted down the runway, warming up.

She hopped up on the vaulting table and practiced the end of her vault.

Just don't fall, Monica told herself. *Nothing else matters.*

Monica watched Kristin jump off the podium and confer with her coach. She felt Grace and Leigh disappear from behind her. Finally.

Everyone was whispering with her own coach. Everyone except Monica, whose coach was across the gym where Grace had gone. Monica got down off the podium and stared at her fingers. She would not look at the board.

By the end of this rotation, she'd fall back a few slots anyway, if she was beating anyone to begin with. Most of the best gymnasts did an Amanar on vault, which scored megapoints compared to Monica's double twisting Yurchenko.

Monica blinked hard, willing her eyes to stay open, her blood to speed up, as Kristin climbed the stairs beside the vaulting runway. The announcer called Kristin's name. Monica watched her friend nervously stretch her shoulders while her coach whispered a stream of words into her ear. Monica would make herself cheer. Kristin was counting on being alternate. And there were three. They could both be alternates.

"Go, Kristin," Monica finally got herself to yell.

By the time the words left her mouth, Kristin was already upside down with her hands on the vaulting table. Monica watched as she launched herself skyward, twisted once, twice, then—*what?* She landed. Kristin put her feet on the ground, took a huge hop forward, and raised her arms to signal to the judges that she was finished.

Even though she wasn't. She shouldn't be finished. She'd missed an entire half twist.

Monica's jaw hung open. Kristin had not done the Amanar. She'd done a DTY. She must be having a terrible day. She'd done the same vault Monica would do.

Natalie was next—a planned DTY.

It was possible that Monica's name was ahead of theirs. That she was beating at least two people. It was possible she still would be at the end of the day.

Ted was nowhere around when Monica's name rang across the gym floor for the last time that day.

Could she be beating Kristin? (Could she be beating Leigh, too?) Could she use this rotation to pull even farther ahead?

Don't look, Monica told herself one last time. She climbed the podium stairs with her eyes on her toenails.

But, when she was standing in the chalk, she lost the battle. Before she knew it, her eyes found the scoreboard and scrolled up for her name.

Not ninth.

Or eighth.

Not seventh, sixth, fifth.

Oh yes, she was beating Kristin. And Annie. And Natalie. And Leigh. *Leigh*.

Fourth.

Fourth. Right after third.

She felt her heart stop. It climbed slowly to her throat, threatening to choke her.

Monica was deep in we-at-least-have-to-talk-about-naming-her-to-the-team territory.

She tried to clear her brain and forced more adrenaline into her muscles. They needed to work like springs. She stood with her toes lined up at the end of the runway. She tried to chase the image of the scoreboard, of the number four far from her brain and to think instead about landing her DTY.

And ten seconds later, when her too-close-to-bare ass slapped against the blue gym mat, when the meet of her life slipped away from her because of one crooked landing on her left foot, when she did exactly what Leigh and Grace predicted, when she *fell*, Monica cursed herself for ever looking.

Not because she believed in bad luck or karma. Not because she thought remaining clueless would somehow have changed her vault.

But because, even though she'd still be beating someone at the end of the day today, even though she'd still end the day ahead of multiple gymnasts, that wouldn't be enough anymore.

And it was all because Grace made her look at the score.

CAMILLE

"Comeback Cammie! Comeback Cammie!" It pulsed through the stadium right after the announcer called her name. But, to Camille, it sounded more like a plea than a cheer. *Come back, Cammie? Come back, Cammie?*

She was back, right? She was here, in the Baltimore Metroplex, at the Olympic trials, climbing the stairs to the floor and preparing to flip and twist and stun and awe for the second time that day like her mother wanted, like her sixteen-year-old self had been itching to, like she would need to do to make the Olympic team.

So she was back. Right?

- - -

After Camille had spent what was supposed to be her Olympic summer recuperating, attending physical therapy, eating pizza and ice cream and the first candy bar since her bat mitzvah, she had insisted on going to actual high school for her senior year.

At first it was scary at the public school, so different from the solitary room with one table and one computer where she'd done her schooling over the Internet since the sixth grade. Camille was short and skinny at the start of the year, constantly knocked around by backpacks and elbows in the hallway, completely overwhelmed by the number of new faces and voices and names that she was expected to learn almost immediately. Seven different teachers. Two lab partners. Four people in her group project in English class. The six girls who invited her to sit with them at lunch. Then there were the students who it seemed like everyone knew because they were popular or unpopular or had some distinct feature like being in a wheelchair or being extremely tall. All of these people had lived in Camille's Long Island neighborhood for most of her life. All of them had histories that intersected and meshed; they were shaped by the story of their neighborhood and even their country, and they were not shaped at all by the specific history that had endless influence in Camille's own identity.

During the first few days of school, Camille watched in awe as girls her own age walked the hallways in bodies that made them look like full-grown women. She marveled at the way they interacted with ease and committed their hearts to other things almost as passionately as Camille had once committed to gymnastics: concert choir or cross-country or school. Some of them seemed disproportionately dedicated to things Camille considered frivolous—fashion or religion or social life.

The first few days were enough to distract Camille from the ache. The yearning for gymnastics. The need to be upside down.

Camille barely spoke to anyone who was not a teacher. She did what she was told, then went home and stared at the television while all the things she'd seen and heard and smelled that day ran on repeat through her head. .

But, too soon, the ache returned.

Before walking home from school one day, Camille had gone back to her English classroom for a notebook she'd left by accident. She'd paused at the doorway because, inside, four girls were standing in a circle, singing softly in harmony with their eyes closed. Camille held her breath and watched, her heart almost still. They were so happy, so precise. They were so sure of who they were at that moment. They were like she used to be.

Their voices faded out and their eyes opened and Camille realized that they had all found her, the short and skinny girl standing in the doorway, watching them dive headfirst into a passion that wouldn't break their backs.

"Um. Sorry," Camille had stammered. "I was . . . I forgot my notebook."

They all smiled and the tall, redheaded one said, "Do you sing? We're trying to start an all-girls a cappella group and we need more members."

Camille shook her head and scurried to the back of the room to retrieve her notebook. A minute later she stood in the hallway with her back against the lockers, sucking in air like she'd just dismounted from the uneven bars.

She had a choice but it wasn't much of one. She'd have to go back to gymnastics and risk her life the way the doctor had explained. Or she'd have to live the rest of her days with a hole in her heart.

"You're not gonna cry, are you?"

Her head whipped to the side. A boy stood next to her. He was a full head taller than her, with curly brown hair and a face full of freckles. He wasn't that cute, at least she didn't think so right away, but Camille felt her personality shrink anyway. She'd barely ever spoken to boys in her life.

She shook her head.

"Good," he'd said. "I can't stand when girls cry."

Camille worked on evening out her breathing. She wondered if it was okay for her to walk away or if that would be rude.

"Ya just got dumped, didn't ya? Freshmen boys can be so stupid."

Camille shook her head again.

"Get cut from the freshmen play?" he'd guessed.

Camille made herself look at him. "I'm a senior," she'd whispered.

He'd smiled and it transformed his face. Suddenly he was adorable. Camille felt her cheeks turn pink.

"Oh, come on," he'd said. "I know all the seniors."

Camille smiled in spite of herself. "I'm new," she said.

"Gymnastics girl," he'd whispered, nodding his head. "I've heard about you."

Camille felt blood rush to her ears. What had he heard?

"Do you want to go get some pizza?" he'd asked. "I'll give you the lowdown on this boring school."

Camille had smiled.

By the end of the week they were dating. By the end of the year, they were inseparable.

It was Bobby who made it possible for Camille to sort through those six months without the gym. With his help, she built herself up from the inside while she stretched from an under-five-foot-and-under-eighty-pound girl into a woman of five feet and one inch with breasts and hips. It was Bobby who convinced her that gymnastics was a choice, that it had always been a choice, that she could still be herself—the same exact girl—if she was choosing something else.

But Bobby was wrong, and when Camille had believed him, so was she.

- - -

Still, Camille thought as she performed across the floor, *it is as impossible to imagine life without Bobby as it had been to imagine life without gymnastics.* She'd survived without gymnastics. She'd maybe even been happier without it, at least without it the way it was now. But when she met Bobby, she had been a completely different person. Different height. Different weight. Different voice. Virgin.

Could she survive without Bobby now?

Camille stumbled on a landing and barely noticed it. She should be thinking about her floor routine. She shouldn't be thinking about her breakup. But it didn't matter how Camille performed on floor. At least not to her mother or her coach or Katja. She was bound to be an Olympian only because of her vault. The floor routine was just for her.

She'd insisted on continuing to train on floor. She'd needed some part of her workout to be about the joy of the gym and not about her mother's dream of gold medals in their living room.

Yet with all of these people watching, she couldn't enjoy it.

Camille dismounted her routine and tried not to hear the chant as it boomed back down on her. She tried to push it away from her brain.

Because she wasn't who they said she was. She wasn't Comeback Cammie. She hadn't come back. She'd made herself new.

If the fire in your eyes like Wilhelmina's was what

got you to the Olympics, then Camille wouldn't be so close to going. Someone with more fire would be able to beat her on vault. But that wasn't the way it was. Talent lit up your gymnastics regardless of fire.

It wasn't Camille's fault if she went to Rome and was miserable while Wilhelmina stayed home and was also miserable.

Camille halfheartedly saluted the judges and made her way to the stairs of the podium. A number, a score, rang through the stadium. And it wasn't hers. Camille froze on the podium stairs and turned toward the vault.

Because that was interesting.

There was nothing she could do to get herself out of this gymnast destiny, but maybe there was something someone else could do. Hope filled Camille's veins in a way it hadn't since the last trials four years ago.

Leigh Becker had changed the game.

WILHELMINA

Wilhelmina stood slack jawed and watched from one hundred feet away as Leigh celebrated with her coach. Leigh bounced on her perky toes, her perky ponytail swinging behind her head, her perky teeth practically glittering in the gym lights as she smiled that huge, huge smile.

Wilhelmina could almost hear the televisions in the homes of gymnastics fans everywhere. "And Leigh

Becker makes gymnastics history by landing the first triple twisting Yurchenko! Three full twists in the air! An entire half twist more than Camille Abrams! The first time it's been landed in competition."

The applause in the stadium was deafening.

The end. That's what the applause said to her.

Wilhelmina had done what she'd sworn she wouldn't. She'd peeked at the score. Before Leigh's vault, she had been in third place. Now she would certainly be shoved to fourth.

Fourth had been her goal, but now she was pretty sure Katja wouldn't take her if she was in fourth.

Also, the best Wilhelmina would be able to do was third on vault because Camille was always going to beat her and now Leigh would, too. Wilhelmina and her calculator had been banking on second for vault. She'd never seen Leigh do a vault that could come close to outscoring hers before. From the way Leigh was squealing and dancing on the sidelines, it was clear Leigh hadn't seen herself do one like that, either.

Leigh would climb ahead of Wilhelmina this rotation.

Wilhelmina knew Leigh didn't blow the entire vaulting competition out of the water just to slash her own personal dreams of Olympic glory. But it felt like an assault.

It seemed impossible that Leigh or Grace or Georgette or Camille or anyone could want this dream as badly as Wilhelmina did herself. She wanted it more than anyone. And she had worked the hardest and for the longest. That was a fact. If effort and desire were what counted, Wilhelmina deserved this the most.

But Wilhelmina was being cast out of Olympic Village and into Alternate-ville. A land she didn't think she could stomach after years of seeing those five rings every time she closed her eyes.

Her parents and Davion and Kerry would never understand it, but she had made her decision: Wilhelmina was either competing in the Olympics, or she was done with gymnastics.

And if Camille was right, Katja would easily pick Maria or Annie or someone instead of her.

So, unless she managed to catch Grace or Georgette, she was done. *Thanks a lot, Leigh.*

After five more routines, a lifetime of work might come to a close.

She almost wished she could be another kind of gymnast. The kind who would message Dylan Patrick something suggestive tonight to get under Grace's skin. The kind who would quote that most recent article about Leigh right to her face: *Pretty good for a linebacker.* She wished she could be the Camille kind of gymnast.

Kerry came up behind Wilhelmina.

"Camille said Katja doesn't like surprises," Wilhelmina said. "Which means she's going to hate me."

Kerry shook her head. "Katja loves winning. More than anything. You're going to help her get there."

"Are you sure? Because—"

But Kerry was shaking her head. "Mina-Mina," she said. She put a finger to her lips.

"I know," Wilhelmina said. "I can only control me. I know, I know." She felt like rolling her eyes. She was the gymnast kind of gymnast, and that was it.

"I've trained you well, huh?" Kerry said.

Shut up, Wilhelmina felt like screaming. Why wouldn't Kerry just tell her once and for all if fourth place would put her on the team? Why wouldn't anyone tell her that? Why did she always have to remind Mina of her limits instead of making promises?

Kerry smiled. "Go get 'em."

Wilhelmina walked away from her coach angry, but as soon as her feet hit the podium steps, she felt her blood slow. She'd be mad again in two minutes. For now she was focused.

Life was easiest when the eyes of a stadium were on her.

Wilhelmina spread the white chalk across her palms and the soles of her feet. She wondered why the chalk always had to be white. Organically, chalk was more of a tan or beige, but gymnastics chalk was always bleach white, standing out on her legs and streaking her arms in obvious ways that would go unnoticed on a milky gymnast like Leigh Becker.

That's what she was thinking about when she heard her name. Chalk. Stupid, trivial stuff. It was nice.

Her brain was similarly clear when the upbeat

drumming that preceded her floor music beat into the stadium.

Wilhelmina took two steps and swung each arm in a graceful arc, embracing the stands. She was inviting them to join her. She was ready for their eyes.

Then the keyboard and horns started in an instrumental Motown medley and Wilhelmina took a breath, bounced on her toes, and smiled.

She was off, running halfway from one corner of the mat to the opposite before launching into her first tumbling run. Her hands hit the ground for her roundoff and back handspring, then they didn't touch it again as her feet and legs propelled her body upside down four successive times in a double layout, double tuck.

The crowd went wild, and when she danced down the length of the square, she heard them begin to pulse with the music. They were clapping. All of them. It didn't matter what she was going to place on vault or where Grace and Leigh and Georgette were. It didn't matter who was ahead and who was the star and who was the Comeback Queen and who was the most famous. Right now, as Wilhelmina did a triple full twist, then dropped to the ground and pushed herself back up on her hands, the entire place was watching her. They were cheering for her. Their hearts were beating with hers, their hopes were flying with her as she soared in an Arabian double back at the end of her second tumbling run. She was the star.

Wilhelmina danced to the middle of the mat and

pointed both fingers to the top of the crowd as she spun in a triple full turn. Again, the cheers rained down on her.

She somersaulted into a handstand and cartwheeled out of it so that she landed in the corner. She did her dance positions, then paused momentarily before her final tumbling run. She was memorizing the moment. She was holding on to it. She had to. She needed these moments to get her though the rest of the meet. The unfair parts. The awful parts.

And then she flipped her way back across the floor, saluted the judges, and bathed in the applause.

I dare you not to love that surprise, Wilhelmina said to Katja in her head. Kerry had to be right. Camille was just trying to scare her.

There was no way Katja wouldn't want that floor routine on her team.

LEIGH

Even though her body had been finished competing for more than twenty minutes, Leigh's heart still beat wildly in her rib cage as she stood next to Grace and smiled at the NBC Sports reporter who pointed a microphone at their mouths.

"So, you did the impossible," the reporter said, smiling at Leigh. "You beat the Queen of the Vault, scoring higher than Camille Abrams on her signature event. How did that feel?"

These questions were so stupid. How did that feel? It felt right. It felt like destiny.

It felt like relief. Because the vault had the highest point potential, her triple twisting Yurchenko more than made up for her screwups on beam and bars.

Beating her crush had been exactly what Leigh was thinking about as she stood on that vault runway. Proving to herself that she was the best by squashing the score of the girl who gave her electric jolts and goose bumps.

But, of course, she couldn't say any of that. She had to be sweet for the public.

"Camille is an amazing vaulter," Leigh heard herself saying with a sheepish giggle. She hoped that Grace and the reporter didn't notice the way her cheeks turned pink just from saying Camille's name out loud. "Of course I didn't set out to beat her. I was just trying to do my best."

"Well, you certainly did that." The reporter smiled through too much sticky-looking hot-pink lipstick. "So, how did it feel?"

That stupid question again.

"Fun," Leigh said. "The higher you jump, the more fun it is." She laughed again.

Leigh felt all puffed up and powerful and, even though Grace was still winning (for now), she felt superior. But she was giggling shyly.

Apparently That Girl was also a liar.

"So, you two find yourself in pretty much the exact

same positions you were in after the first day of Nationals," the reporter's raspy voice went on. "Leigh, will you be gunning for Grace tomorrow? Grace, what will you be doing to try to put some space between the two of you? Or would you both just be happy to make the team?"

"Oh, no," Leigh heard herself continue to lie. "It doesn't really matter."

She wanted to beat Grace. She wanted to beat everyone.

"Grace?" the reporter said. "It must be difficult to always be competing when you two are so close."

Grace laughed one staccato *ha* that was so out of character, it made Leigh turn and pay attention to what she was saying. "Well, we're friends. But we aren't *close-close*. If you know what I mean. There's nothing . . . like, scandalous or anything going on here. *I'm* not like that."

It was like a hammer hitting Leigh in the stomach.

Grace's face flinched into a nasty look and just as quickly it melted back into a sugary-sweet smile.

"We're best friends," Leigh blurted. Although she didn't feel like they were at the moment.

She narrowed her eyes at Grace, trying to make them say, *What are you doing? Why would you try to destroy me right in the middle of the Olympic trials?*

"Yes," Grace said. "We're best friends . . . we're only *friends*. Nothing more."

Leigh almost choked. It was like being stabbed in the back right in front of her face.

"Okay . . ." the reporter said slowly.

What had happened? Only a few minutes ago they were working together to trip up Monica. That whole plot had been Grace's idea and entirely for Leigh's bene-fit. Now, suddenly, Grace was trying to destroy Leigh?

"Well, you're on top now, Grace," the reporter said, trying to get her bearings. "What's your strategy for tomorrow?"

Leigh barely listened as Grace muttered the stan-dard things about hard work and focus and doing her best.

It was a crock. Grace didn't only try to do her best. She tried to keep every other gymnast down.

"Thanks so much, ladies. Best of luck tomorrow," the reporter said, and the two of them waved identically perky waves at the camera.

As soon as it disappeared, Grace rolled her eyes at Leigh. "I hate those questions," she said. "Especially the *how do you feel* question."

She smiled.

Leigh's jaw dropped. "What was that?" she demanded.

"What?" Grace said, innocent.

"Why the hell would you say that? 'We're not *close-close*,' '*I'm* not like that'?"

Grace shrugged, wide-eyed, smiling.

Leigh was going to slap her. If it weren't for the cam-eras still in the vicinity, her hand would be imprinted on Grace's face.

"What's wrong?" Grace said, too high, too nasally, too fake. "We *are* only friends, right?"

She started to walk away. Leigh reached out and caught Grace's wrist with her palm, spinning her too hard so that they would be face-to-face. "Explain," she spat.

"We're only friends," Grace said. "We aren't even best friends, I guess."

"What?" Leigh asked. "Why?"

"You should have told me," Grace said.

"I did tell you," Leigh said. "You're like the only person I've ever told. And you just said it to that reporter—"

"Not that. God, no one cares about that, okay, Leigh?"

Leigh lowered her eyebrows. She told Grace everything. Everything except her crush on Camille. But there's no way Grace knew about that.

What was Grace talking about?

It was for only an instant that the best friends stood like that, staring and unseeing. Then a shadow fell across their tension. They looked up to see Ted standing above them, his hand on Monica's shoulder.

"Get your things," he said. "You'll eat with Monica and me."

Had her dad found the Dylan Patrick messages? Was Grace mad now, a whole day later, that Leigh had tried to have a little bit of fun?

It didn't make any sense. Leigh had sent that message to Dylan last night, last night before the trials even started, last night when they were . . . friends, when she was just . . . Leigh.

Leigh shrunk under Ted's gaze. Her heart cowered

behind a rib. She didn't like Ted. She was tiny in his presence, no matter how well she'd performed that day. And even though her vault was great, Leigh had had far from a perfect day.

Ted put his other hand on Grace's shoulder.

"You were great today, Monica," Leigh said, purposefully leaving out Grace. "I mean, don't worry about the vault. You were so amazing on everything else."

The mousy girl tilted her head and gave Leigh a confused look. Grace and Ted walked away.

"Yeah, sorry," Leigh said. "I know how it feels when you fall. I shouldn't have said anything. I can't stop thinking about my messed-up beam."

Monica shook her head.

"What?" Leigh said.

"Never mind," Monica said.

"No, what is it?" Leigh pushed.

"I heard what you said about me earlier," Monica said.

"Huh?" Leigh said.

"What's wrong with you? You can't just pretend . . . You're . . . you and Grace . . . you're . . . mean."

"Oh," Leigh said. The butt glue. The snickering. Had she really done that? It felt like someone else had said those things and smiled that nasty smile. "I . . . I'm sorry."

Monica was still shaking her head.

Leigh felt even smaller than she had with Ted. Like she was shrinking until she was Monica's size. Like she didn't know where or who she was anymore.

"I'm sorry," Leigh said again. "It wasn't . . . nice."

Monica snorted, then flinched at her own noise.

Leigh faltered. She didn't want Monica to be so mad. She didn't know how to explain that the girl who had made fun of Monica wasn't who she really was. That outside the meets she'd always been nice. That she sometimes had issues with her own butt glue.

Ted called Monica.

Leigh watched the three of them disappear from the gym. Ted, Monica, Grace: they were all mad at her.

A terrifying thought rippled through Leigh's body: What if That Girl wasn't someone she liked?

STANDINGS
AT THE END OF DAY 1

1.	Grace Cooper	60.705
2.	Leigh Becker	60.100
3.	Georgette Paulson	60.025
4.	Wilhelmina Parker	59.850
5.	Maria Vasquez	56.950
6.	Kristin Jackson	56.670
7.	Monica Chase	56.655
8.	Annie Simms	56.455
9.	Natalie Rice	54.050
10.	Camille Abrams	29.985
11.	Samantha Soloman	29.980
12.	Olivia Corsica	29.738

Evening Limbo

GRACE

Grace stood, frozen, and stared. There was a buffet of food for the gymnasts and their coaches spread out across the table along the back wall of the hotel conference room.

Grace gawked at the full salad bar with every type of vegetable that grew out of the ground, chunks of tofu and freshly roasted turkey breast, a platter of grilled chicken decorated with bright yellow lemons, a basket of whole-grain breads and rolls, and bowls of red and green apples, fuzzy peaches, glistening nectarines. The options were healthy, but the sheer amount of food was terrifying. Each basket and plate and platter was brimming over. Each fruit was plump, each veggie plentiful, each roll the size of Grace's fist.

It was such a cruel thing to do to athletes in a sport where a few pounds could mean the difference between being shattered and being immortalized.

Grace was not the only gymnast standing four feet from the table and staring at the food.

She knew that almost every gymnast had food issues. Every one of them could recite her weight down to the hundredth decimal. They all dreamed of pizza and candy and doughnuts when they slept. Each one had her own struggles trying to be healthy and wondering if it was even possible to be healthy when she thought this much about food. Grace knew she was not alone in all of this.

But Grace also knew that her food issues were worse.

For now, she blended in. Or, rather, the fact that her face could never blend in helped her mask the shrinking of her body. She looked like the Chinese-Chinese gymnasts, who were always skinny. So, as she stood with several other girls, no one noticed that she was by far the slimmest among them. It was the one gift her mother had left her: the ability to wither into wires undercover.

The coaches were finished at the food table. They'd selected their food easily, like normal people, and taken a table in front of the girls'.

But Grace's dad sat at the back table by himself, not with the other coaches. Grace knew she would have to join him. So would Monica. Ted didn't like to let his gymnasts eat at the table with the other girls because he was afraid that the chatting and laughter would distract them from the importance of eating correctly, eating the combination of protein and grains and calories that would lead to higher release moves and tumbling passes. If it weren't for all the other people in the room,

Grace's dad would probably make her plate himself. But they were both a little embarrassed about the amount of control he wielded on Grace's life.

She grabbed a dish, feeling the cool edge of the porcelain against her palm like the barrel of a gun.

This is going to be hard, Grace thought.

Because while Grace's father thought he was controlling everything, while Grace was happy to let him control most things, there was one thing he knew nothing about.

She glanced over the white warm-up fabric on her shoulder and saw her father sitting at the back table, staring at her from beneath bushy blond eyebrows as if to say, *Get over here already.*

Monica wasn't even in the conference room yet, so it wasn't like Grace was the only one keeping him waiting.

There was no way around it today. Not with everyone here. Not with her father staring at her that way. Grace was going to have to eat.

She looked down at her chest. *That's what you want anyway, right?* she asked her heart.

Grace made a salad. She piled spinach and tofu and turkey and broccoli and cauliflower and hearts of palm onto her plate. She dressed it with only a little balsamic vinegar, no olive oil. She grabbed a bottle of water and added a small roll that she had no intention of actually eating to the side of her plate.

As she carried her tray back to the table at the back of the room, she passed the one where all the girls were sitting. Leigh's head was thrown back in laughter as she listened to a story Maria was telling about the last Olympic trials.

Well, Grace didn't want to talk to her anymore anyway. Grace was done with friends.

Still, it was stupid that Grace couldn't eat at that table. That she couldn't sit down right next to Leigh and keep punishing her. Why did Leigh do that? Why would she hide something so huge from Grace? Just to win? Leigh was acting like . . . like . . . Grace. It was something Grace would do—keep a major trick in her back pocket and not even tell Leigh she was planning to use it. But Grace hadn't. Grace was desperate to beat Leigh, but she'd never even thought of trying to fool her. Trying to destroy her. In fact, Grace had spent today trying to destroy someone *for* Leigh.

Was this what all the Dylan Patrick stuff was about, too? Was Leigh trying to distract Grace last night so that she didn't ask about new tricks, about strategy? So that she went into the meet blindfolded?

Grace was desperate to win the meet, to beat Leigh. But she'd believed her best friend when she had said that all she wanted was for the two of them to get the top two spots, to make the team and qualify for the individual all-around. Could it be that Leigh was just as desperate to beat Grace? Desperate enough to fake friendship? Desperate enough to hide huge point potential and distract her with a cute boy?

It was worse than that. Leigh had given Grace hope.

Hope that someone else might eventually like her. Hope that there was a space for her outside the four walls of her dad's gym. Leigh didn't know what that hope had meant to Grace. She already had so many other friends. She already had a *life*.

Grace plunked her tray down across from her dad and tried to give him a smile.

He glanced at her food but didn't comment on it. Grace relaxed a little bit.

She was going to eat. It felt weird, but it would actually be good for her gymnastics. It would make it so her heart didn't jump and split like that anymore. Grace picked up her fork and forced a chunk of tomato into her mouth.

One meal will not make you too heavy to fly, she told herself. But she sucked in her stomach before biting down.

"Listen, I'm not mad at you, Gracie, okay?" her dad said.

Grace looked up sharply, so shocked that the thoughts of food were actually gone from her mind. "About what?" she asked.

"Your fan page. I saw it. And it's okay." He smiled a rare smile. Well, rare for Grace. Max got his smile all the time. For learning to tie his shoe or repeating a joke he didn't quite understand. Max—Grace's adorable little brother who chased their awful mother away just by being born with Down syndrome—usually got all of their dad's soft side. But Grace could see a little of it in his eyes now, and it was pointed to her.

"I can't be mad at you because your supposed friend took advantage of your vulnerabilities," her dad said. "That's not your fault. You didn't message that singer guy."

"I didn't!" Grace said. "I swear!"

She was so distracted by this real family moment, she took a bite of cucumber, chewed, and swallowed. Almost without thinking.

Her dad actually chuckled. "I know," he said. "I believe you. You would never spend your meet thinking about some stupid boy."

Grace nodded. She managed another bite. Maybe this conversation would get her through a whole meal.

"I followed the whole thread, Grace, from your fan page to that Dylan boy's to Leigh's. Leigh started the whole thing. Leigh. Your so-called friend. She did it to distract you."

Grace paused mid-chew. That's what she had just thought of, minutes ago. Was the whole Dylan Patrick thing a part of Leigh's strategy?

She had to be careful now, with her words, with her bites.

"She . . . Leigh . . . she said we were just having fun."

"Oh, Gracie," her dad said. "What have I always told you about friends in the gym?"

But this was in the hotel room.

Grace didn't say anything.

"You have to be cautious. Especially when you have so-called friends as worldly and educated as Leigh.

Leigh spends half her time outside the gym. She knows how to be a typical teenage mean girl in a way you just don't."

That was true, Grace conceded.

"But how do you know she was doing it to distract me? How do you know she knows more about being a teenage mean girl than a teenage nice girl?" Grace asked. There had to be some of the nice kind, too, somewhere out there.

"Well, did she tell you she had a triple twisting Yurchenko?"

Grace dropped her fork. "No," she said.

"Listen, don't let all of this get to you. If you spend tonight thinking about Leigh or thinking about some boy, her plan will have worked. You two are both going to be on the Olympic team. You can figure out if you want to be friends with her after the trials are over. Don't think about her tonight. You can't get distracted. You have to do better tomorrow, Gracie," her father said. "I was hoping you'd have more of a lead by now. We don't want this to be like the second day of Nationals."

Grace nodded. She barely heard him, though. She was forcing the cube of turkey to squish between her molars.

"Now, that girl, she had a good day," her dad said. Grace followed his eyes to the door where Monica was walking in, smiling at Kristin.

Grace forced herself to swallow. "You mean *Monica*?" she said.

He nodded. "She impressed me today," he said. "Did you see how she flew on bars? And her legs are so long and straight and perfect? You see, you always have to watch out, Gracie. She's our own and she still came out of nowhere. There will always be younger, newer, talented girls on your heels."

Grace watched Monica load a plate with chicken and vegetables and fruit like she wasn't even thinking about it. At once she was hating Monica's skinny frame and wishing she hadn't interfered, wishing that Monica was still beating Leigh.

Grace flashed back to herself two years ago, at fifteen. She'd still been growing a little bit and with the workouts she was doing, her body would churn up all her calories almost as soon as they hit her tongue. At fifteen, Grace would not have been terrified by this buffet, either.

But would her dad understand that? Would he respect the fact that she'd pared herself down to three hundred or five hundred calories a day just to be able to keep up with the skinnies like Monica who were waiting in the wings? Could he possibly understand that in the past year, since Worlds, her body had slowed down and she couldn't speed it up? That if he kept talking about how high the skinnier girls in her gym flew and how perfect their lines were and how graceful their legs looked, Grace might stop eating completely and then she'd never be able to stay on the bars?

"She's fifteen," Grace said. It was a start.

This whole meal would be better without Monica. Normally, as in back-when-she-was-eating, Grace had enjoyed sitting with her father when the competition was over. He'd let his guard down a little and they would laugh at something silly a fan had written on a poster. They'd talk about Max and all the funny things he and his babysitter had yelled out from the bleachers that day. They would giggle at the girls who were so clearly gunning for her but who had no chance. But her coach couldn't morph back into her dad tonight because Monica was there and she'd have to eat with them as well.

So, in two words, Grace tried to explain the obvious. Yes, Monica was smaller. She was also younger. Two and a half years younger. Max, who was eight, was also smaller than Grace, but her dad didn't hound her about that.

"And she fell on vault," Grace blurted before she could stop herself.

Just then a tray tapped down beside her. Monica sat and began arranging her napkin and utensils and water bottle and pretending she hadn't heard Grace, even though Grace knew she had. Her face burned.

This time she *hadn't* meant for Monica to overhear. Now that she was wishing Leigh would disappear, Grace wanted to build Monica up, not tear her down. The other girls probably thought Grace was mean, the way her dad thought Leigh was mean. But that wasn't quite the truth for Grace. It didn't have anything to do with Monica when Grace talked about her behind her back. It wasn't about being mean: it was about being in control. Monica wouldn't understand that.

Grace looked at her food. How could she touch it now with this skinny mini next to her and her dad smiling at the gymnast who was not his daughter? It was hard to eat in the best circumstances. Now it would be close to impossible.

Monica shoved a huge bite of chicken into her mouth, and Grace's father said, "I was just telling Gracie how impressed I am with your performance today."

Monica nodded.

"You did a great job, kiddo."

Grace's jaw dropped, but it didn't matter. Neither of them was looking at her.

She couldn't believe that silly little Monica was able to pull a compliment out of her father after that average performance. How long had Grace yearned for a sentence like that? One that wasn't followed up with "but" or "just watch." One that was purely a good job? And the little pipsqueak even got a nickname?

Monica didn't look happy. Instead, she looked a little angry, eating wide-eyed, bite after bite like it wasn't a big deal, like a perfect day in the gym isn't the same thing as eating the perfect amount and no more.

"I fell on vault," Monica said finally, between bites.

Grace's dad shrugged. "That doesn't really matter. You were almost perfect outside of that."

Monica went back to her food. Grace's stomach

churned. She didn't know if it was because she was hungry, or because eating that one bite of turkey after so many months of not eating any kind of meat had turned her stomach inside out.

Her father was still talking about how great Monica was. Monica, Monica, Monica.

Grace stared and stared at her food, taking bites of lettuce to her lips but only eating every third one.

Then another burst of laugher erupted from the table across the room. Grace turned to look, to see who Leigh was buddying it up with now. She knew that half of the girls at that table would love to be eating with their families. She knew that most of them hated the way gymnasts were kept separate from all spectators for the duration of a meet, even if it lasted several days. But Grace didn't care. She was jealous of them: both for getting to eat with each other and for having parents who gave them a break from the gym.

Leigh was staring daggers at Grace while laughing with Maria. How did she manage to do both things at once? Maybe she *was* a mean girl.

"I'm getting distracted," Grace told her father. "Can I eat this upstairs?"

He nodded.

In the hallway, Grace almost bumped right into Wilhelmina, who was coming from the bathroom. "Hey," the girl said.

"Hi," Grace answered quietly.

She wondered how long she was obligated to stand and talk to her. It wasn't like the two of them were friendly. And Grace's hands twitched, wanting to be rid of the food between them, wanting to be alone with her phone and the Internet.

"Are you okay?" Wilhelmina asked, her eyes on Grace's salad.

Grace looked up quickly. That was a weird question. Especially from someone Grace hardly ever talked to. "I had a good day," she said. She didn't need Wilhelmina's pity. She was beating her.

"I-I know," Wilhelmina stammered. "You did. I just meant, um . . . where are you going?"

Grace shrugged. "Eating in my room," she said. She hoped her voice didn't waver. She had to get out of here, get out of this, whatever this was. "Bye."

Grace darted past Wilhelmina and didn't turn to see if she was being watched as she stepped into the elevator.

In her room, Grace ate five bites of lettuce and half a chunk of tofu while she played with the message on her screen, writing it and rewriting it until it was close to perfect. She could write back now. Her dad wasn't mad at her. Her dad was on her side. Leigh was against her. If her dad found the reply, she could say Leigh wrote it while Grace was sleeping. He'd believe it.

She swallowed the second half of her tofu chunk just as she hit "send." Chills ran through her chest.

> Thanks for the messages today. It means a lot to know someone is watching me. Especially someone as cute as you.

Then she ran to the bathroom and flushed the rest of her food down the toilet, making sure it was completely gone before Leigh came back to the room.

When she got back to her phone, she already had a reply.

WILHELMINA

Don't be there, Wilhelmina pleaded as she walked down the hotel hallway after dinner. She was hoping Camille would be in Samantha's room watching TV or somewhere, anywhere else. She wanted a minute alone to call her mom and dad, to text Davion. To figure out her strategy for tomorrow.

She didn't want to hear about all the reasons fourth place might not be good enough. Wilhelmina couldn't let Camille get in her head again.

Don't be there.

But she was still two doors away when she heard Camille's voice floating into the hallway. "It's a stupid fan page, that's all," she heard Camille say. "It doesn't matter who writes on it."

Wilhelmina froze. Was Camille's boyfriend upset because some random Out of Touch boy messaged his girlfriend? How did these people have time to worry about things like that?

"It's not a big deal. I don't even like Out of Touch that much," Camille's voice whined.

Wilhelmina shook her head. It hadn't occurred to her to be concerned about Davion getting jealous over whoever might have written on her fan page. Davion didn't even have the official "boyfriend" title, and Wilhelmina was still pretty sure he wouldn't be jealous over some stupid one-sided online flirting. It was disappointing: Wilhelmina never knew Camille was so full of drama.

She couldn't face her. Not the whiny voice on the phone. Not the manipulating voice from earlier today. She marched to the end of the hallway. Ice would be good on her knees and ankles anyway.

The USAG had set up an ice bath in a room on Wilhelmina's floor. A volunteer sat in the hallway with a clipboard to sign the girls in and make sure they didn't stay long enough to get frostbite. After chatting with her briefly, Wilhelmina went into the room and breathed a sigh of relief to find it empty. She sunk her legs into the ice, leaned her butt against the metal rim of the tub, and took a deep breath, sucking in the solitude around her. Thank God she was alone.

She reached to her bag on the table behind her, pulled out her phone, and began scrolling through the texts Davion had sent today.

After vault: You are such a badass.

After bars: Your routine was the bomb. You're the best.

After floor: I don't care what the judges say. You're winning. I'm sure I know more than the judges.

He was there, in the stadium, eleven hours away from their home. He'd driven all that way just to see her. Mina.

She tapped the phone against her upper lip, wondering what to write back.

- - -

Davion had been Wilhelmina's friend and neighbor since they were little kids. That was the only way she was able to meet him, since she had been homeschooled since seventh grade. Davion had been a playmate before the gym ate away all her free time. They'd spent hours playing basketball and hide-and-seek with Davion's brothers when she was eight and nine and ten. After that, even though they lived on the same street, it felt like Wilhelmina did not see Davion for years.

Until he appeared on her stoop.

Wilhelmina had swung open the door, frozen, and stared. He was wearing a red T-shirt that showed off the richness of his brown skin and the muscles in his arms and chest. His eyes were so bright they were almost gold. His smile was adorably crooked. He held a pile of misdelivered mail in the fist by his hip.

Wilhelmina had furiously patted at her short hair,

hoping it wasn't puffy, hoping her elbows weren't ashy and her forehead was pimple-free.

"Wilhelmina," he'd said, almost whispering, almost reverently. And that's when she'd realized that he was staring back. His voice was deeper than when they were children.

It was only a second before his smile and eyes turned goofy. "You know, there's an ice-cream place up the road."

Wilhelmina tilted her head. "I know," she said. They'd both lived on the street her whole life.

"I haven't see you there in about eight years is all," Davion said. "Just wanted to make sure you didn't catch amnesia and forget the best ice cream in town is only a quarter mile from your doorstep. I'm there after dinner almost every night, so I'm sure you haven't been recently." He'd raised his eyebrows, handed over the mail, and left.

It was only after the doorstep had been empty for a full minute that Wilhelmina started laughing.

She was nervous. But she'd marched her butt to that ice-cream parlor after dinner that night and sipped on the Gatorade she'd bought despite all the delicious-looking ice cream. After a few minutes that felt like hours, Davion came through the door with his brothers and sister. The smile on his face told her she'd read his clues right.

"Well, look who it is," he'd said. "Our street's long-lost gymnast. I was beginning to think you were more of a legend than a person. You know, like the Loch Ness Monster."

He'd asked her out then and there and, a few days later, they went to a movie. She let him buy her a ticket, but she had to turn down the snacks because she had practice the next day. He asked if she wanted to go to pizza after the movie, but she had to rest before getting up to train in the early morning. He was funny and cute and Wilhelmina's heart felt soft and warm around him, but she had the rest of her life for dates and cute boys and swooning over crooked smiles.

She had only a few months left to be a prospective Olympian.

Before they said good night he asked her out for the next weekend, but she had a meet to go to. He'd asked about the weekend after that, but she wasn't sure what her training schedule would be then.

By the end of the date she'd had to tell him that, though she liked him, they could only be friends. For now. Until after the Olympics.

Kerry wouldn't have minded if she dated Davion. And, though her parents were supportive when Wilhelmina had deferred her acceptance to college for a year to focus on the Olympics, it's not like they forced her to do it. Wilhelmina had the kind of support that made gymnastics optional, so it was her own decision when she'd asked Davion to wait. And she knew she might lose him. But she also knew she was a nineteen-year-old who'd never been kissed, who'd never held a guy's hand in a dark movie theater, who'd never had a crush. The prospect of all of that was exciting enough to become distracting. If she let him hold her hand once, she'd be fantasizing about the next time constantly. She'd be imagining kissing him in the middle of pirouettes on the high bar. The attraction to him was distracting enough. Mina couldn't afford to add the touching. Not yet.

Davion hadn't become her boyfriend.

He'd become her friend, her fan, her supporter. And, despite her resistance, her crush.

- - -

A light sliced across the dark hotel room. "Hey, Wilhelmina!"

She looked up to see the one person she was hating more than her roommate: Leigh. Leigh, the Mystery Vaulter. Leigh, the Dream Crusher.

"Whatcha doing in here? Just icing? I feel a little beat-up after today, too. We're like old ladies with these aches and pains."

Oh my God, shut up!

Wilhelmina didn't say anything. She looked away, hoping Leigh would get the message.

Leigh reached into the ice machine next to the metal tub where Wilhelmina was soaking and stuck a cube in her mouth before filling up the plastic bucket she was carrying. Leigh smiled right at Wilhelmina with a huge ice-filled smile like she didn't realize she'd personally threatened Wilhelmina's life with one ten-second vault.

"So it seemed like you really rocked it today. Your floor routine was incredible. How are you feeling?" the lucky gymnast asked.

Wilhelmina couldn't help rolling her eyes this time.

It was impossible that Leigh was beating Wilhelmina by working harder. Wilhelmina worked so hard. This girl went to high school. She was bouncy and perky and lucky and Wilhelmina was a workhorse, but luck was winning.

"Are your legs okay?" Leigh nodded toward the ice.

She just wouldn't quit. How much clearer could Mina be?

"Fine," Wilhelmina answered.

Please just leave so I can text my not-boyfriend.

Leigh smiled again. "Hey!" she said. "Did you hear? My brother messaged me. He was reading about the meet online and he said that apparently Katja is giving some interview about us. Tonight. First time she's ever given a mid-meet interview. Crazy, right?"

Wilhelmina stayed very still. It *was* crazy. It was unprecedented. Would she give some clue as to how she planned to construct the team? Would she answer the question: Did she love winning more than she hated surprises?

"Interview?" Wilhelmina said carefully. "Where?"

"Oh, not on TV," Leigh said. "On, like, espnW.com or

something. But, you know, live. With the, like, SportsCenter reporters!"

She said this last bit like it made it all more exciting. Like hearing her name on SportsCenter was akin to competing in the Olympics.

"Yeah, well," Wilhelmina said. "I don't have my computer with me, so—"

"Oh my God!" Leigh squealed. "You should totally come down to our room to watch it. We all should. We can, like, watch it together, you know? Spread the word, okay? Nine o'clock. Room 203."

Wilhelmina said nothing.

This was too weird. If Camille could be manipulative and full of drama, anyone could.

The cube of ice was visible between Leigh's molars. "Okay. Well, see you later," Leigh said, then darted out of the room like she didn't want to be there in the first place.

Wilhelmina dove for her phone and let the number dial in her palm. Forget texting. She wanted to hear his voice.

"Hey, Super Woman," Davion said as soon as he answered.

"Super Woman?" Mina asked.

"Well, you do fly," he said.

"You are not actually here," Wilhelmina said. Her voice sounded like someone else's. She was giggling.

"Why do you say that?" Davion said. He giggled, too,

but it was manly. His was the only manly giggle Wilhelmina had ever heard.

"You did not drive all the way from Indiana just to go to some gymnastics meet."

"Oh!" he said. "Shoot, man, I'm at the wrong meet. I didn't think I was at 'some gymnastics meet.' I thought I was at the freaking Olympic trials. I thought I was watching my friend kick ass at the freaking Olympic trials."

"There's no way you're really here," Wilhelmina said. Even though she knew he was there. Even though she believed him. She wanted to hear him say again that he'd come just for her. She wanted to hear his giggle.

Was this flirting?

"I'll prove it to you," he said.

"Really?" she said. Was he in the hotel? It was exciting, but not allowed. She couldn't see him now. "How?" she asked.

"Tomorrow," he said. "I'm going to give you the biggest hug ever. I've never hugged an Olympian before."

Wilhelmina sighed. "I might not be one, you know."

"So?" he said. "You better be ready for it because I'm gonna hug you either way, Parker. I'll hug you like you've never been hugged before."

Maybe there could be advantages to retiring . . .

When the door swung open again, Wilhelmina hit "cancel" without even saying good-bye. She wanted to keep that voice to herself.

The figure in the doorway was only little Monica.

She climbed up the side of the tub and sunk her own legs into the ice.

"Hi," she said.

Good-bye, alone time.

Wilhelmina hated her instantly.

MONICA

Monica picked up a cube of ice and watched it melt slowly into her palm while avoiding the eyes of the superstar gymnast beside her. She had been hoping to get a minute alone. That was the reason she hadn't wrapped her ankles in ice packs and had instead come down to the ice room in the first place: to get away from Kristin for a little while.

Kristin hadn't known it would hurt, what she said. Or maybe she had. Well, it didn't matter. It did hurt.

I only look bad because you were beating me.

I only look bad because you, Monica, were beating me.

I only look bad because you, Monica, suck.

Monica wasn't the right kind of gymnast. She was the kind whose success only destroyed others—Kelly Moss, Kristin, Leigh almost—instead of counting for something on its own. So at least, in this cold, dark room, her company was someone consistently higher than her on the scoreboard.

Now I know, she thought as she watched the ice turn into a puddle and drip off her palm. Why Kristin always roomed with her. Why Leigh changed from nice to mean so quickly. Being lowest on the scoreboard had been easier on her social life.

At least that's not me, she thought. *At least when I was the one losing every meet, I was gracious to all of them. At least I'm not that ugly.*

"So . . ." Monica said.

Wilhelmina scooted a bit farther from her. It stung in her heart.

Monica used to be Wilhelmina's biggest fan. But she was here now. She couldn't be a fan.

- - -

Five years ago, the National Championships had been held an hour outside of Monica's hometown, and two weeks after her birthday.

Monica had expected a gift on the breakfast table as usual that day, but instead she'd found only a card. Inside there were three tickets.

"Can you believe we get to go?" her mother had cooed. "Can you believe it's so close to home? I thought it was the perfect gift! Because one day you'll be there! One day little girls and their moms will be buying tickets to see you. *My* little girl."

Monica's eyes were wide. "This is a real meet?" she'd squealed. "With real gymnasts? Ones who could be in the Olympics one day?"

Her mom's smile got a little sadder. "Well, I wanted you to be able to bring a friend. And it was sort of expensive. So I only got tickets to the juniors event. But still. They'll be the best fifteen-year-olds on the planet."

Monica ran at her mother and smothered her in a hug. "One day it'll be you," her mother whispered. "It will."

Monica shrugged that part off. Even all of those years ago she didn't like the pressure her mom heaped on her to be better than Monica felt she was. At ten years old, she was already training forty hours a week. She was working on routines that would qualify her for elite status one day. She was hoping to make the national JO team the next year. She was gymnast through and through. But, even at ten years old, Monica knew she wasn't the best.

So Monica had been in the crowd when Wilhelmina was crowned the junior national champion for the first time. Wilhelmina was the first full-time gymnast Monica had met in real life. And she was so nice. After the meet, they lined up to shake her hand and get her autograph.

"I'm a gymnast, too," Monica had said.

Back then, Wilhelmina seemed so much older than her. Like an almost-grown-up.

"Really?" Wilhelmina asked, even though there was a line of other little girls waiting to meet the new junior champion. "What's your favorite event?"

"Bars!" Monica said, at the same time her mom said, "Floor is her best."

Wilhelmina had smiled. "Yeah, the best is not always the most fun."

They giggled together, and then, even though Monica was only one of dozens of girls going gaga over Wilhelmina Parker's double Arabians and DTYs, she stood up, crossed the table, and gave little Monica a hug.

- - -

Monica hadn't even been able to dream that she would one day compete against that gymnast.

It was amazing that Wilhelmina Parker had lasted this long, that she was still here five years later and still in great shape. She was the girl who Teeny Gymnast Monica had swooned over those years ago, and here she was, right now, sharing ice with Current Monica. The Nobody.

This morning this whole thing would have made her happy. But she couldn't be happy now. What was the point of being so good today, of getting as high as fourth on the scoreboard, just to fall on her butt on the last rotation and have everyone hate her anyway?

"I bet you're making it hard for Katja Minkovski to sleep tonight. She loves new gymnasts like you."

Monica shrugged. Wilhelmina sounded nothing like the girl five years ago who stood up and walked around a table just to hug her.

"Seriously," Wilhelmina said. "Katja loves young and skinny gymnasts."

But Monica felt like a failure. She hadn't met her number one goal. She hadn't even factored into the Olympic conversation enough for Ted to say anything to her about the fall; he'd actually said that it didn't matter. Kristin had said the same thing.

"I fell on vault," she said quietly.

Then Wilhelmina did something shocking. She threw her head back and laughed.

Monica lowered her eyebrows. She might not be the best gymnast there, but she was sick of everyone acting like her performance was nothing. Even this girl she barely knew was laughing at her.

"Sorry," Wilhelmina said, straightening out her face when she saw Monica's angry look. "But your vault doesn't matter. You know that, right?"

Yeah, yeah, yeah. Nothing mattered. Her whole life Monica's gymnastics had almost—but not quite—mattered.

"To me," she said, trying to sound strong but instead squeaking like a mouse. "It matters to me."

Wilhelmina nodded. "Yeah, get ready for it," she said. "Lots of things will matter to you that don't matter to anyone else."

Now Monica was mad enough to talk with some actual volume.

"I know I never had a chance. I know it seems like I should be happy with three good performances. Or that I should be happy just to be alive. But I'm not. I wanted to get through the day without falling and I'm sick of everyone telling me to be happy. You wouldn't be happy if you fell."

Wilhelmina stared at her. Monica gripped the side of the metal tub and braced herself to endure a lecture about gratefulness: be grateful you're young and healthy and did an amazing bars routine. Be grateful you're not old and you might have other chances. Be grateful you're not me for one reason or another.

When other gymnasts said these things to her, they were always secretly grateful they weren't Monica. It's not like she didn't know that.

Wilhelmina said, "No chance? You think *you* have no chance?"

Monica shrugged. "I never really had one. Then I fell on vault."

Wilhelmina shook her head. "That's not what I meant," she said. "I didn't mean *you* don't matter. Your *vault* didn't matter because we wouldn't need you to vault. Between Leigh and Camille and Olivia and me, I guess, we have plenty of vaulters. You know, there are only three vaulters in the Olympics."

Monica squinted. What was this girl saying?

"You wouldn't ever vault there anyway."

Monica nodded. Of course she wouldn't. She wasn't going. But Wilhelmina did have a point. There were going to be five people on the team and only three performed on each apparatus. So Leigh's crazy-high-scoring vault had made everything easier for her and Samantha and Maria and Annie and . . . oh, God, it *still* didn't matter. She was never going. There were too many of them.

"You're young and fresh and tiny and great on bars and amazing on floor. You are exactly what the committee is looking for. Believe me. I've been around long enough to know."

Monica smiled. Wilhelmina was wrong, but Monica was sure she meant it because no one gave fake compliments while sounding that angry.

"It's just," Monica said. "I—I don't care that much about Katja and them. I didn't want to fall."

Wilhelmina's face softened. She squinted at Monica, but she didn't say anything.

"You're doing great, though," Monica said.

Wilhelmina sighed. Then she sighed again. Monica could almost see the walls coming down behind her eyes. When she spoke, her voice was quiet. "No," she said. "For me vault is all that matters. And now I'm in third on it." She shook her head and took a deep breath like the next thing she was going to say would be close to impossible. "I've been trying and trying, adding up scores and refiguring them, but I'm in fourth now and I'm scared I'll stay there. So . . . Look, don't tell anyone. I'm trusting you, okay? You're like the only gymnast here young enough to still be a real person."

"Okay," Monica said.

"So . . . if I do come in fourth, if I can't beat Grace or Leigh or Georgette . . . I think they'll name me alternate."

"No," Monica said. "There's still another spot open. You don't have to beat one of them to make the team."

It would be really hard to beat Leigh or Grace or Georgette. The three of them had taken the top three spots in every meet this summer.

"It's not going to go to me," Wilhelmina said. "Even if I come in fourth. Katja is mad at me. She'll make me alternate to spite me . . . and if she does, I think I'm not going. I think I'll retire. If I can't beat one of those three, tomorrow's my last day." Her voice cracked. "Last day as a gymnast."

Monica's eyes went wide. She felt suddenly large, like a hippo balanced on the side of this tub. Big and important. Why would this gymnastics superstar choose to confide in her?

"I think . . . Well, I don't think it'll happen . . . but I'd *like* to be an alternate," Monica said, selecting these new words carefully.

"Yeah, I get that," Wilhelmina said. "But then what would you do afterwards? After the Olympics."

Monica shrugged. "Keep training."

Wilhelmina nodded slowly. "See. I can't do it. I can't hang on another four years." She shook her head. "I'm only nineteen, but I'm so old."

"What about college gymnastics?" Monica asked.

Wilhelmina shrugged. "I gave up my eligibility years ago."

Monica stared. Of course she had. Wilhelmina had

been a huge star, on the brink of a World Championship until that Chinese gymnast beat her by under a point. The endorsement deals probably came knocking in full force before they fell away. So she took endorsements and went pro. Which would mean no NCAA. But Wilhelmina hadn't made it; she wasn't a big enough star to make more money than she'd eventually have to spend on college tuition. Monica knew that was rare. Wilhelmina had probably given up her eligibility for nothing.

"Besides," Wilhelmina said. "I'm tired. All I've wanted is the Olympics for so long, for like six years. Longer than that, but I thought I had a real chance for six whole years. I don't think I could stand the smell of a gym anymore after I miss that goal."

Suddenly, Monica *was* grateful. Grateful the Olympics had never been everything to her. Grateful that she'd be back in the gym on Tuesday no matter how tomorrow turned out.

They were both quiet for a minute, their eyes studying the ice at their thighs, but there was a buzzing energy in the silence.

"Can I ask you a question?" Wilhelmina said. She didn't wait for Monica's response. "How do you even do this when you don't think you have a chance?"

The Important Hippo Monica nodded and tried to take her new role seriously, being the sounding board for this kind of an athlete. She thought about her answer carefully. She turned the question over in her mind like a precious stone. But all she came up with was "I try not to fall."

Wilhelmina squinted at her, so she kept talking.

"I mean, I set a goal like that. One that I can achieve no matter who else is at the gym that day."

Wilhelmina nodded. But she said, "You shouldn't."

Monica raised her eyebrows.

"You should set the goal of beating everyone. Everyone you can beat, mathematically, at this point. You could easily climb above some of us if you perform top-notch tomorrow. And when they factor in who is winning on beam, bars, and floor combined without vault—and they will—it's you. It could be, anyway."

Monica shook her head. She couldn't think like that. It made her brain spin and her heart ache because no matter what goals she set, she knew the Olympics wasn't in her future. She wasn't good enough.

She didn't want it to hurt too badly when her name wasn't called tomorrow.

"Why don't you decide that, then?" Monica asked.

Wilhelmina shook her head. "It's complicated for me." she said. "But when you're in the Olympics, I'm going to cheer for you." She reached across the ice to knock Monica on the shoulder with her fist. "You're the only girl here I actually like."

LEIGH

Leigh had dawdled at dinner as long as she could. She'd been slow and overly careful (and talked way too much) while filling a bucket with ice to munch on until Lights Out. Her steps in the hallway were at a slug's pace. She did not want to go back to her room. She was glad, when she got there, to find the bathroom door closed and the shower running. She flopped down on her bed and pulled out her tablet.

Hip-hop pumped through her earphones.

Grace's fan page glowed from Leigh's computer screen. Dylan had been messaging her all day. Grace had even messaged him back.

Leigh stared and stared at this until a mixture of anger and terror came down black over her eyes. All she could hear was Grace's voice:

"We aren't *close*-close."

"We're *just* friends."

"*I'm* not like that."

The reporter had said, "Okaaaay." Like she felt bad for Leigh. Like she knew. Like everyone in the world would know now.

Leigh thought about the laughs she'd gotten at dinner. She thought about the friends from school who had texted her throughout the day. She didn't need Grace. It was Grace who needed her.

She couldn't let the anger she felt at Grace get mixed up in sadness.She had to protect her secret.

A new message popped up on Grace's fan page, and Leigh realized that Grace and Dylan had been having a whole back-and-forth ever since Grace got back into the room.

And then—suddenly—she knew what to do and exactly how to do it. Grace wouldn't like it, but Leigh didn't care about that anymore. She pulled her phone out of her bag, logged into her own fan page, and started typing.

> Hey Dylan Patrick, why all the attention on Grace Cooper? There are more of us out there you know!

It was ballsy, but so what? Leigh even linked Grace's fan page to the comment so she'd be sure to see it.

She threw her phone on the bed and it dinged immediately.

He'd replied.

> Oh, I noticed you out there, Leigh Becker. They said that vault was the best one in the world. (And you looked good doing it, too.)

He was flirting. With her. Which meant he had no idea. Which meant they weren't talking about that linebacker comment all day on the television.

Which meant she'd better write back.

She typed quickly, something flirty but not sug-gestive:

I'm sure you could vault just as well if you gave that singing thing up.

His reply:

Or maybe you should watch me sing sometime.

Leigh's heart sped as her fingers played on the touch screen. It was weird, this, whatever this was. This flirt-ing with a boy. It was like trying on someone else's skin. Like doing a handstand on the bars while wearing sneak-ers. It was awkward and clunky, but a fun challenge.

This kind of public flirting would keep anyone from looking too deeply into that "Linebacker" nickname or Grace's weird interview tonight. And if Grace outed her completely, she'd have this fan page conversation to point to in order to keep herself in the closet.

. . . because she wanted to stay there. Right?

In some ways Leigh almost wished Grace would have come out and said it tonight. She wished she could admit who she really was and stop worrying about what gymnastics, America, the world would say.

Leigh was so involved in fake flirting that she didn't hear the water turn off. Suddenly a dripping, towel-wrapped Grace stood at the foot of her bed.

"What are you doing?" she demanded.

Leigh shrugged. "What's it to you?" She didn't pull out an earbud. She didn't want to talk to this girl who used to be her best friend.

Grace marched up behind her.

"You're messaging him? You're messaging Dylan? What are you doing?"

Leigh didn't even look up this time. She pretended not to notice, not to know what was happening as Grace lunged across her bed and yanked her own iPad out of her bag on the floor. While her back was turned, Leigh looked at Grace. She was wrapped from head to toe in towels: one secure around her waist and reaching all the way to her ankles. Another plastered under her armpits so that her hips and butt were double-wrapped. And yet another draped over her shoulders.

Leigh's heart cracked. She swore she could hear the creaking sounds as it splintered inside her.

Leigh's mom had told her that sometimes in life she'd face people who didn't understand, who thought they could judge her, who would hate her for simply being who she was. She was scared of how high she'd have to hold her head when she did choose to tell the world about her sexuality. How, as a semi-famous person, she'd be opening herself up to ridicule from friends *and* from strangers. Hate, ignorance, judgment: Leigh knew these things were coming in her life, but she hadn't had to face them yet.

Until now. And now it was Grace—too scared to let Leigh see a bit of skin besides her face and her feet. As if Leigh's sexuality would automatically mean she was attracted to sticklike Grace. As if Leigh was dangerous and scary.

God, it hurt.

She typed. Grace was still linked in the conversation, so she'd see it right away.

Is that an invitation? To a concert?

Leigh watched Grace's shoulders go tight as she read.

Grace slowly sat up, her legs crisscross-applesauce wrapped in the brown towel, and looked at Leigh. Her face was long, the corners of her lips pointing down. Her wet, black hair was dripping all over the top of her white bedspread and it was like she didn't even notice.

"I don't get why you're doing this," she said slowly. "I mean, you don't even like him."

"Neither do you, really," Leigh said.

Grace shrugged. "How do you know?" She was barely whispering now.

Leigh answered aggressively. "Because you're—"

Focused. Boring. Not interested in anything or anyone.

Leigh had only seen Grace look so flat and vulnerable once before: years ago when Grace's birthday had fallen during the Natalia cup and, even though she won the gold medal for the junior all-around, her mother still didn't call. Grace said that was the first time her mother had missed her birthday. They were thirteen.

But that was different. That made sense. Leigh wasn't sure she trusted Grace's long face now. After all, Leigh had been a part of it when Grace had set out to destroy Monica earlier today. And then the target had jumped to Leigh's own back faster than she'd gone over the vault.

Leigh's laptop dinged with a new fan page alert and she saw Grace flinch.

This was sort of fun, this flirting. Maybe she could be straight after all.

But this message wasn't from some boy. It was from Camille.

Did you guys all see Leigh Becker's vault today!?!? AMAZING.

It was a silly promotional post. It was probably something Camille's agent told her to do so that she wouldn't look bitter. It wasn't even real.

But it made Leigh's blood rush to the outer layers of her skin and light her on fire.

"Because I'm *what*?" Grace demanded. She didn't notice Leigh flush and Leigh silently thanked Past Leigh for never telling Grace the whole truth, for never telling her about this crush. "I don't really like Dylan because I'm *what*?"

Leigh was more calm now, though. She didn't

want to hurl any of those insults anymore.

"*Do* you like him?" Leigh asked Grace.

Grace sat silent, studying her pruney fingers. "I'm not allowed to," she said finally.

Leigh did not want to feel sorry for her.

"Do *you* like him?" Grace asked. Almost like she was trying to be funny, like she wanted to be friends again.

Leigh looked at Grace, slowly shaking her head. She knew why she was enjoying the flirtatious replies from someone she didn't find appealing at all. She knew why she'd messaged him in the first place. This was about beating Grace in this stupid way, since she could never beat her in gymnastics. What was the point of being the girl who went to regular high school, who knew how to make friends, who tried so hard to be normal and nice? What was the point carving up her life so that she could never really belong anywhere if the people on the outside of their little gymnastics world weren't going to recognize her as the coolest?

Grace would always win. Even when Leigh had beaten her this summer, the headlines and the stories had been about Grace. SURE THING FALLS TO BEST FRIEND. And WHO DOES GYMNASTICS HAVE IF THE GREAT GRACE COOPER CAN BE BEATEN? Grace would always win in the gym because she was allowed to dedicate all her time there. What was the point of being Leigh, what was the point of *not being Grace*, if Leigh couldn't win in the real world?

Leigh opened her mouth to attempt to explain this,

to attempt to find a truce when they heard a knock on the door. They both jumped, startled.

"Oh yeah," Leigh said. "I sort of invited Wilhelmina and some others over here to watch Katja's interview on espnW."

"Katja's interview on espnW?" Grace repeated.

Leigh nodded. "Yeah. In ten minutes."

Grace and her army of towels darted back into the bathroom and Leigh froze for a second before letting the other girls in.

Was Grace her friend? Or not?

CAMILLE

"Yeah, it's cool. I know it's cool that so many people wrote on my page. Sorry, Mom," Camille said into the phone.

"I'm just trying to enjoy it with you, sweetheart," her mom said. "I only want to be a part of your life, you know. Ever since Bobby started hanging around, you don't let me in anymore."

Camille sighed before she could help it. Was she serious? Camille's mom was the reason she was here right now, the reason she did everything.

"What?" her mom said.

"Nothing. Sorry."

"You're nervous, aren't you? About tomorrow?" her mom said. "That's why you're all upset."

She'd been on the phone for too long. It was ridiculous. Wilhelmina was sure to come back soon and she had to think of a way to fix that situation, too.

So she said, "You know, Mom, if I joined an NCAA team—"

Her mom cut her off. "Are you still thinking about that? You promised—"

"I know," Camille said. She'd promised her mom that if she made the Olympics, she would finally go pro. She'd give her up college eligibility.

"It's not just about the money, sweetie," her mom said. "I want to see you be a star! I want to see you on Subway commercials and Wheaties boxes. I want to go with you when the team is flown to Disney World. I've been dreaming of these things since you turned your first cartwheel, you know. I've been here, by your side and I'm only—"

"Mom, I know," Camille said. "I'm going to go pro if I make the Olympics. I'm just saying if I don't make it—"

"I don't think we need to worry about that, sweetie. You've got the most consistent, most beautiful vault. And Leigh was going to be chosen anyway. I'm sure both of you girls will still get to go."

Camille tried to hide the hope from her voice, tried to sound disappointed when she spoke again. "That might not be what happens. Leigh did a triple twisting Yurchenko. She's the best vaulter now. And then there are a lot of all-around girls who also have good vaults, so it might be—"

"Ohhh," her mom said. "Listen to you, all nervous. You're okay, sweetie. You've got it in the bag. Get some rest, okay?"

Her mom sounded so happy. On the other side of that happiness was a despair so deep, Camille didn't know if they could both survive it again. So, even though she was still sort of hoping she wouldn't make the team now, she dropped it. Camille said, "Thanks, Mom," and hung up.

A knock on the door pulled Camille out of her own head.

"Katja is being interviewed live," Samantha called through the wood. "Leigh's got a computer. Her room. Ten minutes."

Camille put down her phone and left the room. She'd fix things with Wilhelmina after she heard what Katja had to say.

- - -

During her six months of nothing but high school and Bobby, Camille had missed the gym, the power of her limbs, the ability to defy gravity and science's understanding of the human body.

But she didn't miss it enough. Not enough to want to do the hardest tricks, the ones that are required of elite gymnasts. Not enough to risk breaking her back, shattering her personality, redefining herself yet again.

Still, when Camille had stopped training, it was like someone had died. For as long as she could remember, her family had always been her and her mother, and when they lost their common goal of gymnastics glory, they started living with a ghost.

At dinner they would have conversations peppered with silences where the words they didn't know how to not say hung in the air in gray typeset letters. In the mornings, Bobby would drive Camille to high school. High school, where her mother didn't sit behind a glass wall and watch her progress the way she always had been able to at the gym. And Camille could see the other ways her mother was changing: her weight was yo-yoing again, she spent full days without ever taking off her yellow robe, and she often forgot to eat until Camille asked about dinner.

Camille's mom wanted her career back, but Camille was choosing to spend her time and energy on other things. Like Bobby.

Camille loved them both. She wanted to make them both happy.

She refused to go back to her old gym. She would not let her body get mangled and pushed. But Andrew's gym across town was different. He didn't deal with many elite gymnasts. He had never coached an Olympian. His goal was to place several gymnasts a year into college programs with scholarships. When Camille met with him, he agreed to train her only after school and on Saturdays. He agreed that she should keep some of the new weight on her body. He agreed that school and boyfriends and family were also important things. Neither of them mentioned the next Olympics. Camille thought her mother would be happy. She thought maybe she'd be happy, too.

She would compete in college. She would be part of a team. She would be part gymnast and part everything else.

"I think you're throwing your life away," Helen had said when Camille told her the new plan over dinner. Her hair was oily, the gray and blonde roots matted to her skull, and the brownish locks hung from her head in chunks. She picked up her fork again and it waved around in front of her face, her red eyes watching it.

This wasn't fair.

"What about *your* life?" Camille had asked.

She didn't think her mother would understand the jump in the topic. But she did.

"Our life," her mom had said. "You're throwing our life away." Her voice didn't match the anger of the words she chose. She was whispering. "You're a kid, so you don't know it yet. You can choose school and boys and all sorts of other things. You can say I should be happy to have you for so long, but you're wrong."

"Mom, you're not making sense," Camille had said.

"I am," she said. "You just aren't listening. We used to do everything together. We used to spend our whole day in the same room, working toward the same goal, doing it together. All I wanted was to see you be an Olympian, and you can do it. I know you can do it. And I know you can choose not to, but me, I can't. I'm too old. There are no men left for me, nothing else for me to do with my life than to be an Olympic mom. I just wish you'd try."

Then she'd finally taken a bite of fish.

"I want to try the NCAA," Camille said quietly. "I love gymnastics, but I want to be on a team. And I love other things, too."

"Don't you miss it?" her mom had said while she was chewing.

"I did miss it. I was missing it."

Her mom looked alarmed. "Not anymore?"

"Because I'm doing it, Mom. I'm going to be training twenty hours a week. I want to keep going through college and get a scholarship so you don't have to pay for me to go. I'm happy. It's . . . like . . . a balance or something."

"No," Camille's mother had said. "Don't you miss *it* . . . us?"

Camille's eyes had welled up. She did miss that. She loved her time with Bobby. She loved her new gym routine and how it left time for silly stuff like movies and flirty texting. But she missed her mother. She missed the closeness they used to have. Singing Wham! in the car when her mother drove her around. Talking about the highs and lows of every workout before she went to bed each night. Cuddling under blankets and watching the other countries' National Championships on live streaming. She missed sharing a small world with this one woman, this one person who would always love her more than anyone else could.

So she said, "I'll ask Andrew about the Olympics."

Her mom had perked up immediately. "Okay!" she'd

said. "I'll meet you at the gym after school tomorrow and we can ask him together."

And Andrew had come up with the plan to make her a specialist. He'd explained that was how Camille could graduate from regular high school and still have some time for studies (and her boyfriend, though he didn't say that). She'd be a vaulter.

Camille's heart had broken: she loved the floor and the beam. She didn't want to be only a vaulter.

But when Andrew told her mom about the vault, how it had the highest DODs and the lowest chance for deductions, how Katja had consistently chosen the top vaulter for all Olympics and Worlds teams for the past ten years, whether that gymnast could contribute anything else or not, Camille knew it was over. The smile on her mother's face was huge.

"See, Cammie?" she'd said. "It's perfect. You can train part-time and still make me an Olympic Mom."

Camille had swallowed and her cheeks had burned with the lie she was about to tell. "Sounds perfect," she said.

"Let's talk about going professional," her mother had said immediately. "You have such a great story with the car accident, I'm sure we could get your name out there quickly."

Camille had looked at Andrew, panicked, and he'd come to her rescue right away.

"There's no rush here," he said. "The Olympics are still a few years away, and most of the public will not be interested in the athletes until it's over. A lot can happen in a year, as you both know. Camille should hold on to her NCAA eligibility until she makes the team."

"Good idea!" Camille had said. "Might as well play it safe."

And so they'd struck a deal. Camille would keep her NCAA status and she'd become a vaulter. She wasn't worried.

Andrew had never had an Olympian. Andrew would never get her to the Olympics. That's what Camille had thought. That's what it seemed like back then. Camille didn't know she was committing to sacrificing her future. She thought she was only buying her house a few months of peace.

WILHELMINA

They were walking down the hall, side-by-side. It was a comfortable silence. Wilhelmina's legs were tingly from the ice and Monica's were bright red.

Monica's voice was repeating over and over in Wilhelmina's brain. *Just don't fall.*

Kerry would love that goal: it was in Monica's power and control. It was a goal no one else could ruin.

Could Wilhelmina get through a meet with a goal like that? It'd been years, a lifetime, since she thought that way. But Monica and Kerry were right. If she didn't find a goal like that, she was here depending on other gymnasts messing up just a little bit more than she did. Wilhelmina couldn't control how much they messed up. She could only keep herself on her feet.

Just don't fall.

Was that enough?

She looked down at Monica's floppy ponytail. Was this girl a genius or an underachiever?

They reached Wilhelmina's room and she could still hear Camille's voice going-going-going on the other side of the door. Wilhelmina froze. "Hey," she said. "Do you want to come to Leigh's room with me?"

Monica made a face. Wilhelmina thought it must be confusion but it looked more like disgust.

"Katja's doing some interview on espnW. I guess I want to see what she's thinking. . . ." Wilhelmina smiled.

"You do?" Monica asked. "I didn't think you'd care about stuff like that."

"Everyone needs to care about stuff like that," Wilhelmina said.

Monica seemed to shrink. "Oh," she said.

Oh. Like Monica didn't care about what Katja thought. Maybe Monica was only able to focus on herself so well because the rest of the gymnastics world was fair to her.

Oh.

Wilhelmina forced her eyes not to roll. Gymnastics had been so unfair to her. Life was being so unfair to her. How could she explain that to this little gymnast without sounding like a whiner? It was awful that no one ever understood the particular kind of unfairness that plagued Wilhelmina's gymnastics. It should be obvious just to look at her.

"Well, I do care. I want to hear what she'll say. So . . . come with me?" Wilhelmina said. "I can't stand anyone else."

"Okay," Monica said. "Let's do it."

There were already a few girls gathered in the hotel room, and several more wandered in just as Wilhelmina and Monica arrived.

Wilhelmina hovered inside the doorway as the rest of the gymnasts huddled together on the two beds and the floor between them. She watched them link arms, giggle, gossip, theorize about whom Katja loved, whom she hated, what she would say. But they talked about other things, too. She listened to them compare fan pages and celebrity mentions and pictures of crushes. She watched them tease and brag and pout. She observed them as if they were animals on the Discovery Channel: a totally foreign species to Wilhelmina's world.

It wasn't just that she didn't give a flying split leap about white boy bands. It was that she, and apparently she alone, didn't give a flying split leap about boys. She was focused on her gymnastics. Her mind was so firmly rooted in her meet tomorrow that it didn't even matter that she had a freaking awesome boy waiting to give her a huge hug after it was all over. She was making him wait.

Wilhelmina looked around the room for the gymnasts who might beat her. Maria Vasquez and Samantha

Soloman sat on the corner of Leigh's bed giggling and whispering, even though they were both twenty-two and should know how to focus. Leigh Becker was showing something on her iPhone to Georgette Paulson. Grace Cooper, who sat by herself in the office chair at the side of the room crunching ice cube after ice cube between her teeth, could not tear her eyes from the ticker on the side of the TV screen that was slowly scrolling through women's Olympic updates in track and swimming to "Gymnastics Trials First Day Breakdown with Katja Minkovski."

Maybe there was one other pure gymnast in the room.

Grace looked lonely, like Wilhelmina felt. Her legs were much too skinny as she kicked back and forth in the black chair. Her wrists were barely thicker than the cubes of ice she popped into her mouth. Wilhelmina had mortified herself outside those elevators earlier that night. She had thought Grace might be as mad about Leigh's triple-twister as Wilhelmina was. Wilhelmina had been so concerned about that vault that she hadn't remembered until right now what was weird: Grace was leaving dinner with a tray full of food.

Wilhelmina watched the bones in Grace's ankles shift as she swung her chair back and forth. A familiar sickness climbed into her throat. Wilhelmina suspected what was going on. She'd seen it over and over again in so many gymnasts for so many years. But there wasn't anything she could do about it.

Wilhelmina found a spot on the wall next to the door and leaned against it. She pretended to watch the screen while instead she watched the chummy competition around her. At least Camille wasn't there. Maybe Camille was getting ready for bed. Maybe Wilhelmina could stay in Leigh and Grace's room long enough to avoid Camille all night.

Then the door slammed and in she came: purple pj's, wet, frizzy hair piled on top of her head, tiny star necklace hanging around her neck. Damn.

LEIGH

"Yeah, he was totally flirting with you," Georgette confirmed. This plan was working perfectly. Grace was still pissed, Leigh thought. But she didn't care. Grace's feelings didn't matter anymore. And as far as everyone else knew, Leigh was straight.

Georgette passed Leigh's iPhone back to her, and Leigh smiled. She was having fun with Georgette. Leigh took in the long, black braids down her back and her high, dark cheekbones and her vanilla-smelling body lotion and wondered if Georgette might be a good roommate in Rome.

"Flirting? You think?" Leigh asked. She fake-squealed. She snuck a look around to Grace, who was sitting about three feet away from them, to see if she had heard.

Instead she caught a glimpse of a curvy body in purple pajamas.

Camille was here!

Leigh's breath caught. She lost herself for a second, staring at the way her hair was pulled back from her face, the way her necklace rested in the crook of her collarbone, the way the satin fabric moved across her silky skin.

"Totally!" Georgette was saying. "I'm so jealous! I wish someone famous would write on my fan page. Like, someone I actually find hot. Not, like, the governor's husband or whatever."

Leigh shook her head to clear it and tried to give Georgette a laugh. Probably a little too late.

Camille was in her room. Leigh's room. Right now.

It wasn't going to be like it had been in Leigh's fantasies last night. When Camille had sat down with Leigh on her bed and told her she was dumping her boyfriend because she'd realized she thought Leigh was so much hotter. And then had laid down next to her and . . .

But Camille was here. In Leigh's room—well, her room for the weekend. Her feet touching Leigh's carpet. Her hand on Leigh's wall.

Leigh had to stop staring at her. Leigh's eyes fell on her roommate sitting alone in the office chair.

Grace was scowling, but that was usual.

Leigh had invited all of these people into their room

to make Grace squirm. She'd done it to prove, once and for all, that though Grace might be winning in the gym, Leigh was winning everywhere else. (And, okay, a little bit to see if maybe Camille would show up and say something to her about her vault or the fan message or anything.)

Grace spun on her chair and chomped down on a handful of ice.

Leigh wanted to smile, but didn't. She was surprised to see how well this little get-together had worked. She didn't know that gymnasts had this kind of socializing in them, not in the middle of the biggest meet of their lives anyway. There were so many gymnasts she deeply respected in this room—Camille and Samantha and Maria—Leigh decided it had to be a good thing. They all needed a break. They needed to turn their brains off for a minute before performing tomorrow. They needed a reminder that their competitors were also people.

Then Leigh felt Georgette squeeze her upper arm. "It's starting," she whispered.

Katja's face filled the television screen that Leigh had hooked up to her computer. They were suddenly all silent and attentive like good little girls. Good little gymnasts.

CAMILLE

Camille thought about approaching Wilhelmina right there in that crowded, chatty, giggly room. She thought about walking up to her where she stood frowning against the wall by the door and explaining that it had been a mistake. But what would she say? "I don't want to go to the Olympics anyway"? "I sort of wish you'd beat me so that they'd choose you over me"? Wilhelmina wouldn't believe any of that. Plus, she had been kicking butt all day ever since Camille had made her so angry. Maybe Camille should let her stay angry until the end of the meet. If Leigh's vault somehow meant Wilhelmina got to go to Rome and Camille got to stay home, she'd try to explain after that.

It was awful that Wilhelmina was mad at her now. The list of people who hated her always seemed like it was growing.

Camille shot Wilhelmina a weak smile, then plopped on the floor in front of Samantha and Maria. "Hey, fogey," Samantha said, nudging Camille with a knee.

She shouldn't be here, in this room. Katja loved her. Her vaults were quick and easy and fun and probably enough to get her into the Olympics. And she didn't want to go. She should not be here surrounded by these hopeful gymnasts. She could be killing one of their dreams and making herself miserable in the process. Everyone in this happy room should be as mad at her as Wilhelmina was right now. But, the wrath of a gaggle of gymnasts seemed easier to take than the incessant silence of her boyfriend/ex/whatever-he-was-now.

Still, maybe she should leave. Maybe she should stop trying to pretend to be one of these girls, to want what they wanted, to think how they thought. Sixteen-year-old Camille belonged in this room, but that girl was gone. Camille moved toward the door.

Then, suddenly, the crowd hushed. They all seemed to sit straighter. Some even folded their hands.

"It's good to be here, Jim," Katja Minkovski said. "Thank you for taking the time to pay attention to our little sport of gymnastics."

Jim giggled. Several of the girls giggled.

Camille almost retched.

Katja was going on national TV or whatever this was to call gymnastics *little*?

Somehow they were all supposed to believe it was *little*? Like just because the athletes were young and small, the sport was insignificant?

Why had they—why had she—given up their whole life for a sport if the figurehead was going to call it little?

And then, even though she knew it might make some more people hate her, Camille stormed out.

MONICA

Does Katja ever even think of me? Monica wondered as the wrinkly face filled the screen and she explained her role as Olympic team coordinator.

"Each year the rules are different. They are set by the USAG, the committee that determines the rules for American gymnastics in particular. Not the Olympics. Or the FIG, the international organization. So different countries do it differently. This year there is the guaranteed spot and the trials televised from beginning to end. When the selections must be made, it will be quite, quite difficult. I am used to putting the puzzle together with more time . . . and freedom . . ."

Everyone in this room seemed to have an opinion about Katja. Or a relationship with Katja. Or a theory about how Katja felt about her.

Of course Katja knew Monica. She'd known her forever. Monica was on the national team and went to all the camps. She followed all of Katja's rules about food (the right amount, the right kinds) and sleep (eight hours every night) and workouts (seven hours, six days a week, rest on the rest day) and life (only short family vacations, no other sports, no dangerous leisure activities like skiing or horseback riding, plan your calendar around the gym season).

But Monica had never wondered what Katja might think of her.

Jim laughed, like Katja was being charming, while she talked about having her pick and how it was difficult to choose the perfect Olympic team without Olympic selection camp. Monica knew what Katja liked about camp. All the gymnasts knew what Katja liked about camp. But Katja didn't say it. She didn't say that camp allowed her to make her choices in private. She didn't say that it allowed her to play favorites without the rest of the country catching on.

"Wouldn't you pick the top girls anyway?" Jim asked.

"Usually yes, of course. But sometimes . . . the meet goes differently."

Monica didn't know what Katja was trying to say this time, but it was something. Something real. A hidden meaning hung on her words.

Jim didn't see it.

"Well, how do you think our girls did today?" he chirped.

"The meet, so far, is going well," Katja said.

The girls around Monica were still, so still, not even breathing.

"When you see a girl perform to the level that is expected, that is what makes my job the easiest."

"Aha," Jim said, like he understood what she was saying. But he didn't. There's no way. Monica barely understood. And it wasn't the accent.

"She's speaking in code," Wilhelmina whispered under her breath. Monica had to agree.

"And can you give us a sense of who that was?" Jim asked.

"Grace Cooper did quite well today," Katja said. "And Georgette Paulson."

Of course, Monica thought. *And Leigh.*

But Katja didn't say Leigh.

"Still, they'll both need to do as well or better tomorrow to impress me. You see, Jim, we look for consistency. We don't look for who is doing well in one meet only. We look for who is getting better every day. Who is on the up instead of the down. The Olympics are a two-week process. If you are already tired at the trials, you will never make it through the ultimate test. This is why I prefer to have a selection camp after the official trials. It will be much harder to choose girls with stamina when we have only one meet to go off of."

Jim didn't seem to be paying much attention, but the girls in the room were so silent, so alert, like they were eating Katja's words for dessert.

"I see," Jim said. "So you don't want any bad surprises."

"Yes," Katja said. "We don't want those. But if they are going to happen, we want them to happen now. We'd rather weed out a bad surprise at this point than be faced with it in the middle of the Olympics."

Some of the girls sucked in a breath. Monica could feel her shoulders tense. "Weeding out a bad surprise" meant weeding out a gymnast. A person. Katja and Jim both seemed to forget that.

"Also," Katja was saying, "we don't always want good surprises."

"Huh?" Jim said. He tilted his head at Katja. But he was still smiling.

"You see, a good surprise to you is someone like young Monica Chase."

Monica felt all eyes go to her suddenly. She was itchy. Her bones might have torn out of her skin, she was so uncomfortable.

"A good surprise to *you*, I say, because I am not surprised by Miss Chase today. I follow her. She does what she is supposed to. I have seen her get better at one camp and one meet and one camp and one meet until today when she looks like a true elite. Like a star."

Monica's face was on fire. Her throat was twisting in two. She couldn't get a breath down.

Katja was saying good things about her. Good things! Why did this feel so awful?

"But other girls, they do surprisingly well, and I have not seen them along the way. I have not seen the slow progression of developing the skills. How do I know it's not a fluke? If she has been hiding, how do I know I can trust that one to get us the Olympic gold? How do I know if she's tired? How do I know if she's peaking at trials? When a girl shows up like this at trials with tricks and routines we did not know were coming, it feels like a slap in the face to my process."

"Aha," Jim said. "And are you talking about someone in particular now?"

Katja nodded slowly. "There is one athlete I am the most concerned about on this topic," she said.

"Any chance you'll tell us who?"

Monica's jaw dropped as she watched Katja pat the reporter on the arm and fake a giggle. "Oh, Jim," she said. "You are bad. You know I can't do that."

But Monica knew.

Her eyes traveled across the hotel room until they landed on Wilhelmina's sunken face.

And her heart broke for her old hero, her new friend. She had seemed so down and bitter in the icing room today. Enough that it was almost annoying to Monica. But that bitterness came from somewhere real.

Wilhelmina's fear had come true: tomorrow would be her last day as a gymnast.

GRACE

The girls sat in silence for several minutes after Katja's interview concluded.

Finally Maria said, "Well, that was bullshit," and a few gymnasts chuckled nervously.

They all seemed angry. Why did Grace feel proud?

"That wasn't about us, guys," Samantha said, standing up and stretching her hands over her head. "Take it from the fogies. That was some effed-up stuff, but that wasn't about us. That was Katja fighting with the USAG. Playing tug-of-war over the rules."

"And using us as the rope," Maria added. "Of course."

There were some *uh-huhs* and some *of courses* and some more curses, and then the girls were gone.

Leigh flipped the TV to an old rerun of SNL and vanished into the bathroom without saying anything. Grace chewed her cheek. There was something wrong with her. There was something broken about the way her brain worked, she decided. Why was Grace the only one on her phone searching old e-mails for the lists of camp attendees over the past few years while the rest of the girls seemed to get angry and/or heartbroken that one of them—any of them—had been singled out like that? Of the three gymnasts who had been mentioned by name, why was Grace the one no one even glanced at? Why did she seem to be the only one who was happy to be called out like that instead of mortified? What was Grace missing?

Grace had found the name easily. The gymnast Katja was talking about. The one she'd just told the whole world she didn't want on the team. Grace knew who it was. The last camp had been mandatory, so they'd all been there, but one of the athletes in today's all-around had only trained on vault at camp. And that same athlete had missed the two camps before that. And that same athlete had only competed on vault at Nationals.

So, Katja was rooting against Wilhelmina. And Katja hated the USAG. Grace didn't mind her name being used to send them a message. She wanted to be the first gymnast mentioned in any conversation ever.

(Though she did catch Katja's warning that she'd better do as well tomorrow as she had today. Grace knew that warning was for her and not Georgette, who had been consistent all season. But that was okay. It was only a warning telling her to do what she already planned to do.)

"Are you happy?" Leigh demanded when she came back into the room in her shorts and T-shirt.

"No," Grace lied. She was back to herself, which felt close to happy. Back to being sure she could win, even if Leigh had other secret tricks up the sleeve of her USA leotard.

"She didn't even mention me. After that vault she didn't mention me. You give that weird interview, and then she didn't mention me. So the last thing that will be said about me all night long is how you and I are *only* friends, how we aren't *close*-close, how you aren't *like that*. So there you go. You win, Grace. Good job."

Then Grace remembered what she'd done.

- - -

A year-and-a-half earlier, at the February camp, Leigh and Grace were alone in their cabin after the afternoon workout and before dinner. They were both still in shorts and leos, hunting through duffel bags searching for matching shirts to wear to dinner. It was Grace's favorite part of the day, though she knew it shouldn't be. The time of the day that had nothing to do with gymnastics. The time of day that she got to put friendship, Leigh, first.

Leigh tossed a bright pink shirt with blue writing onto the bottom bunk. "What about this one?" she'd said.

"Okay!" Grace said. It was a shirt from camp the year before. They both had it.

She was sitting on the bottom bunk, leaning into the duffel bag, scanning for flashes of pink.

"I have to tell you something," Leigh said.

Grace looked up, but Leigh said, "No, keep looking for your shirt. I . . . it'll be easier if I'm not looking at you."

"Okay . . . ?" Grace said. She pulled her bag onto her lap and found her shirt right away. But she pretended not to. She kept her eyes in her bag, like Leigh asked.

"I have a crush," Leigh said.

Then Grace couldn't help but look up. "Oh no!" she said.

Crushes were not good. Crushes were distraction. Not every coach said that, but her dad did, all the time.

"No, no, it's okay," Leigh said. "I'm not going to do anything about it."

And Grace remembered to look back at her bag. Leigh's face was almost as pink as the T-shirt.

"Look, it's not a big deal. I've had crushes before, too, okay? Lots of crushes. At least, I hope it's not a big deal to you because it shouldn't be, but it's a secret, okay? And I'm trusting you because you're my best friend and—you just can't tell anyone ever, ever, ever."

"About the crush?" Grace said. She kept her eyes in her bag. She didn't dare move. Leigh had never told her a secret before. No one had ever told her a secret before.

"About what I'm about to say next. Promise, Grace. You have to promise."

"I promise," Grace said.

"Look at me now," Leigh said. "Look at me and promise."

Leigh was being weird, Grace thought. But she looked up. She said, "I promise," as sincerely as she could. This moment was about Leigh. It was not about Grace. And that was okay, because this moment was about a crush and not about gymnastics.

"Look away again, okay?" Leigh said. She was standing over Grace, fidgeting with her fingers, tapping her toe. She looked more nervous than she did during any meet. "So . . ." she said. "When I have a crush . . . it's . . . on a girl."

"Oh," Grace said. Her eyebrows raised. Her eyes stayed glued to the inside of her bag.

"Yeah . . ." Leigh said. "That's it. I like girls."

"Oh," Grace said.

Leigh sat next to Grace on the bunk and Grace took this as permission to look at her friend.

"Do you care?" Leigh asked.

Grace shrugged. "No," she said. "Why would I care?"

Leigh smiled. "Good," she said.

"Can I ask you something?" Grace said.

"Look, Grace, I'm just not ready to tell anyone else, okay? I know if it doesn't matter to you, it shouldn't matter to anyone. But it will. It'll matter when people say I'm a bad role model or whatever. Even though those are stupid, ugly people, it'll hurt when they say that. But it'll matter in the good ways, too. I mean, when people say I'm the first lesbian on the USA national team, right? People will make a big deal about that in both ways, you know? I won't be able to be all gymnast anymore, ever, when that happens, and I'm not ready, so you have to keep it a secret, okay?"

"Yeah," Grace said. "That's okay. I get it."

"Oh," Leigh said. "So what's the question?"

Grace bit her lip. In some ways she thought her question would be even more embarrassing and revealing than Leigh's confession had been. "How do you know?" Grace asked.

Leigh raised her eyebrows. "Know that I'm a lesbian?"

Grace nodded.

Leigh said, "Because I like girls."

And Grace nodded again. But inside she panicked. Grace didn't like girls. Grace didn't like boys. Grace had never liked anyone. Was something wrong with her?

"I promise I won't say anything," she'd said.

- - -

Grace had almost broken her first promise to Leigh. The first one she ever made to any friend.

She hadn't meant to do that. As usual, she hadn't meant to be mean. She was only trying to have a little bit of power, a modicum of influence on the world.

"You could have trusted me to keep your other secret, too, you know," Grace said. "I was mad you didn't tell me."

"Didn't tell you *what*?" Leigh demanded. "I have no idea what you're talking about."

"Your vault. You had a TTY."

Leigh sat. "Oh," she said.

"I figured it out," Grace said. "That's why you messaged Dylan. That's why you were whispering about him all day."

"What?" Leigh said. "What does Dylan Patrick have to do with my vault?"

"Everything has been some scheme!" Grace yelled. "You messaged Dylan last night to get me to think about him instead of asking about the meet. You were keeping, like, two whole points in your back pocket so you could be sure you'd beat me."

"What?" Leigh said.

Grace sat on the bed. She looked away. She wouldn't answer.

"Grace, come on. I wouldn't do that. I wasn't even thinking about vault last night. I was trying to have fun with you."

"Then why, Leigh? You never even mentioned you had started training a TTY, let alone that you were going to debut it! You never said anything. You aren't supposed to sneak up on me. You're the one person I talk to. I even stayed friends with you when you beat me, but when you're keeping secrets—"

"Grace!" Leigh said. She stopped. "I'm sorry. I didn't mean to not tell you. It's just—I'm not always thinking about gymnastics when we talk."

"You're not?"

"No!" Leigh shook her head back and forth quick-quick. "I don't think about the gym when I'm not at the gym."

"Really?" Grace asked, shocked.

Leigh nodded. "For God's sakes, really! I wasn't even planning to do the TTY but then I was in seventh place and I had to do something to make sure I'd make the team and I was so nervous and I didn't think I'd land it because I only land it, like, 40 percent of the time in practice but then I did land it and . . . I thought you'd be happy for me."

Grace's breath caught. "I'm sorry."

Leigh deflated immediately and climbed into bed, though they still had twenty minutes before Lights Out. She covered her face with the sheet. Grace wondered if she was crying.

"Leigh, that's why Katja didn't mention you tonight. You're going to be on the team. She's not worried about you. That's it. I mean, I think she only mentioned me to warn me about being consistent."

Leigh didn't move.

"And you like girls. So what?"

Leigh still didn't move. Grace was desperate to have her back. The prospect of going to bed without any more words was terrifying. She kept talking. "Even if Katja figured it out, it wouldn't matter. Or whenever you decided to tell everyone, it won't matter. It has nothing to do with gymnastics."

Leigh snorted.

"Well," Grace said. "It shouldn't."

"Yeah, sure," Leigh said, her voice muffled in the covers. "Thanks."

Grace hated how hurt Leigh looked, how scared she must have been. She hated it now, even though it had been her exact goal a few hours ago.

Grace sat on the side of Leigh's bed. "I'm really sorry," she said. She wasn't sure how she always forgot what happened when she tried to wield that kind of control. Her influence always struck in the wrong ways. "I wasn't trying to hurt you." Even though she had been, sort of.

"Why are you acting all afraid of me, then?" Leigh's voice demanded through the sheet.

Grace's face pinched. "Afraid of you?" she said. "I'm not afraid of you." *I'm better than you. I'm still better than you. I'm not afraid of you.*

"You came out of that bathroom so wrapped up it

was like you thought I'd do something awful if I saw one square inch of your skin. I'm not attracted to *you*, Grace. Just because I like girls doesn't mean I like *you*."

Grace's eyes went wide. The towels? This was about all the towels?

"Dylan probably isn't really attracted to you, either," Leigh added. "You're not, you know, *like that*."

The words stung Grace's skin.

"That wasn't . . . I'm not afraid of you. . . . I was . . ." *afraid you'd see how far my collarbone is sticking out today, afraid you'd notice that my legs are like twigs growing out of the hotel carpet.* "Cold."

She put her hand on the back of Leigh's neck to prove it.

"Really, that's all," Grace said.

Leigh's face peeked out of the sheets, a little pink now like she was embarrassed. "Oh," she said.

Grace rubbed her back.

"But, look, you really can't tell anyone. Even if you're mad at me or I beat you or something. You can't do that again," Leigh said. "You have to wait until I'm ready."

Grace nodded.

"This is important. More important than gymnastics."

Grace sighed. Nothing was more important than gymnastics, but she didn't want to argue. "I won't. I won't hint at it again. I promise."

They froze like that. Leigh under the covers barely breathing. Grace's palm still on Leigh's back.

"Maybe Dylan Patrick could be your beard anyway, though," Grace tried.

Leigh giggled. "My beard."

Grace felt a little better. She went back to her own bed and grabbed another handful of ice from the bucket. There were only scraps left now, floating in the frigid water. Grace liked the way the cold felt against her fingers, reminding her that she was alive, she was here.

"Grace?" Leigh said.

"Hm?"

"Do you ever think you'd maybe like yourself better if you weren't a gymnast?"

Grace turned to her friend, startled.

"If I wasn't a gymnast?" she said. It was like she was mimicking another language.

Leigh's voice sped up, defensive. "I'm not saying I'd be happier or anything," she said. "I'm saying, you know, I'm . . . I kind of think I'm a bitch in the gym."

Now Grace laughed. "You? A bitch?" she said. "I don't think so."

They were quiet again. Leigh sighed. Grace crunched.

How could Leigh be a bitch when it was Grace who almost outed her on national TV, who started the whole Wedgie Queen thing, who was hating all the girls whom Leigh had invited into their room a few minutes ago? Would Grace's brain be this messed up without the gym?

Grace said new words quietly, staring at the ice cup. "I think I might be happier."

Now Leigh was the startled one. She sat up and stared at her friend. "If you weren't a gymnast?"

Grace didn't respond.

"Then why are you one?" Leigh asked.

Grace sucked a piece of ice, thinking, until she said, "Because I might be happier, but I wouldn't be me."

Leigh nodded against her pillow.

Not being a gymnast would change Grace, but being a gymnast didn't. It made no sense. And something about it was terrifying.

Leigh got up to wash her face. They pretended the conversation had not happened.

But later, after they had climbed into their side-by-side beds, after Leigh had called her parents to say good night and Grace had called Max, after their assistant coaches had stopped by the room to ensure the girls were there and in bed, after they had said good night to each other and Grace had snuggled under the duvet and dug the side of her head as far into the pillow as it would go, Leigh spoke again.

"Grace?" she said quietly, like she didn't want to wake her up if Grace was already sleeping. Grace thought about not answering, but she wanted to be friends with Leigh again. This evening had been too lonely.

"Hm?"

"Grace . . ." Leigh said, trailing off until Grace propped up her head and looked at her. "What about when we aren't gymnasts?"

Grace's blood sounded like the ocean in her ears as she pictured her last dismount. Not her last dismount from tonight, her last dismount ever. It was the worst thing she could possibly think about right before the biggest step of her life: the fact that this big step would also be a giant leap toward the end of this life. "I don't ever think about that," Grace said. "It's scary, isn't it? This is probably going to be our only Olympics."

"Yeah," Leigh said, turning back to face Grace. "What will we do after we retire?"

"I don't know. I hate it that it has to happen." Grace sighed. "When I do think about it, I decide maybe I'll coach for my dad or take the test to be a judge or something. After college, I guess."

Leigh nodded. Grace felt like the conversation was missing the point somehow, like Leigh wanted something else out of it, something deeper. After what she had done tonight, Grace owed it to Leigh to keep it going.

"What about you? What will you do?" Grace asked.

Leigh rolled onto her back and stared at the ceiling. "I don't know," she said. "Something completely different. Something cheerful like teaching elementary school or being a personal stylist."

Grace chuckled.

"I don't want it to feel like my whole personality is changing just because gymnastics is over, you know?"

"No," Grace said, suddenly serious. "Of course it will. Everything will change. Everything about you.

And me. It has to."

Leigh didn't answer. After a few minutes, Grace heard Leigh's heavy sleep-breathing. She fell asleep without answering.

Maybe she hadn't cared.

Maybe she would never be able to care about Grace, to trust Grace, as much as she used to. Maybe Grace had messed up that much.

Grace folded herself into her sheets, imagining her long, lean lines for tomorrow, her perfect, small body flipping around the bars and beam and vault and floor.

Maybe Grace didn't deserve Leigh's secret in the first place. After all, she'd never even thought about telling Leigh hers.

Day 2

Daytime Limbo

WILHELMINA

When the alarm between their beds beeped, Wilhelmina stretched her arms over her head and sat up without yawning. Despite being attacked publicly last night, she'd slept soundly. She woke feeling rested and peaceful.

It had been the confirmation. It was everything she needed to know.

First, Katja hated her. But she hated Katja back, too, now.

Second, fourth place wasn't good enough. She had to come in third. Or maybe even second. She had to come in third or second, and she couldn't think about trying to come in third or second because she couldn't control what happened to anyone else. That was the hardest part.

That's what she'd told Monica when she had followed Wilhelmina back to her room to offer comfort.

"I'm not sure what to say," Monica had said. "That was really gross. What she did."

Wilhelmina had almost teared up. It took serious

guts for any gymnast to speak ill of Katja. It took knowing beyond a doubt that you were right.

And yet, it was so touching to have someone on her side. To have someone *get* it. How she'd been screwed over. How she'd never been given the chance the rest of them had.

"I'm okay tonight," Wilhelmina had said. And Monica had started to walk away, but Wilhelmina had called after her. "But . . . if I don't make it . . . come find me tomorrow. After. Okay?"

Now, Wilhelmina watched Camille as she groaned and pulled her pillow over the massive brown bun in the back of her head. Camille curled farther into her bed.

What's her problem? Wilhelmina thought.

Camille groaned again and flipped over in the bed.

Wilhelmina said it out loud. "What's your problem?"

Camille mumbled a "good morning" back, then buried her face back in the pillow.

"Cut the crap, okay?" Wilhelmina said. "You're here at the Olympic trials again. You get a second chance to be a star when most people only get one. Whatever's going on with you, just hide it from me, okay?"

Camille emerged from the pillow and said that weird thing again. "You really want to go."

This time it was a statement, not a question, so Wilhelmina just stared at her.

"I want you to go, too, okay?" Camille said. "Look, you don't have to win. I think if you beat two of them, Katja will have to choose you. She's definitely going to take Leigh, Grace, and Georgette. It'll look really weird to everyone if you come in second and she doesn't take you. She'd have to take three gymnasts you beat, then. Do you think you can come in second?"

Wilhelmina's head was tilted so far, she might have strained her neck. What was Camille talking about? Why was she acting like she was on Wilhelmina's side? Didn't she realize that Wilhelmina could see right through this?

"It's going to be hard to beat two of them now that Leigh is the best vaulter," she bit back.

Camille collapsed back on the bed. "Pick one," she whispered. "You can't be mad at me for both."

"Huh?" Wilhelmina said.

"Pick one," Camille said. "You can't be mad at me because it seemed like I was going to be the best vaulter, and then be mad at me because I'm not. Do you realize that Leigh vaulting like that means maybe I won't get chosen?"

"Uh—" Wilhelmina said. She hadn't thought of that. Her face was starting to burn. But Camille cut her right off again.

"And if I don't get chosen, Leigh becomes the best vaulter. That means there's another spot open. And maybe the team would be all all-arounders. And that would help you."

"Why are you talking about me?" Wilhelmina asked. "You're at the Olympic trials, too."

Camille sighed. "You can't be mad at me for both,"

she said again. But she didn't say it angrily. She said it quietly. It was a surrender.

Wilhelmina wasn't supposed to be thinking about these things today. She wanted to try it a new way, to pick a goal that only involved her own gymnastics.

"I'm not mad at you at all," Wilhelmina lied. Then she stormed into the bathroom.

She brushed her teeth with ferocity. She couldn't believe she'd gotten herself back into that kind of conversation with Camille. That was it. She was done. She wouldn't be angry at her or Leigh or Grace or anyone else. Wilhelmina wouldn't let anyone into her head today. She needed control. She needed a new goal.

If you're really here today, she texted Davion, watch out for this. This is what I'm going to try to do. *Don't fall* would be too easy for her. But Monica had the right idea. Maybe if Wilhelmina focused on something specific, something totally within her control, she'd be able to approach the meet like Kerry wanted her to. 9.5 or better execution score, she texted. Four times in a row. If that happens, I promise I'll be happy.

Don't think about the team, she told herself. *Just think about nine-point-five.*

You can do that, he texted back. And you don't have to promise me anything.

Wilhelmina laughed through the toothpaste in her mouth when she saw that text. She had taught him well. She'd told him time and again that she couldn't promise him anything. Not yet. Not until after the Olympics.

The promise is to myself, she wrote back. And it was. Those 9.5s could, mathematically, put her in at least third place, with a fighting chance at second. She was pretty sure Camille was right. Second place would mean the Olympics. Third was a toss-up.

But she couldn't control third, second, fourth. She had to stop thinking about the math.

His reply came quickly: Can't wait to see you soar. Live. Because I'm here.

Still don't believe it. ;-), she replied.

A short time later, the girls gathered for a quick breakfast in the same ballroom where they'd been fed last night. Wilhelmina noted that, like yesterday, the food was correct but the amount was ridiculous. They would eat before heading directly to the gym for some light conditioning and training. They would need a few nutrients to coat their muscles, but no one would want to fill up her stomach completely before running it around in circles and flipping it upside down. After their workout, they'd get to eat a more substantial meal, take some time to nap or rest or ice or get athletic massages, then they'd prepare for the early-evening conclusion to the meet. The hotel had set out enough food to feed a dozen football players, which equaled about one hundred gymnasts.

Wilhelmina watched the younger girls stare at the food from afar like they were afraid it would attack them. She tried not to see the way Grace was pacing back and forth in front of the table without touching any-thing. She tried not to think about Grace's full tray after dinner, her bony legs last night. There was nothing Wilhelmina could do to help her. Even if there was some-thing wrong, no one would believe Wilhelmina was anything but jealous of the winner.

Grace was probably fine.

Wilhelmina grabbed a granola bar and an apple. Shedding that fear of food was one advantage of being a veteran for Wilhelmina.

When Kerry sat down next to Wilhelmina and said, "So, what's the plan today?" Wilhelmina smiled at her. She knew it would sting if she managed her four 9.5s and still, at the end of the meet, had to watch Leigh and Grace and Georgette and Camille and whoever else cele-brate their positions on the team knowing that she could have helped them win the team gold if she were given a chance. Even with four 9.5s she'd be hard-pressed to come in second and might not make third. She was al-ready in the hole. And Grace and Leigh and Georgette all had higher all-around DODs if you added up their poten-tial on each apparatus. So there was nothing she could do but her best.

"I think I finally get it," Wilhelmina said. "That thing about only worrying about what I can control. About doing what I can and hoping the committee does the rest."

Kerry nodded and took a bite of her peach. "And?" she said.

"I have a goal—"

But another body cast a shadow across their table before she could say any more. Wilhelmina looked up to see Katja Minkovski's wrinkled face looming over them. She looked hard, like she was carved out of stone. She carried a plate brimming over with all the breakfast foods gymnasts could never eat: french toast and syrup, bacon, and doughnuts.

"I thought you would only be competing vault, Miss Parker," she said in her thick Russian accent. In more relaxed moments, Wilhelmina had heard her accent sound like a simple personality flare, like something charming to remember her by. But right now she seemed to be using it to wield intimidation.

Thank goodness, Kerry spoke up in response.

"We entered the meet in the all-around," she said calmly.

"Yes," Katja said. "But based on what I'd seen at camp, I expected you to only look to compete on vault. Now, you are hoping to compete the all-around? In the Olympics, no? Wilhelmina?"

Katja stared at her. Kerry turned to look at her, too. Wilhelmina felt herself shrinking. She managed a tiny nod.

"You are a talented gymnast," Katja said. "But that is a huge request to come through the gymnastics world at the last minute."

"Gymnastics world" equaled Katja Minkovski and Katja Minkovski alone, and all three of them knew it.

"You know we do not like to have things shaken up so close to the Olympics," Katja said. "I'm sure your hopes are not too high. I know you're not going to make this difficult for me. I assure you that will backfire."

Kerry was shaking her head. "We only do our best, huh," she said.

"Your best may have been enough to put you on the team, Miss Parker, if I had known about it before now. At this point, I don't know you. I can't possibly trust your gymnastics after seeing it for only two days. There's no more time for you to convince me you belong on the team. Enjoy today, Miss Parker. But don't expect it to get you anywhere." She paused and studied Wilhelmina's face. Wilhelmina was barely managing not to cry. "And again, don't make this difficult. I only want to do what's best for our country."

There was the answer. Wilhelmina felt her body get smaller and her eyes get larger. A hot fire burned in her gut and she swallowed to keep the anger there. Gymnasts are not supposed to be angry.

But she was sick of it. Apparently, this was her last day as a gymnast. She was going to be herself.

"I understood your concerns after the interview last night," Wilhelmina said.

"What?" Kerry asked.

Katja gasped. "I . . . I . . ." she faltered.

Wilhelmina didn't know what to do. She'd never seen Katja at a loss for words before.

"What interview?" Kerry said.

"I gave an interview with espnW last night." Then Katja turned to Wilhelmina. "Did you see it?"

"Yes," Wilhelmina said quietly.

Katja's face didn't look so hard anymore. Her accent softened.

"Did all of you see it?"

Wilhelmina nodded, confused.

"Oh," Katja said. "Well. I suppose you and I are clear now."

Then she walked away.

Wilhelmina filled Kerry in on everything that had happened the previous night.

Kerry patted Wilhelmina's back and leaned toward her ear so she could speak in the lowest possible voice. "I'm so sorry, Mina-Mina. I was not expecting this. I know you can help the USA win the Olympics. . . . You are one of the most skilled gymnast in the country, the world, but . . . if that's not enough . . . what could I do for you?" Wilhelmina nodded, but Kerry kept talking. Almost like she was convincing herself. "If you had been to all of those camps, if you had been competing the all-around for all of these years . . . you'd be so tired. You would have—"

"I would have broken," Wilhelmina interrupted, letting her coach off the hook.

"You are such a fantastic gymnast. I am so sorry," Kerry said.

Wilhelmina nodded. If Kerry thought it was over, it was over. DODs and math and strategy. They were all over. If Katja hated her this much, Wilhelmina didn't have a chance.

She took a deep breath and tried to calm her heart. She forced her words past the black disappointment that was infiltrating the front of her brain. "I want an execution score of nine-point-five on each event. That's all I'm looking for. If I do that, I'll be happy," she whispered to her coach.

I'm not going to the Olympics. She tried to not let it take over her body. She had the rest of her life to be disappointed but, before that, she had four more routines to execute. Her last four.

Kerry nodded. "Good girl," she said. "That's a huge goal, challenging goal. But one you can accomplish, huh?"

Wilhelmina loved to see Kerry smile like that, like Wilhelmina was something special to be around.

So, it would be enough. It had to be.

Life had never been fair. She was used to it by now. She could make herself used to it again.

And, tonight, as soon as the cameras and newscasters disappeared, as soon as the gymnasts were officially divided into the team and the losers, she could kiss Davion. She would. She'd wrap her arms around him and press her lips to his. He'd be so surprised, but then, after a millisecond, they'd be making out and Wilhelmina would enjoy it more than all the other times that she had seen his adorable smile and been tempted to pull his face close to hers. Because she'd waited until it was over, until she had gone out with a bang, until she was ready to break up with gymnastics and find a new love.

Hopefully, one that wouldn't hurt her as badly.

LEIGH

Leigh did her back handspring back tuck. For what felt like the thousandth time today, she landed crooked: one foot half off the beam to the right, the other to the left, her torso out of sync with her hips and legs. She swung her arms behind her head to attempt to keep her balance, then gave up and hopped off the beam. Over and over again this morning, she'd failed to complete that series. The hollow banging of the beam between each hit kept knocking her in the brain.

"Leigh," Phil said too loudly. "It's not difficult. Stay on the beam."

Leigh turned to stare at him. It *was* difficult. Everyone who had talked about or participated in or even watched one gymnastics meet one time knew that staying on the balance beam was the hardest thing these girls had to do.

Phil was getting frustrated with her. That didn't happen often.

"Get back on there, Leigh!" he said.

She was tempted to start thinking cruel things

about him, to start calling him names in her head. She was tempted to say something back that would hurt his feelings. But Leigh was going to try something new today: she was going to be nice. She was sick of being parceled up into Gymnast Leigh and Regular Girl Leigh.

Last night Grace had said, "Everything will change." She had said that nothing would be the same once the gymnastics life was over. But Leigh didn't think she could handle changing completely just because this part of her life was over.

She wanted the Olympics. She was willing to give up so much to get there—dates and friends and vacations and the chance to try other sports. And anonymity. She had even begged to give up high school. Leigh was willing to give up so much of her present and past. But she didn't think she could give up her future, too. So when Leigh had closed her eyes last night, she had made a promise to the Gods of Gymnastics or the Universe or whoever was in charge out there. *Tomorrow, I will be me, and I will still win. I will win while being nice.*

"Do it right," Phil grunted. "If you want a chance to compete in the all-around in Rome, you have to nail the beam tonight. Nail it. Now."

Leigh made her face be still. She put her hands on the beam to hoist her linebacker body the four feet back up.

"Leigh," Phil said again.

She hopped off the beam as quickly as she'd pulled herself onto it.

Caela Carter

Phil came over to the side of it and stood right in front of her. He said, "I'm sorry for yelling. That doesn't help. It can be hard to remember, but I know that."

Leigh nodded. She worried her bottom lip between her teeth.

Her coach was nice. She was lucky to have found a coach who was successful and still nice. Why did she have such a hard time balancing those things?

"But you have to tell me," he said. "What's going on?"

Leigh wanted to answer but she didn't know. It had been easy enough to be nice at breakfast. She'd taken a seat with Kristin and Annie and talked to them about *Pretty Witches*, that guilty-pleasure show all the gymnasts watched. And she'd even managed the next part. When they were heading out of the ballroom, Leigh had caught sight of the GymCade crew and pulled on Monica's sleeve to ask her to stay back a minute. Then she'd apologized. Monica had nodded, her dull brown ponytail swinging behind her head. And, for the first time, Leigh had wondered if she was maybe more like Monica than she was like Grace. Monica's hair was neat but not in some superslick fancy style like Grace's. Monica had a crumb from her granola bar stuck on her knee and the left strap of her practice leo was twisted. Maybe it would be good for Leigh to have another gym friend, one who wasn't so perfect all the time.

Conditioning had gone fine this morning, too. While they ran and did leg lifts and handstand drills and all the rest, Leigh had managed to smile at each gymnast. (Well, except for Camille. And that wasn't cruelty. That was shyness.)

But then there was the beam. The sound of it. It had gotten into her head. She didn't know how to force herself to focus, to force her brain to ignore her size and the constant banging, without forcing all of that niceness down.

"What's going on?" Phil demanded again.

"I don't know," Leigh said finally.

Phil sighed. "Is it the same thing?" he'd asked. "The noise?"

Leigh had to remind herself that his frustration might not be with her, it might be with that *Sports Illustrated* reporter who had called her the linebacker and whom he'd called an asshole. He'd called him an asshole just for hurting Leigh.

"Only partly," she said.

"What else." He said it like a statement, not a question. He said it like Leigh had better hurry up and tell him so she could get her butt back on the beam, because she had the four most important routines of her life coming up in a few hours.

Leigh pretended the black strap of her practice leo needed straightening so she wouldn't have to look at Phil when she said it. It would sound so stupid coming out of her mouth.

"I want to be a nice gymnast," she said.

"What?" he almost shouted.

"I want to go to the Olympics being me." She didn't think it was as stupid as it sounded. And part of being herself probably meant being herself with Phil.

Phil raised his eyebrows and lowered his voice. He looked scared. "You know, kid, I always said I'd respect your decision on when to tell the world. And I will. But . . . you know . . . distraction is . . ."

He stopped. Leigh was shaking her head frantically. There were too many people around and she was terrified that if he kept talking he'd out her accidentally. Even though it seemed like it shouldn't matter. Her gymnastics had nothing to do with her sexuality. It was the secret of it that got twisted up into her brain.

"I'm not talking about that," Leigh said. "I mean there are going to be young kids who look up to me, if I go to the Olympics, you know? And I don't want to be the gymnast who only cares about herself for hours. I want to be a nice gymnast. A role model."

Phil sighed and it seemed like he was almost going to laugh. "Girls," he said. Like that answered everything. Like being nice and being a role model had more to do with your gender than your personality. "Okay," he said. "I don't know what to do about that. I think you're plenty nice. But I have an idea about the other thing."

He looked around the gym, swinging his head back and forth. "Grace!" he shouted. He said it so loudly, Leigh jumped before finding her friend with her eyes. Grace was standing beside the bars, watching Monica. Grace and Ted turned to Phil, and Monica stumbled on her dismount.

"Christ, Phil," Ted said. "What do you need Grace for?"

"Just a favor," Phil called back. "Help out a friend."

Ted shook his head. "She's training," he said.

Leigh knew that's what Ted would say. *There are no friends on the gym floor.*

Grace stared at her toes. Leigh and Phil looked at Ted, and Ted looked at Phil, and Monica looked at Leigh, and Grace looked at her toes.

"I'll help." The voice was behind Leigh, close. It was smooth and it danced across her skin. "What can I do?"

Leigh turned and there she was. Camille.

"Uh . . . Can you do a back handspring back tuck on beam?" Phil asked.

Camille nodded. "Think so," she said. "It's been a while, but it'd be fun to try."

"Are you sure?" Phil asked.

Leigh almost said the same thing. Was Camille crazy? She was going to climb up on beam in the middle of the Olympic trials and try a back handspring back tuck when she hadn't competed beam in years. Did she *want* to get hurt or something?

"Sure, I'm sure," Camille said.

She performed the series easily on the line taped to the floor.

Camille wanted to help her? Camille wanted to help Leigh so much that she would risk her own Olympic trials? Leigh's heart was pounding so hard in her chest, she was sure Camille would be able to see it moving through her leo. She was trying to keep her crazy-person smile under control, but she was sure she was failing.

"You don't have to do that, you know," Leigh said. "I mean, I don't want you to get hurt or anything. Not that you would, I mean. Because you could do it right on the floor, so why wouldn't you be able to do it on the beam, right?" Leigh felt her cheeks getting hotter and hotter as the words refused to stop walking out of her mouth. "But you know, I mean, I don't want you to, like, get hurt. Just in case you get hurt. Or, like, in trouble—"

"Will your coach mind?" Phil said.

Leigh had never been so grateful to be interrupted.

Of course he will, but let her do it, anyway, Phil. Let her help me.

Camille shrugged. "Don't think so. We're still waiting for Wilhelmina to finish up on vault. I said she could have a few more minutes."

Leigh was so excited, her skin was practically vibrating.

Phil nodded. "Okay, then. Hop up there."

Leigh watched the contours of Camille's legs stretch and retract as she hoisted onto the beam. She was mesmerized. She wanted to watch Camille's muscles and curves turn upside down and right-side up again.

But Phil made Leigh sit beneath the beam with her eyes closed. "Listen," he said.

And she heard it: *bang-ba-bang-bang.*

It sounded just like her. Of course it did. Camille was a big gymnast. She was built like Leigh.

But Camille was also gorgeous.

And talented. Crazy talented.

And popular with the fans.

And beautiful . . .

Leigh opened her eyes. Camille was standing on the beam, staring down at Leigh. Leigh's heart was in her throat.

Leigh hated this crush. It was unfair—Dylan might have distracted Grace yesterday, but Leigh was the only one with hormones that would let her actual competitors distract her.

Leigh also loved the crush.

She'd have to find success on the beam now that Camille helped her.

Camille hopped down and started jogging toward the vault. Leigh managed to call out a thank-you after her.

Phil squatted in front of her. "Leigh," he said. "Everyone makes noises on the beam. Everyone."

Leigh nodded. *At least all the big girls do. All the girls like me do.*

"You know what *does* happen because you're bigger?"

Leigh shook her head.

Phil nodded across the gym to where Camille was now sprinting down the vaulting runway. "Watch her. Watch Camille. Study her Amanar."

Leigh's breath caught as Camille's body spun and

twisted high in the air. Her Amanar was stunning. She was beautiful.

"You know what happens because you're bigger?" Phil said again.

Leigh didn't say anything. She watched Camille bounce back down the runway with an ache in her chest.

"You fly higher."

Leigh gave him a smile. He was trying. She looked from his face to the beam and told her heart to save its crush for later.

"I hate those noises," she said.

Phil sighed. "Look, I get the role model thing. I don't want you to think about that right now, but I can't tell you what to think. And I do understand. So, you can be nice to all of your competitors and to the other coaches and the judges and the selection committee and all the little girls in the stands. But . . . can't you be mean to the beam?"

Leigh laughed.

The beam would not defeat her again. The beam would not win. She would pound it with her hands and feet. She would make it scream. She'd focus so hard, she could burn the four-inch surface with her retinas.

Leigh hopped back onto the apparatus and smiled at her coach. Phil had given her the key. The way to win while being nice.

Back handspring back tuck. *BANG*. Perfect.

CAMILLE

Camille was seriously considering not going over the vault that night.

That was the answer. She'd let Leigh be the best vaulter. She'd take the question of whether she'd make the team out of her brain.

She'd keep her NCAA eligibility. But would any school actually take her on their team if she quit in the middle of the Olympic trials?

Somehow this debate was working for her. She was nailing Amanar after Amanar without a step. Gymnastics is all about muscle memory and her muscles were doing their job without the help of her brain.

Skip it. Step onto the podium, signal the judges, and step off. Don't go over the vault.

Bobby would be watching from home. And if he saw her quit mid-meet, he'd think it was the most romantic thing ever. He'd greet her tomorrow with flowers and plans for them both to attend NYU in the fall.

NYU. With no gymnastics team.

Camille's hips knew how to twist her body the full two-and-a-half rotations in the air. Her wrists knew exactly when to flex against the horse to propel her off it. And her feet were perfect at squeezing the mat when they landed in order to keep her upright and in one place.

Her brain had no idea what it was doing.

If I disqualify myself, Wilhelmina will be happy, too. But . . . Mom.

Camille had to keep her mother happy. And healthy. It was Camille's responsibility. All she had to do was vault. A simple vault that would propel Camille into gymnastics fame and glory.

Then the endorsements would roll in, even more than they were now. She'd give up her eligibility. She'd honor her promise to her mother.

Her own desire to join an NCAA team was impossible no matter whom she chose.

"Yes! Yes!" her coach kept yelling as she landed. Camille would smile, slap him five, and jog back to the end of the runway thinking, *I have to go over that vault tonight. I owe it to my coach. To my mom. To myself, my old self.*

But by the time she was sprinting down the runway, she was thinking, *If I do this tonight, I'm going to the Olympics. I'm staying on the huge stage. I'm training full-time for another few months: the preparation in Italy, the games, and then the Tour of Champions. I'm staying exhausted and risking more pain. I'm giving up more than Bobby.*

Bobby still hadn't called or texted or anything. Camille had tried to reach him several times last night and this morning. He'd gone silent on her for the second day in a row. Camille was starting to get angry. First he had promised he'd be there. Then he didn't show up. Then he dumped her and disappeared at the most important moment of her life—or her post-accident life anyway. What had happened to the supportive boyfriend she met in high school? When did he change?

- - -

"I made elite again," Camille had told Bobby last summer. "I'm going to make the national team. Andrew says I might be his first Olympian." They were sitting in his car in the gym parking lot. She was sweaty and her hair was extra frizzy and it was pointless that Bobby had shown up to take her home because her mother had been in the observation room through her entire practice. But he was here anyway. Because he loved her, Camille guessed.

Bobby didn't say anything. His jaw tightened underneath his rust-colored stubble.

"He said we'd try only on vault. I think I convinced him to let me train floor, too, just for fun. But still, that's only two events," Camille was saying. "So you don't need to worry, I'll only practice a few extra hours a week. He says with an Amanar like mine I have a chance at it." Camille tried to sound as enthusiastic as possible, tried to get Bobby to smile. She felt tired. "What would you think of that: an Olympic girlfriend!"

"I thought you were excited to go to NYU with me this fall. I thought I was enough," Bobby had almost whispered. "I put off college for a year just to be with you in that stupid gym."

I didn't ask you to do that.

Camille said nothing about the picture that flashed in her brain anytime someone mentioned the word *college*: her, in the crowd of fifteen or so gymnasts in matching leos, her competing in the NCAA. Where the gymnasts seemed to truly love each other. Where they danced in unison on the sidelines as their teammates rocked creative floor routines. Where they trained a maximum of twenty-five hours a week.

Camille as a part of a team. It was a piece of her childhood she'd missed. Teamwork.

She swallowed her dreams in that car with Bobby.

If she could hold him off a little longer, she could make them both happy. First her mom training for the Olympics. Then Bobby with retirement.

Ultimately, it was only herself she'd have to disappoint.

She hadn't expected to have a chance to get to the Olympics with Andrew. Camille didn't know that within a year she'd be considered one of the best vaulters in the world, that she'd make the US national team quickly, that she'd do better in this new gymnastics body than she had in her first one.

Camille hadn't expected any of it.

For the past year Camille's heart had been a piece of putty being pulled and yanked by her mother and by Bobby. It was so out of shape, she couldn't recognize it anymore.

- - -

Camille landed yet another Amanar.

"That's enough for today," Andrew said with a chuckle. "I think you've got it."

Camille stopped her jog back to the end of the runway and turned to face her laughing coach.

"We don't want to wear you out, right?" he said.

She nodded. "Right," she said.

But inside there was a strange queasy feeling. Disappointment.

Camille realized that she'd been having fun with this parade of perfect Amanars.

Had she just turned her last Amanar ever?

It was both freeing and heartbreaking.

GRACE

Grace finished practicing her floor routine. She posed in the far corner with her arms thrown over her head as she always did.

Then she hopped off the podium and reached for the water bottle in her father's hand. Her stomach was rumbling despite the five apple slices and tablespoon of peanut butter her father had forced her to eat at breakfast.

"Nice job, Grace!" Monica piped up. She'd gotten taller or something ever since that stupid interview last night. Like it counted for something. Like Katja wasn't just saying Monica's name to put down the other gymnasts.

Grace gave her a look. They were the only two present who had to share a coach and Grace was sick of it. She wasn't used to her father splitting his time. She had been looking forward to the break from his constant scrutiny during this meet, but she thought they would split her father's attention 80/20 or 70/30. Now, it was feeling like Monica was getting close to 50 percent of his time, and it wasn't fair. Because, first, Grace was more than his gymnast. She was his daughter. And second, Grace was better.

The worst thing about the morning was the compliments. First, there were all the compliments that her father kept giving Monica. After almost every routine he would say, "Good job, kiddo." And that was it. Even when Monica's toes weren't pointed. Even when there was a separation between her legs. Even when her beam routine was full of so many balance checks, she looked more like a Mexican jumping bean than a gymnast. He'd still say, "Good job, kiddo." And when she fell, on beam once and bars twice, he said, "It's okay. Get up there again, kiddo."

Then there were the constant compliments that Monica was giving Grace. She was making herself look better, superior. What made her think she could decide what a "nice job" was? Who was Monica to judge Grace?

"That was pretty good, Gracie," her father said. "You need to watch that bobble on your landing. And keep your knees straight when you pike."

Grace nodded. *Seen and not heard.*

She was sick of him acting like Monica was the talented one. There was only one way in which Monica was better than Grace: she was smaller.

And by the end of the morning practice, it felt like that was all that mattered.

Grace toweled off her face and took a few gulps of water before pulling on her sneakers and heading into the locker room. She put her hand on her stomach and told it to shut up.

She'd had a good workout. Her dad had said almost one-third positive things. That was well above average. And Grace had to admit that she might be steady because of the protein in that tablespoon of peanut butter.

Grace needed to be consistent tonight. Katja had pretty much said that to the world.

So, Grace left the gym determined to eat a regular lunch. She'd eaten a regular breakfast and gotten through the entire workout without one moment of a wobbly heart. She would force herself to have a few bites of meat, a full serving of vegetables, a little skim milk. Then, she'd shower and chill out in her bed in the air-conditioning, her wet hair feeling refreshing against the back of her neck.

Grace was not going to let her heart or her stomach interrupt her tonight. She'd seen Leigh fall over and over again on beam in practice. If she went into tonight as steady as she had this morning, she might be able to beat her, TTY and all.

There would be no stupid message distracting her. Even if Dylan started messaging her again before or during the meet tonight, Grace would not look. There would be no focusing on being Leigh's friend or on food or on anything. She'd think about gymnastics.

But lunch was not a buffet. Instead, the gymnasts were seated and the staff of the hotel brought them turkey sandwiches on whole wheat bread, oranges, full glasses of skim milk.

Grace sat across from her father and stared at the food on her plate. She wished for the thousandth time that she was allowed to eat with the other gymnasts so she could see what they were doing. There was no way they were all going to eat two full slices of bread. It was loaded with pointless carbs. And there was no way they were going to eat an entire orange, with all the fructose.

Beside her, Grace heard crunching. Monica had taken a bite of the sandwich like it was no big deal.

But what were the older, mature, wise gymnasts doing? What were Wilhelmina and Leigh and Maria and Samantha doing with this meal? She wanted to eat like a normal gymnast, not like a normal person. She didn't want to eat so much that it coated her stomach, hung in there like a weight, and made her hit her hips against the bars.

"Don't get distracted, Gracie," her dad said when she turned to look at the other gymnasts behind her. "Eat."

Monica crunched beside her. Grace wanted to elbow her in the ribs.

Grace peeled the top layer of bread off. She figured if she ate the lettuce and turkey out of the sandwich, that would be good. She wished there were more vegetables. She had been ready to eat a full serving of celery or broccoli or cucumber or carrots, not a full serving of meat or bread.

"Just eat, Grace," her father said again. "This is a good lunch. Eat it."

He glanced at her plate. He almost looked suspicious. And she couldn't let him know. He could never find out. If he found out that she was only on the top because she was barely eating . . . If he knew she was a total fraud . . .

Grace took a small bite of the sandwich. At first her taste buds rejoiced at the flavor of the grain and the freshness of the turkey. The lettuce crunched between her teeth. A bit of mustard slipped onto the tongue, a spicy surprise. But her throat closed against it when she tried to swallow.

She had to talk to it. She put her hand on her larynx and said, *Swallow it. It seems bad for you, but it will be good for you.*

But she didn't believe her own words. If she ate this entire meal, she'd consume more calories than she'd had in a single meal in weeks.

Grace played with her phone. She untied and retied her shoe.

The food from her first bite was still stuck between

her molars when Monica finished off half her sandwich.

"Grace," her dad said. "Eat." His eyes were wide. It was a command.

So, Grace took small bites and was sure to chew them until they were nothing but a flavorless paste in her mouth before swallowing. She took several sips of water and a small sip of milk between each bite.

A plan hatched in her brain but she didn't let it distract her from eating as slowly as possible.

Grace knew her father's patience was limited. She could stretch this out. She would outlast him.

Monica finished most of her sandwich and a few bites of her orange and all her milk before Grace had eaten five bites of her sandwich. Grace would not eat the orange.

Monica left. Most of the other gymnasts and coaches left.

Her father finished eating and started fooling around on his phone while Grace took another slow bite.

Finally, when Grace was about a third of the way through the first half of the turkey monster, her father gave up on her.

"Finish eating and get some rest. Make sure your head is in the game, okay?" he said.

She nodded. She took another small bite for good measure.

Then, her dad did something remarkable. Shocking. He stood up, walked to Grace's side, and leaned over and kissed the top of her head.

"You're so close to winning this thing. If we do it like yesterday, like this morning, you're winning. I can feel it. I can taste it. I'm so glad you're my kid."

Grace nodded, this time telling her tear ducts to suck the tears back in.

That kiss woke up the part of her brain that she had almost succeeded in shutting down completely: Grace as a non-gymnast daughter. Where was her mother? *Why isn't she here? Why do we have to stick Max with a babysitter? What's wrong with me that I could lose my own mother?*

Her dad was gone. Grace turned off those thoughts like it was as simple as spinning a faucet.

Grace looked down at her plate. She'd eaten close to half of the first half of the sandwich. She'd drunk a quarter of the milk. It was more than she'd consumed in a long time.

She had to do it like yesterday. Like this morning. Like her dad said. He thought she needed to eat, but he had no idea how little had been in her system yesterday. She had to stop eating.

Grace looked around. She was the last person in the ballroom except for a few of the staff who were cleaning. Slowly, she stood. She walked her almost-full tray to the garbage can and, with only a millisecond of hesitation, she dumped it. She spat the bite in her mouth out and into the black hole for good measure.

She would win. She had to.

It was only when she looked up that she saw the two eyes watching her through the doorway.

Wilhelmina.

MONICA

Monica was terrified. But she didn't look it.

She looked ready. She had never looked more ready.

There was someone watching her. Katja had followed her career.

She had to treat herself like she mattered. She had to believe she mattered.

Katja had used Monica's career to insult Wilhelmina. Monica couldn't let that be what her gymnastics was all about.

Monica snapped the sleeve of her bright blue leotard in place on her wrist and studied herself in the bathroom mirror. Thanks to one of the USAG volunteers, her dark hair was done in twin French braids that twisted in the back of her head and formed a bun at the bottom of her skull. Her blue eye shadow matched the blue of her leotard and made her usually dull skin look creamy and mysterious. The star-patterned gemstones on her leo's sleeves glistened in the light of the bathroom. And her butt glue was carefully applied and would do a better job than yesterday. She hoped.

Monica smiled at her reflection and for once her

cheeks looked high instead of puffy, her big eyes looked beautiful instead of mouse-ish.

She looked like *her*. Like that gymnast she'd always dreamed of becoming.

Monica felt like she'd finally figured it out. She had observed carefully all morning while Ted critiqued her teammate but barely said a word to her. She had watched Kristin after returning to her room last night when she had scrubbed away her makeup and untwisted her hairdo and transformed back into just some girl.

Monica could make herself look like an Olympian. She could make herself feel like an Olympian. She could make herself perform like an Olympian. The one thing she couldn't make herself was an actual Olympian.

She couldn't dream the way Wilhelmina had said she should last night, but she'd let herself get part of the way there: *Today, I'll beat at least one person. Today I won't lose.*

Then, she'd get a new coach. One who believed in her. She'd keep fighting. She'd try for the Olympics the next time.

The thought was terrifying. The cameras in her face yesterday at the gym. Her name on Leigh's television speakers. Being relevant brought all sorts of attention and a lot of it didn't feel like attention she wanted.

But the Olympics one day? That was worth it. Monica was going to let herself try. Hope.

Besides, Monica thought as she smoothed another layer of red lipstick on her thin lips, *everyone might be this terrified. Everyone might just be better at pretending than I am.*

With one more twirl in the bathroom mirror, Monica told herself, *This is it.*

Then she marched to the elevator to meet Grace and Ted in the lobby.

There was a hand strangling her elbow as soon as she walked out the elevator doors.

"I have to talk to you," Grace hissed.

Monica shook her arm free. "What?" she snapped, pretend-confident.

Grace whipped her head around. The lobby was starting to fill with gymnasts and coaches. She seized Monica's elbow again and dragged her into the corner.

Stay confident, Monica told herself. But she was shaking a little already.

"I don't know what you think you're up to," Grace said. "But this crap has to stop, okay?"

Monica stared at her.

"You tried to get me yesterday, all right, but you failed. I am still ahead, still winning. And you're not going to get me today."

"I—I didn't." Monica didn't know what to say. She didn't try to beat Grace. She didn't try to beat anyone. She hadn't believed she could do it. But she couldn't admit that out loud.

"Just shut up with the goody-two-shoes compliments crap, okay? You're not going to be my new bestie. You're not going to be Leigh's new bestie. And you aren't going to the Olympics. Stay away from me today and I'll stay away from you."

There were tears now. Some had even made it as far as her eyelashes. Why was Grace being so mean? What was this all about?

Be *her* be *her* be *her*.

"Sounds good to me," Monica spat back. Then she stormed away.

An hour before the competition was scheduled to continue, the athletes and coaches gathered in the locker room at the Metroplex. They sat on benches or folding chairs or the floor with their backs leaning against the blue steel lockers. They extended their legs out before them or rolled their toes and ankles; they stretched their arms over their heads. Monica sat with her ice-taped ankles out in front of her and, like the others, didn't pay much attention to Katja Minkovski and the other three members of the Olympic selection committee who stood in front of them.

Most of the girls weren't making eye contact with Katja. Everyone in the room seemed a little uncomfortable. The more Monica had replayed the interview in her brain, the angrier she'd gotten. Even the small moments, like when Katja called gymnastics "our little sport," started to bug her. It was like she needed permission to be angry. Wilhelmina gave it to her, and then the anger kept coming.

Maybe the other girls were angry, too, deep down.

They all knew what Katja would say anyway. That,

after the final rotation, they should gather back in this room and wait until the selection committee was finished meeting. Then the committee would join the girls in the locker room and announce the five members of the next Women's Olympic Gymnastics team as well as the three alternates. Because of the tight schedule this year, all eight of those gymnasts and their coaches would be expected to board a plane tomorrow for three weeks of training in Italy before the start of the Olympics. It was crazy: Monica had no chance of going, but she'd still had to pack as if she were leaving for a month instead of a weekend.

Katja did say all that. She said the words that the girls knew they would hear while they ran through performances in their heads and worked kinks out of their legs.

"Keep in mind that you must be physically present in this locker room at the conclusion of the meet in order to be placed on the team. If you leave the Metroplex for any reason, you will be automatically disqualified," she said. Monica and the rest of the gymnasts began to gather their bags, shift, stand, figuring she was finished. But then Katja kept talking. "The USAG and the Olympic selection committee have agreed to do something a little unconventional today. We will be changing the squads and mixing up the gymnasts in order to look at different pairings. Do not try to analyze your new placement. Simply have your best meet while resting assured that the Olympic Committee will make the best decision for our country with the talent that we have in this building. Okay?"

She looked around the locker room like she wanted the girls to nod or say okay or something. They all stared. Monica had never heard of a shake-up in the middle of a meet. It was unfair to ask them not to analyze it.

It would be obvious, Monica knew that. She braced herself for what was coming. She would hear her name in the Nobodies column. She could not let this break her. She couldn't stop pretending; she couldn't be the cowering, terrified girl with a crushed face or slumping shoulders. She had to keep looking like this confident gymnast with braids and red lipstick and blue eye shadow. She grabbed the back of the bench she was sitting on, squeezing her shoulder blades and pushing her heart forward and begging herself to be strong. There would still be plenty of gymnasts to beat. She could still beat one person. She could do it. This didn't need to change her goals at all.

Monica was talking to herself so loudly in her brain that she almost missed the names being called.

"Starting on bars," Katja said, "Kristin, Annie, Natalie, Samantha, Camille, and Olivia. Starting on vault: Maria, Leigh, Monica, Grace, Wilhelmina, Georgette."

Monica's jaw dropped. She felt both Kristin and Ted turn to stare at her. Kristin's eyes were full of nails and Ted's were full of question marks, and she knew why.

She was in the better squad.

She'd tricked them. She'd dressed herself up and stood tall and now they believed she could be worth something. It worked.

The gymnasts and coaches shifted, gathering their bags, pulling on their warm-ups.

"Hold on!" Katja exclaimed.

They all froze. Silent. Like good little gymnasts.

"I'd like to have a word with the girls," she said. "Alone."

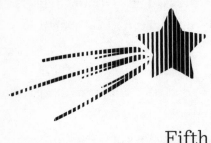

Fifth Rotation

CAMILLE

Camille sat in a straddle on the matted floor in the locker room as the committee spoke about the Olympic selection process. She wasn't listening.

She pulled her right arm across her body and held it with her left elbow, stretching her shoulder. *I am going to vault today,* she told herself. *I'm choosing Mom. Bobby left me.* She ignored the way the corners of her mouth tugged downward when she made this decision. One side of her brain argued so persistently, so constantly, that the other side, the one that wanted to curl up on her mother's couch with Bobby's body snuggled behind her, finally gave up. *Thank God vault is first.* She wasn't sure she could hang on to this determination for too much longer.

And then *boom.* Katja made her announcement. The squads would change. Camille would start on bars. Vault would be last. Camille would not even compete for the first half of the meet.

She was still slack-jawed with surprise as the

gymnasts began to stand. How would she make it through those first two rotations with nothing to do but panic?

The girls around her were acting like this was normal, pulling on gym bags and adjusting ponytails and leotards as if everything had not just changed.

"Hold on!" Katja's voice cut through the room and halted all the action around Camille.

When only the Olympic team coordinator was left in the locker room with the gymnasts, Camille watched as her face changed. It was like Katja took off one mask and put on another. She went from competitor to grandmother in seconds.

Camille sat on the floor and kicked her legs out in front of her. She bent toward her ankles. Truthfully, she wanted to get up and stalk out of the locker room right there. This woman was never a gymnast. She didn't know how it felt. How much fun it was. How painful it was. How it etched itself into your soul so you couldn't be sure quite who you'd be if you ever stopped flying.

She'd called their sport *little*, for God's sake. She'd called their *lives* little.

"It is time for me to apologize," Katja said. She smiled and a million tiny lines appeared on both of her cheeks. She looked soft and dainty. "I did not know that word had gotten out about my interview on espnW. You all know I want nothing but the best from USA Gymnastics. I was doing what I thought was right for the sport. For our country. For us," she said. Camille squinted. Calling them insignificant was best for them? What was this woman saying?

"But none of that was meant for your ears, okay?" she said.

And then Camille realized she had missed most of the interview. What had Katja said after she left the room?

"No matter what you thought you heard, it meant nothing." Katja's eyes bounced all around them while she said this. Camille tried to follow where they went. "Here in this small room, among us, are the five ladies who will win me Olympic gold." Katja somehow managed to smile wider, to multiply her wrinkles. "Why would I ever do anything to hurt them?"

Camille's heart was swinging like a punching bag in her chest. What did this woman mean? What had she said?

"And you should all know how I work by now," Katja continued. Now Camille could follow her eyes easily. Now Katja was staring directly at Wilhelmina. The grandmotherly smile was still there, but her eyes had turned hard as marbles. "If I had a message for you personally, I would get it to you personally." Her eyes swung and landed on Camille herself. "If you don't hear it from me *in person*, don't believe it."

They were frozen in silence for a few seconds until Katja finally said, "Now go! Do your best! Make our country proud!"

Camille sat still on the floor as the other gymnasts

around her rose and began to file out. She tried to make her face stay calm while her brain freaked out behind it. What was happening? What had Katja said? Why did this matter when there were events to compete out there?

Camille wished there was one aspect of this sport she loved that wasn't touched by Katja. And there was: the NCAA. But Camille would never get there.

Someone lowered herself onto the bench behind Camille, and she turned, expecting her coach. But it wasn't him.

Katja Minkovski. Leaning to Camille's ear. Giving her that so-called personal message.

"Do not worry," she whispered. "Do not worry about your rotation today."

Camille felt her eyes widen.

"It means nothing," Katja was saying. "I saw you—we saw you—this morning. You are the best vaulter in the world. I need you on my Olympic team. You are consistent. Despite Leigh's performance yesterday, you are our best weapon. You are our key to beating the Russians! All you need to do is stay in the gym. . . ." Katja's lips stretched back into that smile. It looked a little more fake this close up. "And you will finally be an Olympian."

Camille hadn't paid attention to the rest of the names. She hadn't realized that she'd been placed opposite Grace and Leigh and Georgette and the others who would likely be named her teammates later this evening.

Her heart turned heavy. Leigh's vault wouldn't help her after all. There was nothing she could do anymore.

Camille felt her face betray her. She smiled back. She nodded. She said, "Thank you." It was a lie. So was the smile. Why did she always have to be so obedient?

Camille joined the other gymnasts who gathered in the gray cave under the bleachers, waiting to be announced for a second time. Some of them hugged each other the way they did yesterday. Some of them stood still with their hands clasped, praying or meditating. Some of them stretched and jumped up and down. Some of them chatted in whispers.

Camille leaned against the wall. Her heart beat wildly. Her eyes spun in her head.

What could she do? Katja said she'd be an Olympian and so that was it. One vault would seal her fate.

Unless I don't go over it.

If only vault was first. If only she could march right out of the gate and immediately launch herself into this dream she didn't want anymore. If only she didn't have to get through two hours of self-torture before obediently committing herself to this dismal Olympic future.

Camille didn't want to be a weapon or a key. She wanted to be a person. A gymnast, yes. But a person even more.

When Camille watched those NCAA meets on TV, she rarely looked at the actual competitors. Instead, she watched the sidelines. She watched as a group of young women acted like a sponge, enveloping the competitor who had just dismounted from beam or floor. She watched the line of athletes on the sideline of the floor who waved their arms and shimmied their shoulders and kicked their legs, dancing in unison with the one member of their team who was competing. Camille wanted a team to dance with.

So maybe she didn't want to go over the vault.

But she had just decided she would!

It was so exhausting.

Camille sunk into a sitting position on the floor. How could they still be here? How could this meet have not even started yet?

Camille saw Wilhelmina chatting with Samantha on the side of the crowd and she turned her head away. The last thing she needed was to see the fire in Wilhelmina's eyes right now.

When two blue sneakers appeared next to her eyes, she was sure it was Wilhelmina coming over to yell at her some more.

She looked up hesitantly, but it wasn't her roommate.

It was Leigh. America's Golden Child. Grace's number two. Despite the fact that everyone was predicting that all three of them would be on the Olympic team, Camille had barely ever spoken to Grace or Leigh. They were only a few years younger than her, but in gym time, they were a different generation.

Right now, Leigh looked down on her with wide eyes and a concerned smile. "Are you—are you okay?" she mumbled.

Camille shook her head no. Though she would deny

it to her mother or Bobby, or even Wilhelmina, she didn't owe this gymnast, this one who had actually beaten her vault score, anything.

Leigh sat cross-legged next to Camille. "Is this okay?" she asked. "I just thought, you know, you helped me out earlier today, so maybe I could help you out, if you want, I mean."

Camille looked at her. She was wearing barely any makeup, and her dark blonde hair was in a simple ponytail and almost as frizzy as Camille's. She was pretty, but in some ways she was regular-girl pretty, not gymnast pretty. She had the scores of a young gymnast with the body of an old one.

"You go to high school, right?" Camille asked. She'd read this whole article in *Sports Illustrated* about how Leigh was single-handedly improving the face of gymnastics by being a balanced leader, by going to high school, and, most importantly, by actually eating. The article ignored the fact that there had been a mix of muscle among the stick-skinny gymnasts for a decade now.

The article made Camille feel invisible. Camille had enjoyed it.

Leigh nodded.

"Do you think that makes your life more normal?"

Leigh rolled her eyes. She leaned back against the concrete wall next to Camille. "I don't know. I mean . . . I have some normal friends. You know, who aren't gym ones? So, I guess. But . . ."

"But what?" Camille asked.

"But I still always wonder, you know? What it would be like to *be* one of them. To be normal. To only work out to stay in shape, to get to hang out after school, or try a new sport each season? To worry about your grades and stuff? To be able to tell . . . We all wonder these things, I guess."

Camille nodded slowly. *I know that answer,* she thought. *I'm probably the only one here who knows that answer.* Maybe that's why it was so hard this time.

"So . . . what's wrong?" Leigh asked again.

Camille shuddered, but she said it. "It's hard to make a comeback," she said.

Leigh raised her eyebrows. "But you're killing it! You're the face of comebacks. I mean, do you see all of these posters? People love you. And your vault—I mean, I know what happened yesterday but my vault isn't, like, consistent or whatever. I think I'm gonna do an Amanar today anyway. Oh . . . I probably shouldn't have told you that. Um . . . So yeah, your vault is, like, the best. Or whatever. Or . . . yeah."

Camille was almost shaking. "No," she said. "I don't mean it's hard to get your tricks back. That's not easy, but that's the part everyone knows about. It's so much harder than that." Now that the words were coming out of her mouth, Camille couldn't stop them. "To do it. Just to do it. It's almost impossible and it's almost impossible not to. To give up that normal life once you've had it. To go back to gymnastics but change your personality and body and style and to be entirely unsure who you are . . ."

Leigh was nodding. Leigh shouldn't be nodding. Leigh shouldn't have to hear this. Still, Camille couldn't stop. "To have felt your body break . . . to know that gymnastics almost killed you once . . . and to still . . ."

"Line up!" The meet coordinator's voice interrupted their moment. "Get in order in your heats and line up!"

Leigh was staring at Camille wide-eyed, though. Like she was shocked.

"Don't tell anyone, okay? Please?" Camille asked her. "It'll just—"

Leigh interrupted. "Don't worry. I have . . . secrets . . . too."

Camille nodded. "It's okay. I won't tell anyone about your vault plans today."

And she wouldn't. Her face was already on fire. Her heart was a stone in her chest. She shouldn't have told Leigh all of this. Camille had scarred her, scarred another gymnast before she'd even managed to apologize to Wilhelmina.

Leigh stood and reached down to pull Camille to her feet. Camille turned to line up with the other heat when she felt Leigh's arms thrown over her body in a tight, desperate hug.

"I had no idea," Leigh whispered, "what you were going through."

"Look," Camille said, wiggling out of the hug. "Don't think about it, okay? Don't worry about it. It's not that bad."

Leigh let her go abruptly and they lined up.

Stupid, stupid. Camille told herself. All she'd done since she got here was rain negativity on the happy gymnasts.

Camille marched behind Annie, out of the dark cave and into the applause. The other gymnasts would suck it in, savor it. It made Camille shrink inside herself.

One fan in the crowd started the "Comeback Cammie!" cheer.

Camille turned to smile at him the way she was supposed to. And her eyes went wide. He was in the first row. Green shirt that highlighted piercing eyes. Curly brown hair. Freckled face. Wide smile.

Bobby was here?

WILHELMINA

Wilhelmina realized she was free. Without Katja and the Olympics on her mind, she could focus on herself. She'd do this meet differently.

Today was about Wilhelmina and Wilhelmina only. And that magic 9.5.

Later, when the meet was over and they were all out to dinner—Wilhemina and her parents and Kerry and, she guessed, Davion and his brother, whose presence would be a surprise to everyone else—she and Kerry would have to accept her family's hugs of congratulations and be grateful to them on top of the impossible-to-avoid disappointment. But then Wilhelmina would announce her retirement to all of them. She knew her parents wanted the Olympics for her, too. She knew that Kerry had worked as hard as she had, or maybe harder, and that she would love to bring another athlete to the Olympics, even as an alternate. She knew that Davion, while he might be happy, would also be worried that she was leaving this dream behind for him, somehow. That it was his fault. They would all worry that she was just plain quitting, that one day she would regret it. And she would have to explain that there was nothing to be gained for her physically or emotionally or spiritually by busting her butt invisibly while the Olympics happened nearby. They might not understand. They might never understand. But the whole thing would be easier if Wilhelmina made sure that everyone had fun today. Especially Wilhelmina herself.

(And later-later she'd have a different kind of fun. A kissing kind of fun. That would get her through the day.)

Wilhelmina led her new squad of gymnasts out of the locker room and onto the floor, and the crowd erupted as they marched toward the vault. The first thing she did was scan the crowd. It was hard to make out anything up there, in the dark above the lights that shined down on the gym floor, but Wilhelmina found them anyway, in the second row where she knew they would be. Two brown faces in a sea of mostly white ones with two smiles that lit up the stands. Her parents.

She waved. She raised both of her hands over her head and waved like a maniac, a happy maniac.

She'd never done that before. She'd never bothered to think about her parents in the stands when there was a scoreboard to worry about.

Next, she found Monica stretching her legs on the podium. Monica would be up first, but Wilhelmina wouldn't be watching. She liked Monica. Monica was quiet like Wilhelmina but smart like Kerry. Monica had given Wilhelmina the key to getting through this meet now that the dream was dead.

Wilhelmina plopped down next to where Monica was stretching, swinging her feet off the podium.

"Where's your coach?" Wilhelmina asked.

Monica shrugged and looked around. Her eyes landed on Grace, who was sitting slumped in a chair with the two girls' coach leaning over her.

"Oh." Wilhelmina wanted to tell Monica that she was up first, so Ted should be talking to her. She wanted to tell the girl that she needed a new coach.

But instead she lost herself for a second, studying Grace's skinny legs as they hung off the folding chair. Wilhelmina swore she could see through Grace's quadriceps to her femur. Even when Grace was bent over, her hip bones were visible. Wilhelmina didn't want to know that Grace had a problem, but she knew. Watching Grace toss her entire lunch in the garbage today—and spit out the bite that was already in her mouth—was only the confirmation. Grace might try to claim she didn't eat her full lunch today because of nerves, but Wilhelmina could see all her bones, and they told a different story.

Wilhelmina had seen too many gymnasts end up out of the sport, in hospitals, screwed for life because of what gymnastics did to their relationship with food.

"Does she ever . . ." Wilhelmina tried. Monica looked at her.

. . . *eat?*

But she couldn't finish the question.

It would do no good. Grace was winning the meet and Katja had pretty much told Wilhelmina she had no chance this morning. If Wilhelmina reported Grace, Katja wouldn't believe her. She'd think it was some sticky political plan. And if Wilhelmina didn't say anything about watching Grace spit that one bite of sandwich into the garbage over the top of her lunch, Grace might . . . She could . . . It didn't matter. Wilhelmina couldn't do anything about it. Besides, today was supposed to be about Mina-Mina-Mina.

"I wanted to wish you good luck," she finally said.

"You too," Monica said. She added, "Thanks for talking to me last night, too. I needed to be put in my place."

Wilhelmina laughed. "You're the one who helped me."

Monica had opened her mouth, like she was going to question this when they both heard Ted's heavy voice say her name. "Monica. You're up first. Go chalk up."

Monica climbed the podium and Wilhelmina turned her head. She heard the crowd clap politely when the announcer called Monica's name, but she didn't register anything else. She paced with her back to the vault and meditated on her own Amanar. She'd be next.

She wouldn't watch anyone else. She wouldn't think about anyone else: not their gymnastics, not their fan pages, not their eating disorders, not their boyfriends. She'd only have one thought all day: *nine-point-five, nine-point-five, nine-point-five.*

Then Wilhelmina was on the podium, her toes lined up on the end of the runway, staring at the vault. *There you are, old friend,* she thought. It seemed impossible that she had stood in this exact position only twenty-four short hours ago with stars in her eyes and dreams so big, they didn't fit in her heart. How many times had she stood on a vaulting runway like this for the past twelve years? How many times had she stared down the mat and envisioned herself landing a perfect ten, the way she was right now? How many times had she dreamed those big dreams?

And it came down to this: to these ten seconds that were about to begin the last meet of her life.

MONICA

Monica felt her smile disappear as soon as Wilhelmina's feet hit the mat and stayed right where she put them. Monica was clapping. But her heart was sinking farther into her tiny frame until it was almost hiding behind her spinal cord.

It would be harder than she thought, competing with this squad, she realized.

She turned to glance at Ted and Grace, their heads bent together, Grace's perfect black braids so shiny they almost reflected Ted's blond crew cut.

She had been repeating her goal in her head: *One person. Beat at least one person.*

She'd performed her DTY well and then said it to herself again and again. *One person. One person. One person.*

But the people she had a chance to beat were far away on bars. And she was here with the stars on vault. Monica knew it was flattering to be placed in this squad. Just like it was a compliment when Katja had mentioned her last night. She knew that Katja had big plans for her one day, and that was thrilling. But it was all sort of weird and uncomfortable and embarrassing.

Everyone was wondering why Monica was in this squad.

But she only had to keep her mind on her own goal. She only had to fake her confidence. She only had to pretend.

Monica saw Ted release Grace's shoulders from his grasp and send her toward the podium.

Go wish her good luck, Monica told herself. She had to make up for the way Grace had scared her in the lobby of the hotel. She had to make sure Grace knew she couldn't destroy her.

She's your teammate! Monica reprimanded herself. *Get over it. Go talk to her.* Grace was hugging Leigh. They were right next to her. In less than a minute, Grace would climb onto the podium and Monica would be relegated to cheering like a fan instead of whispering good wishes like an equal.

Monica had proven herself as close to equal as she possibly could. Monica was placed in Grace's squad. The better squad.

Monica turned when Grace and Leigh pulled away.

You have to stop being so afraid of these people.

Finally, just before Grace took her first step up to the podium, Monica pulled on her elbow. "Good luck, teammate," she squeaked.

God, why did she have to sound so pathetic?

Grace smiled with too many teeth. "Thanks, you too. And"—she shrugged—"sorry your rotation got switched. I hope you're okay competing with Natalie and them from across the gym. You know, it was really hard on my dad yesterday when we were so far away from each other. They must have figured it would be easier on him if they put you with us."

Grace gave her another smile and Monica tried to imitate it.

Grace was being mean, but still.

All of that was probably true.

"You should be able to beat them, though, you know. You should be our alternate," Grace said. It was like she'd forgotten all about the threat she'd leveled on Monica only a few hours ago.

Was that a real smile or a fake smile? It was so rare for Grace to smile in the gym that, even though they practiced in the same building for six to eight hours a day, Monica didn't have a frame of reference for what Grace's smile should look like.

"You have a chance at alternate, really," Grace said. "Just do your best and don't watch the scores, right?"

Monica nodded. She made herself say, "You too."

But she didn't mean it. Was this what it was like to be Grace?

GRACE

Grace stood at the end of the runway, smoothing the chalk over the soles of her feet while her body buzzed with adrenaline or nerves or weakness. Grace couldn't tell the difference anymore. It felt like her blood was running in teeny zigzags through her veins. Was that normal? Was this how she always felt at the start of the meet, full of nerves and excitement, tingling with anticipation? Or did the buzzing mean something else?

She was glad they were starting on vault, though it bore an advantage for Leigh. Grace had managed to finish yesterday as the leader, but only by a hair. And Leigh was so good at vault, if she did a triple twisting Yurchenko like yesterday, she'd pull ahead in this rotation.

And, Grace thought, *if they wanted to keep any mystery to these new rotations, the committee should have changed which apparatus the squads were starting on.* It was clear that all the leaders, all the best gymnasts, were put into the same heat. Having this squad move through the meet in Olympic rotation made it more obvious. Grace had basically been placed on the Olympic team already.

That wasn't enough. She needed to win the meet.

But, despite all of those logical issues and disadvantages, Grace was glad to be starting on vault. Even if it meant Leigh would be beating her for at least one rotation. She was glad to be starting on vault for one reason: vault was the shortest.

And Grace wasn't sure what was going on inside of her right now. Was this buzzing a sign that her body was betraying her again?

It wasn't fair. Grace had eaten. She'd had all of that peanut butter at breakfast and then so many bites of turkey sandwich. She'd had the equivalent of at least three normal-people bites. Grace looked down at her legs and she swore she could see the peanut butter on them already, coating the inside of her thighs in a layer of fat that brought them closer to touching. Clearly, if she'd eaten enough to see the fat obliterate her bones and muscles, she must have eaten enough to keep her body calm, to keep her heart in one piece, to keep her organs under her control.

Just before she knew the judges would raise her green flag, Grace pressed her hands together, squishing the zinging veins in her left wrist against those in her right. *Calm down*, she told them. *Act normal.*

For so long, for months and years and in some ways

for as long as Grace could remember, her focus had been her food. Her focus had more than made up for the calories she cut. It had kept her graceful and helped her add new tricks and kept her on top.

Her focus filled her up. There was no Monica or Dylan Patrick in the back of her brain. There was no confusion over Leigh flirting with boys. There was no fear over Leigh making other friends. There was no missing mom. There was no food. There was nothing in her brain or her body except gymnastics. That's all Grace was: focus and gymnastics.

The green flag was raised and Grace took a deep breath. *Let's do this.*

She took off down the runway. By the third step she was calm again. Her blood ran normally. Her vision lasered in on the vaulting table in front of her. She felt the mat press against the bottom of her toes and the air rushing by her face as she ran.

And then she was over it, safely on the other side with heavy breath and a toothy smile for the judges. She'd done it. Not a hop or a stumble. Not a single organ out of rhythm or splitting into pieces in the air. Grace was Grace again. She'd done so well, her dad gave her a big hug.

Leigh would still catch her this rotation, but Grace should be able to get her lead back by bars and then keep it.

Clearly it had been only nerves. Her focus was still on target. Her body was perfectly happy with her.

LEIGH

Leigh was mortified. Too mortified to focus on her vault even as her competitors went over it one by one and her turn got closer. Why had she sounded so corny? Why had she given Camille that hug?

Why couldn't she ever shut up?

When Leigh had approached the veteran gymnast, she was sure Camille was upset about being placed in the other squad, the B squad. She'd thought of a few things to say. She had reminded herself of Camille's help at the beam earlier that day and talked herself up until she managed to approach her crush.

She hadn't been ready for what Camille said.

It made Leigh think more about what she and Grace had discussed before going to bed.

It made Leigh think more about the normal girls who were her friends from school. Or they were kind of her friends from school. They were friends because they talked about homework and complained to each other about teachers. Leigh knew who their boyfriends and best friends were. She sometimes knew what they did over the weekend. Maybe, if they happened to ask on an off day, Leigh might go to a movie with them. They were nice girls because they let Leigh be a periphery friend. Because they still invited her places, even though she said no eleven times out of twelve. Because they shared tidbits of their lives, like what their boyfriends got them for Valentine's Day or why their mothers grounded them, without insisting that Leigh also share things about her own outside-of-school life. And Leigh never did. Because she couldn't. Because regular girls who think about boyfriends and movies and groundings would never understand what it's like to be a professional sixteen-year-old. Sometimes it felt like she only bothered trying with those normal girls because it made her parents happy.

But, Camille had asked Leigh if she was normal, if she was one of them. Camille hadn't been able to tell that the high-school life was her other life, her second life, that Leigh was just like the rest of the gymnasts. Except she wasn't.

No one understood her. To one group she was the professional teen, and to the other she was the one who went to high school full-time.

Even Grace had never really understood Leigh. Leigh saw that now. They were being friendly like usual but something had shifted last night. Leigh wasn't sure she and Grace would ever be whole again. She wasn't sure she'd ever trust Grace like she once had.

Leigh felt like Camille felt. Totally misunderstood. She wondered if that's what she had recognized in Camille in the first place.

Leigh was staring at the empty air above the vault. She wasn't seeing anything.

Phil grabbed her arm as he walked by. "Focus!" He

almost spat the word in her face. "There's no point in Nice Leigh if you can't focus!"

She nodded and shook him off her. *Focus,* she told herself. *Focus on your Amanar. On sticking the landing.*

They were using her normal Amanar today because it was much more consistent than her TTY. And she didn't need the extra points from a TTY anymore. If Leigh hit on her Amanar, she'd get enough points to pass Grace, who only did a DTY. She'd be on top at the end of this rotation. The challenge would be staying there.

Leigh climbed the podium, chalked up, and stood ready for her green flag. *Stick the landing,* she told herself. But she wasn't even hearing her own internal warnings. Inside she was still cringing and wondering what Camille thought about that stupid hug.

Leigh glanced around. Phil was staring at her. Grace was not. She was digging through her bag. Monica was pulling on her warm-ups. Camille was pacing next to the bars. Were her friends from home watching? Or had That Girl been alone the whole time?

The green flag went up and Leigh was running over the mat before she even knew it.

The lightning nerves jolted her again. *What do I do? Oh, God, what do I do? Why didn't I visualize it?*

Leigh's hands were on the mat. *You can do it,* she told herself, but she could feel she was off. Her right hand landed inches ahead of her left on the table, so she was a little twisted; her body got into the air but not as high as yesterday; she stumbled sideways on the landing but still stood it up.

Not great. Not a disaster.

"You have to focus," Phil whispered as he pulled her off the podium. "You gotta get your head out of your being a nice kid. Friends are for later. Focus!"

Leigh nodded.

Then she heard her score. She turned to the scoreboard and watched as the scores updated. And her jaw dropped.

She was now tied for first place. In the Olympic trials. With Grace.

Leigh felt her heart speed up but she took a deep breath to calm it.

She couldn't make this about beating Grace. That wasn't nice. That was something Grace would do.

STANDINGS AFTER THE FIFTH ROTATION

1. Grace Cooper   74.905
1. Leigh Becker   74.905
3. Georgette Paulson   74.705
4. Wilhelmina Parker   74.700
5. Maria Vasquez   71.250
6. Kristin Jackson   70.620
7. Monica Chase   70.555
8. Annie Simms   70.410
9. Natalie Rice   67.150
10. Samantha Soloman   45.205
11. Camille Abrams   30.980
12. Olivia Corsica   29.738

Sixth Rotation

MONICA

As she walked behind Georgette from the vault to the bars, Monica glimpsed the scoreboard. Okay, she looked at it. She made that ultimate mistake and turned her head and looked for her name.

Worse, she forgot herself for a minute. She forgot all her rules and rituals. She looked from the top down.

Seventh.

At the end of the third rotation yesterday, she'd been in fourth. Two rotations later, she had plummeted, and Natalie and Annie were right on her tail.

All of that happened despite the fact that, a minute ago, she'd beaten yesterday's score on vault.

The precise makeup and the sparkly leo and the braided hair didn't mean anything. She wasn't good enough.

Her mom and dad and grandmother and stepdad and brothers and sisters and stepbrothers and stepsisters were all here to watch her fail. And if anyone had finally recognized her face on the TV, that person was watching her fail now, too.

Monica's cheeks burned as she put her bag on her new chair and waited her turn to warm up on bars. Grace was right. She was only placed in this squad because they needed a sixth gymnast and they didn't want to make Ted run back and forth constantly like he had yesterday. How could she have let herself believe that this was where she belonged? That she mattered?

Monica mounted the bars for her warm-up. Maybe it was time to go back to her old goal, the one Wilhelmina had convinced her wasn't big enough. *Don't fall.* If that was her focus, it wouldn't be so disappointing when Natalie or Annie climbed past her on the scoreboard.

Except Monica had seen that four next to her name yesterday.

No matter what, she'd go home disappointed. Monica hated how hope compounded on hope until she built herself up to be higher than she could be, and all of those piles of hope meant that she was never happy. It was why she usually tried not to hope at all.

No falls, Monica told herself as she swung through a series of giants. *No falls and no looking at the scoreboard.*

Monica landed a watered-down dismount and hopped off the podium.

"Nice dismount," she heard Grace's garbage voice say.

Monica turned her head, startled. She hadn't realized anyone had been watching. She hadn't seen Grace approach.

And before she knew it, she'd rolled her eyes.

Grace's own eyes grew in surprise. "What?" she asked.

Oh, come on.

"I just said it was a good dismount. You know, you stuck it."

Monica shook her head.

"What?" Grace said again.

You're not my coach. I don't have to care what you think.

She looked around. Ted was sitting slumped over at the end of the row of folding chairs. He had his phone in his hand. He hadn't even seen her warm up.

Even her own coach didn't think she was worth the effort. What was she doing here?

"I'm being nice," Grace whined.

Monica was sick of it. She was sick of Grace and Ted and Leigh and everyone.

She was sick of hoping. But Monica didn't think she could stop the hope from pulsing through her veins anymore, so she dove into it. She wasn't going to make the team, she knew that. But she was going to get as close as she could.

She was going to believe in herself. Alternate. Olympic team alternate. She had three more rotations to get there.

"That wasn't my real dismount. And you know it," Monica said to Grace. Then she marched over to their coach.

"Do you have anything to say about my warm-up?"

she asked. She tried to make her voice strong, but of course it sounded squeaky.

Ted looked up. He lowered his bushy eyebrows in surprise. "You did great," he said. He looked back at his phone.

Monica didn't move. She didn't care that she was only in her leo and totally exposed to everyone in the stands. She didn't care that she was tiny and she probably had chalk in her braids and streaked across her thighs. She was at the Olympic trials. She was alive. And though she wouldn't make the team, she owed it to every gymnast who hadn't made it this far for one reason or another to try her best, push her hardest.

Finally Ted looked up again. "Yes?" he said.

"Did you see it?" She hated how her voice sounded weak and raspy when inside she was finally feeling strong.

"Huh?" he said.

Behind Monica, Georgette mounted the bars and began her official routine. Monica would be up next, in only a few minutes.

"Did you even see my warm-up? Did I miss a handstand? Did I bend a knee? Did I look strong on the first release?"

To Monica's surprise, Ted smiled.

"You want my real critique?" he asked.

Monica felt herself shrink. She'd started this conversation so confident. But he was smiling at her like she was a three-year-old with a messy lollipop. Monica didn't want to be cute. She wanted to be good.

Still, she nodded. "For real," she managed.

"You hit your handstands," he said. "But you almost always have an inch or two between your ankles. Your release move is precise, but I always think you're about to hit your foot on the bar on the way down. You barely get any height."

Monica nodded.

Ted kept talking. "When you kip to the low bar, your right hand always looks too loose on the bar. And if you think you're making that connection between your release moves, you're fooling yourself. You hesitate half the time, almost. The judges will always see that, always, no matter how well you cover it up."

Monica stared at him wide-eyed. *Now? He chooses to tell me this stuff now? For the first time?*

"Oh, don't give me that look," he said, wrinkling his face in a way that made him look like his daughter. "Don't give me those big hurt eyes. You asked for it. You marched up here and demanded a real critique, so there you have it."

Monica's eyes fell to her toes and she shook her head. But she wasn't hurt. "What?" Ted said.

She was pissed.

If you've known that all along, you should have told me before. If you were taking me seriously, maybe I'd have taken myself seriously. Maybe I'd have a chance.

"Nothing," Monica said.

Ted turned around and went back to his chair.

But, a few minutes later, when Monica's name was called, he stood and walked to the side of the podium. "Ankles together," he yelled. "Remember, keep those ankles together." She nodded. She mounted the bars and, ninety seconds later, when there were red half-moons on each of her inner ankles from being pressed together through her whole routine, Monica knew her score would be even higher than yesterday's.

But she didn't look.

GRACE

Grace spat into her grips and rubbed the wet chalk across the leather. There was a camera circling her like a kid at a roller rink.

She thought about what they'd be saying on television right now:

"And here we have one of our leaders. She made a good case for the guaranteed position yesterday, didn't she, Jim?"

"Why, yes, she did, Cheryl. The top spot is certainly on her mind right now. But we've seen some mistakes from her in the past."

"Mistakes or no mistakes, are we going to see this one competing for our country in Rome?"

"Cheryl, I'd be shocked if Grace Cooper wasn't on that Europe-bound plane tomorrow."

Grace remembered watching meets as a child. The announcers had made it all seem simple. She thought it was simple. Gymnasts were talented girls who wanted to win the meet. Who enjoyed hugging each competitor after each routine. Who were friends with their athletic enemies. A gymnast was able to be happy for people who got what she herself wanted, what she had worked hard for. A gymnast cared more about her country winning gold than herself going to the Olympics.

A gymnast would be thrilled to take a step to the left on the podium and share that gold medal with her best friend. She wouldn't hate her for tying her score.

Even Dylan seemed to think this way. After Grace's vault he posted: I'm still watching you, Grace Cooper, even though it seems pretty obvious you and Leigh are both going to the Olympics. Woo hoo! Can't wait to watch you there.

For the announcers and spectators it was as simple as "she wants it, and she wants it, and she wants it, and she wants it, but only one of them will get it, and, hey look, they're all friends." They *were* friends, some of them. But.

The announcers and spectators didn't know what it was like to have fire running in your veins because you just heard your name for the sixth time at the Olympic trials and you know you're less than two hours, only three quick rotations, away from the final step to achieving your wildest, grandest dream and that the only thing possibly standing in your way of going to the Olympics as the world's best gymnast is your best friend, who is now tying you, and how that's the most exciting and scary and overwhelming place you've ever been.

Grace had to stare at the bars, to narrow her eyes, and to tell her veins to cool down, her heart to stay steady, her stomach to feel full, because there were way too many tiny things that could pull the dream right from her fingertips.

Bars was Grace's best event and Leigh's worst. This tie would be over soon.

Grace got the green flag, signaled the judges, and mounted. It was time for her to turn back into the willow tree.

She spun around the high bar in a giant, added another half giant, and landed in handstand. She was slightly short on it but she wasn't even sure if the judges would catch that.

So far so good.

She transitioned to the low bar, flew around it in a straddle, and swung herself back up the high bar for a double pirouette.

Her toes were pointed, her knees were straight, her arms were strong. Her body was full of long, lean lines, like her father and everyone else would say.

Still good.

Something was different from yesterday. The crowd was fidgety or something. She didn't feel every eye on her, every pair of lungs holding in their breath, every face calm.

She didn't feel calm. She felt nervous.

But she'd competed like this before and gotten great scores. Everything she was doing was technically perfect.

Grace did her Cooper with her legs splayed and her free arm circling the bar like a ribbon. Then she re-grasped the bar with her left hand for a pirouette. She hit it perfectly, up and down.

Still good. Almost done.

But that's when it happened. Her arms were suddenly spaghetti. Her stomach was slush. Her eyes saw black. Her body almost crumpled off the bar and whacked it before falling 8.2 feet to the floor. The entire crowd gasped with shock and surprise and horror, terrified she would fall.

She caught herself just in time, tightening every muscle from her fingers to her biceps to her abs to her lower back and quads and calfs and toes. She swung herself into another giant and another handstand. Two tricks she wasn't planning on, tricks that she'd already done, so they wouldn't add anything to her score. She hadn't fallen. But the entire crowd had inhaled with surprise. It was noticeable. And now she had no idea what she was doing.

She had to figure it out in a millisecond.

She was exhausted. Her palms were ripping apart, her muscles were burning, her lungs were fighting for air.

If she missed her Mustafina dismount and fell, her save would have been pointless.

But she had to do something. She kipped as usual. She could feel that her knees were slightly bent and her toes were not quite as curled as they should be. God, her joints were so tired.

There's no way she could make her muscles do all the twists and flips in a Mustafina.

She released the bar and did a simple, and sloppy, single backflip dismount. She stumbled on the landing.

Grace turned to the judges and barely put her arms in the air before jumping off the podium.

That was it. Leigh would take over. Leigh didn't even look at her as she climbed onto the podium herself and dipped her hands in the chalk.

Grace hung her head and approached the folding chairs, instructing her neck not to turn, not to watch as Leigh stole the top position out from under her.

Oh, God, Grace thought. *What is Dad going to say?*

But she wouldn't wish her mother was there. Her dad was wishing it. He never said anything, but Grace knew he was always wishing their lives had gone differently. He was always wishing that his wife was still here.

He didn't have that kind of wife. Grace didn't have that kind of mother. She had the kind who disappeared, and she couldn't wish for anything different. She couldn't do that to herself.

By the time the announcer said Leigh's name, her dad still wasn't by her side. He wasn't there. Grace looked up and glanced around for him. Was he talking to Monica? Was he in the bathroom or something?

No. He was standing five feet away and ignoring her. Like Grace had wanted to mess everything up. Like she'd done it to punish him.

Grace turned back to her gym bag and opened her phone. Maybe someone who knew nothing about gymnastics would have a nice word for her. Maybe there'd be one person who understood. But, for the first time in six rotations, there was nothing. No message. Even Dylan was disappointed in her.

Grace looked up again and couldn't help catching Leigh's perfect release move in the corner of her vision.

It would be impossible now. Leigh had messed up a little and Grace had wasted the opportunity by messing up a lot. In order to beat Leigh, Grace had to have a higher score on bars. Leigh's degree of difficulty was too close to hers on beam and slightly higher on floor. It would be impossible now.

Unless Leigh fell.

LEIGH

No, Grace! No!

In the fraction of a second that Grace went weak on top of the uneven bars, Leigh almost screamed. She almost rushed the podium to stand beneath her friend with her arms out, as if she could get there in time to catch the crumbling gymnast. She almost cried.

In that tiny moment, all Leigh could see was the confusion in Camille's eyes an hour ago. The fear. The loss. All she could hear was Camille's voice, choppy like waves during a thunderstorm, saying, "It's hard to make a comeback," over and over again.

But Grace maintained her grip and Leigh exhaled. When Grace exited the podium after a downgraded dismount, Leigh wanted to rush at her. Leigh wanted to throw her arms around her best friend and say, *Thank God you're okay.*

Instead, Leigh walked past Grace silently as she made her way to the chalk bucket. She knew better. Grace didn't understand Leigh, but Leigh sure understood Grace.

Grace didn't ever think about life without gymnastics. Grace didn't sit in her high-school Algebra II class and stare at the girls who were passing notes and wonder what it would be like to be the kind of high-school girl who would pass around her secrets on folded up pieces of paper. Grace's brain never left the gym. There was no way she realized how close she almost came to leaving it forever.

If it was that hard for Camille, who was well-rounded and smiley and rock solid, it would be impossible for Leigh's friend Grace.

I'm going to win now, Leigh thought. She knew it in her gut. And though she was being nice enough to feel sympathy for Grace from the sidelines, Leigh would win. Letting Grace win was not the kind of nice she wanted to be.

Leigh felt calm as she stood beneath the high bar for the second time in this meet. She remembered the series of crippling fears that had rattled her bones the previous evening, but today they were absent. She might mess up. She might miss a connection or slip on a handstand or fall on the dismount. But she would be herself.

She was Leigh Becker. National champion. A girl so close to making the Olympic team. A girl so close to her dream.

And she was also Leigh Becker. Public high-school student. Friend. Daughter. Confused, closeted lesbian.

Leigh couldn't talk about all the parts of herself but she would still *be* them. She'd win this meet being her whole self.

The flag turned green. Leigh signaled the judges. It was like her entire body was smiling. *Here we go.*

She ran at the springboard, grabbed the high bar

with both of her hands, and swung herself into a hand-stand.

The bars were her enemy. The bars were her servants.

Leigh swung around in a giant, then sailed over the high bar, folded her body in half across her straddle, and flipped in her first release move. She reached to re-clasp the bar and found herself with her arms spread, ready for contact long before necessary. She was sitting in the air. She was actually flying.

The crowd awarded her with happy gasps and hoots.

Yes! Leigh thought. *I've never gotten that reaction on bars before.*

She performed a Pak salto to the low bar. Her legs were straight and tight together. Her toes were pointed.

She transitioned right back to the high bar, once again flying higher than necessary. One handstand, double pirouette, two giants before her dismount. She nailed them all. The crowd whooped and clapped and enjoyed.

From her final giant, Leigh used her elbows and biceps, wrists and forearms to catapult her body as high as she could above the high bar. Then she swung her feet over her head and twisted twice. She felt the floor coming toward her backside so she rushed her final twist. Her feet found the floor.

She hopped forward about four inches but found her balance easily. The smile for the judges was already on her face.

She ran to the edge of the podium and jumped

directly into Phil's arms. He swung her around, yelling, "That was it! That was it!"

He put her down and leaned over to whisper in her ear. "If that's Leigh as a nice gymnast, I'll take it."

She smiled back at him. "I wasn't being nice to the bars."

They both laughed.

Then she felt a warm hand on her shoulder. She turned.

"Great job, Normal Girl," Camille said. Then she was being hugged. Again.

"Thanks . . . I mean, thank you. You know, for coming over here. For . . . Thanks." *Shut up, Leigh!*

Camille smiled but it was only a half smile. Did she know? Did she suspect?

"I need to talk to Mina," she said. "But I caught that routine and . . . Wow."

Leigh bit her lips to keep herself from *I mean*-ing all over this beautiful girl one more time. She nodded.

Then Camille was gone and everything else was the same. Phil was smiling at her. Her scores were high. She was winning. And it seemed like, once again, no one noticed, no one guessed her secret.

It was an almost-perfect moment. But part of Leigh wished she could steal that microphone right from the announcer and claim that final part of herself. She would declare to the whole stadium, "I am Leigh Becker; I am winning this meet; and I like girls. Deal with it."

WILHELMINA

Grace had almost melted on bars. She'd almost dripped into a bloody puddle on the purple mat beneath the high bar and Wilhelmina felt like only she knew why. She'd kept her back turned to the bars the whole rotation until that gasp from the crowd made her head pivot without thinking. And what she'd seen was a girl breaking in two, a person whisking into nothing, a gymnast dissolving. Why was she the only one seeing this?

Wilhelmina could not report Grace.

Grace would be right: Wilhelmina didn't like Grace. Wilhelmina didn't want Grace going to the Olympics, stealing her own destiny. But Wilhelmina didn't want the girl to shatter, either.

And what if Grace broke like that, and somehow Wilhelmina won the meet? She'd be going to the Olympics with Katja hating her the entire time. Would it be worth it?

It was so unfair.

Don't think about this today.

Wilhelmina squeezed her eyes shut and tried to meditate on the 9.632 execution score she'd gotten on vault. She tried to picture it on the scoreboard next to her name. She'd heard it announced but she hadn't looked at the standings. She was focused on her own gymnastics. She was good at avoiding the scoreboard until the end of the meet.

Bars would be her hardest test. Judges were picky on bars, and they weren't built for girls like her anyway. In order to get that 9.5 or better, she'd need to keep her legs glued together (as much as possible, considering her bulging quadriceps). She'd need to keep her toes pointed. She'd need to nail each handstand, landing exactly perpendicular to the high bar. She'd need to fly on her release moves and catch the bar at the exact right second. She'd need to be strong and sturdy, like the bars were an extension of her own limbs.

And bars were hardest for another reason: if Wilhelmina did get that 9.5, she'd have the highest score on bars today, on *bars*, on her worst event. She'd have the highest score on her worst event on the second day of the meet. And even if that happened, she still wouldn't get chosen. She was never going to be chosen. She had to win the meet or else she'd be out. And unless terrible things happened to Grace and Leigh and Georgette, it was impossible for her to win the meet.

Wilhelmina had to keep the bitterness from stinking through her sweat glands. She had to focus on her gymnastics.

Later, she'd complain to Davion. And he'd hug her. And she'd kiss him. And he'd kiss her back. They'd sit on the hood of his car and his arms would be around her waist and . . .

All right, so Wilhelmina was *mostly* succeeding in

her quest to think only about her gymnastics.

The announcer called her name. Wilhelmina stepped up to the bars feeling like Babe Ruth must have on the mound. Like she knew exactly how to do what she needed to do. Like she controlled not just her muscles but gravity and physics. Like she could make all the forces that would want to pull her body down irrelevant by the sheer determination to succeed according to her own definition, the sheer destiny of 9.5.

She mounted the low bar and, ninety seconds later, she was halfway to her daily goal.

Wilhelmina turned immediately from the judges to Katja. *How do you like that?* she asked the old lady in her head. *I bet you want that bars routine representing America.*

But Katja was staring back at Mina with an expression so cold, she was sure it would freeze the blood in her veins if she looked at her for too long. Katja hated her. In the frigidness of that stare, in the aftermath of her threats, it became clear to Wilhelmina in a new way. Katja would hate her more and more the better she did. And if Mina somehow managed to make the team, Katja would make her life miserable.

Not. Today, she told herself.

Wilhelmina kept her head twisted away from the scoreboard as she ran through the obligatory hugs and thank-yous that come after a successful routine. Camille was at the end of her receiving line.

"What are you doing over here?" Wilhelmina said.

"I wanted to cheer you on," Camille said. She followed Wilhelmina over to the folding chairs and plopped down as Wilhelmina rubbed lotion over her knees. "And"—Camille's voice got quiet. Wilhelmina looked up at her—"I want to apologize. I'm sorry. For what I said yesterday and this morning. About Katja. I shouldn't have stuck my nose in it. I shouldn't have—"

Wilhelmina shook her head. "You were right," she said.

Camille shrugged. "I wasn't trying to hurt you or mess you up or anything. It just popped out of my mouth." She paused. "And who really knows what Katja's thinking? I didn't hear what she said last night, but it sounds like she might not have meant it. You still have a chance . . ."

Wilhelmina squinted. *What would have happened if Camille hadn't said that yesterday?* she wondered. She would still be jittery. She'd be staring at the scoreboard. She'd be trying to control Leigh's and Georgette's and Maria's and even Camille's performances. She'd be so concerned about Grace's DODs that she wouldn't see her failing body. She'd be thinking about the Olympics all day, and then it would still be over.

"It's weird," she said to Camille. "But it actually helped me."

Camille bit her bottom lip like she was nervous about something else. "So . . . are we friends? Because I could use one."

Wilhelmina stopped her eyes from rolling. She stopped herself from saying no. There was more to life than gymnastics; there had to be or hers wouldn't be worth living after today. She wasn't going to focus on the rest of them—Grace or Camille or Monica or anyone—as gymnasts today. But that didn't mean she couldn't think of them as people.

Wilhelmina nodded. She sat next to her friend and focused on her face, making sure Maria and the bars were totally out of her vision.

CAMILLE

Camille spilled her guts. She let all the words fall out of her and pile up at Wilhelmina's feet: how she was always worried about her mother, how she was always disappointing Bobby, how she never knew the right thing to do.

How Bobby had dumped her and then showed up out of nowhere.

Camille didn't know why she was talking. She'd never said this stuff to anyone. Not even the people she trusted the most. But now, Camille wasn't sure if she cared whether any of this got repeated. She'd been balancing them alone for too long now: her mother and her boyfriend. She felt like she lived her life standing on her left foot with her arms spread outward and her hands turned upward. Her mother sat on one hand. Bobby sat on the other.

She'd been thinking so much about what they wanted, she'd never even stopped to think about what she wanted. Until Leigh beat her on vault. Until she'd almost gotten it.

She wanted the NCAA. But that would hurt both Bobby and her mom.

Somehow, she had lost her right foot and the ability to stand still and balanced.

She didn't—she couldn't—tell Wilhelmina anything about the real debate going on in her brain: to vault or not to vault? She couldn't tell that to anyone. But she wasn't sure she could figure it out without talking to Bobby first. She needed someone to give her permission to break the rules, sneak into the bathroom, and call him.

"He's up there," Camille said. She nodded to the stands behind them and they both turned to look.

There he was. His curls bouncing as he waved his phone at her.

"He wants me to call him," Camille said.

Wilhelmina shook her head. Her words came slowly, like she didn't really know what to say. "You're in the middle of a meet. You're not allowed to talk on your phone."

Camille sighed. "I know. But he came all the way here and—"

Wilhelmina cut her off. "No. He's a selfish jerk. Don't ruin your meet over him. Get your butt over the vault."

Camille felt her defeated heart speeding up.

"You're going to the Olympics!" Wilhelmina shouted. "Who does that kid think he is?"

"Yeah," Camille lied.

She'd been stupid to think that maybe Wilhelmina would understand, that maybe since she was an older gymnast, she would also have a little bit of gymnastics fatigue or competition fatigue or whatever it was that was weighing on Camille and making her wish she wasn't here.

Wilhelmina was angry. "You're the best vaulter here. You can't give that up for some guy."

Camille's mouth dropped open. She struggled to say something, anything that would make Wilhelmina, or her mother, or her coach, or anyone, anyone understand.

"It's so unfair, Camille! I mean, Katja loves you, right? She didn't have any *private messages* for you. And yet you're the one who's going to risk the Olympics for some jerk's phone call?"

Camille remembered Katja's words. Her promise. All Camille had to do to get to the Olympics at this point was show up in the locker room at the end of the meet. Wilhelmina was mad, so Camille didn't want to tell her about her private moment with Katja.

She felt her cheeks go pink.

Then, something dawned on her. "Wait," she said. "Did Katja have a private message for *you*?"

Wilhelmina fell quiet and Camille swore she could see her heart break across her face. She shrugged. "At breakfast," she whispered.

"What?" Camille said, borrowing some of the anger that her defeated roommate was letting go. "What did she say?"

"I'm too late," Wilhelmina mumbled. "She said she can never trust me. She asked me not to make it difficult for her. She basically asked me not to try to make the team because, well, she said that would backfire."

"But . . . but . . ." Camille started.

"But, what?"

"But that *is* unfair!" Camille blurted.

Wilhelmina shook her head. "I know that. That's what I'm saying. Everything has always been unfair for me." She wouldn't look up at Camille.

"Well, that's what—" Camille started.

But Wilhelmina cut her off. "I shouldn't . . . I don't want to talk about it. I mean, don't want to think about it. I'm trying to be . . . healthy. I'm trying to enjoy today. That's what I want. I want to enjoy today."

Wilhelmina looked up then, and Camille nodded. There wasn't much to say to that. Who didn't want to enjoy today?

And it was working: Wilhelmina was rocking it. But she was in fourth place yesterday. The math alone made it pretty unlikely that she'd be able to surpass Georgette and Leigh and Grace. Gymnasts rarely moved more than one spot after the first day of a meet, unless there was a major fall. And no one ever wished for falls.

"What do *you* want?" Wilhelmina asked. "If you

forget your mom and that jerk. What do you want?"

Camille scrunched her eyebrows. "Part of it," she said. It was what she always wanted. But she'd never admitted it to anyone.

Wilhelmina looked at her like she was crazy, but it didn't matter. Camille knew what she meant.

She wanted a balanced life that wasn't controlled by gymnastics. Her mother would hate that.

She didn't want to give up gymnastics completely. Bobby would hate that.

If she tried to make either of them happy, she'd never be happy herself.

Did it really matter what Camille wanted?

"You're not going to call him, are you?" Wilhelmina demanded.

Camille shrugged. She wasn't any closer to a vault solution.

"I can't be talking about this now," Wilhelmina said. "I'm not trying to be mean, but I can't let this Bobby screw up my meet, my day. Let's talk after the meet. Ignore him until then."

Then she was gone.

Camille slumped in her chair, her head down so Bobby would know she wasn't looking at him.

"Well, I get it," a voice said beside her. "I think I get what you mean."

Camille jumped. She turned to her right. *Monica.* Had she been sitting there the whole time? Had the girl been so much of a nonfactor in Camille's brain that she didn't even realize she'd been sitting there, privy to Camille's innermost thoughts?

"It's harder to be talented than it looks, huh?" Monica said. She said it like it was really a question. Like Camille had the answers.

"It's hard to be . . . us," Camille said. "I think. I mean, it's hard to be a person and also be, like, a . . . commodity. Like, the product. You know?"

"I know." Monica shrugged. "There's more to gymnastics than the Olympics, though."

Camille nodded. *For you, maybe. I wish there was for me.*

"And there's more to life than gymnastics," Monica said. "I get why you'd want to go call your boyfriend."

Camille was surprised. But that was the permission she needed.

STANDINGS AFTER THE SIXTH ROTATION

1. Leigh Becker   90.405

2. Wilhelmina Parker   90.325

3. Grace Cooper   88.705

4. Georgette Paulson   88.704

5. Monica Chase   85.555

6. Maria Vasquez   85.505

7. Kristin Jackson   84.845

8. Annie Simms   84.405

9. Natalie Rice   80.650

10. Samantha Soloman   60.405

11. Olivia Corsica   59.550

12. Camille Abrams   30.980

Seventh Rotation

MONICA

Monica climbed onto the beam to start her warm-up. Out of the corner of her eye, she saw Ted stand and approach the podium. He was watching.

That's good, she told herself. But her knees were shaky. She walked to the end of the beam and sprung her body through the first tumbling pass. She landed, her right heel hanging off the end of the beam, her left pinkie toe hanging off the side. She squeezed her legs and feet to keep her body upright. *Crap.* That was not good. She had to land that trick during her routine.

Once she regained her balance, she hopped off and walked on the mats to the end of the beam. She climbed on again and tumbled again. She landed crooked again.

Damn it! She hopped off to try yet another time.

Some gymnasts warm up by running through their entire routine, but Monica always went for a watered-down version. Usually, without the pressure of the eyes from the judges and the crowd, she would do her tumbling perfectly in her warm-up. Then she'd do a few full turns, her leaps, a dismount and be done with it. That gave her muscles enough spring and herself enough confidence to feel good mounting the beam for her official routine a few minutes later.

But Ted was standing there, staring at her, ruining her confidence and the whole point of her warm-up. He wasn't telling her what to do; he wasn't even saying his usual "good job, kiddo." He was staring.

Monica hopped off the beam yet again after screwing up for a third time, and Ted sat. He pulled out his phone.

Now, of course, she did a perfect double-handspring back tuck. She did a few full turns without the slightest balance check. She practiced a split leap. Perfect.

Why was it so much harder to perform when people were watching?

Monica hopped off the podium and the next girl mounted the beam for her warm-up. Monica felt good. But then she heard Ted's voice, gruff and mean. "Monica."

She looked up at him.

"What was that?"

He said it so loudly, she ran over to him, hoping that if she was right next to him, he'd stop the hollering and everyone in the gym would stop looking at her. Grace was staring at her with a scrunched nose like Monica was the most pathetic piece of worthlessness gymnastics had ever seen.

"Is that how you warm up for beam?" Ted was saying. "Just do a few run-throughs and don't worry when you fall off? Just do a turn for the hell of it? La-la-la, I'll do whatever I like."

He was mocking her. Monica felt herself grow shorter, her cheeks grow brighter.

Her blood ran hot.

It was amazing that she could feel this small, this insecure, this terrified and at the same time be so angry.

"I—" Monica started.

"You what? You thought your warm-up was a suggestion? Thought we talk about muscle memory because we like the sound of our voices?"

"No," Monica said, "I didn't—"

"Don't tell me you didn't know," Ted said. He was quieter now but his voice still cut through her heart like a steak knife. "Don't tell me that here you are, at the Olympic trials, the second day, having the meet of your life, and you don't know how to warm up."

There were so many people looking at them.

Is this what it meant to have Ted as a coach? You either get ignored or you get mocked?

Monica felt tiny and scared, but she couldn't stand there and let him yell at her while everyone watched. She couldn't keep the anger in her stomach anymore. She felt the words simmering in her throat. "This is your fault," she mumbled. She wasn't sure she even heard her own voice, but Ted did.

"Excuse me?" he said.

"You should know that's how I warm up. I did the exact same thing yesterday. You should know." She wished she could sound as angry as she felt.

Ted's mouth snapped shut. He nodded once. Monica thought that was going to be it. She was ready to go back to being ignored and belittled. Anything was better than mocking.

But Ted smiled. It was a weird smile, like Grace's.

He pointed to the line that was taped on the floor. "Do it again," he said. His smile disappeared as soon as he spoke.

"What?" Monica squeaked.

Ted pointed to the floor. "You want a real warm-up? Fine. I'll teach you now. Do it again."

Wide-eyed, Monica backed up until her feet were on the tape. She did the first of her double handsprings.

"Stop!" Ted said. Monica froze, knees bent, hands in the air, ready to spring her body over again. "Start at the beginning. Your whole routine," Ted said. "That's how we warm up."

She ran through her entire routine on the floor. Ted pointed out every balance check, every slipped foot, every bent elbow.

Monica's heart stuttered every time she heard his voice. His eyes focused like lasers on her feet and it made her jumpy. She flipped down the length of the fake beam and her toes landed half a foot away from the end of the tape.

"Well, that's great," Ted said. "You just leaped off the end of the beam."

This is what I want, Monica told herself as she walked back. *He's paying attention to me. I have to listen to his words and erase that disgusted tone from my ears.*

She finished her routine and turned to her coach.

"Do it again," Ted said.

He's here because he thinks I matter.

Grace herself was warming up on the beam by now, but Ted kept watching Monica. "Balance check," he said over and over again. "Point your toes. Get those ankles together. Come on, Monica, you know better!"

And Monica did matter. Her gymnastics mattered. It mattered to her: that was most important.

By her third run-through Monica was smiling. There was something good about being terrified of Ted. It made it impossible for her to be terrified of everyone else.

Minutes later, her name was called. She stared at the beam, focusing on it like it was the only light in a room full of darkness. She ran through everything Ted had told her. Then she put her hands on the surface and raised herself into her handstand.

And a word went through her head. *Alternate.*

Olympic alternate.

She could do it. She knew she could.

GRACE

As her name boomed across the Baltimore Metroplex for the second-to-last time, Grace watched her father lift her competitor from the balance beam podium. She watched him lean over the girl he maybe loved best now, the girl Katja probably loved best now, and whisper in her ear. She watched him put her on the ground and pat on her lower back. And then he sat.

He did not come over to Grace to give her any last-minute strategy or warning or advice. He didn't even look up as she climbed the steps to the podium.

Grace glanced back at the stands, hoping to see Katja's eyes on her as they usually were, but no.

Katja had asked Grace to be consistent and she wasn't. There was no way Katja would see her as consistent now. But Grace had to make Katja happy in order to qualify to compete in the all-around, which would lead to her one shot at Olympic gold. And now there was only one way to make Katja happy.

Grace had to beat Wilhelmina Parker.

Grace was the only one who had bothered to figure out what—really, *who*—Katja was talking about last night, and now she could use that to her advantage.

Katja needed Grace to kill Wilhelmina's story. Because Wilhelmina could prove that you can be a real person and still be a gymnast. Wilhelmina could prove that you can use your brain, that you can do something different from what Katja decided, and still make the Olympic team.

And Grace was the opposite. Grace did everything exactly as Katja preferred it.

If Wilhelmina beat Grace, she would nullify Katja's whole training philosophy, Katja's whole job, Katja's whole life. But if Grace beat Wilhelmina, Katja would be validated.

Grace would stay in Katja's favor.

Grace had to show them all that Katja's way was the right way.

Because it was the only way she knew how to live. Katja was the third most important person in her life. Dad, Max, Katja, Leigh. That's all Grace had.

If Dylan were into me . . .

If Mom were here . . .

Grace squeezed her eyes shut and tried to shut her entire face. What was happening? What had flirting with Dylan done to her? It had been so long since she'd let herself miss her mother.

Grace wiped the pain off her face and signaled the judges.

This was not the way it was supposed to be. It should not feel this awful to be coming in third at the biggest American gymnastic event in four years. Later today, Grace would hear her name listed among those going to the Olympics. In only a few weeks she would be on an international stage fighting to etch her name into history next to Nastia Liukin and Gabby Douglas and Carly Patterson and Mary Lou Retton. Right now, the stands were full of Americans who had followed her career. They were full of people who believed in her. Her little brother, Max, was up there, somewhere in the dark, waving a sign around and screaming her name.

Yes, she was in third. Yes, she might stay there. *But still*, Grace thought, *this should feel better.*

She should feel confident, proud, excited. Instead of mortified and hurt and like a terrible daughter and a terrible gymnast and a terrible friend.

Her heart was pumping sludge, sinking lower and lower in her torso, and it would keep sinking until it was caught by the hip bones that protruded from her navy leo. Her arms felt so heavy that it was an effort to lift them over her head when the flag turned green.

But luckily Grace's gymnastics did not depend on her emotional state. She squinted at the beam, like her coach had taught her, and watched it grow. She flipped the switch. She erased her feelings. She let her brain and heart die, and her body took over.

Foot, she said to herself as her left foot launched her off the springboard. *Foot*, she told herself patiently, and her right foot landed on the beam.

Spin. She did a full twist with her left leg kicked out to the side. It was a difficult trick and the audience—the crowd of thousands whose belief in her somehow still couldn't erase her father's disappointment—awarded her with applause.

By the time Grace stood with her toes lined up on the end of the beam, her arms raised over her head, ready to catapult her body into its first tumbling run, she was herself again. *Hand-hand-feet.* Her roundoff. *Feet.* Her back layout. *Feet.* Her back tuck.

She landed squarely on the beam, her right foot in front of her left in ballet's fourth position. She posed with her arms over her head and smiled toward the ceiling. That was it. Her body was listening again.

Grace felt her confidence build. She let her body do what it always did, let her muscles take her through the routine, let her spirits rise with her body's abilities. *Standing back tuck. Check. Switch leap. Check. Dance poses. Perfect. Second tumbling run. Awesome.*

Everything connected. Everything square.

By the time she landed her double-tuck dismount, the applause falling down on her like the confetti that would after she was announced to the team, she didn't need to force her smile.

So what if Dad was ignoring her? She always knew exactly what he'd say anyway. She could do it without him. He hadn't said anything to her, hadn't looked at her for over an hour, and she did it. That amazing beam routine. That close-to-perfectly executed and extremely difficult beam routine.

She'd be closer to Leigh and Wilhelmina at the end of the rotation. If one of them messed up a little bit, she'd be ahead.

Take that, Dad. I'll do it without you.

This time her father was there to meet her when Grace exited the podium. "Where was that on bars?" he said.

Grace shrugged and tried to move past him.

He followed her over to her gym bag. "Well, good job," he said.

Grace braced herself for the "But watch—" or the "Only—" that was sure to follow. It didn't. He left it at good job. Then he went over to say something to Wilhelmina's coach.

Grace breathed a sigh of what she knew should be relief but it came out shaky. She watched the back of her father's head and wondered why a simple "Good job" didn't feel like she always thought it would. It felt empty. It felt shallow. It felt . . . like he was giving up on her.

She watched her father walk over to Monica and whisper to her. Is that how Monica always felt?

Grace knew the look on his face: he was critiquing Monica. Whispering to her about unpointed toes or space between her knees or even strategy while Grace sat on a folding chair five feet away, drinking water and telling her empty stomach that it was full.

Leigh mounted the beam with her signature front-tuck mount and the crowd cheered as if it were the hardest trick in the books.

Why don't you ever fall?

LEIGH

I hate you, Leigh told the beam as she stood at the end of it, following her first tumbling pass. She had to have the beam routine of her life in order to be chosen as an all-around gymnast in the Olympics. Right now she was winning the Olympic trials; she had set herself up to make the team, no questions asked. For the third time this summer, she was on top at the biggest meet of her life. She couldn't let the beam defeat her now.

I hate how skinny you are, how high off the ground.

At some point gymnastics came down to math. And the math was on Leigh's side. She couldn't let the beam defeat the math.

I hate those stupid noises you make.

Leigh was less than 180 seconds away from being a front-runner for Olympic gold, from being a gymnast who would be discussed all across not only America, but Russia and Great Britain and Romania and Japan and China. One hundred eighty seconds from magazine covers and television interviews and autographs. This sixteen-foot plank of fake wood could not take all of that away from her.

You can't stop me.

Leigh did her standing tuck on the beam. It said *bang.* But Leigh closed her ears. She did her dance poses, trying to go for a little extra flair, to raise her leg a little higher, to wave her arms a little more confidently. To be her cheerful self, even when she was on the beam. She made her way to the end and took a deep breath. *Don't listen,* she told herself. Just flip.

Leigh felt the air rush by the bottom of her body from her ponytail to her pointed toes as she completed two back handsprings and a back layout. Though she landed squarely, the wall of applause from the crowd was so loud it almost knocked her back off the beam. She smiled. She'd never gotten that much height before.

She followed it up with a long, high flip, a connected switch leap, and an almost perfectly solid full turn. Leigh felt the muscles in her body work to keep her upright and balanced. She felt them flex and release, allowing her to scale the air, defying gravity by more than should be humanly possible.

And she understood. It was good to be big. It was maybe also good to be graceful and balletic like Grace. But for Leigh, it was better to be the linebacker.

Leigh the Linebacker.

She would embrace it. She would use it. She would use it to win Olympic gold in the individual all-around.

So as she began her second tumbling run, Leigh opened her ears again. She let the banging of the beam confirm that she was doing things right. She was flying high above it. She was landing squarely on it. She was a gymnast. She was herself.

Bang. Boom. Bang.

She bathed in the sounds she was making.

Leigh felt every eye in the stadium on her, every mouth in the stadium smiling as she danced the five hundred centimeters down the beam, as she did a standing back tuck, as she leaped and twirled and landed herself at the back of the beam.

She took a deep breath. *Back handspring, back layout, full in–full out. Get enough height to stick the landing.*

Leigh took off with speed and agility and power. She was like a cheetah as she flipped down the length of the beam; she would always land on her feet; she always knew where the surface was; she could never mess up because her muscles and her power wouldn't let her.

After her layout, her feet released her off the end of the beam, straight into the air above it. The audience gasped at how high Leigh got. She tucked her body into a ball and turned it over with a twist. First her head was up, then her head was facing away from the beam, then it was facing the flag behind her, then it was down, then *bang.*

A hammer bashed into her forehead just above her right eye. Her body stiffened and her blood was sharp and painful, like razors running through her veins, and her eye was going to fall out and roll on the floor, that floor, which was coming up beneath her limbs much too quickly, and then, thankfully, she blacked out.

CAMILLE

Camille sat with her warmed-up bottom balancing on the edge of the toilet bowl and hissed, "What are you doing here?" into her cell phone. Her breath was short from the floor routine she'd just nailed.

"Supporting you," Bobby answered, like it was no big deal.

"You told me you weren't coming," Camille whispered.

"I think you're making a mistake," Bobby said. "But I love you, Camille. I want to be with you, even when you make your mistakes."

"Bobby . . ." Camille didn't know what to say. Yesterday she'd wanted nothing more than for Bobby to show up, to call her, to text her, to anything. But now that he was here, she felt confused. He'd broken up with her right before one of the biggest events of her life. That didn't feel loving. She couldn't magically morph back into the person she was before he said they were breaking up.

And even in that moment, things hadn't been perfect. When was the last time the air between them felt like magic?

"I thought you'd be happy to see me," Bobby said quietly.

"I am," Camille said. Though she wasn't sure it was true.

"You don't sound like it," Bobby said.

Camille sighed. "Let's talk about this later, okay? I'm not even supposed to be on the phone right now."

"Come on, Camille. I came all the way down here and . . . I was hoping maybe you'd let me . . . take you home?"

"I'll talk to you about it after the meet, okay, Bobby?"

"No, Cam, that's not what I mean. I mean, don't finish the meet. Just leave. With me. Now."

Camille thought for a second. She pictured herself leaving the meet. She pictured the locker room without her at the end of the night. Everyone who was named to the team would want to go. She could stay right here. It would solve so many problems but it still didn't seem quite right.

Camille heard the door to the bathroom open and breathed a *shhh* into the phone as she listened to someone else wash her hands and then leave.

"I gotta go, Bobby," she said. "They'll disqualify me if I keep talking to you now."

Bobby chuckled. "Then let's keep talking," he said.

Camille immediately saw a picture of her mother in her mind's eye. Her mother in her faded robe, bent over a dinner Camille had made that she refused to eat.

Why did that sound like something her mother would say? Her mother would never tell her to skip a meet, but something about it was familiar.

"If we stay on the phone," Bobby was saying, "you'll get kicked out of the meet and you'll be free."

Camille wanted to be free. But she didn't want to be banished from gymnastics. What was she yearning to break free from?

She thought about those college athletes dancing on the sidelines. She'd never get to dance along, but that's what she wanted.

Bobby was trying to be funny, so Camille laughed to rush him off the phone. "I doubt I'd ever even be welcome on a college team if I left like that."

"But," Bobby said quietly, "I thought you were going to go to college with me."

That was it. Something bright lit up in Camille's brain. She was shocked she'd never seen it before. The way Bobby fed her pizza and soda and made her feel like she wouldn't look good without the extra pounds. The way he convinced her to trick her mother into believing in her second-rate coach. The way he put off college for a year so that she would go with him. The way he broke up with her and when she didn't come running back, showed up where he swore he wouldn't.

It wasn't that Bobby thought gymnastics was bad for Camille.

It was that Bobby didn't want to share Camille with gymnastics.

"You're manipulating me," Camille said quietly. *Like Mom does.*

They were both using their relationship with her as leverage to convince Camille that she had to do what they wanted.

No wonder it was so hard for her to figure out what she wanted for herself.

"What?" Bobby was saying. "No, Cam, I—"

If her mother hadn't been so manipulative, Camille probably wouldn't be here, and she might be happier. But there was nothing she could do about that now. For now, she had to think about what to do from here, how to proceed. And she didn't want to be an Olympian, but she also didn't want to be a quitter. Not with a body that could fly over the vault like hers could.

"I'm going over the vault," she said.

"Don't do it, Cam," he said. "Run away with me. You don't want to be a gymnast anymore."

"Maybe not forever, but right now I do. Right now I'm at the Olympic trials. I shouldn't be hiding in the bathroom talking to my ex-boyfriend," she said.

"Ex?" he said, like that was the part that mattered.

"I'm one of the best gymnasts in the world. I *am* the best vaulter in the world. And it's awesome to be the best at something. So, whether or not I should be, I'm here, and while I'm here, I will enjoy it."

"Camille—" He tried to protest again.

"No," she said. "Not now. I have an Amanar to land."

Camille hung up before he could say anything else. She tucked her phone into the waistband of her warmups and rushed back into the arena.

She was feeling better than ever when she jogged through that gray tunnel. She was running past the bars toward the beam, wishing she could keep running until she went down the runway and catapulted herself over the vault. Out of the corner of her eye she was watching Leigh flip-flop through a dismount and then—

It was like slow motion. Leigh's body went straight up instead of up-and-out. Leigh's head plunged toward the beam. Camille tried to run. She felt like a million tiny wires were wrapped around her wrists and ankles, dragging her backward, as she fought to get to Leigh in time. She didn't know what she would do. What could she do? But she needed to get there.

"No!" Camille shouted. She shouted so loudly that all the spectators and gymnasts and coaches who had been watching floor routines turned to see it happen.

Leigh's head whacked into the corner of the beam. Leigh's body went stiff, then fell four feet and crashed like a baby bird on the sidewalk. A deafening *pop* rattled through the stadium. Leigh had popped.

Leigh didn't move.

Camille didn't, either. She stood stock-still between the bars and the beam. Her legs were still, one in front of the other. Her arms were frozen in front of her like her hands were trying to push the reality of the scene away from her.

"This can't be happening. This cannot be happening *again*," she mumbled to herself. Over and over.

It was all her fault. She'd freaked Leigh out. She'd messed up the meet for Wilhelmina and for Leigh and still managed to send herself to the Olympics. This was not how it was supposed to be.

Camille saw Leigh's coach signal for more help. She saw the paramedics get her on a stretcher. She saw them carefully pass the stretcher from the podium onto the main level.

She did not move until she was in the way of Leigh and the four men who were carrying her.

She wanted to deny everything she'd said before about comebacks. Even though it was true, she wanted to take it all back and let Leigh make up her own mind.

She wanted to apologize.

She wanted to clutch Leigh while they talked about how hard it is to give up the one and only thing that defined your entire childhood.

"Where are you taking her?" Camille yelled out once they were almost past her.

One of the paramedics shouted, "Johns Hopkins."

Camille had to get there. Fast.

WILHELMINA

The arena was freezing. As if when they carried Leigh out through the gray tunnel under the bleachers, she took all the warmth with her. No one was moving. No one was on floor. Wilhelmina was not on beam. The coaches were not walking toward their gymnasts. The gymnasts had not turned their heads. The stands above them were still, because none of the forty-five thousand spectators were thinking about the bathroom or the snack bar or even calling out to their own beloved gymnast.

Instead, ninety thousand eyes stared at the black hole through which Leigh the Gymnast had disappeared.

Wilhelmina wasn't sure if it was seconds or minutes or hours or days before she started to feel the energy shift back into the room. Some of the people in the seats wiggled or sneezed or whispered to each other or answered their phones. Some of the gymnasts shook their heads. Some of the coaches put an arm around their athletes.

Wilhelmina didn't move.

She could see the gym in front of her, technically. She could see Annie climb the floor podium and slowly step toward the chalk. She could feel Kerry's hands touch her shoulders lightly.

But the image of Leigh's head snapping back with the force of the beam blocked everything out. Leigh's neck about to crack and her skull about to roll across the floor. Leigh's leg folded under her hips at a grotesque angle when she landed. Leigh's toes still pointed even when she was being transferred to the stretcher, unconscious. All Wilhelmina could hear was the sound that ripped through the stadium when Leigh's skull hit the wood of the balance beam.

She could have died.

Wilhelmina knew she didn't. But still.

"It's your turn," Kerry said softly in Wilhelmina's ear. "Get your nine-point-five."

Wilhelmina looked at Kerry. Was she serious? Did they really think Wilhelmina could climb onto the beam right now like nothing happened? Would Wilhelmina be expected to perform even if her fellow gymnast *had* died?

But somehow, making her jaw work—asking Kerry how she could expect Wilhelmina to get up on that tiny four-foot-high platform and be powerful and beautiful and perfect right after another girl's entire world had shattered—seemed even more impossible than flipping and spinning.

So Wilhelmina took a step toward the chalk. She was surprised her body knew how to move.

Grace was standing next to the chalk bowl. She might have been the only person in the stadium who had stayed still longer than Wilhelmina.

When Wilhelmina dipped her hands into the bleach-white chalk, Grace turned her head to look at her. Wilhelmina was shocked to see tears dancing in her eyes.

Grace opened her mouth.

But before she could say anything—before Grace could yell at Wilhelmina for thinking more about gymnastics and competition than Leigh's life—Wilhelmina spit out the words, "I don't want to hear it. It should have been you."

For a second they were both shocked. It was so unlike Wilhelmina to stoop to mean comments in the middle of a meet, at least outside her head. But she hadn't intended the words to be cruel. It *could* have been Grace.

It could have *more easily* been Grace. Grace was starving herself into nothing when she could have been the best in the world. It made Wilhelmina hot-angry.

Even more surprising, Grace nodded. "I know," she said. "I'm a terrible friend."

Wilhelmina was too mad for the pity party. She wiped her chalky hands on her thighs, leaving white streaks on her muscles. "That's not what I meant. I know, okay? You haven't been eating. It's so stupid, Grace. Do you want to get hurt? Do you want to make sure you'll never be as good as you used to be? You can't survive in this sport if you don't eat."

Grace had tears in her eyes. But she didn't yell. She said, "Use it."

"Huh?" Wilhelmina forced the syllable out of her mouth.

Grace said, "Use it. Use your anger. Leigh would. Leigh would use it."

So Wilhelmina nodded. Gymnastics had been unfair to Leigh, too. She finally wasn't alone. Leigh had been minutes away from winning the Olympic trials, and now she was, at the very best, disqualified. And Wilhelmina had been handed the massive job of performing right after her.

She took a big, shaky breath and climbed the stairs to the podium.

She looked up into the stands, hoping to find Davion. Hoping he could give her a wink or a smile. Something to build her up.

But her eyes landed instead on Katja. And the woman very carefully stared at Wilhelmina and shook her head back and forth, back and forth. As if she was telling Wilhelmina not to do well on beam.

And Wilhelmina didn't care. She knew she wouldn't go to the Olympics for this woman, no matter what. Even if she did make the team now that Grace seemed broken and Leigh had fallen, she wouldn't get to bask in the glory of it. She'd have to deal with Katja constantly putting her down, telling the media and anyone who would listen that Wilhelmina was only an alternate promoted too soon.

Wilhelmina deserved to go to the Olympics honestly. Like a star. With her country behind her. Katja would never let that happen, even if Wilhelmina won the meet today.

So this was it. Two more routines. Then she was through.

She squinted at the balance beam until the images of the past few minutes were blocked from her vision. And she mounted.

STANDINGS
AFTER THE SEVENTH ROTATION

1. Wilhelmina Parker   103.780

2. Grace Cooper   102.930

3. Georgette Paulson   102.704

4. Monica Chase   100.305

5. Maria Vasquez   100.230

6. Kristin Jackson   99.350

7. Annie Simms   98.655

8. Natalie Rice   94.550

9. Samantha Soloman   60.405

10. Olivia Corsica   59.550

11. Camille Abrams   42.500

12. Leigh Becker   WITHDRAWN

Eighth Rotation

LEIGH

I'm lucky to be alive, Leigh told herself.

It doesn't matter, Leigh told herself.

Her body felt exhausted between the too-starched, too-white sheets of her hospital bed; her muscles were too tired to remember they were in pain. An hour ago she'd been planning to flip and twist and contort this body in ways that would delight the judges and the Olympic selection committee. Now Leigh couldn't imagine turning her head to tell her mother, who was trying not to weep at Leigh's bedside, that she was squeezing her hand too tightly.

She wanted to ask her mother why she was crying—was it about the Olympics? Or was it the residual fear from Leigh's fall? Or was it because Leigh's whole life up to now had been pointless? Was she crying because they'd moved to Virginia? Because Leigh had given up flute and soccer and every possible after-school activity to end up in this hospital bed?

Leigh wanted her to be quiet already.

There was a knock on the door and Leigh was suddenly able to move her head. She swung it to look at the door and ignored the way a stabbing pain fired through her forehead. She was hoping for the doctor to come into the room and finally end the waiting.

She was hoping for good news.

The pain in her head was a good sign. If it was a concussion . . .

Stop, she told herself. *You're lucky to be alive.*

It was only Leigh's dad. He handed her mom a cup of coffee and she stared at it, spacey.

"How ya feeling, Leigh-bee?" he asked. He put his hand on her cheek.

"Okay," she said. "I feel okay now."

It was true. Other than the top of her eye, which still felt like it was being rammed with a sword, she felt usual, like she had just finished a meet. Her muscles were tired but that was probably only because of the way they stiffened before she passed out. There were currents of pain zipping back and forth under her left knee cap, but that was normal. That was why gymnasts walked around with bags of ice taped to their torsos and shins and elbows and wrists and back. Zipping pain was an athlete's silent reality.

"I feel okay," she repeated again. *I feel like a gymnast.*

Her parents looked at her doubtfully.

"You know what's going on, right, Leigh-bee? What being here means?" her dad said.

Leigh sighed. "Yeah. It doesn't really matter how I'm feeling."

His eyebrows jumped. They hated when she said things like this. Things that made it seem like she was all gymnast and nothing else.

"I mean it doesn't matter what the doctor says. I'm out no matter what. When I left the Metroplex, I disqualified myself for the team. That's what they said in our meeting before the meet started."

Her parents nodded, looking relieved. But Leigh clutched hope to her chest. Maybe it was only a concussion. If it was, they'd change the rules for her. The USAG changed rules constantly. They changed the rules so much that it was impossible to remember them all, to predict what would happen one year based on the last year, to determine how many gymnasts would be on a team or how many would qualify for the all-around or how many would automatically qualify based on the trials. Nothing ever stayed the same. Everyone felt like victims of the USAG's and FIG's shifting policies, but where there were victims of circumstances, weren't there always the opposite? Wasn't there always someone for whom the unfairness bore advantage?

Well, that would be Leigh. They wouldn't let a silly concussion keep America from winning team gold. Surely, they'd want Leigh on the team once she was cleared to compete.

They'd announce five gymnasts tonight. Grace, for sure. Wilhelmina, now. Camille and Samantha and Georgette. Then, once they learned that Leigh had nothing more than a concussion, that after a day or so of rest she'd be completely fine, they'd put her back on the team.

She'd been winning when she nose-dived into the beam, after all. They wouldn't punish her for leaving the Metroplex. Not on a stretcher.

"Let's talk about what we'll do when we get home," her dad said, forcing a smile. "There are so many things you haven't gotten a chance to try. We'll find new activities that you can enjoy."

He was endlessly cheerful, annoyingly optimistic. This is probably how Grace often felt about her, but now, when she was in a hospital bed awaiting the verdict on whether all her sacrifices had been smacked out of relevance eye-socket-first, the optimism was grating. Or it was wrong.

Leigh was optimistic, too. She would be a gymnast again. Next week or the day after tomorrow she'd be back to conditioning and spinning around the bars and twisting over the vault.

"What'll be your first meal when you're free from the nutrition plan?" her dad asked. "Ice cream?"

"Pancakes?" her mom added, sniffling.

"I'm tired," Leigh said.

She shut her eyes. She imagined herself in an Olympic leo, climbing to the top of the podium as they played the American national anthem because she had won the women's all-around.

"Leigh," her father said. "We know you want to go

back, honey. We're hoping for good news for you, too. But . . . it'll be easier to be . . . to be yourself . . . if it's not so public."

Her mother squeezed her hand even harder. Leigh was worried it would be even more injured than her knee.

"It's true," her mom said. "You might be able to come out in school, you know? If you have to be out of the gym for a while. You can do it quietly, right? Maybe date a few girls."

For a second, Leigh let the picture drift in her mind. Herself and a cute girl from her school all dressed up for the next dance. A nice girl who messaged her the way Dylan had last night. A hot girl who kissed her like—

But no.

Phil said it was all about focus. She would focus now. She would focus so hard it would fix whatever might be but probably wasn't wrong with her body. She'd be like Grace. She'd use her mind to put her body back together.

A knock at the door, and her eyes flew open.

The doctor came in, her sandy-brown hair falling across her face so Leigh couldn't even see her eyes. She studied a clipboard, which rested against her middle, between the flaps of her white lab coat. She didn't even bother to look up at Leigh when she said it. She didn't even think about the words as they left her mouth.

"The good news is you'll walk again," she said. Flat. Unfeeling. Hardly even negative. Like she was telling

Leigh that the light blue of her hospital gown was the wrong color on her.

"Walk again?" Her mother gasped.

The doctor nodded curtly. "You will. And without surgery. We were concerned based on the swelling of your knee when you came in that you might have torn your ACL, but it turns out you only subluxed the kneecap."

Only, Leigh thought. She said *only*. Only was good. Only meant it wouldn't change her life too much.

Leigh had done it. She'd focused hard enough.

As if the doctor could hear her, she said, "You'll recover. This should not affect you long-term."

Leigh's heart was doing a jig in her chest, she was so happy.

"We want to take an X-ray in the morning, once the swelling goes down, to be sure the tendons heal. And you have a bad concussion, so we're going to keep you overnight."

The doctor turned to go.

"Wait!" Leigh called out.

The doctor turned back around. Leigh tried not to see how she was tapping her thigh impatiently.

"You said I'll recover. But when? When will I recover?"

"We will send you to an orthopedist when you get back to the DC area."

I'm not going to the DC area, Leigh corrected her. *Rome. I'm going to Rome.*

"If it turns out your knee is subluxed as we are predicting, you will need to be completely off it for about two weeks, then we will slowly transition back into exercise with a knee brace. You'll be in a brace while exercising for a few years."

"Years?" Her mother gasped.

"Weeks?" Leigh almost screamed.

The doctor finally looked up. "You'll live a normal life," she said.

"But—" Leigh cut herself off before she finished. She snapped her jaw shut.

But I don't want a normal life.

"You were inches away from a much more bleak conversation," the doctor concluded.

She had glasses perched on a tiny nose. She was tall and lanky and her nose didn't fit her body at all. She didn't look like that much, Leigh decided. She didn't look like she was always right about everything.

"And?" she said, when Leigh still hadn't said anything.

Finally, Leigh whispered, "The Olympics."

"Oh," the doctor said. She clicked her pen against her clipboard. "Yes. Well, there's always next time."

MONICA

After her floor warm-up, Monica found herself sitting between her terrifying coach and her terrifying teammate. Grace hadn't warmed up at all. Almost no one seemed to care about the floor exercise anymore.

Seeing Leigh fall had cracked everyone's focus.

Monica still wanted to finish this meet up well. She still had that word running through her mind: *alternate.* But it was scary now, too. She'd never heard a human body pop before.

Grace looked at her. "You should be warming up."

Monica shrugged. *I did warm up. YOU should warm up.*

"I . . . I can't. I can't warm up," Grace said as if she'd heard Monica's thoughts.

Monica lowered her eyebrows. "Why?"

"It's my fault," Grace said quietly.

Ted whipped his head out of his hands. "Don't say that, Gracie," he commanded. Then he shuddered. "It's mine."

"Listen," she said, her voice shaky, like she was going to cry. "I made her fall. It was me."

Monica started to get up, feeling suddenly like she was in the middle of a family moment, but Grace put her hand on Monica's elbow and pulled her back into the chair.

Grace looked at Monica, her eyes so tense, her mouth so serious, Monica froze and stared back. "I said this awful thing last night. I totally betrayed her. I'm sure that's what Leigh was thinking about," Grace was saying desperately. "And even worse: I wanted her to fall. I wanted to win so badly, I wanted her to fall. I *wished* for it. I think I accidentally *prayed* for it."

Monica's eyes widened. She opened her mouth. What could she say?

"You're wrong, Gracie," Ted's voice said behind Monica's head. He was still looking at his shoes and Grace was still staring at Monica and Monica decided to go back to being the quiet little mousy girl and try to be invisible to get through this moment. "It's my fault," Grace's dad was saying. "Why do you think you wanted her to fall? I'm the one who taught you. Who told you all those things. *There are no friends on the gym floor.* What kind of lesson is that? What kind of coach am I?" He paused. "Or father?"

He used that word like a weapon against himself.

Monica's heart was beating so quickly. Her quiet time was negated as soon as Leigh went down, but any remnants of calm were erased by this bizarre argument she was suddenly filtering.

"You need a new coach, Grace," Ted said. "I need to focus on being your parent. Your dad."

Grace, shocked, finally let go of Monica's elbow. A white ring stained her skin where her teammates' fingers had been.

Suddenly Wilhelmina was in front of them. "Monica," she said softly. "They called your name. You're up."

She hadn't even heard her own name.

She stood. But then she turned. She wasn't afraid of them anymore. In fact, in some ways, she was smarter than them.

"You know," she said to Grace and Ted. "Neither of you did that to Leigh. You aren't gods."

Father and daughter stared back at her. She wasn't

sure if they heard her. But Ted reached out and put a hand on her forearm. "Don't fall, Monica, okay? Don't fall."

Don't fall. The words, her old goal, took on a new meaning.

Monica smiled. It was almost like she had taught Ted something.

She climbed the stairs to the floor podium, visualizing her routine on repeat in her brain. She was about to turn herself upside down seventeen times. She was about to pound her legs and her arms, her ankles and her wrists, her back and—potentially—her head.

Don't fall.

God, why did they do this to themselves? Why did she spend her entire life learning to do the tricks that could potentially keep her from ever doing them again? Why did she spend all of yesterday wanting to be Leigh when Leigh could un-Leigh herself so quickly?

Monica's floor music started and she danced into the middle of the floor.

Don't fall.

But Monica could feel the tension, the depression, the worry filtering out of her body through her pointed toes, her arced arms, her soft smile, her pliés and split leaps. Her muscles flexed and sprung, balanced and flew.

She backed into the corner, her heels lined up in front of the floor's boundary, ready to flip herself around the mat for her first tumbling run.

Don't fall.

She said it one last time. Monica was relaxed now. She was relieved that she didn't have as far as Leigh to fall. She wasn't four feet up on the beam. And more importantly, her name wasn't at the top of the scoreboard.

Monica didn't fall.

GRACE

Grace landed her first tumbling run on a twisted left foot. Her right foot landed behind her left ankle so her body was contorted, and she stumbled trying to straighten her stance. She felt the fuzzy floor on the soles of her feet as she took step after step backward for what felt like minutes, hours, days to regain her balance. By the time she found it, she was so far out of bounds, she had to jog back to the floor and put her hands over her head.

Her face burned with embarrassment.

You shouldn't even be here, she told herself. *You should fall on your head.*

Grace moved into her dance positions, stumbling on a simple full turn. She could almost feel her father turn his back, turn away from the Olympic disaster that was his daughter and his athlete. His athlete who wasn't even his anymore. She tried not to care.

But she did.

You're a terrible person, she told her herself as she backed her ankles into the southwestern corner of the floor.

You're a terrible person, but you could be winning the Olympic trials again.

Shut up!

She saw the red flag go up. She'd gone out of bounds again, this time on a simple step. She was imploding.

It wasn't on purpose. She was trying to focus. Even if it made her a terrible person, she was trying to hold on to her spot, to get ahead of Wilhelmina again.

Wilhelmina was right about Grace, but Grace wanted to prove her wrong anyway. Grace wanted to prove that she could beat the girl who was trying to disprove Katja, even without eating. She wanted to prove that she could be the best, she could go to the Olympics, even without eating.

The rest of them needed food like Wilhelmina said, but Grace was different. Grace was so much gymnast, she was practically magical.

It wouldn't be fair to go to the Olympics while Leigh sat rotting on a couch and watched her on TV. Not when it was maybe her fault that Leigh wasn't focused on beam, that Leigh was obsessed with her stupid secret instead of thinking about her gymnastics, that Leigh was . . . that Leigh was . . . where she was right now.

The truth was Grace didn't care about what was fair and what wasn't. Grace was awful, and even in her awfulness she couldn't force herself to think more about her friend in the hospital than her own gymnastics career.

Because without her gymnastics, who would she be?

A girl who loved her brother but had no idea how to communicate with him? A girl who was totally alone in a house with no mom? A girl who never had anything to say to her father when he wasn't her coach? Without gymnastics, Grace would disappear.

She tripped out of a full turn.

It wouldn't matter. No one thought the USA could win gold in Rome without both Grace and Leigh; there was no way the Olympic selection committee would make a team without either one of them on it. And without Leigh, Grace would certainly get a chance to compete in the all-around.

Grace thought this even as she lurched through another landing of a tumbling run. She managed not to go out of bounds, but she was totally off at this point. The music was two full bars ahead of her. She had to improvise some dance moves, move parallel to the northern boundary of the floor and launch right into her final tumbling run.

Her brain flipped back and forth between Leigh's broken body and Wilhelmina's stern voice.

But it wasn't because she hadn't eaten enough that she was imploding. That couldn't be it. She wasn't focused, that was all.

It wasn't fair for her to focus, not fair to Leigh who didn't have anything to focus on anymore.

It didn't matter what was fair. It didn't matter if everyone fell on their heads. It didn't matter if she starved or if everyone starved. Grace was scaring herself but if she was honest, it might not matter if everyone died.

She wanted to be an Olympian.

Even if it meant being without Leigh. Even if that was all her fault.

WILHELMINA

As Wilhelmina watched Grace cave into herself on the floor, she found it impossible not to think about the huge hole, the missing link, the gap that Leigh had left. The spot that would need to be filled.

Everyone there could see it clearly. Not just in the empty folding chair where Leigh would normally be sitting. Not just in the silences that would usually be filled with Leigh yelling, "Come on, Grace!" You could see the hole in Grace's gymnastics. You could see it in Maria's tentative landings, in Kristin's lip-biting, in Monica's sad brown eyes. You could see it all over.

Wilhelmina had managed a close-to-perfect beam routine, managed a 9.587 execution score, even right after Leigh changed the way they were all thinking. And still, she wouldn't be going anywhere. Right now, Wilhelmina was the best gymnast in the room. She knew it. She was better than this shell of Grace, and Leigh was gone. She was the best. And she was about to perform for the last time.

Even if Leigh's injury meant Wilhelmina won the meet. Even if that happened, Wilhelmina wouldn't go.

She didn't want to go to the Olympics and be the bane of Katja's existence if Katja could tell the other countries' coaches and espnW and Kerry and even Wilhelmina herself that she was only there because of Leigh's fall.

Wilhelmina wanted to go honestly. She deserved to go honestly. She wouldn't go as some second-choice alternative who had to talk about how great Leigh was to every reporter the whole time.

Her whole life Wilhelmina had settled for less than she deserved. She wouldn't do that for the Olympics.

Stop! she told herself.

She bent down to stretch her hamstrings, to stop looking at Grace, to stop thinking about Leigh, to tell herself, *Nine-point-five, nine-point-five, nine-point-five.*

One more nine-point-five and I get to kiss Davion. To be a real girl. To spend the rest of my summer making out in the back row of the movies and exploring beaches and theme parks with my hot, goofy boyfriend.

Grace spun on the floor in front of them, stumbling over her toes. Wilhelmina was scared for her. She was in a more dangerous situation than Leigh. But Wilhelmina couldn't do anything else about it, not until later.

Kerry came up beside Wilhelmina and she straightened up.

"Nine-point-five, huh," Kerry said. "So far so good." She was smiling, but sad.

"That's the plan," Wilhelmina said.

She hated that she'd have to hurt Kerry when she chose to slip out the back gym door.

Kerry nodded and stared into the distance. Grace's floor music plunked to its conclusion and there was a spattering of polite applause throughout the arena. Grace looked close to tears as she exited the podium.

"There's another thing," Kerry said. "Now."

Wilhelmina's heart fell. In about thirty seconds her name would be announced and she'd have to chalk up and focus. She was looking forward to it. To forgetting the way Leigh's head slammed into the beam. To being able to choose her last routine when her competitor hadn't had that choice.

So she shook her head. She didn't need Kerry to suddenly turn cutthroat like Ted. She didn't need the added pressure of trying to climb on top of an injured gymnast the way others had tried to climb on her tired body for the past three years.

It was impossible not to think about the new hole in the Olympic roster. But Wilhelmina and Kerry didn't have to talk about it.

That's not what Kerry said.

"This is a sad stadium, now, huh? Everyone is thinking about the poor girl. Everyone is thinking about the end of dreams, about the price of your kind of a life, a childhood."

Wilhelmina stopped shaking her head and studied the dark blue eyes of her wise coach.

"Maybe if you put on a performance like bars today for you, maybe you will help everyone smile for a little, huh? You can show everyone the joy of your kind of life.

Maybe you can give Leigh credit for the way she spent hers so far?"

And that was a good enough goal for Wilhelmina's last routine.

She took a step toward the podium thinking Kerry might be her hero in life, not only in gymnastics.

Get ready for some real gymnastics, she prepared the crowd. *Get ready for joy. Leigh, this is for you.*

CAMILLE

I have to get out of here. Camille turned her phone over in her palm like a precious stone. She looked over her shoulder to see that yes, Bobby was in the stands.

Camille went to the side of the floor to cheer on Wilhelmina. She would watch her friend clinch the meet, then she'd leave.

Camille wanted to go over the vault. She didn't want to go to the Olympics. But she was already here. She wanted to spend the ten seconds it would take to give herself the thrill of landing that Amanar.

But she couldn't now. She had to get out of the room. The depression was stifling. It put weights on Grace's ankles so she stumbled all over the floor. It curved all their coaches' lips into permanent frowns. It slowed down the floor music; it divided the clapping; it hung in a taut tension over the shoulders of the fans and the coaches and the families and the gymnasts.

Camille had to get to Leigh. Camille was responsible. And Camille was the only person who knew what she was going through, who could comfort her. Also, Camille *could* get there. She was probably the only person in the entire room who had a spectator who would drive her away from here, who would support her choice to leave.

But she didn't want to ask him for something. She didn't want to owe him anything anymore.

Camille studied the face of her phone. She opened up a text window and typed letters and deleted them. She did that again. She did it again. She had about three letters when something made her turn and face the meet.

It was a sudden sigh of relief from the collective population of the gym.

It was a loosening of the shoulders, a straightening of the frowns, a hoot here, a yelp there. It was one person, then more, then more enjoying themselves again.

Camille felt her arms part and her hands come together, smacking her phone in the middle of her own clapping. She was joining in the pulse of the audience as Wilhelmina went through her first series of upbeat dance moves in the middle of the blue floor. Wilhelmina opened her arms and arced them so that in one swift move she was able to point to every spectator and coach and gymnast, every individual in the room, and their clapping got louder.

Camille dropped her phone, turned off her brain, and watched her friend. She gasped as Wilhelmina leaped and flipped off the floor. Five feet in the air, then ten, then twelve. She whooped with the audience when Wilhelmina landed her double Arabian. Camille stuck out her hip and waved her arms in unison with Wilhelmina during her second dance series. She skipped and leaped on the sidelines as her roommate did the moves on the floor. She squealed and jumped when Wilhelmina took her final pose and stood smiling at the audience, her chest pumping to suck in air, her eyes shining with something between laughter and tears.

A few minutes later Wilhelmina sat pulling on her warm-ups next to where Camille stood.

"I'm sorry for cutting you off earlier," Wilhelmina said.

But Camille didn't care anymore. "How did you do that?" she asked.

Wilhelmina shrugged.

"You changed everything," Camille whispered, sitting down next to her.

Wilhelmina flashed Camille a smile. "I don't know," she said. "I was just . . . enjoying it."

"I have to get out of here," Camille whispered. She felt like Wilhelmina could help her, like Wilhelmina could do anything. "I have to get to Leigh."

Wilhelmina's eyebrows knitted together. "The Olympics—"

"I don't want to go," Camille cut her off. "I'm tired. I'm done." Her own jaw dropped along with her friend's. She couldn't believe she'd said it out loud. Finally. Her shoulders felt light, like she had never put on all of that weight that she'd worked so hard to keep. "I never wanted this kind of comeback." Camille studied her friend. "Maybe this makes me selfish or crazy or something, but . . ." She trailed off.

Wilhelmina nodded, like this made sense. "A day ago . . ." she said. "A few hours ago, even, I would have hated you for saying that. But . . . I get it."

Camille nodded. They'd be calling her name any minute now. Once they did, she'd have to get to the vault and go over it. She'd be sealing her fate if she didn't run away soon. She flipped open her phone.

"I'm not going, either," Wilhelmina said.

Camille froze. "What?" she asked. She didn't have time to hear the answer. But she needed to hear it anyway.

"I . . . I don't know," Wilhelmina said. "I haven't seen the scoreboard. I'm probably not going to win and if I don't, Katja won't choose me. I don't want to be an alternate. And if I do win because Leigh fell . . . well, Katja hates me. She'll tell the whole world I'm only there because Leigh fell. She'll make me miserable. It's just . . . It's so unfair."

Camille shook her head furiously. Alternate? What was Mina thinking? She was *winning* the meet. *She would have beaten Leigh anyway,* Camille thought, *if you added up Leigh's scores from yesterday.*

"Or even if they put me on the roster because Leigh won't be on it. Or you. Or whatever . . . I'm . . . I can't do that to myself. I deserve to go honestly."

"Honestly?" Camille asked. What did that even mean? "I—" Camille started. Then she shook her head. She couldn't get into a long conversation right now. She had to get out of there. "Okay. Look. Text me from that locker room. Or call me? Before you announce that decision, talk to me."

"Why?" Wilhelmina asked.

"I—I'm sorry. I—I have to . . . go."

"What's the rush?" Wilhelmina said.

"I have to get to Leigh," Camille said. "I can . . . I can help."

"Oh," Wilhelmina said. "Then you can tell me if she's okay?"

Camille nodded. "So . . . I guess . . ." Camille shrugged. "I guess . . . I'll call Bobby. I don't want to, but . . . He's here. He'll take me."

"No!" Wilhelmina shouted.

Camille's head shot up.

Wilhelmina was smiling. "Don't call him. Don't give him the satisfaction," she said. "I have a plan."

Camille nodded. Somehow she wasn't surprised that Wilhelmina could figure this out.

"But," Wilhelmina said, "don't you want to go over the vault one more time before you disqualify yourself?"

"Yes," said Camille. "Yes, I do."

Five minutes later, she stood at the end of the vault runway.

I'll stand here again, she told herself. *There will be*

a school that forgives me for quitting this meet to check on a teammate. College gymnastics is all about teams. I'll stand here for University of Florida or Alabama or UCLA or Stanford. I'll be an NCAA vaulter.

It wouldn't be the same, and that was good thing. But she wanted to remember it like this.

Camille closed her eyes to soak in the "Comeback Cammie" chant that was pulsing through the stadium. She let the sixteen-year-old inside her enjoy it for a moment. Then, the twenty-year-old Camille took off on the last elite runway sprint of her life, her hands hit the mat, her feet bounced off the springboard, her elbows launched her higher than ever off the vault, and she spun. She spun in the applause that echoed from the stadium walls. She spun above the ground, both her young self and her older self full of the joy that comes with weightlessness.

And after she landed, she didn't stop walking until she was in the parking lot.

FINAL RESULTS

1. Wilhelmina Parker   119.555

2. Georgette Paulson   117.929

3. Grace Cooper   115.840

4. Monica Chase   115.225

5. Maria Vasquez   114.730

6. Kristin Jackson   113.945

7. Annie Simms   112.515

8. Natalie Rice   108.105

9. Camille Abrams   60.950

10. Samantha Soloman   60.405

11. Olivia Corsica   59.550

12. Leigh Becker   WITHDRAWN

The Verdict

WILHELMINA

Wilhelmina's phone buzzed in the pocket of her warm-up pants as she followed the rest of the gymnasts into the locker room. She lowered herself onto the bench in the back, next to Monica, and snuck her phone into her hand.

Davion: The eagle has landed.

Wilhelmina smiled. She clutched tighter at the happiness she'd felt during that floor routine. She had to keep it. At least until she was alone with her family and the neighbor boys and Kerry. Safe. She'd done the best she could do to be both a good person and a great gymnast. She'd helped the stadium see the joy in gymnastics for Leigh and she'd gotten Camille to Leigh's side. She'd met her 9.5 goal on each apparatus. And she hadn't looked at the score once. Not even now that the meet was over.

Wilhelmina was pretty sure Georgette had won the meet. Georgette had started in third place and had a solid day. But on the off-chance Wilhelmina had won, she wanted to hear it from her enemy herself. She wanted to hear her name come out of Katja's mouth, to see the hatred on her face one last time, to face it down before she said no thanks and left the gym forever.

Wilhelmina was calm in this tense locker room. Wilhelmina was minutes away from retiring, hours away from her first kiss. But she was calm.

Tonight she'd cry into the privacy of her pillow. Oh, she'd cry. She'd cry because her career was over. She'd cry because any dream worth having would be painful to lose. But that was later.

Now, she had one thing left to do.

"Hey," she whispered to Monica, "you need a new coach. You know that, right?"

Monica nodded. "Yeah," she said.

"You don't need to be treated like that. There are nice coaches out there," Wilhelmina said.

Monica nodded. She looked nervous. Everyone in the room was nervous, probably, expect for Wilhelmina.

"You should talk to Kerry," she said.

Now Monica smiled, surprised. Wilhelmina smiled, too. She was glad Monica was happy, but she wasn't doing this for her new friend. She was doing it for her coach.

"You'd want me as a teammate?" Monica asked.

Oh. Why hadn't she prepared for this question?

She turned to whisper into Monica's ear. "I'm done, Monica. I'm done. And Kerry needs a new star. She could make you one. You have time. But I . . . I can't."

Monica's eyebrows lowered into the most confused

look and Wilhelmina panicked. She'd said too much. Before she could backpedal, before she could ask Monica to keep it quiet until she had a chance to tell Kerry herself, the selection committee came through the locker room door.

"Quiet, quiet!" Katja shouted, even though it was already silent as a grave in the room.

"First, we all need to congratulate the athlete who has placed automatically onto the team," she said, stone-faced. "And she is Wilhelmina Parker."

Mina's jaw dropped and the locker room filled with a smattering of applause. Her brain rewound through the day, through every thought she'd had, through everything she'd felt, and tried to make it all make sense.

I won, she told herself. *I actually won.*

"Come stand by me," Katja said.

"I—" Wilhelmina stood. "I—" She was trying to speak but no one was listening. She was trying to say, "That's it. I'm done. I retire."

But Wilhelmina was surrounded by naked hope. Now there were gymnasts looking at her, wishing they were her, the same way she had looked for years at Camille and others. Wilhelmina couldn't quit in this moment, in this locker room. These girls would start to hate her the way she hated them.

It was confusing. Everything in her life had been unfair until this moment. And everything would be unfair from this moment forward. This was the one moment she should be enjoying. And Katja was making that impossible. Or the hope radiating from these other girls was making it impossible. Or something. Something was making this moment different from what it should be.

Mina should be allowed to be happy. But she was confused.

Monica was hugging Wilhelmina. Wilhelmina was frozen.

"Get up there," Monica said.

But as Wilhelmina walked toward Katja, the locker room swung dangerously in her vision. Georgette had to reach out and catch her.

"Overwhelmed?" Georgette whispered with the joyful tone of someone who was sure she was about to be chosen for the Olympic team and treated fairly once she got there.

Wilhelmina managed to make it to the front of the room and stood next to Katja. She focused on kissing Davion. She couldn't begin to think of the enormous task she had ahead of her now: quitting even when she'd won the trials and made the team. She was an Olympic athlete and her life still wasn't fair.

"And now," Katja said, "will each of today's athletes please come forward?"

Wilhelmina watched as the girls slowly rose from the bleachers or the floor or the walls they were leaning against. She watched Maria step carefully over a bench and stand, facing Wilhelmina. She watched Grace fall in line next to Maria, Monica next to Grace, Kristin next to Monica. Annie. Natalie, Samantha, Olivia. Their eyes bore into Wilhelmina's heart and she was almost knocked over by the solid wall of hope standing in front of her.

Each girl here wanted what Wilhelmina had just gotten. What Wilhelmina was about to give up.

Because she *was* about to give it up. She deserved something better than this. Right?

Then she saw it. It was Grace who started it. Grace, the broken girl.

Grace raised her arms so they were at ninety-degree angles, flipped over her hands, and offered up her palms to Monica and Maria. Within seconds they were a line of gymnasts clinging together, bound by a tangle of fingers and their insurmountable shared hope.

"Alphabetical order. If you hear your name, come stand by me," Katja was saying.

But Wilhelmina didn't want to be on this side anymore. She didn't want to be facing Grace or Monica or Samantha or any of the others when their hearts got broken. She wanted to be with them. She wanted Grace on her team, Monica on her team, Georgette on her team, Kristin on her team, Annie on her team, Samantha on her team, Maria on her team: all of them. She wanted Leigh on her team. It was awful that they had to be divided. They had all worked so hard, all given up so much.

Maybe they all deserved it, or they all deserved better than they were going to get. Maybe that's what made this moment so confusing.

Just as Katja opened her mouth to say the first name,

Wilhelmina broke from her side. She backed into the line of gymnasts and it opened to accept her. She squeezed Grace's hand in her left palm, Monica's in her right, and she sent hopeful vibes to all of them. For a second they were all connected.

Wilhelmina realized they always would be. She would quit the sport. She'd talk to her publicist after this meet and she would make an announcement that she could no longer comply with Katja's rules. She'd be out. But even then, she would still be connected to these girls. She would not be a gymnast anymore, but she would forever be an ex-gymnast. She would always carry the girl gymnast in her bones. And only this chain of girls would ever really understand that.

"The first gymnast selected is . . ." Katja paused for dramatic effect. "Camille Abrams."

Oh yeah.

The locker room was silent and still. Then everyone's heads started whipping back and forth. Wilhelmina looked at the floor and bit her lips to keep herself from grinning. At least Camille had gotten what she deserved. That was one person.

"Where's Camille?" Katja asked the crowd.

Only Wilhelmina knew the answer.

"I . . . I'll go find her!" she said. And she darted out the door before anyone could stop her.

CAMILLE

The smell. It hit her like a wall when she sprinted through the automatic glass doors in the front of the Johns Hopkins Hospital. She wasn't expecting the smell. Of sterilizer and lemon cleaner. Of nursing scrubs washed too many times in discount detergent and of upholstery cleaned so often it was mildewy anyway. Of tile and bright ceiling lights and pure white sneakers.

It was the smell four years ago, the smell of lost dreams.

Camille almost gagged. She ran back out the door and watched as Davion's navy Camry drove up the hospital driveway. She could run after him or call Wilhelmina and tell her to tell him to come back. It wasn't like Leigh was expecting her.

But where would she go? Not to the Olympics; she'd slammed that door shut, thank God. Not to NYU with Bobby.

Camille had nowhere to go. Maybe she had to be back in this smell in order to truly come out of it.

She called her mom. "Camille!" Her mother's voice came through clear and excited. "Camille!"

"Yes, Mom—"

She cut her off. "Did you get it? That vault was the best I've ever seen, did you get it? Are you in the locker room? Did they name the team yet? Oh, I wish I could be with you."

"Mom," Camille said. Her voice was small.

"Oh, honey," Camille could hear her mother's broken heart in her words, in her tone. "Oh no. Oh, no. You did everything you could, right? You vaulted like a champ. I can't believe they wouldn't take you! What does that mean—is Leigh Becker all right after all? We should have known she had the triple-twister. That was sort of dirty of her, don't you think?"

Camille took a deep breath. "Mom, I left. I'm at the hospital."

"What?" Her voice was shocked and worried, more worried than disappointed. Camille felt her heart warming. Maybe her mother did care more about her well-being than her gymnastics.

"No, no," she said quickly. "I'm okay. I'm just . . . I came to see Leigh. I disqualified myself. I . . . I don't think I ever really left that last hospital."

"What?" her mom said.

"I came because I thought Leigh would need me. I thought I'd be the only person who could possibly understand her. And I think she might be the only one who can understand what happened to me, too."

"What?" her mom said again.

She expected her mother to yell. To tell her to get her butt back to the Metroplex and beg forgiveness.

Camille couldn't let Bobby run her life, so she had

dumped him. It wasn't easy, but it was possible. She couldn't dump her own mother. But she couldn't let her run her life, either.

Helen said, "I really wanted you to go to the Olympics." She didn't sound angry. She sounded depressed. That was worse.

"I know, Mom," Camille said. "But I didn't want to go anymore."

"Why? Why couldn't you do this one thing for me?"

Camille didn't want to have to explain this when the smell was everywhere, when she was rushing to get to Leigh, when she was so close to tears. "I want to go to college, Mom," she said. "I want to go now. Or soon. When I'm still sort of the same age as the other people on my team. I want to be a part of something: classes and gymnastics teams and all of that. I want a chance at the parts of school I missed before it's too late."

Helen didn't say anything. Camille could hear her breathing heavily through the phone.

"Is that okay, Mom?"

"It's your life, honey," her mom said flatly.

"Is it?" Camille asked. "Is it my life? Are you going to forgive me for making this call?"

Her mom was speaking so slowly, Camille had the image of her from two years ago. Emaciated. Depressed. "I wanted you . . . I wanted to be . . ." She trailed off.

"I know," Camille said. "But . . . I'm not."

Camille didn't know what to do. She couldn't abandon

her mother. But she couldn't live for her, either.

"Will you come, Mom? Will you meet me at the hospital? It's . . . it smells the same. I need you."

"Okay," Helen said.

"Really?" Camille said.

"If you need me, I'm there. All I want is for you to need me. . . . And without gymnastics . . . you won't need me anymore."

"I need you now, Mom," Camille said.

"Then I'm on my way."

She knew that it wouldn't be easy. That she and her mother would need help turning their relationship into a productive one. That there would be bad days when her mother was bitter and Camille would miss Bobby. But she still breathed a sigh of relief. She'd never known she could ask her mother for anything. Yet her mom was on the way.

Camille held her breath when she went back through the doors. A nurse appeared in front of her. She was young, with violet scrubs and smooth brown hair pulled back with a part down the middle. She looked Camille up and down, and Camille knew. This was a fan. She could spot them from a mile away, the fans that were more than once-every-four-year fans, that recognized her in airports and supermarkets. The nurse walked right up to Camille and said, "I'll take you to Leigh."

GRACE

Grace's fingertips were starting to go numb in Georgette's and Monica's hands. Her heart was getting pins and needles, too.

Where the hell is Camille?

Grace took a deep breath, pushing her hope through her arms and into the other gymnasts. A minute ago, she had looked at them all standing beside her, yearning for the same thing as her, with sore muscles like hers and lives on the line like her own. A minute ago she had felt like one of them, like she belonged here.

Grace was trying to stay that nice. She didn't want to be the twisted, deranged girl anymore.

"Well, now we've lost Wilhelmina," Katja said. "Guess it's no surprise that one didn't stick around." She was speaking under her breath, pretending they couldn't hear her. But she knew they could.

And Grace realized: she didn't want to be like Katja anymore. *Katja* was twisted and deranged. Katja was like the worst parts of Grace.

But she still wanted the woman to say her name.

"Kristin, check the bathroom," Katja said. "Samantha, check the floor." The gymnast chain broke.

The wait was not good for Grace. Once she heard her own name, she could go back to wishing and hoping and dreaming for everyone else. But she didn't know how much longer she could wait without her dark side surfacing again. Her brain twitched with insulting thoughts about all the other gymnasts. Her mouth wanted to put down Monica again. She hated when she wasn't in control.

But for now she held that part of herself in check.

Her name would be next. She needed to hear it. She needed it to happen soon, please. To be relieved that she could keep working with her father, keep using her gymnastics to fill in the spot where her mother should be. She needed to hear her name to keep being herself. Grace was so tired. She wanted to hear her name, and then go directly to bed.

If Leigh were here, she'd maybe still be squeezing Grace's hand.

If Leigh were here, her name would be next, alphabetically.

But Leigh wasn't here. The guilt seized Grace's heart like a cold, dead fist.

Kristin ran back into the room. "Camille's not in the bathroom," she said. She paused, then added sort of loudly, "But Wilhelmina is. That's where she is. She didn't leave."

A few of the gymnasts smiled at Kristin's guts. Grace didn't have guts like that. Grace would never have the guts to stand up to Katja Minkovski. But she'd find the courage not to want to be her anymore.

Grace twisted her right fingers in her left hand. *Was Camille gone? Could she have given up on herself?*

Samantha ran breathless through the door. "She's gone," she said.

Elite gymnasts are stoic, so there were no gasps or jumps or startles. There was only a long row of jaws dropping.

Wilhelmina knew, Grace realized. *That's why she looked so dizzy up there. She knew that Camille was gone before Katja called her name.*

"I ran into her mother walking out the door," Samantha was saying. "She said Camille went to see Leigh. In the hospital."

The icy fist squeezed harder on Grace's heart and she was sure that it would burst again into a million moths that flew around her rib cage and reminded her that she wasn't perfect. But this time it wouldn't be because she failed to eat. It would be because she failed to care.

Camille had managed to love her best friend better than Grace did. Wilhelmina had helped Camille to care for Leigh. Grace was the worst.

"So . . . Camille is disqualified," Katja was mumbling. She clucked her tongue and ran a pencil down her clipboard.

Grace would not be mean. She'd channel the best parts of Leigh to cover up the worst parts of herself.

Grace squeezed Monica's hand again. She gripped Georgette hard enough to leave a black-and-blue mark. She was terrified that the committee would go back behind the closed door to figure out what to do now before announcing the rest of the team, before saying her name. She wanted her fellow gymnasts to form a wall and keep Katja here, force them to decide right here in this room.

"We will name the rest of the team, then the alternates. Then we will go back to decide who to promote."

Grace breathed a whoosh through her teeth.

Here we go, she thought. *Here we go. I'm next.*

In a mere second she'd hear her name, she'd be officially on the team, the torture would be over. Once she heard her name, she could deal with everything else. Like whether she had a best friend anymore. And whether she had a coach anymore. And whether she even wanted either of them if they hurt her gymnastics. Grace had big questions to figure out about who she was and how much of her was a gymnast and how much was a feeling, thinking human. But she could figure all of that out in the next part of her life, the part that would start in a fraction of a moment when she was standing next to Katja as a part of the team. She'd figure out those big questions as an Olympian.

"And here are the Olympic team members." That was all Katja said and Grace's grip was already loosening. She was Cooper. She'd be called first. Only Becker was before her. "Wilhelmina Parker, Georgette Paulson, Samantha Soloman—

She didn't hear any more names. A buzzing started inside her brain. It vibrated from one side of her skull to the other. How had she messed up that much?

I'm not on the team.

MONICA

Monica was clutching hands so tightly, she thought she might break them.

It felt like a short chain of girls now, though. They were dropping like flies. Leigh was injured. Camille was disqualified. Wilhelmina was so surprised she won the meet that she was off getting sick in the bathroom somewhere. At least that's what Monica suspected.

But Monica wouldn't let that affect her. She wanted to be team alternate. She hungered for team alternate. She'd had to talk herself up to wanting it and now she was likely to be it. She would be happy.

"And Maria Vasquez," Katja finished. "So that's your team: Georgette, Maria, Samantha, Wilhelmina. And one of the alternates. We'll promote someone to the spot Camille vacated."

Monica felt the hand in hers go dead. She turned.
Grace.

Grace hadn't made the team. She was staring, her skin ashen, her face so broken, Monica was afraid she'd cry.

But she couldn't worry about Grace right now. Right now it was almost her moment.

"And the alternates are," Katja said, "Monica Chase. Grace Cooper. Kristin Jackson."

The chain of girls broke into the nine separate links, each one of them with open jaws and pounding hearts.

The committee filed out the back door to discuss the last member of the team. For an instant, it was silent.

It was silent inside Monica, too. Nothing in her brain. Only Olympic rings in her vision. Only the sound of her own rushing blood in her ears.

Olympic team alternate.

She'd made it.

The locker room burst back into life, Olympic gymnasts clutching each other's arms and dancing in circles, non-Olympic gymnasts hugging and rubbing tears into each other's shoulders, Olympic team alternates standing hunched and tense awaiting that final name.

Monica was too shocked right now for the joy. She was too happy for the tension. She was too sympathetic for the sadness.

She backed up a few steps until the back of her knees found the wood of the locker room bench, and then she lowered herself onto it and sat. She was the frozen pebble in the middle of the swarming activity and emotion.

It happened. She did her best. She believed in herself. She was going to Italy.

She wanted to see Wilhelmina, Monica realized. She wanted to run to her and make sure she wasn't serious about quitting. The girl couldn't quit now: she'd won the Olympic trials, for God's sakes. But Monica didn't dare leave. She didn't dare lose this spot.

Grace lowered herself onto the bench next to Monica. "Good job," she said.

Monica tried to keep her smile contained. "Grace," she said. "I'm sorry that—"

"Don't be," Grace's words bit. "I'll be on the team in a minute. I'm the one they'll promote. I'm better than Kristin and *you*. Everyone knows that."

Monica bit her lip, then forced herself to smile again. No one was going to ruin this for her. Not even Grace.

LEIGH

Leigh was numb in the bed. Maybe it was the drugs. Maybe it was the exhaustion. Maybe it was that without gymnastics she didn't know what to hope for, what to think about, who to be. Her parents were quiet, too; they'd finally gotten the hint.

The door opened and shut. Leigh didn't pick up her head. She wasn't a gymnast. She didn't have to be polite for the cameras anymore. There would be no cameras anymore.

"Well, isn't this nice!" her father exclaimed, his voice too bright and cheerful.

Her mother stood up by her side. "Oh, it's good to have friends at a time like this," she said, trying to sound as cheerful as her father, but failing because of her tears.

"Leigh," a voice said. It was musical, magical. It sparked goose bumps all over Leigh's useless body.

She picked her head up, ignored the pounding in her skull.

"Camille!" she said, too loudly. Her face burned again. She was numb and broken, but she still managed to embarrass herself.

Then her parents were gone.

Camille stood right inside the door and shifted from foot to foot. Leigh had never seen this gymnast look nervous before. She was always confident, always in control, always solid. But right now Leigh could tell she didn't know what to say.

What was she doing here? She couldn't know how Leigh felt, right? Leigh hadn't told anyone.

Unless it was that stupid hug.

Could Camille possibly feel the same way?

"Hi," Camille said. "You okay?"

Yes, Leigh thought. *Because you're standing in front of me right when I thought I'd never have a reason to smile again.*

No, Leigh thought. *Because I'm here in a hospital and not going to the Olympics.*

Leigh said, "Who made it?"

"I don't know," Camille said. She walked toward the bed.

Leigh's eyebrows jumped.

"I left before the team was announced," Camille said. "I disqualified myself."

"Why?" Leigh hoped Camille couldn't hear her heart pounding. *Camille has a boyfriend*, she reminded herself. *Camille is not thinking like you are right now.*

Camille sighed. She dropped into the chair next to Leigh's bed, where her mother had been. "Because I'm like you."

"You are?" Leigh asked, her vision filled with shooting stars for a split second before she realized that there was no way Camille meant *like you* the way Leigh was hoping, because no one even knew Leigh was a lesbian. It would be easier if Camille knew. It would be easier if she didn't have to hide it.

"I mean, how? How are you like me? You aren't hurt, are you?"

"No, no," Camille said. "I shouldn't have said all that stuff about comebacks. I feel like I cursed you. All I've done since the trials started is mess up my friends."

Friend. She called me her friend. It was both thrilling and disappointing.

"It wasn't your fault. I hit my head on the beam. I didn't get enough height."

"Well—"

"I mean, it's nothing like what happened to you, actually, you know? I mean, you were in a car accident and you weren't even the one driving. So, like, it was someone else's fault when you—" *Shut. Up.* "You know what I mean."

Leigh bit the insides of her lips.

I feel a lot like I did before we even started today, she realized. Then, she was under the bleachers and on top of the scoreboard, ready to kick some butt. Now, she was in a hospital bed and erased from gymnastics stats everywhere, ready to wear a knee brace. But something in her was the same.

Camille said, "I didn't mean to—"

But Leigh cut her off. "It wasn't your fault, okay? It was mine. Or it was gravity's. Or something. I'm a good gymnast, I know it. All athletes get injured sooner or later, if they stick with it for long enough. It was really bad luck that my injury happened then."

"Wow," Camille said. "You're smart, you know that?" She reached out and clutched Leigh's hand, her face more serious than Leigh had ever seen.

Don't hold my hand. It's confusing. I know it's normal to hold someone's hands if she's in a hospital bed, but for me it's confusing. There's no way you could know this but I have a crush on you. And it hurts too much to have you cluelessly holding my hand like this.

"So," Camille said. "What did the doctor say?"

"I'm in a knee brace for a long time. Like, for weeks constantly and then, like, years while working out."

Camille's eyebrows raised.

"And I have a concussion," Leigh said. "So they're keeping me here overnight."

"And that means . . ." Camille said. "I know it's not all about the Olympics and all that . . ." She trailed off.

"I can try again next time if I want to," Leigh said.

Camille squeezed her hand a little. "Will you?"

Leigh let her head fall into the pillow. Would she? She wanted to. She couldn't be finished. She wasn't ready.

But why did the thought of another Olympic season make her so tired?

Camille's phone rang. She glanced at the screen. "I have to take this. Sorry. I'll be right back!"

Then she was gone.

WILHELMINA

"Okay, I'm calling you," Wilhelmina said as soon as Camille answered. "It doesn't matter, though. I can't do it. I can't go to the Olympics with that witch who did everything to keep me from getting there, and she would have too if—"

"Hold on! Hold on!" Camille shouted back. Wilhelmina shut up. Camille was in a hospital. She probably shouldn't be yelling at her.

Wilhelmina pulled her legs up onto the window ledge where she was sitting. She was in the bathroom closest to the locker room and it was a public bathroom, too. One that was supposed to be open to anyone in the stands. But Wilhelmina had dead-bolted the main door to the outside so the row of metal stalls and the two sinks and the window in the back were all hers. It was selfish. But she was only going to be selfish like this for a minute. Sometimes you need to take care of yourself.

"Now," Camille whispered. "What happened?"

"I won. So Katja had to name me to the team." Wilhelmina had been dreaming about saying this very sentence at the outset of the meet, yet now she felt miserable. "She was forced to."

"Why do you sound so upset?" Camille asked. "You told me you really wanted to go. Now you get to go."

"I wanted to get there on my own. Without anyone falling. I wanted to get there fair and square. And I want it to be good once I'm there. Instead, if I go, Katja is still going to hate me the whole time."

"So?" Camille said.

Wilhelmina felt like punching her. "So, nothing has ever been fair for me, okay? Last Olympics I would have gotten to go but then the FIG said I was too young. By four days. Only four days!"

"That happened to a lot of girls," Camille pointed out. "All over the world. That wasn't just you."

"But—" Wilhelmina couldn't say what she wanted to say. *But I was the best.* It would sound snobby but she wasn't being snobby.

"But what?" Camille asked. "Go to the Olympics. You want to go, you go. Don't let Katja stop you."

"But it's all unfair again," Wilhelmina said. "I wish I could be like the rest of you. I wish things had happened the way they were supposed to for me."

And Camille laughed. A huge, loud, insulting laugh.

"Don't laugh!" Wilhelmina pleaded. She was finally being honest. She didn't need to be laughed at.

"No," Camille said. "Listen."

Wilhelmina had never heard Camille sound this serious. She nodded, stupidly.

"You think things were fair for me? You're right that this was my second trials. And four years ago, I made the team, too, like you did today. But I didn't go, because my mom got into a stupid fender bender, and she'd kept me on such a strict diet I slipped right out of the seat belt and broke my back. In some accident that should have been nothing. Was that fair?"

"No, but—"

"And what about Leigh?" Camille said. "Leigh was winning the Olympic trials. She made a mistake, yes. I guess that was her fault. But not all mistakes mean you're injured during the Olympic trials. That's not fair, either."

"I know it's not fair, what happened to Leigh," Wilhelmina said.

"And Grace, she has to deal with her dad. You can't say *that's* fair. And how about Georgette? She's always third to those two all-stars, always listed third. And now today is finally the meet in which they both mess up—and then you come out of the blue and steal it from her."

Wilhelmina's eyes were wide. Her heart was going wild. Camille was right.

"And even Monica," Camille said.

"Monica?" Wilhelmina said. That was one she was sure gymnastics was fair to. Yes, she had Ted as a coach but he wasn't nearly as cruel to her. And she was young and fresh and Katja loved her.

"Monica worked her butt off and now she's an alternate. But if she had one more year, if the Olympics were next year—"

"She'd be a star," Wilhelmina cut Camille off. "So you think I'm crazy," she said.

"No," Camille said. "I know what you mean. Katja isn't fair to you, that's true. She's worse to you than anyone else who was there today. But that's not what this is about."

"It isn't?" Wilhelmina asked.

"No," Camille said. "This is about you. You did what you set out to do. You got to the Olympics your own way, and you still can't enjoy it. At some point you have to stop blaming other people and look at yourself . . . Sorry, that was harsh," Camille interrupted herself suddenly. "I'm trying to learn to speak up but . . . that was too much, maybe."

"No," Wilhelmina said. "You're right."

"Katja might be unfair to you in particular," Camille said. "But gymnastics? Gymnastics isn't fair to anyone."

Wilhelmina's eyes were huge. Her hands were shaking. Her heart was exploding.

Camille was right. What was the point in proving Katja wrong if she didn't go to the Olympics after all? Now Wilhelmina had made the team. Katja couldn't stop her anymore. The only person who could stop her now was herself.

Thank God for her old friend Camille.

"Mina?" Camille said.

"Camille . . ." she said. "I'm sorry."

Camille laughed and Wilhelmina knew she wouldn't

get it. But she still had to apologize for thinking the worst about Camille yesterday. And for thinking her life had been perfect.

"I'll be okay," Camille said. "I'm going to try for the NCAA. I think one of the coaches or teams might listen to me. They might not ban me forever for quitting during the trials if I can tell your story about how you had to defy Katja and deal with her hating you openly just so you could go. But in order for me to do that, you have to go!"

"I'm going," Wilhelmina whispered. "I'm . . . I'm an Olympian."

"Go for the gold, baby!" Camille cheered. Then she said, "Oh, sorry," to someone else. "Look, I gotta go. Go celebrate, okay? Text me as soon as you find out the whole team, okay?"

"Okay," Wilhelmina said.

And now she was laughing and crying and spinning and squealing in her private bathroom. Wilhelmina splashed some water on her face and snuck back out the bathroom door. She had to get back to the locker room. She had to explain where Camille was and she had to find out who else was on the team. *Her* team.

The hallway was still deserted. Everyone in the crowd was glued to their seats, awaiting the announcement of the Olympic team. Wilhemina felt sort of guilty for making them wait so long, but she knew she needed to do it this way. She'd needed to come this close to quitting, to be *okay* with quitting, in order to truly do her best out there.

"Mina?" She was steps from the locker room when she heard her name behind her. It was a boy who said it.

She turned.

Davion.

He looked so good. He was wearing a black T-shirt and one of the sleeves was rolled up a little bit. It wasn't on purpose, but it gave Wilhelmina a glimpse of his muscle, almost as toned as her own. He was smiling. He was rushing at her.

"You won! You won! I can't believe you won!"

Then she was in his arms, and he was spinning her around, her feet off the floor, her head right next to his face. She could feel his jaw muscle against her ear as he said it over and over. "You won! You won!"

When he put her down, she looked at him, smiling.

Her heart was in her mouth, her lips. Her heart was pulling her toward him, yanking on her feet and shoulders and chest.

Kiss him. Kiss him. Kiss him.

Her whole body was chanting.

She took a step closer, so there was no distance between them, so his black T-shirt was brushing up against her Team USA warm-ups. She could smell his cologne and his hair oil.

She tilted her head up toward his face. She stood on her toes. She was going to do it.

His eyes went wide for a second and then he closed them like he knew what was coming.

She was almost there. Her lips were just a centimeter away from his. She could feel his breath on her mouth.

He flinched.

"It's okay," he said. "I . . . I can wait."

Wilhelmina's eyes were wide. He didn't want to kiss her? He drove eleven hours to watch her gymnastics meet and he didn't want to kiss her.

Her face was burning. She took a step away from him and hunched her shoulders. She wished the stadium would swallow her whole and spit her back out in Rome.

"It's not that I don't want to," Davion said. "It's just that there's still the Olympics . . . And I know everything you said. I don't want to distract you."

Wilhelmina brightened and stepped toward him again. "No, it's okay. I learned a lot of stuff today."

Davion leaned in again like he was going to let their lips touch.

But then he shook his head. "I'm sorry. It's just . . . what if you were right before? It's too much. I want to kiss you more than anything but . . . this is the Olympics. I can't mess that up for you."

No. No. NO, Wilhelmina was screaming, but only inside her head. *I figured it out. I know how to be more than just a gymnast now.*

Davion's eyes looked sadder than she'd ever seen. "You'll be back in a month," he said. "We'll see what happens then. It's been a year. What's one more month?"

Nothing. Everything. Both.

MONICA

The selection committee was back too quickly. Monica didn't want to hear the final name. It would be Grace, obviously, and Monica didn't want to deal with Kristin being inconsolable to be on the same level as Monica herself. She stayed frozen on the bench as the committee took their places.

The gymnasts were separate now. Ten links of a busted chain. It happened so quickly. Monica would always miss that hope they had all shared through their interlocking fingers a few minutes earlier, but it was gone forever.

As soon as she thought that, there was a hand squeezing Monica's shoulder. She looked up and found Wilhelmina standing behind her.

"You okay?" Monica whispered.

Wilhelmina nodded. "Yeah. I'm . . . I'm good. I'm going. To be an Olympian. After all."

Monica smiled.

"You really helped me," Wilhelmina said. "You and Camille. I came into this meet hating everyone, but I couldn't have done it without you two."

"No," Monica said. "You—"

Wilhelmina interrupted her. "You did. You might not think so, but I needed to talk to you last night in order to have a day like today."

"You're the one who helped me!" Monica said.

Wilhelmina laughed. "Well, let's not argue about it," she said.

Monica relaxed. The next few minutes would be easier to get through with this new friend at her side.

"This was not an easy decision," Katja said finally. "We have to think about who can perform best where and how to put the team together. And we have to consider that this is the Olympics. That the athlete we choose could potentially compete for several days, several competitions back-to-back. She must have stamina. She must be continually improving. She must show growth. She must not have already hit her peak."

Around her, the other gymnasts and coaches were nodding. They were half-listening. But Monica listened carefully because the committee did not usually explain decisions. Such a long explanation probably meant they weren't going with her teammate, the obvious choice, but also, the gymnast who had fallen apart halfway through the second day of every important meet all year. And Monica braced herself. If it wasn't Grace, Grace would crumble.

Monica felt something she hadn't ever felt for Grace before: empathy.

She turned to look at her teammate. Grace's face was frozen in anticipation and dread, her whole body leaning toward the committee like if she got close enough to them, maybe they'd remember her.

"The new alternate will be Annie Simms. And . . . the

fifth member of the Olympic team is," Katja began.

If it wasn't going to be Grace, then it would either be Kristin or—

"Monica Chase."

And now the joy exploded out of her, tears streaming out her eyes, her feet jumping up and down. She knew that her teammate was disappointed and that there were brokenhearted gymnasts everywhere, but she also knew that she deserved this. That she was the best choice for the USA. That she would be an Olympian and make herself proud. And that as much as she hated hope when it first came for her, when she first saw those Olympic rings in a hazy version of her future, this moment would never have happened if she hadn't hoped for it like she did.

Then she was hugging someone. She was being swung back and forth by someone else who was crying her own tears onto Monica's shoulders.

"I told you you could do it," Wilhelmina whispered in her ear. "I told you."

She craned back to look at Monica. The two were mismatched in every way: an old gymnast and a young one. An experienced gymnast and a rookie. A powerful gymnast and a classical one.

"So, roommates? In Rome? At the Olympics?" Wilhelmina asked.

Monica nodded and they laughed and jumped and let the joy seep out of them.

She turned to find Grace, to say something to make it better . . . but Grace was already walking toward the back door. For a second Monica's heart clenched, worried, but, just before they disappeared from the locker room, Monica's teammate turned and waved at her. Her look was sad, but genuine.

So that's her real smile, Monica thought.

CAMILLE

Camille held her phone between her palms and smiled. She hadn't known she could speak to someone so forcefully, but in the end that seemed to help Wilhelmina. Camille couldn't make decisions only because they'd make someone else happy, any more than Wilhelmina could make decisions only to spite someone else.

Then, too quickly, Camille remembered where she was, that this was not a place for smiling. And there was someone else a room away who probably wouldn't want to see a smile. But when she walked back into the hospital room, Camille swore Leigh's face brightened.

"Sorry about that," Camille said. She sat back in the stool next to the hospital bed but Leigh quickly folded her hands across her chest, so Camille kept hers in her lap. "So, what were we talking about?"

And then, to Camille's surprise, Leigh laughed.

"What?" Camille said, but Leigh was still laughing. "What?"

"I can't believe it," Leigh said, "but we were actually talking about the *next* Olympics."

Camille joined in the giggling. "We're the most pre-dictable people ever. Gymnasts," she said.

"Yup," Leigh said. "So. You really didn't want to go? You really didn't want to be an Olympian?"

Camille sighed. "You know . . . I did. Four years ago, I did. But now I don't. I really don't."

"What do you want to do?" Leigh said.

Camille squirmed. For some reason this was mak-ing her uncomfortable. "It's okay," she said. "I came here to comfort you. We don't have to talk about my drama."

Leigh shrugged. "Well, I'm stuck in this bed. I can't decide what I'm going to do four years from now today, can I?" She snorted. "I mean, you know, I'm thinking about it but . . . I'm stuck here all night. So we may as well talk about you. I mean, it's okay to talk about you sometimes, you know, Camille?"

Leigh's face turned bright red like it did sometimes and she tried to shrug off what she'd just said, but the words slapped Camille in the face.

It's okay to talk about you sometimes.

It's okay to talk about you sometimes.

And it was.

"So, like, are you done?" Leigh asked. "Retiring?"

Camille shook her head slowly. "I know it's weird but . . . and Andrew will be all upset with me today, obvi-ously, but he's nice and I think he'll get over it and help me . . . and, well, I don't want to go to the Olympics. I want to go to college."

Leigh laughed. "Yeah, that's good."

"No, I mean, like the NCAA." Camille's heart was beating wildly. "I didn't admit this, even to myself, until today. My mom always wanted me to go to the Olympics and my boyfriend, well, ex now, he always wanted me to quit all gymnastics and I . . . I lost my voice in the shuffle. But . . . I figured it out when you vaulted yesterday. I was happy when I thought your vault maybe meant I wouldn't make the team. Because if I just *didn't make it,* I knew there were a ton of NCAA teams that would take me, and that's what I want.

"I'm not sure if it'll be the same now that I disqualified myself but, I mean, you're my teammate. Someone will understand, I hope. I just want—"

"You want to be a Bulldog. Or a Gator. Or something!" Leigh finished her sentence gleefully. "I think that's cool. That's so cool."

"Really?" Camille said.

"Yeah," Leigh said. "I mean, people do that. People decide to be a serious gymnast but only, like, as a part of their lives. Like, my parents made me do that. But you're doing it on purpose. That's cool. And unique. And like, independent." Leigh's face was bright red again and she cleared her throat before saying, "So who was on the phone?"

Camille's brain was still making plans, still thinking about marching out of this hospital and calling Andrew and telling him everything. She only half heard herself say, "Wilhelmina."

But Leigh's eyes went wide. "Oh! So do you know now?"

"No, but—" Just then her phone buzzed and the results were in her hand. "Well, I do now," Camille said. "That was Wilhelmina. She made it. With Georgette, Maria, and Samantha. And then they were going to promote one of the alternates, since I'm not there."

Leigh's jaw hung open. "So no Grace?" she said, stunned. She looked sadder than she had since Camille first walked in the room.

"Oh," Camille said, realizing how surprising this was for the first time. "I guess not. Not unless she's who they decided to promote."

"She's not." The voice came from the open door behind them. "I'm not," Grace said. "And, you know, hi."

GRACE

"Grace!" Leigh cried out from the bed.

Grace's head began pounding immediately at the sight of Leigh all wrapped in sterile sheets. *I'm not a god*, Grace reminded herself, over and over. *I didn't make her fall.*

"How'd you get here?" Leigh asked.

Grace shrugged. "My dad drove me," she said. "He's in the lobby with your parents."

She stayed in the doorway. She was still worried that Leigh was mad, maybe not about the falling, but about all the other awful, twisted things Grace had done. It was easier to see them now, looking back over the past few days, now that she'd fallen off her own pedestal.

"Get over here. I can't move. Get over here," Leigh ordered, and Grace flew across the room and squeezed her best friend.

And it was like they were in their hotel room again, like they were alone. "I'm so sorry," Grace said and Leigh said and Grace said, back and forth.

Finally they broke their embrace.

"You're . . . You, Grace Cooper . . . You're not going?" Leigh asked.

Grace shrugged. "I'm the alternate," she said. "So . . . I'm going. Just. Not how we planned."

"Grace," Leigh said. "I'm so sorry. That's so unfair. Who—"

"Monica. She got the last spot."

Leigh's face flashed into something close to horror, but Grace shook her head. "Don't. Don't," she said.

Leigh nodded.

"I'm . . . I'm okay. I think? Maybe I . . . Maybe I didn't deserve to go?"

"You?" Leigh shouted, aghast.

Just then an orderly came into the room rolling a cart of food. The smell of cafeteria roast beef and green beans from a can almost knocked Grace over. It was gross food, and it still sung to her empty stomach.

"What do you mean?" Leigh asked when the orderly was gone. "You're the World Champion. The *World* Champion!"

"I guess . . . I don't know, I guess . . ." Grace watched

Leigh reposition herself in front of her tray and try to cut into her meat with a useless plastic knife. She was close to telling Leigh everything. That she hadn't eaten more than six bites of anything all day that day. That she'd thought starving herself would make her better somehow but it had clearly backfired and that that was her own fault and not Katja Minkovski's. But then Camille coughed behind them and Grace jumped, startled.

It was one thing to tell Leigh. She didn't need to tell the whole world.

"Next time?" Grace asked her best friend. "Are we going to try again?"

Leigh's fork froze on the way to her mouth. "Will you, you think? Will you try again? It seems so . . . hard."

Grace shrugged. She sat on the edge of Leigh's bed. "I don't know," she said. "Will you?"

Then Leigh looked at Camille, so Grace did, too.

"You'd tell us not to, right?" Leigh asked.

Camille shook her head. "No," she said. "I'd say only do it if you want to."

The two of them nodded seriously but Camille burst out in laughter.

"What?" Grace asked.

"I just—it's so obvious. That's like the most obvious advice ever. Why couldn't I give it to myself?"

They laughed with her. When they were calm again, Camille kept talking. "The real advice is this: If you're going to do it again, you have to be careful, okay? You have to treat your body differently when it's older. You have to let yourself get bigger. And you might have to drop an event or two. You have to let your gymnastics change." Camille paused. "Well, I guess I'm done with her for real now, so I'm just going to say it. Wilhelmina was right: if you want to do it again in four years, you can't play by Katja's rules."

Leigh and Grace giggled shyly. They were both nodding.

Then Camille looked right at Grace. "You've got to gain weight. Muscle. If you're going to try again in four years—"

Grace cut her off. "I have to eat."

"Well, yeah," Leigh said with her usual cheer. Leigh didn't get what Grace was saying.

"No, I mean . . ." She took a deep breath. It didn't matter if Camille heard her, because she was about to tell her dad. If she wanted to keep being a gymnast, she needed help. Just like Wilhelmina said. "I mean I have to eat more. I mean I haven't been eating. I mean, the reason I almost fell off bars today, and the reason I fell at Nationals and Classics—" Their eyes were so wide. They were horrified. Leigh was going to hate her forever for this secret. "I haven't been eating," Grace said.

It was the bravest thing she'd done all day. Ever.

"Oh, Grace," Leigh said. "Oh, Grace." She almost seemed sad. "You can get help for that, you know. You need to get help. Olympics or not."

Grace nodded. "My dad already said I need a new coach."

"That's a good idea," Camille said. "Tell him you need a new nutritionist, too. . . . There are a lot of girls who struggle with food. Not just gymnasts either. So there's a lot of help you can get."

Grace nodded. It was going to be awful. It was going to be almost impossible to let her body change from feather to rock. But she had to do it now. Leigh would make her do it. That's why saying it out loud was the hardest part.

"Come here," Leigh said again, and Grace leaned in to hug her.

Just then her phone buzzed in her pocket. "Check it!" Leigh squealed.

"It won't be Dylan," Grace said. "He stopped messaging me as soon as I messed up on bars."

But Leigh laughed. "Dylan does not care enough about gymnastics to know you messed up on bars," she said.

And it was Dylan.

Congrats, Grace Cooper, Olympic team alternate! I had a lot of fun watching you the past two days. Being the alternate is probably similar to being the backup dancer in a boy band. We have something in common, I guess. :-)

Grace stared at the message, dumbfounded. Could it be that someone, somewhere in the world would understand what it was like to try and try and try and never quite get what you were aiming for? Could it be that someone, somewhere in the world would understand Grace?

LEIGH

Camille stood and joined the hug, her arms wrapped around both Leigh's and Grace's backs so that all of Leigh's broken body was on fire.

I'm the same girl I was yesterday, she reminded herself. So many parts of her would stay the same even if gymnastics went away.

"Um," Camille said when the hug was over. "I don't want to sound, like, I don't know. Don't judge me too harshly for this or anything. But, should we maybe go get your dad now, Grace? I mean, I'll go away or whatever. But maybe you should, like, tell him when you have Leigh here to support you and before—"

Leigh couldn't believe it, but Grace was nodding. "Before I lose my nerve."

Camille turned toward the door. "Should I go—"

"Wait!" Leigh cut her off. She'd shouted again, but this time she wasn't embarrassed. This time everything on her mind was too important for a crush to get in the way of it. "Wait, Grace, does that mean you're trying again? Does that mean you're keeping this going four more years?"

"I don't know. Are you?" Grace said. "Are we still in this together?"

But Leigh wasn't sure yet. The thought of losing that part of her life—the workouts and the competition and the camps and the friends—was so painful, it stung.

But the rest of it. The secrets. The parceling up her life. The twisted line Grace and Leigh had to walk between besties and competition. Four more years of that. It seemed so exhausting.

Too exhausting.

It wasn't worth it.

But maybe she could fix that. She could fix their friendship. She could glue all the pieces of her life back together.

They were her secrets anyway.

They weren't even bad secrets.

And if Grace was brave enough to tell a secret like *that*—

"I want to go to the Olympics," Leigh said. "But I want to do it as your friend. If we try again . . . can we be better?"

Grace shrugged. "Be better?"

"No, I don't mean like better tricks or DODs or whatever. I just mean . . . can we be better to each other?"

"I hope so," Grace said. Her eyes were on her sneakers. "I'm really sorry, Leigh. I get all confused because gymnastics . . . I mean, it's everything to me. It didn't make sense to me that you're thinking about other things but . . . I can be your friend even if gymnastics is only part of what's important to you. I can make friendship a bit part of my life, too, you know? I don't want to quit after this Olympics, but I also want to be happier. I want to like myself more. So, don't worry. I won't tell anyone you're gay. I really won't."

Leigh's eyes went wide and straight to Camille. Grace's followed hers. She clutched her hands at her chest. Leigh's face was so hot, she couldn't think. Grace looked pale enough to pass out.

"I—oh my God, I didn't—I suck. Oh God, Leigh, I suck. I didn't even mean to—I was trying—Camille, you can't tell anyone, okay? Leigh doesn't want anyone to know and I just—oh my God, Leigh, I'm so sorry, I didn't mean to—oh my God."

And then Grace'e eyes spilled over. The blood left Leigh's face. Her breath returned to her lungs. Grace was crying about something that had nothing to do with gymnastics. Grace was crying for *her*.

"I can be better, too, Grace. I can be better to you. I can forgive you. It's different this time. Because you didn't mean to."

And part of Leigh was relieved anyway. Part of her was grateful.

"Well, I wasn't supposed to hear that," Camille said, clearly trying to lighten the mood. "But I just retired from elite gymnastics, so I'm pretty sure I don't even count anymore."

You count. You should count more than anyone, Leigh thought.

"It's okay, Grace," Leigh said. "Your friendship should be more important to me than some secret that shouldn't even be a secret."

"And yours should be more important to me than gymnastics," Grace said. "Camille, will you get my dad now?"

She was brave. So brave. Grace was brave and Leigh was brave and Camille was brave and in that hospital room their courage multiplied on itself.

Camille left and Grace said, "So we're doing this again? Four more years?"

Leigh nodded. "Four more years as gymnasts, but not only-and-everything gymnasts. Four more years as friends, too. Okay?"

And Grace said, "I'll try."

And that was enough.

GLOSSARY OF GYMNASTICS TERMS

AERIAL CARTWHEEL: A move in which a gymnast turns her body over like a pinwheel (as in a standard cartwheel) without using her hands for support

ALL-AROUND: A gymnast who competes in all events; for women this refers to vault, uneven bars, balance beam, and floor

ALTERNATE: A gymnast selected to train and prepare for the Olympic games in case one of the Olympic gymnasts cannot perform due to illness, injury, or another reason. Olympic Alternates rarely get to compete, if ever, and they do not stay in the Olympic Village

AMANAR: A gymnastics move on vault (named for Romanian gymnast Simona Amanar) in which a gymnast performs a Yurchenko with two and a half twists

APPARATUS: The significant piece of gymnastics equipment for each event; i.e., the vault, the uneven bars, the balance beam, and the gym floor

ARABIAN: A tumbling move that starts as a back flip and finishes as a front flip

BALANCE BEAM: A piece of gymnastics apparatus and an event in which the gymnast performs tricks on a beam that is 4 feet high, 4 inches wide, and nearly 16.5 feet long

BARS: A term commonly used to refer to the uneven bars

BEAM: A term commonly used to refer to the balance beam

CLASSICS/US CLASSICS: An annual national gymnastics meet held each summer and regarded as the start of the serious gymnastics season

DEGREE OF DIFFICULTY (DOD): A rating that reflects the difficulty of a gymnastics move. DODs are added up, then added to the execution score to determine a gymnast's score on an event

DISMOUNT: Term used for the last element in any routine, used to get off the apparatus in beam and bars

DOUBLE TWISTING YURCHENKO (DTY): A gymnastics move on vault in which the gymnast performs a Yurchenko with two full twists

ELITE: The top level of gymnastics as determined by the FIG; gymnasts must be an elite in order to qualify for the national team

EVENT: Term used to refer to the four standard performances in women's gymnastics: *vault, bars, beam, and floor*

EXECUTION SCORE: A score based on the quality of a routine regardless of the difficulty of tricks; execution scores all start at 10 and deductions are made based on mistakes or imperfections during a routine

FIG (*Fédération Internationale de Gymnastique*): The governing body that determines the rules and the code for international gymnastics, including the Olympics

FLOOR: A shortened term for the floor exercise

FLOOR EXERCISE: An event in women's gymnastics in which athletes compete a routine made of tumbling and dance moves set to music over a 40-foot square spring floor

FULL TURN: A 360-degree turn performed on either floor or beam

GIANT: A move on bars that involves a 360-degree swing around a bar from handstand to handstand with the body in full extension

GRIPS: Equipment made of leather that gymnasts fasten around their hands and wrists to improve their handling of the uneven bars

HANDSPRING: A tumbling move on floor or beam in which the gymnast moves from both feet to both hands and back to both feet; it can be performed forward or backward

HIGH BAR: The top bar of the uneven bars

INTERNATIONAL GYMNAST/IG: The most popular magazine about national and international men's and women's gymnastics

JUNIOR OLYMPICS/JO: The program of gymnastics for those too young (or not yet skilled enough) to compete on the elite level

KIP: A basic gymnastics skill on bars in which the gymnast moves from a hanging position to a fully extended handstand

LAYOUT: A move on floor or beam in which the gymnast flips with her body held straight or arched, but not tucked

LEO: A shortened term for leotard

LEOTARD: A one-piece fitted garment made for competition in gymnastics

LOW BAR: The lower of the two uneven bars

MOUNT: The first skill used in any routine; in beam and bars this refers to the move used to get onto the apparatus

MUSTAFINA: A dismount on bars named after Russian gymnast Aliya Mustafina in which the gymnast does a double back tuck off the high bar while also twisting her body 180 degrees

NATIONAL CHAMPION: The winner of the Nationals meet; regarded as the best American gymnast until the next Nationals meet, or the Olympics if it is an Olympic year

NATIONALS: An annual gymnastics meet among the best American gymnasts, held to crown a yearly national champion; many countries also host their own national championships

NATIONAL TEAM: A select group of elite gymnasts required to train together several times a year; all the international teams such as Worlds and Olympic teams are selected from this group

NCAA: National Collegiate Athletic Association, also used to refer to college athletics in general

OLYMPIAD: The period of four years between Olympic games

OLYMPIC ROTATION: The preferred and standard order for a gymnast to compete on the events; this order is always used unless there are multiple groups of gymnasts, in which case the order remains the same but may start on a different apparatus; the order is vault, bars, beam, floor

OLYMPIC SELECTION COMMITTEE: A small committee of people who are committed to gymnastics who work together to determine the makeup of the Olympic team, often including past Olympic athletes, past coaches, etc.

OLYMPIC TEAM COORDINATOR: The member of the Olympic Selection Committee who establishes the training and preparation required for all Olympic hopeful gymnasts, advises gymnasts and coaches, and makes many decisions about US Olympic gymnastics

PAK SALTO: A move on bars, named after North Korean gymnast Gyong Sil Pak, in which the gymnast releases the high bar, does a backward flip, and catches the low bar

PIKE: A body position used in moves on floor, beam, and bars in which the legs are kept straight and the body is bent at the hips, preferably in an angle over 90 degrees

PLATFORM: The raised surface upon which the apparatus is placed in big events

RELEASE MOVE: Refers to any move on bars in which the gymnast lets go of the bar and does a trick in the air before grasping the bar again

ROUNDOFF: A move on floor or beam that starts similar to a cartwheel, but both feet land on the floor at once; often used to begin a tumbling series

ROUTINE: A combination of skills and tricks that one gymnast performs in a certain order on one apparatus

RUNWAY: The line of mat that a gymnast runs down when approaching the vault

SENIOR: A gymnast who is over sixteen years old, or is fifteen but will turn sixteen within the calendar year, and is therefore eligible to compete in the Olympics and other international and national meets

SPECIALIST: A gymnast who competes in only certain events and does not do the all-around

SPLIT LEAP: A move on beam and floor in which a gymnast starts on one foot, completes a split in midair, and lands on the other foot; ideally the split will be more than 180 degrees to showcase flexibility

TUCK: A position used during flips in which the body is bent at the hips and knees or curled into a ball

TUMBLING PASS: A series of connected tumbling tricks that gets the gymnast from one side of the floor or beam to the other

UNEVEN BARS: An apparatus and event consisting of two fiberglass bars, one 148 centimeters high, the other 228 centimeters high

USAG: The governing body for US-specific gymnastics

VAULT: An apparatus consisting of a runway, springboard, and vaulting platform; an event in which a gymnast sprints down the runway, punches off the springboard, performs flips and tricks, and ends up on her feet on the other side of the vaulting table

WALKOVER: A move on floor and vault in which a gymnast moves from a standing position into a handstand and back to standing by "walking" on the air with her feet

WOLF JUMP: A jump performed on floor and beam in which a gymnast has one leg fully extended in front of her and one bent sharply at the knee with her body in a pike position

YURCHENKO: A move on vault, named for Soviet gymnast Natalia Yurchenko, in which the gymnast hits the springboard with her hands and performs a back-handspringlike movement over the vault, then twists before landing

ACKNOWLEDGMENTS

This book taught me a whole new meaning of the word "revise," and both the book and myself are so much better for it! An immense thank you to my editor, Leila Sales, for the brilliant insights, the endless patience, and the consistent belief that I could make this work. I am a better writer because of you. Thank you also to everyone at Viking, especially Janet Pascal, Tricia Callahan, everyone in publicity and marketing. And thank you to Nancy Brennan for the cover!

Kate McKean, thank you for believing in this project when it was just a tiny idea and thank you for believing in it every step of the way! I'm blessed to have you as my agent.

This book had many early readers whose insights were priceless to making sure I had a story, and one with five distinct voices. Thank you to Jessica Verdi, Allary Montague, Corey Ann Haydu, Dhonielle Clayton, Mary G. Thompson, and Sona Charaipotra for your thoughts on my first pages and on early drafts. A special shout-out to Alyson Gerber and Amy Ewing for sticking with me through many revisions and for letting me lose my mind and then helping me find it again.

I'm also blessed to have many communities who

support me. Thank you to The New School, The Lucky 13s, The Class of 2K13, and the Binders. Thank you to my friends in writing, in life, and in both: I count on you in so many ways.

Thank you to my family: Beth and Bill Carter, Dan Carter, each of the Larssons, and all my aunts, uncles, and cousins.

Thank you to my Buddy.

And, always and forever, thank you to Greg.